Donna Alward lives on Canada's east coast with her family, which includes a husband, a couple of kids, a senior dog and two crazy cats. Her heart-warming stories of love, hope and homecoming have been translated into several languages, hit bestseller lists and won awards, but her favourite thing is hearing from readers! When she's not writing she enjoys reading—of course!—knitting, gardening, cooking... and she's a Masterpiece Theatre addict. You can visit her on the web at DonnaAlward. com, and join her mailing list at DonnaAlward.com/newsletter

USA TODAY bestselling and RITA® Award-winning author **Marie Ferrarella** has written more than two hundred and fifty books for Mills & Boon, some under the name Marie Nicole. Her romances are beloved by fans worldwide. Visit her website, marieferrarella.com

Discover more at millsandboon.co.uk

CHRISTMAS BABY FOR THE BILLIONAIRE

DONNA ALWARD

BRIDESMAID FOR HIRE

MARIE FERRARELLA

MILLS & BOON

First Published in Great Britain 2019
by Mills & Boon, an imprint of HarperCollinsPublishers,
1 London Bridge Street, London, SE1 9GF

Christmas Baby for the Billionaire © 2019 Donna Alward
Bridesmaid for Hire © 2019 Marie Rydzynski-Ferrarella

ISBN: 978-0-263-27265-9

1019

MIX
Paper from
responsible sources
FSC™ C007454

This book is produced from independently certified FSC™
paper to ensure responsible forest management.

For more information visit: www.harpercollins.co.uk/green

Printed and bound in Spain
by CPI, Barcelona

CHRISTMAS BABY FOR THE BILLIONAIRE

DONNA ALWARD

To Mum.
The older I get, the more I admire your strength
and your capacity for unconditional love.
Your children and grandchildren
have been incredibly blessed.

CHAPTER ONE

THERE WERE MORNINGS when a girl just didn't want to get out of bed, but she had to because a) she had to pee and b) she had to go to work because no one else was going to pay the bills.

Tori closed her eyes, gathered her get-up-and-go and threw off the covers. It wasn't that she didn't like her job; she loved it. The Sandpiper Resort was her life. She'd started there doing housekeeping as a teenager and had worked her way up to assistant general manager, overseeing many of the day-to-day operations. Stepping inside the doors each morning felt as much like being at home as entering her own small house, bought just last year.

So even though she was bone tired, despite having slept all night, she flipped on the light switch and turned on the shower. At least the morning sickness had been fleeting, lasting only a few weeks and consisting mostly of inconvenient nausea. Now in her second trimester, she simply got tired more easily. And was in the process of overhauling her wardrobe. Things didn't fit anymore now that her baby bump had made an appearance.

Thirty minutes later, hair blow-dried and makeup on, she left the house with her decaf coffee in a travel mug and made the five-minute drive to work. It had been mild for November, and she didn't have to scrape the frost off her windshield this morning, which was a plus. On arriving at the hotel, she stepped inside, inhaling the fresh scent of evergreens. Once Remembrance Day had passed, the

Christmas decorations had come out, turning the resort into a fairyland of white twinkle lights and pungent pine and spruce boughs punctuated with gorgeous red and gold bows. She greeted the staff at the front desk with a smile, then stopped at the kitchen to ask for a toasted bagel and some fruit—her usual breakfast fare.

"You need some eggs for the little one, there?" Neil asked, his chef's hat bobbing. "Mamas need protein."

She grinned. "When are you gonna stop pampering me?" she asked, taking a sip of her coffee. For a few weeks, she'd been turned off the smell of the brew. Now she inhaled the richness of it and sighed.

"Never," he replied, his eyes crinkling at the corners. Neil had been working in this kitchen since before she'd started cleaning rooms. Pretty soon his granddaughter would be looking for a summer job.

Eggs did sound good this morning, so she smiled. "You know how I like them," she acquiesced. "Thanks, Neil. You're a gem."

"You betcha."

Ten minutes later one of the waitstaff brought her breakfast, as well as a glass of milk. "Neil says you need your calcium," Ellen said, and even though she was younger than Tori, her voice came across as motherly.

"Neil is being overprotective and I love it," she remarked, smiling up at the waitress who'd joined their team last May. "Thanks." She unrolled her cutlery from the napkin. "Everything going okay in the dining room?"

Ellen nodded. "Slower now that the leaves are gone and no one really comes for the beach."

"I know. I'm sorry about the cut hours."

"It's okay. It's a seasonal thing. We all get it."

"We've got some holiday events planned, so if you're up for working those, I'll make sure you're on the list for scheduling." The ticketed events always meant decent tips, and Ellen's eyes lit up.

"I'd appreciate that. Thanks, Tori."

"No problem. It helps a bit when regular hours are short and Christmas is coming." Besides, Ellen had proved herself to be competent and reliable. Throwing a few extra hours her way was small reward.

Once Ellen was gone, Tori dug into her breakfast. Neil had added cheese to her eggs, and a little parsley... delicious. There were two slices of honeydew and a little dish of fresh strawberries, plus a whole-grain bagel with her favorite topping—plain cream cheese sprinkled with cinnamon sugar.

They really were a family around here, taking care of each other. Which was good for Tori, because it was only her and her mom now. Her mom, Shelley, was a nurse and had taken a job at the hospital in Lunenburg. It wasn't far away, but after Tori's father had died of cancer, Shelley had moved into an apartment right in the town for convenience. It put her about fifty kilometers away—close enough for weekly visits.

Tori put her hand on the swell of her belly. Now she was going to have her own family. And she *was* happy, deep down. The question of whether or not to have the baby hadn't even been brought up. She didn't have much family, and now she'd have a baby to love, and he or she would love her in return. Her mother would have a grandchild. Circumstances weren't ideal, but Tori had started thinking of this pregnancy as a surprise blessing.

The bagel caught in her throat and she took a deep drink of the milk to wash it down along with the unease that kept nagging her when she thought of her decision not to tell the father—at least not yet. Every time she'd determined to say nothing, she heard her mother's voice telling her that Jeremy deserved to know. The problem was, she agreed with her mom. She wasn't going to be able to keep this from him forever. She just had to figure out the logistics. The right way.

Jeremy Fisher… What had she been thinking, getting caught up with him last summer? It had been two weeks of sheer bliss, during which time she'd completely lost her head. They'd agreed it was a holiday romance, and boy, had they made the most of their time together. When it was over, he'd gone back to his life in New York and she'd been left behind in small-town Nova Scotia, in a tiny house on the water. And that had been exactly as she'd wanted it. She wasn't a fairy-tale kind of woman, with dreams of being whisked away to a lavish lifestyle and a happy ever after. Well, she had been, once. She'd been swept off her feet by a handsome man with tons of plans. Riley had seemed perfect on the surface. And she'd fallen for him, hard.

Until she realized he'd been living a double life. He'd showered her with gifts and affection, but behind it all was a history of defrauding people and going into debt. For a long time she'd blamed herself for being so stupid.

She bit into a strawberry and considered her summer affair. Perhaps her "relationship" with Jeremy had been different because from the start there had been no question that it would be anything other than a fling. Indeed, it had been quite out of character for her, considering he was a guest at the resort. But they'd been discreet. And after two years of hard work, losing her dad and feeling alone, she'd given herself permission to enjoy this one thing.

She hadn't thought there'd be these kinds of consequences.

The power dynamic hadn't mattered during those few weeks. But it mattered now. Jeremy was a rich, powerful man, and she was…well, not *nobody*. She had enough self-esteem to give herself that much. But she certainly didn't have the same clout and resources at her disposal, and it made for a very uneven balance between them.

She shook her head and pushed her plate aside, eager to get to work. The hotel manager, Thomas, was on vacation this week, so it was up to Tori to steer the ship. She spent the morning at her desk, then met with the housekeeping manager and the catering manager about requirements for a holiday function scheduled for mid-December. There was a Christmas wedding planned for the weekend before the twenty-fifth, and another on New Year's Eve, where the ceremony would actually begin just before midnight so the bride and groom would be the first married couple of the new year. They were making a number of special accommodations for that event, from late checkout the next day to food service at one in the morning. The couple was willing to pay, so the hotel was willing to take their business.

It was mid-afternoon when she got up to do a walk-around, to get out of her office and to talk to staff and see what was happening. It was her favorite time of the day, actually, chatting with the staff, wandering through her second home, caring for it with love and affection. She made a note of a ding in a corner wall that would need to be touched up with paint, and gave a mental check mark to whoever had cleaned the public bathrooms on the lobby level. They sparkled and smelled like the hotel's custom lemongrass-and-ginger scent. She greeted staff by name and made a few more notes about additional Christmas decorations that could be added to the dining room and small on-site gift shop. Maybe business was slower this time of year, but for those who did arrive for an escape or a special dinner, the hotel would show to best advantage.

She was just returning to the administration offices when the front door blew open, bringing in a smattering of brown leaves and rain; a man was propelled in with them, shaking his arms to rid his coat of water droplets.

She turned to the sound…and froze.

"Tori?"

She'd never known that a person could feel blood rush out of their face, but she felt it now.

No.

No, no, no, no, no.

He couldn't be here. This was all wrong.

"Jeremy."

He grinned widely, his thousand-watt smile hitting her right in the solar plexus. Why did he have to be so handsome? "I hoped you'd be here. What's it been? Four months?"

Four months, three weeks, and five days, she wanted to answer, but nothing came out of her mouth. What was he doing here? And could she escape without him noticing the obvious?

No such luck. At her silence, his gaze swept down, then back up, and his eyes were filled with questions and confusion. Of course, she'd chosen today to unveil her new maternity wardrobe. Her *condition* was perfectly plain for all to see.

"Why don't you step into my office?" she asked, pulling herself together. "We can catch up. What brings you back to the Sandpiper?" Her voice came out smooth and steady, thankfully. It wouldn't do for him to see her discomposed.

She turned her back and started toward the offices, her body trembling. Not just because of the lie of omission he'd caught her in, but because just the sight of him still had the power to turn her knees to jelly.

It had been a very good few weeks, after all. Too good.

She heard his steps behind her and once they were in her office, she shut the door. Staff might be family, but they didn't need to hear every conversation, and no one here knew the identity of her baby's father. She and Jeremy had tried to be discreet.

Her office was small, and felt smaller still with him in it. She turned around and faced him, finally, attempting to put up an emotional wall so she could maintain her objectivity. It was harder than she'd imagined. Jeremy had a presence about him that was magnetic. Today he was dressed in a charcoal-gray suit with a precisely knotted tie, and an overcoat that protected him from the cold Atlantic wind. His hair was tousled, as though the ocean breeze had fingers it had run through the strands, making them seem carelessly styled, and tiny drops of rain sparkled on the top. And his eyes… Right now his eyes were the same steel gray as the white-capped waves along the shore. Cold and unhappy. Her tummy turned over with anxiety.

"What brings you back to the area?" she asked, feigning a smile, skirting around him to sit behind her desk. Her tummy was hidden that way…

"Real estate. And I thought I'd look you up again while I was here. I didn't expect to find you pregnant."

The blunt statement hit her like a slap. So much for the hope of him not cluing in. It had been a long shot but she'd held out a smidgen of hope that her top might have camouflaged her bump.

She shrugged. "To be honest, it was a surprise to me, too."

"Is it mine?"

Her stomach plummeted. There was no beating around the bush with him. Never had been. Right from the start, he'd been up front about his attraction to her. He'd been staying in their best suite and she'd checked in on him on the first day to make sure everything was okay. They'd ended up chatting for a long time, about the area and about how different it was from his life in the Big Apple. When he'd invited her out for a drink she'd said yes, and it had been over a pomegranate martini that he'd told her she had the most intriguing eyes of anyone he'd ever met. She'd been charmed…and wooed.

She'd admired his confidence and honesty then, though she wasn't such a big fan of it at this moment.

For the briefest time, she considered saying no. It would solve a lot. But that simple answer was complicated by the small matter of her conscience. She had already been struggling with the fact that she hadn't yet told him about the pregnancy. Then there was a certain amount of integrity at stake. There had been no one else. He'd been the only one.

"Of course it is. I don't…make a habit of what happened between us."

He regarded her dispassionately. "How was I to know that? And were you ever going to tell me?"

Curse her and her honesty. She held his gaze, determined not to cower. "Eventually. And thanks for that wonderful endorsement of my character. It's always pleasant to be shamed by your baby's father."

He let out a breath and turned away for a moment, before turning back again. His gray eyes were contrite. "I'm sorry. That was uncalled for. It's just… This is a hell of a surprise, Tori."

"Yes," she said, "I'm sure it is."

"When…how…?"

Tori picked up a pen and played with it, resolving to keep up her appearance of strength. "We both know the answer to that question. Early July, and presumably one of the times we had sex."

She did not call it making love, though it had certainly felt like that at the time. Her cheeks heated as a memory swept through her. As hokey as it sounded, she had a feeling that she knew exactly when it had happened. They'd spent the day at the beach, splashing about in the water and having a picnic on the sand. And then in the late afternoon they'd gone back to her place and had finished off the day by taking their sweet time with each other.

He'd been a fantastic lover. Gentle, attentive, passionate.

Now, with him standing in her office, at the very least unhappy and very likely angry, those sweet memories were somehow tarnished.

He let out a huge breath. "May I sit?"

She held out a hand. "Of course." She wasn't exactly in a position to deny him anything right now, was she? The fears she'd had about him knowing about the baby were all crammed into her brain and she fought hard to ignore them. Perhaps she could put him off somehow, so she could prepare what she wanted to say to him.

He pulled out the guest chair, then shrugged out of his coat and laid it over the back before sitting. He leaned forward onto his knees, resting on his elbows. Tori bit down on her lip. It wasn't fair that he was so handsome. His brown hair and strong chin were reminiscent of JFK Jr., to her mind, but instead of his eyes being a rich brown, they were gray and heavily lashed. And right now they were looking at her with something like accusation and disappointment in their depths.

"I'm going to be a father," he said, his voice rough. "You're halfway through your pregnancy... When were you going to tell me?"

Her hands shook so she folded them on top of her desk.

"I don't know. I was waiting for the right time, and I've been going back and forth about it every day." She figured honesty was the best policy here; Jeremy would see through any attempt to mollify or placate him, and he'd definitely sense a lie.

His voice hardened. "I have a right to know."

This was the hard part. Just this morning she'd come to work like any other day. There was comfort in that. More than anything, Jeremy transported her out of her comfort zone and she struggled to find her feet in order to deal with this conversation.

She met his gaze again. "Our circumstances are a bit unique, you know. We had a fling. We live far apart, in two very different worlds. And I have no idea how to structure a co-parenting arrangement with someone who is, in many ways, a stranger." She took a breath. "You have resources I don't and I would lose in any sort of power struggle if you made a play for custody." There. She'd said it. No sense beating around the bush.

He sat back then, the questions in his eyes replaced by... Could it be? He was hurt by her last statement. Or at least offended. Her pulse was hammering so hard right now she couldn't quite trust her observations.

"Do you really think I'd do such a thing?"

She sat up straighter. "As I said, we don't really know each other, do we? It wasn't a chance I was willing to take. I'd die before letting someone take my baby away."

Jeremy tried to breathe through the cramping in his chest. He'd been looking forward to surprising Tori today. Work had brought him back to the area on behalf of a client and he'd imagined reigniting the flame that had raged between them last summer. Truthfully, he hadn't been able to get her out of his head, and this work trip on Branson's behalf had given him the perfect excuse to get her out of his system once and for all.

Instead he'd found her carrying his baby. The pregnancy shook him to the core, but the veiled accusation he'd just heard…that was a real gut punch.

He was a straight shooter and liked to think he was a good man. But right now he held back the words forming in his brain and those already stuck in his throat. Because he was confused, and angry, and another emotion he couldn't quite place. Hurt was part of it. And maybe disappointed. It was just a mess.

With his child stuck in the middle.

This was his worst nightmare. A family, kids—a wife, even—were not on his agenda.

"We used protection," he said numbly.

"Which isn't a hundred percent reliable. We were pretty careful, but…" Her hazel eyes met his. "Not careful enough, I guess. Believe me, this was not planned."

His suit jacket felt too tight, and his tie strangled his throat. But he kept his hands firm on the arms of the chair. His gaze stole to her midsection again, though most of it was hidden behind the desk.

His child. With a woman he barely knew, someone with whom he had simply enjoyed a few weeks during a summer trip. And he'd come here with the sole objective of hooking up with her again. He ran his hand over his face.

He should have known that someday his behavior was going to land him in trouble. That eventually his casual approach to relationships would come back to bite him. No words of *I love you*, no commitments, no strings. That was how he liked it. And even though he'd enjoyed his time here, a few states and an international border had made Tori Sharpe seem like a perfectly safe…distraction.

He wasn't really a player, but he'd classify his approach

to romance as…cavalier. His best friend Cole called him a serial dater. Branson had silently agreed with the assessment. He hadn't had a relationship that had lasted over a month since college.

He let out a breath and tried to relax his shoulders. "Okay. So the news is out now, like it or not." He pinned her with his gaze. "And I have no idea what to do."

The lines in her face softened. "That's okay. I do. I don't expect anything from you, Jeremy. I'm not going to come after you for exorbitant amounts of child support or anything. I'm going to raise this baby right here. I have tons of friends I can count on, and my mom is here, and we'll be as happy as anything. I'll even sign papers if you want."

No child support? No contact? And raising the baby in this small town that was nearly dead in the off-season?

"Anything but that," he replied.

CHAPTER TWO

AFTER JEREMY'S LAST statement, tensions had ratcheted up again. Tori had asserted that nothing was going to be decided that afternoon and perhaps they could pick up the discussion later after they'd both had time to think. He hadn't looked happy, but Tori knew they could have gone around in circles indefinitely. It was going to take time to sort out, and she needed time to decide what she really wanted and how best to present it to Jeremy. Being caught on the fly had only made her panic, though she'd tried to cover it up as best she could.

She could compromise on a lot of things, but not on the basics. The baby would live here, with her. As far as his involvement went, that was negotiable. Now that he knew, she could hardly shut him out of everything and pretend he didn't exist if that wasn't what he wanted.

If she tried to cut him out of the baby's life, she had the suspicious feeling he'd start throwing his weight around. And he had the money and connections to make things difficult. The fantasy bubble in which she'd held the memories of their time together was truly popped. It was like her mom said—if it seemed too good to be true, it probably was.

What a tightrope she was going to have to walk. Hopefully he was in town for only a few days.

He'd gone to check in to his room and she logged in to the reservations system to get the details of his stay. To her dismay, she discovered he'd booked twelve days.

That took them well into December. And it was more than enough time for things to go seriously wrong. She tapped her fingers on her desk. How the heck was she supposed to navigate this?

She thought back to earlier, when she'd admitted flat out that she'd lose in a power struggle. His gray eyes had looked so shocked that she'd even think such a thing. He'd run his fingers through his hair, and his throat had bobbed as he swallowed. Her words had left their mark, and it boded well as far as being able to reach him. He wasn't a cold and calculating monster, though she knew he was a tough negotiator when pushed. Watching him work closing deals last summer had shown her that, and she'd admired him for it at the time.

His wounded expression had also touched something in her heart she wished didn't exist. She cared about him. Two weeks together in the summer had been more than enough time for her to develop feelings. Not love, certainly, but definitely affection. It hadn't all been sexual. He'd been charming, and funny, and smart. In fact, he'd been nearly perfect. Even if she'd been absolutely fine knowing their time together would be no more than a whirlwind fling, it was hard to erase all of those memories and see him dispassionately as the father of her unborn child. He wasn't just a sperm donor.

One morning they'd basked in the sunlight streaming through the bedroom window and he'd told her about why he loved real estate. It wasn't just about the bargaining or the money. As his fingers had traced down her arm, he'd said it was about finding homes for people, places where they belonged and could be happy. And when he'd realized he'd let her in, he'd immediately backtracked and said it was just a big bonus that his clients were all stinkin' rich.

But it had been a defense mechanism, she was sure.

And she'd liked that glimpse into the man, and not just the fantasy.

Perhaps the best way to reach him was to approach the situation on a very human level. She could do that and still keep her other feelings locked away, right?

She put her hand on her tummy, wondering when she was going to start feeling the baby move. So far she had the bump but she hadn't really felt much. A few times she wondered if she might be feeling flutterings of movement, but she'd been told they were probably just gas.

Either way, she'd do what she had to in order to make sure her baby was loved and secure.

Whatever it took. Even being super nice to Jeremy Fisher.

The mile-long beach in front of the Sandpiper Resort was beautiful, even in late November. The waves were now more gray than blue, and the wind was raw, but there was a wildness to it that Jeremy loved, and the sound of the waves soothed his troubled mind.

Because he was, indeed, very troubled.

He'd left his running shoes on, meaning he'd have to shake them out later as the sand, even in the November chill, was still soft and thick. The wind whipped his hair around and made his jacket billow out behind him. Just a few months ago he'd walked this very beach with Tori. She'd worn a red bikini and had left her hair down, damp with seawater. They'd had so much fun; fun that had been missing in his life for too long. For those two weeks he'd put his troubles aside and let himself go. She had, too, or at least he'd thought so. They'd shared a blanket on the beach and soaked in the sun's rays; nibbled at a picnic prepared by the hotel kitchen; plucked seashells out of the damp sand that she said she was going to keep in her bathroom.

And then she'd taken him to her house and they'd spent hours exploring each other.

Just the memory made his body react, and he briefly considered jumping into the ocean, fully clothed, to cool off.

It had been easy being with her, because he'd known all along that he'd be leaving again. She wasn't his usual type of woman; his family and his money generally ensured that his dates were not of the small-town, girl-next-door variety, and being with her had been utterly refreshing. Now he'd be tied to her forever, because she was having his kid and there was no way on earth he would abandon his own child. He'd never planned to have any children, but he had to deal with the reality that he was going to be a father, and he was determined to be a better one than his own had been.

But how could he demand that Tori uproot her life? That wasn't fair either, and as much as Jeremy was used to getting what he wanted, he was a fair man. Or at least he wanted to think so.

He needed a plan. He was having a hard time formulating one because he was still stuck on the idea that he was going to be a dad.

The idea was terrifying.

The raw wind bit through his jacket right to his bones as he carried on down the beach. His own parents had divorced when he was two, and he barely remembered his dad. Too often he'd been a pawn in battles between his parents, to the point where he'd often felt like a commodity rather than a son. His mother had remarried when he was four, and his siblings had been much older than him. By the time he'd started high school, his sister had been eighteen and starting college, and his brother, ten years his senior, had already been working in Silicon Valley. Jeremy had gone to prep school, away from home.

From the outside he'd certainly looked like a child of great privilege. There had always been money. There hadn't been a lot of love or warm fuzzies.

He stopped and stared out into the white-topped waves. Yesterday he'd watched as Tori cradled her gently swelling tummy and he'd seen the beatific expression on her face. That sort of maternal affection was completely foreign to him.

No matter what, he wouldn't take this baby away from her. And he or she would never be a pawn in some battle. Not if he could help it.

He started the mile-long walk back to the resort, his thoughts still churning. It would be different if Tori forced his hand. What if she tried to shut him out? He wouldn't try to shut her out, but he wasn't about to let her keep him from being a part of the baby's life. He didn't want his child growing up feeling unloved, or that he didn't care. The situation had to be handled with delicacy, that was for sure.

When he was almost to the resort, he looked up and saw a figure moving around the deck that in the summer had been a patio restaurant. The woman wore a heavy coat and a headband covered her ears, a dark ponytail keeping her hair tamed and out of her face in the brisk wind. The swirl of tension in his gut told him that it was Tori, even though her back was to him. On closer examination, he saw that she was stringing lights along the railing.

He jogged up to the main resort building and climbed the steps leading from the beach to the deck. "That's a cold job," he called out, and her head snapped up, the strands of lights forgotten in her fingers.

"Sorry," he apologized. "I didn't mean to startle you."

"I didn't hear you over the wind and waves."

He opened the gate and stepped onto the deck. He had gloves on his hands, but her fingers were bare and red. "You should be wearing gloves."

"They make my fingers too clunky," she answered, going back to the string of lights.

Jeremy moved forward and took them from her, then removed his gloves, tucked them beneath his arm, and took her hands in his. They were icy cold, and he chafed his fingers over hers to warm them. "Here. Put these on."

"Jeremy, I'm—"

"Shh. They're warm." He tugged the gloves over her fingers. They were too big, but she flexed her hands and he knew the material still held some of his heat.

Moments ago he'd been ready to take her on if she decided to play hardball. Now he was giving her gloves for her cold fingers. For a moment he wondered if he was a weak man, but then he reminded himself that being on good terms would only help matters in the end.

"Let me do a few of these. You show me how you want them."

"I'm just looping them on each post, see?" She held out a hand full of tie wraps. "Putting these on them, and snipping the ends with cutters."

Unease slipped through him. She was looping them, certainly, but he went back and saw how she did it and tried to re-create the same positioning of the string, though it took a few tries. And the tie wrap… He figured out that one end went through the other and he had to pull it tight, but it was a foreign sensation. He was not a handy kind of guy, in any sense. Someone had always done that sort of thing at home. He had many talents. Being handy was not one of them.

Ugh. He really was a spoiled brat, wasn't he?

She reached into her pocket for her cutters, then tightened his wrap a bit more and snipped the end. "Have you never hung Christmas lights?" she asked.

"First time," he admitted, pulling on the strand until it was taut again. His fingers were already getting cold; how had she managed to put this many up without getting frostbite? But he pushed on because he didn't want her to think he was a wimp or completely inept. Together they positioned, fastened and clipped the lights into place. Once they traded gloves so he could warm his hands, too, and then he put the lights up and over the arched entrance to the deck. "Will anyone even come out here?" he asked, trying hard not to shiver. He was pretty sure he couldn't feel his ears anymore.

"No. But we always put the lights up and a lit tree out here. It looks nice from the beach and also from the dining room."

He clapped his hands together for warmth. "You mean we still have to do a tree?"

"What's the matter, not used to the cold?"

New York got plenty cold in the winter, but the icy wind off the ocean was going right through him today. When he didn't answer right away, she laughed—a soft, musical sound that suddenly made him feel lighter. "Your ears are pink. We'd better get you inside. Don't worry, we set up the tree inside and then move it out. Thanks for your help, though. My fingers appreciate it."

"You're welcome." Despite the cold, it had been kind of fun.

She looked at her watch. "It's nearly noon. Do you want to come in for some lunch? Or do you have appointments?"

He shrugged. "I don't have an appointment until two, so I have an hour to spare."

She opened the door that led from the deck to the dining room. "Our chef, Neil, does a curried carrot and ginger soup that is amazing. Definitely cold-weather comfort food."

They went inside and he watched as Tori went to the bar and spoke to the server behind the counter. When she came back, she led them to a table near the fireplace and hung her jacket over a chair. "Phew," she said, sitting down. "I'm not going to lie, that fire feels wonderful."

There were a handful of guests in the dining room, but it was otherwise quiet. "Not your busy time of year, huh?"

She shook her head as he took the chair opposite her. "No. The weekends are busier. People out for dinner, and our Sunday brunch is amazing." She looked up, and he got caught in her eyes again. Today her hazel eyes looked more green than brown, and her thick lashes made them seem bigger. He wondered if their baby would have her eyes.

"I'll have to try it while I'm here."

He sat back when the waitress came over with a basket of warm rolls and pats of butter. "Your lunch will be right out, Ms. Sharpe."

"Thank you, Ellen."

Tori looked up at him, a smile on her lips. "You warming up yet? Your ears aren't quite so pink."

He chuckled a little, his gaze stuck on her lips. Just his luck he couldn't quite forget kissing them. There could be none of that now. "The fire is helping. The wind is so bitter today."

"So why were you walking the beach?" she asked, picking up a roll and breaking it in half.

"Thinking," he replied, meeting her gaze. "I had a lot to think about."

"And did you come to any conclusions?"

Her voice was calm, but he could see a tightening around her mouth. She was nervous about this, too. It gave him a little comfort. The lives they'd both built—separately—were about to be disrupted.

"A few," he admitted. "But I'm not sure you're ready to hear them."

CHAPTER THREE

UNEASE SETTLED THROUGH HER, making her limbs feel heavy and her breath short. This was never going to be easy, but despite all the thinking she'd been doing the last twenty-four hours, she felt ill-prepared for whatever was going to come out of his mouth next.

She nibbled on a corner of the roll, though her appetite was diminishing rapidly. "Oh?" she asked, keeping her voice deceptively light.

He met her gaze and held it. "One thing is for sure, Tori—I can't go back to New York and pretend that this isn't happening. I'm going to be a father. I'm not going to abandon you or my child."

Tears stung her eyes and she looked down at the napkin in her lap. It was lovely to know that he accepted the pregnancy and wanted to be a part of their baby's life. But it stung that they were no more than an obligation to him; that he was tied to them out of duty and DNA and not affection.

"Thank you," she whispered.

"And whatever you need, you only have to ask. You need to know I'm willing and able to support you financially."

Financially. She clenched her fingers into fists under the table.

"Tori?"

She'd been silent so long he reached over and touched her arm, prompting her to look up. She took a deep breath, met his gaze and said quite clearly, "Thank you, Jeremy. But I'm quite able to provide for us."

His expression grew puzzled as his brows knit together. "Then what do you want from me?"

"Honestly? I don't know. Time, I suppose. To figure this out."

He looked at her tummy and then back to her face, and a hint of a smile quirked at the corner of his lips. "Well, we are on a bit of a ticking clock, don't you think? And it's halfway to midnight."

She raised her eyebrow in response. "I'm hardly Cinderella. Or a damsel in distress that needs rescuing."

At that moment their lunch was served; piping-hot bowls of soup along with bacon-and-avocado paninis that seemed to satisfy some sort of craving of Tori's right now.

"This smells delicious."

"It is. I'm kind of addicted to these sandwiches. I'm not sure if it's the avocado or the bacon that the baby likes so much, but it's my favorite."

They ate in silence for a few moments, and then Jeremy spoke again. "This feels so weird. Last summer..."

His voice trailed away and Tori's cheeks heated. Last summer she'd felt about ten years younger and stupidly carefree. Days on the beach, toes in the sand, love in the middle of the day. She'd told herself she deserved a bit of fun, but she'd been careless. They both had.

"Last summer was just...what it was." She wiped her lips with her napkin and tried to calm the rapid beat of her heart. "We got carried away. We were impulsive, and now there are consequences. We can't be impulsive this time, Jeremy. We have to make the right decisions."

"I know."

She thought of her mom, who was both dismayed at how the pregnancy had occurred and ecstatic about being a grandmother. There were just the two of them now. She was an only child, a bit of a miracle baby, really, since her mother had been told she'd probably never conceive. Her grandparents lived in Newfoundland and she rarely saw them. Her father had died two years earlier. Tori felt a certain responsibility to be there for her mom. Without Tori, Shelley had no family.

She looked at Jeremy. "Do you have brothers and sisters?"

"One of each."

The topic had never come up during their few weeks of bliss. Now that Tori thought back to those sun-soaked days, she realized that anytime she had gotten close to talking about his family, he'd changed the subject. Even now, he didn't offer any explanations. Just "one of each."

"And your parents? Are they both back in New York?"

"My mother is in Connecticut. My father lives in the Virgin Islands. They divorced when I was little."

He picked up his sandwich and took a bite, but his face was set in a grim expression even as he chewed. Her heart sank a bit. It would be a shame if he wasn't close with his family. What would that mean for their child?

"Cousins? Favorite aunts and uncles?"

He swallowed and wiped his fingers on his napkin. "What's the point of this family tree examination?"

All the warmth from earlier was gone from his voice, and she withdrew a little bit. "We just…don't know much about each other, that's all. And it seems strange under the circumstances. Besides…" She lifted her chin a bit. "These people are going to be our baby's family, too. Isn't it right I know more about them?"

He took a drink of water and put down his glass, then placed his napkin on the table as he rose. "I'm sorry, but I really should head out to my appointment. Thank you for lunch."

He took a step to pass the table and she reached out to

put a hand on his arm. "Is your family so bad you won't even talk about them?"

He looked down at her, and she couldn't read his eyes at all. They were flinty gray and shuttered, keeping her from seeing anything too personal. "It's not something to discuss over lunch."

"Then later?"

He moved his arm out from beneath her hand. "I've got to go, Tori."

The way he said her name at the end told her he wasn't as closed off as he appeared. Perhaps what they really needed was some time away from prying eyes to discuss properly what the pregnancy meant—to both of them.

"Drive carefully," she replied and shifted in her seat, letting him off the hook.

When he was gone she tried to finish her sandwich, but her appetite had gone with him.

The hot shower was exactly what Jeremy needed after the long day. This afternoon he'd visited three different properties along the South Shore, looking for the perfect home for his client, Branson Black, who was also a former classmate and one of his closest friends. Black was nearly as rich as Jeremy, but he wanted little to do with the money, which Jeremy couldn't quite understand. His instructions were to find a property with a view of the ocean and away from just about everything else. Jeremy was all about giving the client what he or she wanted, but he worried that Bran was trying to hide away from life and not just recover from recent trauma.

Still, he'd found one that he felt was perfect, and under three million. It even came with its own lighthouse, which, of course, was defunct but still lent the property an air of history and uniqueness. He had appointments to see several others during the week, though, before narrowing the choices down to send to Bran.

Being next to the ocean all day, walking the properties, had chilled him to the bone. He'd warmed himself during walk-throughs and by cranking the heat in the car, but the hot shower and warm hotel were more than welcome once he returned.

The hotel might be cozy, but Jeremy's thoughts were not.

He kept messing things up with Tori. He should have known that she'd start asking questions about his family. She was that type. Girl-next-door, nurturing, home-and-family type. He'd always been able to spot them because theirs had been so very different from his own upbringing. Last summer she'd talked about her mom a lot, and missing her dad, and Jeremy had always changed the subject. She didn't need to know that his dad had walked out when he was a little boy and that his mother hadn't been much of a mother at all; she'd left that to the nannies—plural, because his mother tended to hire young women looking to gain some "adventure" by working for rich families for a year or two and then moving on. Some had been nice. Some had been tolerable, more excited about the money and their days off. The last one had had an affair with his stepfather, and that had been the end of the nannies and the beginning of the talk about boarding school. His stepdad had stayed. Jeremy had been sent away.

But it had been a blessing, really. When he'd finished middle school, he'd been sent to out-of-the-way Merrick Hall. And there he'd found his family—of sorts. Including Branson.

He tugged on a warm sweater and called down to room service for dinner. When it was delivered forty minutes later, he opened the door to find Tori's soft face behind the cart.

"Room service," she said softly, and offered a timid smile.

He couldn't find it in himself to stay irritated. He opened the door wide and let her in, watching her hips sway as she moved the cart into the room. He swallowed thickly. Tori Sharpe was no less attractive now than she'd been five months ago. There was a subtle sexuality about her that was alluring. And when she turned around and the gentle swell of her tummy was visible, his heart gave a little thump. That was his child in there. He had no idea what to do but he knew for sure he wanted to be a better dad than his own had been.

"It's late. I didn't think you'd still be working," he said, then realized how critical he must sound right now. "Thank you for bringing it," he added, trying to be less of a jerk. After all, he'd walked out of their lunch like a coward.

"I waited for you to come back," she admitted, her dark eyes troubled. "I didn't like how we left things at lunch, and I wanted to say I was sorry for prying."

"You had a right to ask those questions. It's not your fault I don't like answering them."

She folded her hands in front of her. "You should eat while it's hot. Let me set this up for you."

He watched as she set a place at the small table and chair by the window of the suite, poured his beer into a glass and whisked the cover off his entrée to reveal a glistening steak surrounded by roasted potatoes, grilled asparagus and button mushrooms in garlic butter. It smelled heavenly, and his stomach growled in response.

"Have you eaten?"

"I have," she said. "So please, sit down. I'll leave you to it."

She turned to go and was almost to the door when he said, "Tori? Stay."

The moment she paused seemed filled with…well, surely not possibility? There was a change though, somehow. As if the invitation marked a willing step toward discussion. Intention, rather than dancing around the topic or taking the temperature of the situation.

And when she turned back around and faced him, his stomach quivered. He didn't let himself get too personally involved with anyone, but he was going to have to with her, wasn't he? At least if he wanted more of a relationship with his kid than sending a support check every month.

"Are you sure?"

He nodded. "I was rude this afternoon. I'm sorry about that."

She took a single step toward him. "Neither of us knows how to navigate this. It's an unusual situation."

He gestured to the seat across the table from his food. "Come sit. Do you want some tea? Or anything else sent up?"

"There's water on the cart. I'll grab one of your glasses and have some. That's all I need."

He waited until she had her water and then they sat together. It felt wrong, eating while she wasn't, but the food was delicious and by her own admission she'd had dinner already. The asparagus was done to perfection and the steak mouthwateringly medium, just as he'd requested.

"Your chef is very good," he said. "This is delicious."

"Tastes here aren't terribly adventurous, so he does simple things well and adds a bit of flair when he can. But no one leaves hungry." She smiled. "Neil has been here a long time, and the rest of the kitchen staff have trained under him. It makes for a consistent culinary experience."

The resort wasn't as glamorous as some he'd stayed in, but he had no complaints.

"And you've been here a long time, too."

She lifted her water glass. "Since I was in high school. I started in housekeeping. Then moved to waitressing when I was legal age. Front desk for a while, too."

"You trained yourself to know the different departments," he observed, and her cheeks colored a little.

"I wanted to be in administration. For a while I was the events manager, in charge of special functions. Then when the assistant manager retired, I applied for the job and got it. This week, I'm acting manager since Tom is away on vacation. Saint Lucia, lucky thing!"

"And your mom is here. You have strong ties."

"The strongest. My mom doesn't have anyone else, really. As far as family goes, that is. Of course, she has friends."

"As do you."

Her brow furrowed. "Well, yes."

"And so you probably wouldn't consider moving."

Her hand stilled halfway to the table, the glass trembling in her fingers. "Moving? As in…"

"Nearer to me. So our baby could be close to both parents."

"Not *with* you."

His eyes widened. Did she think he was going to ask her to move in with him? Or "do the right thing" and propose? Their affair had been amazing, but there wasn't love between them.

"This isn't the fifties. We don't have to get married to parent this child. But I did wonder if you'd consider moving somewhere closer to, well, me. Of course, I'd look after everything financially."

Her throat worked for several seconds while she studied her fingers, then looked up. Her eyes were clear and there was no censure on her face, either. "It's a generous offer, Jeremy. But my life is here, as you just heard. I'm truly glad you want to be a part of his or her life, but I'm not prepared to completely uproot mine to make that happen, any more than you're willing to uproot yours."

She was right. If the shoe were on the other foot, he'd never agree to leaving his life behind and moving to small-town Nova Scotia. They were from totally different worlds.

"I respect that," he said, putting down his knife and fork. "I really do. But I thought I should at least put the possibility on the table."

"Of course."

"We don't have to decide right away, right? You've got a few more months to go."

She nodded. Then her expression softened. "About today... I'm sorry if I picked at a sore spot. Was your childhood awful? Is that why you don't talk about your family?"

He sliced into the steak and considered. She was going to find out at some point, wasn't she? All she had to do was get on the internet and do a bit of digging and she'd find out who he was. "My older sister works on Wall Street. And my big brother moved to California straight out of MIT. He worked for a few start-ups right out of college and then started his own. Now he's CEO of a Fortune 500 tech company."

"Wow."

"Yeah. Being in property, I'm kind of the underachiever of the family."

"But property is a huge investment," she contradicted, and he was amused and a bit flattered that she jumped to his defense. "And you don't sell average houses. Your clientele are all rich, right?"

"Yeah. Dropping a few mil on a house is no big deal for them." He realized she had no idea exactly how wealthy he was, and it both amused and pleased him.

"It's a whole other world."

He looked at her and held her gaze. "They're people, just like anyone else. They have their own pressures, insecurities, heartache. It's true that money can't buy happiness, you know."

"But it sure can help take some of the stress off," she remarked, leaning back in her chair. "So how much are you worth, Jeremy?"

She said it lightly, teasing even, but he figured now was the time to be honest.

"One point two billion," he replied.

She burst out laughing, then stopped abruptly as he merely kept watching her. He knew it was a crazy sum of money. Some days he didn't believe it himself.

"Wait. You're not joking."

"No, I'm not."

"You've made that much money in realty?" Her lips dropped open in disbelief.

"Hardly." He pushed his plate away, leaving a few little potatoes, and reached for the beer. "But I had a big trust fund—the one thing my dad left me. And I have a sister on Wall Street who manages my money for me. Add all my assets together…and you get that number."

She breathed out a couple of curse words that made him grin. "I always knew you had money, but…holy—"

"Our child won't have to worry about a thing, and neither will you." On impulse, he leaned over and took her hand. "I don't know what this is going to look like, but I do know this. I promise that I will never abandon you or our kid. If that means we're just friendly and we co-parent, then that's how it'll be. But if you need anything at all, you just have to pick up the phone. I'll be there for you."

He meant every word. He also knew that what he'd just said had essentially tied him to her for the rest of his life.

What had he just done?

CHAPTER FOUR

TORI TRIED TO quell the thrill that slid through her as Jeremy took her hand and promised to be there for her and their child. He was a tough man to resist at any time, but right now, with her hand in his, and the knowledge that he was a freaking billionaire swimming through her brain, she was quite overwhelmed.

She didn't care that he had bags of money. It wasn't that. It was just that she'd never met anyone quite this rich before. She certainly hadn't known last summer. It shouldn't change him in her eyes, but it did. He was so out of her league.

Not as a person; she knew that money and character were two very different things. But in worldly ways, he was on a whole other plane of existence.

"I don't know what to say," she responded, biting down on her lip. "I had no idea that… Well, Jeremy." She let out a big breath. "I'll make you a promise in return. I promise that I will never exploit the fact that you have money. I don't want us to use money against each other, you know? Either how much we have or the lack of it."

"Me, either. I want us to figure this out in a way that's best for our baby."

"You really do believe everything, don't you? About it being yours and everything?"

He let out a sigh. "I didn't react so well when I saw you were pregnant. But yes, I believe you."

"When the baby is born we can do a DNA test. I wasn't

going to do an amnio if I could avoid it. The idea freaks me out."

"A what?"

"An amniocentesis. It's a test where they insert this needle and withdraw a bit of the amniotic fluid—"

He shuddered. "Ouch, and gross."

She laughed. "Yeah. And there are some risks involved. I didn't want to take any chances."

"So you really do want the baby."

She nodded. "I do. It wasn't planned, but I... I don't have much family. And I like children, a lot."

Her clock hadn't really begun ticking yet, not at twenty-eight, but she couldn't lie. She'd been starting to think about a family the last few years. This pregnancy was inconvenient and a shock, yes. But also a blessing.

"I'm not close to mine, as you might have gathered." He took a long pull of his beer and pursed his lips. "I'm closest to my sister, and we both live in New York so we see each other most of anyone. But my brother... He's on his third marriage already and does his own thing."

"And your mom?"

"She's still at the family home in Connecticut. Married to my stepfather. Socializing with the right people, that sort of thing. My dad left and she got the house. Not much else, but we all had our trust funds and she married again within a few years. She made sure she was looked after."

There was a bitterness in his voice he couldn't disguise, and Tori wondered about the little boy he must have been. "I take it she wasn't the nurturing type?"

He laughed—a short, mocking sound. "Not an ounce," he replied, then drained his beer glass. He got up, went to the minibar, and took out a bottle of Cape Breton whiskey, adding a significant splash to a highball glass. He swirled it for a moment before turning and looking at her.

"My mom was a social climber. I didn't know it then, but I know it now. I see the type. And when Dad left, she lost her ticket. She would have had to sell the house and finish bringing us up on her own. Instead she married Bruce, and since she came with the house, he brought the rest of his money and status was restored. Some investments on her part paid for our college. Bruce, apparently, was more than happy to pay my four years of tuition to boarding school. I wasn't really home after I finished eighth grade."

He downed the whiskey in one gulp, and poured another.

She sat quietly. First of all, clearly the topic was painful to him, because he was fortifying himself with alcohol. And secondly, as much as his words were delivered in a factual, who-gives-a-care way, she could tell that the lack of affection had left its mark on him.

Tori couldn't imagine not loving your own child, or considering them in the way. Or sending them away, at such a difficult age.

"Where did you go?"

"Merrick Hall, an all-boys school in Connecticut. Very *Dead Poets Society* with old buildings and rituals and dormitories. Top-notch learning, though." He must have seen her alarmed look because he attempted a smile and went to her. "It was fine, really," he assured her. "I belonged there. I met my best friends there. And despite my cold family, I do have some really great friends."

Tori let out a breath. "Oh, of course you do. But now I understand your reluctance. Do you still see your mother? Your stepfather?"

He nodded. "Now and again. Despite everything, she *is* my mother."

Tori was glad. Estrangement could be such a horrible thing.

"So now you know what I didn't want to talk about over lunch." He sipped at his drink this time, to her relief. "I don't know what kind of father I'll make. But I promise to try. Any kid of mine is going to feel wanted and loved. Not in the way."

He said it with such finality that Tori's heart broke just a little. She'd been brought up in a home with so much love. It was incomprehensible to think of a parent being so careless and dismissive, but she knew it happened.

She looked up at Jeremy, at his dark hair and stormy eyes and cheeks, slightly flushed from the day's wind and the warm whiskey. She wanted to reach up and brush the errant curl off his forehead, to smooth the creases on his forehead, to see his lips curve in a smile again. But she kept her hands to herself, knowing that touching him, kissing him, would only make matters more complicated than they already were.

"Then we're going to be fine," she whispered, twisting her fingers together to keep from reaching out. "Because that's what I want, too. And we'll figure out the rest of the details somehow."

Their gazes held for a few seconds, and then a few seconds more, long enough for something to stir between them. Her body remembered what his felt like and ached to feel it pressed against her again. She remembered how he tasted, the way he angled his head to kiss her, and how he nibbled at her lower lip before taking a kiss deeper.

She stepped back, unwilling to cross that line again. "I should go. It's getting late and I'm on shift again tomorrow."

"When do you get a day off?"

"On Thursday, when Tom is back from his holiday."

"I'll have narrowed down some properties by then. Why don't you come along for some second walk-throughs?

Some of these places are really stunning. You can tell me where we should eat lunch and we can make a day of it."

She frowned. "Are you sure that's a good idea?"

"How are we going to manage to parent together if we can't get through a day in each other's company?"

He made sense, even though Tori knew it was simplifying the matter. "Well, all right. If the weather is good. And as long as nothing comes up here."

"Of course."

She began to clear his plate and dinner mess and put it back on the room service cart. "You don't have to do that," he said.

She laughed. "Sure I do. I work here, remember? I'll drop it off at the kitchen and then go home."

He opened the door for her and she wheeled the cart out into the hall. Then she looked back at him. "Thanks for telling me about your family, Jeremy," she said. "I know you didn't want to."

"It's out there now," he replied, leaning on the door. "Just please…don't judge me on the basis of my relatives. I've tried very hard to be…different."

"I judge a person on what I see them do," she answered, and gave him a smile. "So far you're in the clear."

He smiled back then, a sexy sideways little slice of amusement. "I'll see you soon." Then with a little laugh, he backed up and shut the door.

She wheeled the cart down the hallway to the elevator while trying to calm her thrumming pulse. Amity was better than enmity, for sure, but how was she going to deal with a smiling Jeremy? Because she still found him incredibly attractive. Still got that light feeling in her chest when he smiled at her. And with their baby on the way, she couldn't afford to let her head get into the clouds.

Life wasn't made of fairy tales. It just had reality, and this was hers. She'd better figure it out.

Thursday dawned bright and clear, and after a brief meeting with Tom to bring him up to speed, Tori bundled up in her warm parka and gloves. Her knee-high boots and leggings were comfortable and warmer than she would have been in a skirt. The jacket was a bit snug around the waist, and she tugged on the zipper to get it over her growing bump. She supposed a new coat would be on the shopping list, but she hated spending the money on something she'd wear for only one winter.

Jeremy was waiting in the lounge sipping on coffee when she emerged from her office. To be honest, she was looking forward to the morning. There were worse things than wandering through luxury homes. She loved flipping through magazines and seeing the fancy decor. Now she could see some in person. Maybe even get some ideas for the hotel.

"Hi there."

Jeremy turned around and she tried not to stare. He was in suit pants and shoes, with a soft wool coat and plaid scarf around his neck. His hair was finger-combed back from his face, making it seem groomed but carelessly so.

"Hi, yourself. Do you want a tea for the road? Something hot?"

"No, I'm fine. I had a decaf in the office with Tom this morning. You're ready?"

"Just let me get this in a travel cup and I will be." He flashed her a smile—another jolt to her heart—and beckoned for the waitress to grab him a cup. Within seconds he had his hand at the base of Tori's spine, solicitously leading her out to his rental.

It was a freaking Jaguar.

He held the door and she slid into the sleek interior, the soft leather cradling her like it was shaped to her bottom. It was cold, but in moments he had the heater turned up and her heated seat on. A map on the console flashed and he hit a preset for one of the properties, and then they were on the road, heading toward Bridgewater.

"Where are we going first?"

He tapped the wheel along with the satellite radio station that was playing. "A house in the Pleasantville area. On the LaHave River."

"I know the area."

"Branson's looking for a place to…well, regroup, I guess. He's had a rough year."

"Branson?"

"My client. And my friend."

"How has his year been rough?"

Jeremy frowned. "It's not really my place to say, you know? He's a private guy, and I respect that. But if he wants to be invisible, I'm going to help him get what he needs and make sure it's a good investment. I don't think he'll live here full-time, at least not after a while." He looked over at Tori. "As his friend, my hope is he'll put himself back together, and use this place as a summer home. Get back to throwing parties and having fun. He needs to smile again."

Tori wondered what could be so awful that Jeremy couldn't talk about it, but she respected his desire to protect his friend's privacy. "He's one of your Merrick friends?"

Jeremy nodded. "Yep."

The drive to Pleasantville wasn't long, and Jeremy had just finished his coffee when they pulled through iron gates into a long drive.

At the top was a gorgeous gray-shingled house with a three-car garage attached. Tori's breath caught—it was so cozy looking despite its size. "How much did you say this was?" she asked, scanning the yard, which was covered with a thin layer of snow.

"One point four."

"It doesn't seem quite that grand."

He chuckled. "You wait. It's three acres on the water, and the bottom floor is a walkout. It looks much bigger from the back than the front."

He led her to the front door and then opened the lockbox, giving them entry. She stepped inside and gasped. It was so airy and light and beautiful!

She took off her boots and left them on the rug at the door, then stepped onto the silky hardwood. "Okay, so you're right. It's bigger inside than it looks from the outside."

He took her on a walk-through. The kitchen walls were a pale yellow, with white cupboards and woodwork, and granite countertop along the counters and the center island. Stainless steel appliances gleamed in the morning sun, and Tori couldn't stop herself from oohing over the double wall ovens. Their footsteps echoed through the rest of the downstairs rooms, and then they went up the curved staircase to the next level, where several of the rooms had windows overlooking the water. Even the en suite bathroom was perfectly situated so that one could soak in the oversize tub and look out at the river and a huge tree standing sentinel by a small dock.

"A dock for a boat."

"Yes. And a short sail down the river to the ocean. What do you think?"

She laughed. "It's beautiful and ginormous. You've seen my cottage. What would I ever do with this much room?"

She could feel his gaze on her as she wandered to the windows of the master bedroom again. "But it is lovely. Truly. And despite the size, it feels like a home. That's nice."

They put their shoes back on and wandered around the outside for a bit, and Tori discovered he was right. The house's most impressive aspect was from the river, looking in. Three stories of large windows shone in the sunlight.

"Kids could play here," she mused. "It's just a gentle slope to the water. And gardens. Are there gardens in the summer?"

"Yes, though, of course, we can't see them now."

"Wow. Is this the kind of place you always show, Jeremy?"

He laughed. "Yes and no. This type of property would cost a lot more in other areas. And some of the properties in Manhattan would stop your heart."

"Like yours?"

He shrugged. "I live on the Upper East Side. It's not known for being cheap."

She put her hands in her pockets and squinted up at him. "How much was your place?"

He met her gaze. "Just over four."

"Million?"

He nodded. "It's pretty modest. I didn't need someplace huge and empty, you know?"

"Oh, my—"

He burst out laughing then and she joined in, just because it all seemed so incredulous and the sound of his laughter filled her with some sort of strange joy.

"Come on," he said, holding out his hand. "Let's go see the next one."

They left the house behind and journeyed a short way to a property that was more isolated and right on the ocean. A small cliff separated the property from the sea, and at once Tori was taken with it.

"If the last one was homey, this one is wild," she said, stepping out of the car. The wind off the water whipped her hair off her face and she turned into it, loving the feel even though it wrapped around her with icy-cold fingers. "It's incredible here!"

She had to shout to be heard, but she could see the look of admiration on Jeremy's face and knew this was a favorite of his, too. She rounded the hood of the car and met him on the crushed walkway to the house. "You love it, don't you?" she asked, tucking a swath of hair behind her ear.

"I do. And you'll see why in a minute."

When they got inside, he swept out an arm. "Now do you see?"

Past the foyer was a center area with a small table in the middle, holding a bouquet of flowers. And to the left was the beginning of a circular staircase that climbed up…and up…and up. Tori went to the middle and looked up. There was a skylight at the top, so that a perfect column of light fell from the roof right to the spot where the table sat, and the column was framed by the dark wood of the railings and the creamy white of the steps' risers.

"That," she said definitively, "is a conversation piece. Amazing."

"Isn't it? And there's a sauna downstairs, and an exercise room…"

"No private beach?"

"There is, but it's not direct access because of the cliffs. I'd show you, but I'm afraid it's a bit icy and I don't want you to fall."

There was a room on the side that was rounded, like a hexagon, windows all around to provide a 270-degree view. A stone fireplace was in one "corner," with granite along the bottom of the wall, giving it a rustic feel.

"Can you imagine," she said, unable to keep the awe out of her voice, "sitting here with the fire blazing and a storm outside, with a glass of wine and a book?"

"Yeah," he said softly. "I can."

Their eyes met. This house was not for them. They weren't even a *thing*. But walking through it together was…intimate in a way she hadn't expected. She cleared her throat. "Come on, show me the rest, then."

On top of the porch was a railed deck, with French doors leading from the master bedroom. Tori had never seen such luxury in her life. Even with the furniture moved out, the rooms were commanding in their size and the views were incomparable. Two more huge bedrooms, each with their own bath, finished the upstairs.

"You want to recommend this one, don't you?" she asked. "You like it a lot."

He nodded. "I think it suits Branson, but it's pretty isolated. And did I mention the best part? It has its own lighthouse at the edge of the property. Look."

He pointed southeast, where the land jutted out into the ocean. It wasn't huge, but sure enough, a red-and-white lighthouse stood sentinel, looking a little worse for wear. "Is it still active?"

"No," he replied, sounding disappointed. "But the owner assures me it's still in working order. Solid as the cliff it's built on."

It was undeniably romantic. Who wouldn't want to have their own lighthouse?

"Can we see it?"

He shook his head. "It's a different key, and I don't have access to it."

"Oh."

They wandered through some more, and Tori was quite taken with it all. When he told her the price tag, she laughed and said a girl could dream, but then laughed again and asked what she'd ever do with all that space.

It needed people to fill it up. It needed not only priceless views but life and laughter.

They headed back toward Liverpool, went past the exit and on to a third house that was on Jeremy's short list. She didn't like it nearly as well, though. It was in the same price range as the others, but was a little too avant-garde for her in its design. The house itself looked like a giant block dropped on the sand, and inside it was nearly as austere.

"You don't like it," he said as they walked through.

"It has every amenity a person could want," she remarked, "but I feel off balance. I don't feel at home here. And I know it sounds weird, but I feel like it could just tip over into the Atlantic."

He laughed. "Fair enough."

She put her hands on the cold railing of the stairs and said, "It's the kind of place that people call 'innovative' and 'remarkable' but there's not a lot of comfort here."

"So let's take it off the list."

She looked at him with some alarm. "Oh, gosh, don't take anything I say into account! I have no idea about real estate."

He came over and stood next to her, his hand on the railing close to hers. "But you do know what goes into making people feel comfortable and at home. It's part of why the Sandpiper is such a success. That's what my friend needs right now."

Her heart stuttered a bit. He was a surprise for sure. "Which one gets you the biggest commission?"

He laughed. "This one, actually. But it's never about that."

"It's not?"

"I don't need the money. But I like finding people places to live. I like to imagine them happy there."

"You surprise me, Jeremy."

"Why?"

She put her hand on his chest. "Because in there is the heart of a man who is looking for a home."

His face closed off immediately and he stood back. "That's just you being sentimental."

She'd touched a nerve; it didn't take a genius to figure that out. She dropped her hand. "Oh, maybe. I still think it's nice that you think about what suits the person and not just the biggest payoff."

He lifted his chin, gesturing toward the front door. "Should we find some lunch?"

Her stomach had been growling for an hour, so she readily agreed. "I know just the place."

He followed her outside, and she waited while he locked up. All the while Tori realized she was getting a better glimpse of what made Jeremy Fisher tick. And so far, what she saw made her heart soften. He could deny it all he wanted, but she'd been right. He was looking for home.

She'd always known what home meant. She'd always been wanted and nurtured and valued. What must it be like to have to search for those things?

CHAPTER FIVE

JEREMY WAS STILL shaken by Tori's observation back at the house. Was she right? Did everything come down to wanting to find a place he could call home? He'd done that, hadn't he? He loved his place, with the view of Central Park and the bustle of New York all around him. He was in the middle of it all. Work, restaurants, theater, museums.

But still, there was something missing. And how astute of Tori to realize it.

He buckled his seat belt and turned to her. "Okay, so where are we going?"

She took him to a little hole-in-the-wall restaurant with scarred wood tables and plastic tablecloths, and ordered them both fish and chips. "It's the house specialty," she insisted, and when the food came he goggled at the size of the platter. The whole plate was covered in crispy fries, with two pieces of battered fish on top, a paper cup of tartar sauce and a dish of coleslaw on the side.

"Vinegar?" the waitress asked, as she put down the steaming plates.

"Oh, yes, please."

Jeremy watched as Tori liberally shook vinegar on her fish and fries. "Come on," she said, grabbing her paper napkin and putting it on her knees. "Dig in."

He cut a piece of fish off with his fork and popped it in his mouth. Delicious. Light batter, perfectly crispy and flaky haddock inside. "Mmm."

"See?" She grinned at him as she speared a fry and dipped it in some ketchup.

He took another bite, then ate a fry and then tried some of the tangy coleslaw. Everything was amazing. He was glad he'd had only a fruit cup at breakfast with his coffee. The portions were huge.

"Why didn't we come here last summer?" he asked. It was close to her place, close to the Sandpiper.

"Because you can't get in the door here in the summertime. It's packed." She grinned up at him and let out a breath. "I need to slow down."

"Don't do it on my account." Truthfully, her love of food amused him. The last few dates he'd been on, the women had barely tasted their food and then insisted they were full. It had never made sense to him. People needed to eat to survive. It was also an experience to be enjoyed. Seeing Tori's grin as she bit down on a french fry made him happy for some reason.

"You're probably used to nicer restaurants," she said, pausing to take a drink of water. "Honestly, last summer I had no idea you were so rich. I would have recommended a few places. Particularly in Halifax."

He met her gaze. "At the time I was happy with whatever filled my hunger."

Her cheeks colored as she interpreted a double meaning he hadn't intended. But it was true. He'd been hungry for her. He still was, if he were being honest with himself. Knowing she was carrying his child only made her more beautiful, if that were possible. He had no trouble remembering the taste of her lips or the softness of her skin, the scent of sunscreen filling the air and the tangle of her hair in his hands. It was what had driven him to come back here in the first place. Branson's request had simply given him the excuse.

He shifted in his chair and dug into the fillet once more. Then he changed the conversation to safer topics, like the houses they'd already looked at. "You're going to recommend the one on the bluff, aren't you?" she asked.

"I think so, yes. I'll show him all three and give him my impressions, but overall I think that's what he'll pick."

"It was my favorite. I love how the ocean is so wild there, right on the point."

They'd made it through their fish and half the fries when Tori pushed her plate back. "Okay, I really have to stop if I'm going to have dessert."

He gawped. "Dessert?"

She laughed. "Yes. Because they make all their pies on-site and the coconut cream is my favorite."

He wasn't sure where he was going to put it, and he wouldn't have to eat for the rest of the day, but when the waitress came back, they ordered pie—the coconut cream for her and butterscotch for him, something he'd never had before. He had another coffee and she ordered a decaf, and they lingered a long time, sipping and picking at their dessert.

"This was nice," she said, absently fluffing her fork through some of the cream on top of her pie. "I think it bodes well for us getting along."

"Me, too. Though we didn't really talk about the future."

Her face turned troubled, with her lips tightening and her lashes cast down. He wondered why she did that, because he'd noticed it a few times now when there was the potential for conflict.

"Hey," he said softly, making her look up at him. "We'll get there. I've got more time here. Another week, anyway. I've got to go up to Halifax for a few days, too. You can take some time, and I will, too, to see if we can come up with a plan."

She nodded. "I know. It's fine, really. I just realized that this really wasn't how I'd planned to start a family. With his or her parents living in different countries."

"It's not ideal, but it's the reality we have to work with." At her downcast expression, he put his hand over hers. "Hey. Look on the bright side. I have the means to come visit, or have you come to New York. That sounds okay, right? We won't have to stress over money."

Her eyes brightened. "You mean you'd be okay with us staying here?"

He hadn't meant to agree to that so readily. Truthfully, he'd thought about how great it would be to have her move to New York so he could see his kid whenever he wanted. But he didn't want to get into that now, and mar the great day they'd been having. "There are a lot of options," he deflected, pulling his hand away and reaching for the last of his coffee. "So maybe what we need to do is think about what we each want and then sit down and have a discussion about it. See if we can find some middle ground."

"That sounds fair," she agreed. "I mean, so far we've managed not to argue about anything, and that's quite an achievement, considering."

He nodded, but something felt a little bit off. Like they hadn't argued…yet. And that something was going to come along and cause some friction, and he really didn't want that to happen. He didn't want to argue with her at all. Quite the contrary.

Jeremy frowned as he picked up the check. That was part of the problem, wasn't it? He still desired her, and now that they were spending more time together, he was discovering he still liked her, too. The woman he'd met last summer was the real Tori—smiling and easygoing, easy to be with, and a knack for making him smile. He'd been drawn to her charm and easy laugh, and had felt like he could simply be himself.

The combination made her more dangerous than she could imagine. Because the last thing he wanted was a ready-made family. He didn't know the first thing about how real families worked. His had always been dysfunctional. His most normal relationship had been with the gardener who had come around twice a week to look after the grounds and cut the grass.

Lord, what would Mr. Adley have to say about this predicament?

He'd tell him to do the right thing. The only trouble was, Jeremy had no idea what the right thing might be. It certainly wasn't a slapped-together marriage for the sake of a baby. For a marriage, there needed to be love, and Jeremy was relatively certain that he wasn't capable of that particular emotion.

They got in the car and headed back toward the hotel, where Tori would be able to pick up her car and head home. When they were maybe five minutes away, Tori sat up straight in her seat and pointed. "Slow down...there." She looked over at him and then pointed again, right at a small for-sale sign on a stake at the roadside. "Turn in here, Jeremy. Please!"

She said it with such urgency that he immediately braked and turned into the side road. "What are you looking for?"

"There was a for-sale sign, and there are only a few houses in here. I'm curious."

They'd finished their viewings, and it was still early, so he figured he might as well indulge her. "It's definitely off the beaten path."

"And straight down to the beach. Not the one by the

inn, but a kilometer or so down the coast. It's not as big, but it's lovely. And it's on private property."

They found the for-sale sign close to the end of the lane, but the gate was closed. Tori looked so disappointed that he picked up his cell and dialed the number for the agent.

Then he turned to Tori with a smile. "He can be here in twenty minutes. It's vacant—do you want to get out and walk the property?"

"I could stand to walk off some lunch," she replied, her eyes brightening again. "I'm gonna confess, Jeremy. I've always wanted to see this property. I've seen it from the water. I had no idea it was for sale, though."

"Then let's go."

He parked the car along the side of the lane, then took Tori's arm as they navigated their way around the small gate that was more for show than security. The drive was about a hundred and fifty yards long through a stand of trees, but then it opened up to a cleared yard and a property that was smaller and less grand than the others they'd seen, but impressive just the same.

"Oh, wow," Tori breathed, letting go of his arm as she moved forward. "Look at that."

The outside of the house was done in gray siding with white trim, with an oversize front door and stone steps and a stone walkway leading toward the drive. He'd seen and dismissed this property listing earlier in the week; at under three thousand square feet and a price tag below a million, it was less than what Branson was looking for. That didn't detract in any way from its charm. Under the film of snow, they saw stone gardens dotted with evergreen shrubs, and other areas that would no doubt sprout into a profusion of perennials come spring. The back of the house faced the water, and a path that ended in a set of steps led to the white-sand beach below. A quick assessment told Jeremy that the property probably included about three hundred feet or more of shoreline.

Tucked away in a corner was another smaller building, what Jeremy would have assumed was a converted boathouse. It too was gray, but with shaker shingles and a charming red front door. He was acutely aware of Tori at his side, eyes wide, falling in love with the place.

Her current house was about the size of the boathouse, certainly under a thousand square feet. Charm galore, but tiny.

"Oh, isn't this lovely?" She peeked into the front window. "It could be a guesthouse, or…" She turned to him, her eyes bright. "Something the owners could rent out or something. I mean, it's nicer than renting a room or basement. Guests would have their own space. I wonder if there's a little kitchen. It's cute as anything."

She was beautiful like this, so animated and with her eyes full of possibilities. It was what made her sweet, what made her entirely suited for her job at the Sandpiper. As she circled the little house, he realized with a sinking heart that she belonged here. She wasn't the kind to be happy in the city, was she? She loved the ocean, the open spaces, the wildness. It was as different from New York as sun from rain.

And he couldn't live here. Oh, financially he didn't need to work another day in his life if he didn't want to. But he'd be miserable otherwise. He needed a purpose. A challenge.

By the time she'd finished examining the lot, the Realtor arrived and was ready to show them the house. Inside was just as stunning as he'd imagined, with surprises in some of the detail, such as the iron-and-glass doors to a hidden patio. The iron was in the pattern of lilies, scrolling up through the glass. It was one of the nicest custom-made pieces he'd seen, and that was saying something. There were three large bedrooms upstairs, sweeping views, a chef's delight of a kitchen, and a garden with a stone firepit in the back.

"Oh, look. That's so pretty! And you could put chairs around it and have fires and roast marshmallows in the summer. And hear the ocean." Tori stood at the window, her face nearly touching the glass. "I know you said it wasn't on your list, but this is my favorite one yet."

"It's a bit small for the client. But you're right. It's a wonderful property. How long has it been on the market?"

The Realtor, who'd been wisely letting the house speak for itself, stepped forward. "Since September."

"Really." Jeremy lifted an eyebrow.

"It's not really a seller's market at the moment, as I'm sure you know." There was no harm in saying it, Jeremy knew exactly what the market was like and the other man knew it. "But the owners don't want to sell it for less than it's worth."

Of course not. And in truth, they could have added a good fifty-to-one-hundred thousand to the price and it would still be a good deal.

"I'll keep it in mind for other clients," Jeremy said, offering his hand. "Thanks for coming out today."

"My pleasure."

They stepped outside the house again and walked down the lane to where they'd parked the car. Tori lifted her hand in a friendly wave as the Realtor passed them on the way by. He smiled to himself; it was such a small-town thing to do.

They settled back into his car and started on the short drive back to the hotel. Tori sank into the seat and let out a sigh, resting her hand on her tummy. It was such a maternal gesture that his heart wrenched a little. She was going to be a good mother. There was genuine warmth and gentleness to her and he was at least thankful that his child would be in a happy, nurturing environment.

He cast his eyes back onto the road again. He was already thinking in terms of his child living with her as if everything was already settled. Was that really what he wanted? To just back off and leave his kid here, while he returned to his previously scheduled life, with occasional visits so his son or daughter at least knew what he looked like?

He thought back to his upbringing, and his gut twisted. He actually couldn't remember what his father looked like, and it had taken many, many years for him to stop hoping that one day Brett Fisher would show up for his birthday or for Christmas, and take him away from the cold, lonely life he led. He refused to let any kid of his feel that way—always looking out the window, wondering if his father would come, disappointed when he didn't, only to have his hopes raised and dashed again and again.

What was the alternative?

They arrived back at the hotel and he got out and opened Tori's door before she had a chance to. She smiled up at him and his stomach twisted again, this time not out of pain but out of confusion. In some ways Tori was a stranger. They'd spent a few weeks having some fun, and now a few days talking. But in other ways, she was more than that. His feelings were complicated by desire and concern and, he realized, a bit of fear.

Because he liked her, dammit. And wanted her. And the baby they'd made would join them together forever.

"What's wrong?" she asked, putting her hand on his arm, concern etching her face. "You're frowning."

"Just thinking," he replied, but consciously relaxed his

features. "I should probably go up and put my thoughts together for Branson, and give him a call."

"Right. I keep forgetting today was work for you." She smiled, then looped her arm through his as they walked toward the lobby doors. "It was fun for me."

He tried to ignore how good her arm felt around his, her body pressed close to his side. "It was for me, too. Not every day is like this, though."

"Do you think your friend will put in an offer?"

"Perhaps."

"Why Nova Scotia, instead of somewhere else? I mean, there's Cape Cod. Or the Maine coast. What about the Hamptons? Don't all the richest people live in the Hamptons?"

She was so sweet and artless. She was looking up at him with a playful smile and he fought the urge to simply turn her into his arms and kiss her lips. "I think there's a family connection somehow," he replied, swallowing against the urge to make a move. And that was all he'd say about Branson's connection to Nova Scotia. The rest would require explaining about events of recent months, and he valued Bran's privacy too much.

They stepped into the lobby, straight into warmth and hospitality and holiday cheer. A new addition—a ten-foot Christmas tree—was front and center, with sparkling white lights and blue plaid ribbon wrapped around its evergreen fullness. Clear, silver and blue ornaments shone from the tiny lights. "The Nova Scotia tartan," he murmured, nodding at the tree. "The ribbon. Whose idea?"

"Every year a different department gets to decorate the tree. This year it was housekeeping." She let go of his arm and walked to the tree, then plucked off an ornament and shook her head. "Oh, look at these," she said, holding it out in her hand.

He took it from her palm and turned it over in his fingers. The ball was white but transparent, and in silver paint was the word *Dream*.

There were others, they discovered. Some said *Rest*. Others *Relax* and *Indulge*. "I bet Miriam made these," Tori murmured, hanging one back on the tree. "She's amazing."

His mother would die before having handmade ornaments on her tree, and yet here he was in a luxury hotel and it was celebrated, not discouraged. The ornaments were as nice as any he'd seen, simple but elegant. At the top of each one was a perfect bow made from the same tartan pattern.

"You have some talented staff." He ran his fingertips over the sharp needles of the tree. "And you let them thrive."

"Everyone brings talents to the table. What kind of place would we be if we didn't take their ideas into account? Some of them are very, very good."

"You're incredible," he murmured, standing way too close to her. As if they suddenly realized it, he took a step back and Tori shifted away. But then the distance gave him a chance to see what was above her head. A large sprig of fresh mistletoe hung from the archway, and Tori was directly beneath it.

Before he could talk himself out of it, he stepped up to her and put his hand on the nape of her neck.

Alarmed eyes met with his. "What are you doing?" she whispered.

And then he pointed up, to the mistletoe above their heads. And when she looked back at him again, the confusion was gone and her face reflected back to him what he was feeling. Longing and fear together.

He leaned forward and touched his lips to hers, softly, testing. She was stiff, as if holding her breath, but the moment he paused and slid his fingers an inch through her hair, she relaxed and her lips opened a little. Just a bit, but enough that their mouths fitted together with a sweetness that shook him to the soles of his feet.

This woman. This moment. Carrying his child.

His head said he should not be kissing her. But to his heart it felt…right.

He didn't let the kiss linger too long; he slid his fingers over the curve of her neck and moved away, a few inches at a time, marveling at the quick beat of his heart from such an innocent bit of contact. Her cheeks were flushed and her lips pink and plump, open as if in surprise.

"I couldn't let perfectly good mistletoe go to waste," he murmured, and he ran his tongue over his bottom lip. It was a mistake, because the taste of her lingered there. He'd be a liar if he said he didn't want more.

"Then I think we should just say Merry Christmas and good-night," she replied, taking a shaky breath.

"It's not even dinnertime yet."

"Then…goodbye, then. I mean… Damn. I said *then* twice. I just mean…"

Her stammer was adorable, and told him she was just as affected as he was.

"I'll see you later. *Then.*" He added the last word and smiled, and before he could change his mind, walked to the stairs that would take him to his suite.

What she did for the rest of the evening was none of his business. None at all.

CHAPTER SIX

SATURDAY AFTERNOON TEA had become a weekly ritual, as long as Tori's mom wasn't on shift at the hospital. This weekend was no different from any other, except that Tori was anxious about telling her mom that Jeremy was in town. While Shelley was supportive, she wasn't a fan of how the pregnancy had happened, during a summer fling. Neither was Tori, to be honest. It would be different if it was an accident in an actual relationship based on love and not just…lust. But they had both agreed that since nothing could be changed, it was about looking to the future.

Now she was sitting in her mom's living room, nibbling on a gingersnap as her mom brought in a teapot and a little jug of milk, no sugar. Neither of them liked it in their tea.

Tori poured a cup and handed it to her mom, then poured one for herself. She took a sip of the hot brew and felt her muscles relax. There was nothing like a cup of tea to settle her thoughts.

"You're feeling okay?" Shelley said, looking over the rim of her mug with worried eyes. "You look a little pale. Is your iron low?"

"A little tired, maybe. I've had a lot on my mind lately. But everything's fine. I go for my ultrasound in a few days."

"When?"

"Tuesday."

"I'm on day shift. I can see if someone will switch if you want company."

Her mom's eyes lit up when she said it, and Tori got

the idea she was looking for an invitation. But Tori wasn't sure she wanted company. She almost thought she wanted to go alone and have some time with the baby. It didn't really make sense; the baby wasn't even born yet, and she was "alone" with him or her all the time. Maybe it was just because she was overwhelmed.

"That's okay. I'll get pictures and everything and show you, okay?"

"Okay. If that's what you want." Shelley smiled and reached for a cookie, but before she could take a bite, Tori blurted out the truth.

"Jeremy's in town."

Shelley dropped the cookie. It hit the coffee table and sugar sprinkled everywhere.

"*The* Jeremy? The father?"

She nodded and focused on her cup. "Yeah. He came on business and thought he'd look me up. And found me like this." She pointed to her stomach.

Shelley sat back on the sofa. "Oh, honey. Well, at least now he knows."

Tori looked up at her mom and grimaced. "Yeah. That decision was taken out of my hands."

"Maybe it's for the best. I know it's awkward, but I always thought he should know."

"I know. And me too, really. I'm just…scared."

"Scared that he'll what? Leave you alone? Not be supportive?"

On the contrary. Tori took another fortifying drink of tea. The other day, looking at houses, that kiss… All it had done was remind Tori of how much she'd enjoyed being with Jeremy in the first place. Yes, their relationship had been mostly physical over the summer. But she'd *liked* him…a lot. While she hadn't fostered any dreams of being whisked away to a fairy-tale ending, she had cherished their time together and had tucked the memories away as something very special. Her biggest fear was how to negotiate parenthood without letting her heart get involved. He was a good guy, underneath. He could have made things difficult for her, and instead he was taking his time, not making any demands. But for how long?

She was sure that at some point there was going to be a price to pay.

"You're quiet, so I guess there's more going on here than you want to talk to your mom about." Shelley's eyebrow lifted in a wry expression, but it wasn't condemning. They were close, but Tori had never really shared all the details with her mom.

"He's rich, Mom. Like lots-of-zeroes rich. And if he wanted to, he could make things really difficult."

"Do you think he would?" Concern overtook Shelley's face and her eyes darkened.

"I don't want to think so. He's nice. Caring, really. He hasn't made any demands. We're just…talking."

"Talking is good."

"He wants to be a part of the baby's life."

"That's good, isn't it? It shows he wants to step up. Be responsible."

"It also means I'll have to see him. And I wonder if he'll change his mind about how much custody he wants. If he decides that, I can't afford to challenge him. I'm scared, Mama." Her lips quivered a little on the last word; she rarely called her mom "Mama." "I love this baby already."

"Oh, honey, of course you do." Shelley moved over to the love seat where Tori sat. "You have to have faith, you know? You say he's a good man. I'm sure, then, that you can work this out."

"He is. We spent the day together on Thursday. It was

fun. He said if we are going to co-parent, we need to be able to spend time together."

"He's not wrong." Shelley looked at Tori a little more closely. "But is there more? I mean, there's a reason why you got pregnant. Is that still a factor?"

"I don't know." She let the words out on a breath. "Yeah, I still find him attractive, and there's still…something. At least for me. And I think for him, too. He…"

She halted. Swallowed against a lump in her throat. That kiss had been…something. More destructive to her defenses in its sweetness than any passionate overture might have been.

"He what, honey?"

"He kissed me under the lobby mistletoe."

Shelley laughed lightly. "Sweetie, you could do worse than kissing a good-looking millionaire in the lobby."

"Billionaire," she corrected. "Jeremy Fisher is a billionaire, thanks to his trust fund, his business, and apparently a sister who is a genius with stocks."

Shelley's mouth fell open. "Well."

"How do I prepare myself for this, Mom? I couldn't care less about his money, but it does change things. We live in different countries and are from different worlds. And we're having a kid together. It's such a mess."

Shelley reached for her hand and squeezed it. "You get through it just like you get through anything else. One day at a time, making the best decisions you know how. And then you trust everything will work out."

"You have a lot more faith than I do."

"I don't think so. Just keep an open mind. And if you do everything for the right reasons, chances are it's gonna be fine in the end." She let go of Tori's hand. "Now, have another cookie and drink your tea. Do you want to stay for dinner?"

"Of course I do."

"Good. Then I can send you home with potpie leftovers."

Jeremy switched the phone to the other ear as he sat at the table in his suite, his laptop open in front of him. "So it's down to the one on the river, or the one with the lighthouse, yeah?"

Branson's voice came over the line loud and clear. "I trust you, Jer. You know what I need right now."

His friend needed time and space. "I'm worried you'll become a long-haired, shaggy-bearded hermit who yells at kids to get off his lawn."

A rare, rusty laugh from Branson came over the line. "I don't like beards."

Which was true. But still, Jeremy worried. "You're sure there's no place closer to the city? Or south, somewhere warm?"

"No one knows me up there. No one will recognize me. I need that for a while. And when the house outlives its purpose, I'll sell it again. No big."

"Then the lighthouse one. It's a better value, and to be honest, the location is spectacular enough it should move on resale within a reasonable time frame."

"Put in an offer. I'll pay the asking price. And a quick close."

"You're going to move north during the winter. Are you nuts?"

"I need to get out of here. The house is too full of ghosts."

Which was fair enough.

"Hey, Bran? Can I unload something on you for a minute?"

There was a pause. "Yeah, of course. I owe you a ton in therapy minutes."

They both chuckled a little. It wasn't like they kept score.

"So, remember the girl I told you about? From last summer?"

"Yeah, the fling. You said you were going to look her up again. How'd you make out?"

"She's pregnant."

When he said it all the air rushed out of his lungs. It was almost like until this moment it wasn't really official. He hadn't told anyone until now. Because sometimes you needed your best buddy to give your head a whack.

"Nice work, Romeo. And she didn't tell you?"

"It's complicated."

"Well, duh." There was a pause. "So what now?"

"I don't know. I won't ignore my kid, you know? I can't do that."

"Of course not. And you're a good catch, you know. The electric bill will always be paid on time."

"I'm not sure she's ready for New York. And I'd be bored here within a month."

"So you split your time."

"I guess."

"Your mom know yet?"

"Hell, no."

"Well, my one piece of advice is if you consider making a play for this girl, you be up front with what your family is like before it's all settled. Don't blindside her with it after you've brokered a deal."

"Parenting isn't like buying a house."

Bran laughed again. "Good, I'm glad you came to that conclusion all on your own. Feel better?"

"Yes and no. But thank you. I'll be in touch about the offer."

"Just send me what I need to sign. I trust you."

They ended the call and Jeremy rested his forehead on his hands for a few moments. Bran was right. He needed Tori to meet his family. And he wanted to meet her mom, too.

What an unholy mess.

He made another call and verbally made an offer on the property. Considering he was offering asking price, he was relatively sure that it would be a simple transaction. Once that was done, he ventured down to the business center to take care of the necessary paperwork. As he was sending it off, he realized this meant he no longer had to be at the Sandpiper for more than a few more days. He could pack his things and head back to Manhattan. Get ready for Christmas.

It seemed odd and empty to think about now.

"So, did your friend decide on a house?"

He startled, jumping in his seat as her voice came from behind him.

"Sorry. I didn't mean to scare you."

"I was just thinking." He clicked his mouse and then looked up at her. She was glowing, dressed in black leggings and heels that accentuated her long legs, and a maternity top in a blue that matched the tartan on the Christmas tree. "You look good. Feeling well?"

"I slept a lot on the weekend and read a good book. It was heavenly."

She'd slept and he'd been doing some business in Halifax. They hadn't seen each other at all over the weekend. "I'm glad. And yes. Unless something falls through, it's the house in Kingsburg."

"The one with the lighthouse!" Her eyes lit up. "Oh, that's great. It's so impressive." Then she looked at him thoughtfully. "It does mean that you'll have a good friend in the area."

He hadn't actually considered that before. It was true. At least for a while, Bran would be here. She would be here, and their baby. He had ties to the South Shore without ever intending to.

"It also means I'll be leaving to go back to New York in a few days."

"I suppose it does."

Did she look disappointed? He almost hoped so. Plus they hadn't really come to any conclusions.

He wasn't sure quite what to say when her face changed and her hand went to the swell of her belly. "Whoa."

Alarm skittered through his veins as he shot up from the chair. "Are you all right? What's wrong?"

"Nothing." She looked up at him with wide eyes. "I think the baby just moved."

He guided her to the chair. "Really? What did it feel like?"

"I don't know. Like butterflies, kind of, but running in a line down my belly. I've felt similar things lately, but not this strong. Oh, my, maybe the baby has been moving and I didn't know it!" Her face broke into a smile. "Oh, there it is again."

She reached for his hand and put it on her top, pressed against the solid curve. He didn't have time to react or hesitate; one moment he was standing there and the next he was crouched by her side, palm pressed against her navel. He waited, holding his breath, and then felt the tiniest flutter against his hand. "Is that it?"

She grinned and nodded. "You can feel it? I wasn't sure it would be strong enough."

It was. His child was in there, moving around, and his mother looked like a flipping angel, a perfect picture of motherhood. Something joyful and expansive filled his chest, while a balancing cold trickle of fear ran down his spine. This was amazing! And absolutely terrifying.

He waited, but there was no more movement, so he reluctantly took his hand away and stood again. She let out a huge breath, and then looked up into his face. "You okay? You've got a bit of a deer-in-the-headlights look about you."

"I'm all right. Terrified, but all right."

"I know. It takes some getting used to."

"It just got really real today, I think. I told my friend Branson, too."

She stood and went to him, putting her hand on his shoulder. "I've had a few months of pregnancy so I'm past the surreal part. You've got some catching up to do."

She'd gone through finding out and dealing with the first weeks alone, and an internet search had quickly told him what she'd probably gone through. He'd found out just yesterday that the baby was probably roughly the size of a banana now.

"Jeremy?" She called him back out of his thoughts. "I'm a bit late having my ultrasound, but it's scheduled for tomorrow afternoon. Do you want to go with me?"

Pictures of his baby. His! He felt as if he were being thrown into the deep end so very quickly, but he also knew there was really no other way. "I'd like that. A lot."

"It's in Bridgewater. Kind of close to that first house we saw last week."

"That's fine. You just tell me when we need to leave and I'll be ready."

"Okay." She reached down and took his hand. "It's going to be okay, you know. We'll figure everything out. My mom told me this weekend to have faith, and that's what I'm going to do."

Faith. Jeremy smiled but his heart wasn't in it. He didn't have faith. Not in anything, or really anyone. And Tori was making a mistake if she was placing her faith in him. He could try to live up to it, but chances were he'd fail. There was a reason that he was still single at thirty-six, and never been married. The women who liked him, he didn't like in return. And the ones he liked, he didn't trust. The guys were right. He was a serial dater. It kept him from being lonely, without the messiness of emotions and expectations.

He liked Tori, liked her too much. And he wanted to trust her. But faith? That was just asking for trouble.

Tori had thought what she wanted was to go to the ultrasound alone, but as she sat in the waiting room with Jeremy, she was glad she wasn't alone. And that he was there. He was the baby's father, after all. It seemed right that they share this moment together.

"Are you nervous?"

She looked over at him. His knee bounced up and down. "I think you're the nervous one."

He stopped bouncing his knee and smiled sheepishly. "It feels weird. I never imagined I'd be a father."

"Really? You never wanted a family?" She appreciated how well he'd accepted the situation, and his promises to be there, but it worried her that he might not have seen this role as part of his future.

"It wasn't so much wanting or not wanting," he revealed. "It's more… I just didn't have a great example to follow, and believe it or not, dating is hard with my money."

She gave the obligatory laugh, but then put her hand on his knee. "It must be hard to figure out who's genuine and who's after your bank account. I don't have that problem." And then she laughed again. And hoped he realized she didn't care about his money, either.

"Yeah, there's that. Some women want the status. But I have my own issues. I don't trust easily. Other people, or my own intuition. When it comes to relationships, anyway."

"Then this situation must be driving you crazy," she said, jostling his shoulder. "Because now there's a baby mama in the mix."

"You're being awfully chill about this."

She shrugged. "I am what I am. I can't make you believe that I'm genuine, that I don't want your money or that I'm out for anything. All I can do is tell you my truth. You're the father. I can and will do this by myself if you bail. I can support me and my child, and I'll be okay. So there's no pressure from me on your bank account. Just room for you to be a father."

She turned sideways in her chair and met his gaze squarely. "My only demand is that if you choose to be involved, you're consistent and honest. I don't want our kid always to be wondering if you're ever coming back or if you care."

To her surprise, his eyes softened. "I *was* that kid, Tori. I won't do that to my own." He swallowed and his throat bobbed with the effort. "I promise you I will not be that dad."

"Then we will figure everything else out."

The door across from them opened. "Victoria? We're ready for you now."

They went in together. Jeremy waited to the side while Tori got on the bed with the paper sheet beneath her. The room was warm, thankfully, and in a few moments they'd adjusted her clothing so that her shirt was up and the waistbands of her leggings and underwear were rolled down right to her pubic bone. She looked over at Jeremy and realized his eyes had widened, looking at her belly. He hadn't seen it before, not like this. She smiled up at him, reassuringly. "You gonna be okay, Dad?" she asked lightly.

He nodded. "Yeah. Yeah."

"Okay, then," the technician said. "Let's get started." She squirted gel on Tori's belly, then began, the pressure from the probe firm. Tori couldn't see the screen, though she wouldn't know what she was looking at anyway. The tech made clicks here and there, saying that she was taking measurements first. Then she turned the screen around. "Okay, are you ready to see?"

During Tori's first scan, at only eight weeks, there'd been very little to see. This time, however, was different. The image shifted, but she could make out the head, and the ridge that was the spine, and appendages. "Look at the little toes," she whispered, tears forming in the corners of her eyes.

She tore her gaze away to look at Jeremy, who was staring at the screen in wonder. "That's our baby. My kid." His fingers flexed and unflexed. "I just… I can't…"

"Do you want to know what you're having? I can't tell you today, but the report will go to your doctor."

Tori looked up at him. "I don't mind it being a surprise. Gender's not important to me anyway." Her only concern was that the baby be healthy. Besides, she didn't go into all the pink and blue stuff and gender-reveal things. She'd already started decorating her tiny second bedroom with a Beatrix Potter theme, something neutral. Peter Rabbit and Squirrel Nutkin were way too cute.

"If you want it to be a surprise, then that's fine with me," he said.

"You're sure?"

"Whatever you want." A smile broke out over his face. "Wow. That's our kid in there."

It was the genuine smile that did it. He'd moved past the looks of alarm and panic to that of... Well, looking at him right now all she could see was joy. Relief swamped her heart as well as a feeling of...happiness? Was that possible? Their relationship was still something they didn't talk about. Nothing had been decided about how they were going to make this work. But she remembered what her mom had said only a few days earlier. One day at a time. And today she was going to enjoy this lovely moment.

"Do you want to see the heartbeat?" the tech asked.

"Yes." There was no hesitation from Jeremy and Tori laughed.

She pointed to a spot on the screen where the *ba-bump*, *ba-bump* flash flickered in a little heart.

Jeremy went around to the foot of the bed and sat, covering his mouth with a hand. Tori watched him as he stared at the monitor, feeling her heart slipping bit by bit. He said he didn't trust. He'd had a loveless childhood, from the sounds of it. And yet he was capable of so much feeling. He was good, underneath it all. She truly believed that. Could she keep her feelings for him under wraps? Wait it out until they faded? Wasn't it natural to have feelings about the father of her baby?

Even if they weren't returned...or couldn't lead anywhere?

She looked back at the monitor again, and the form of her unborn child there. Every decision she made had to be for the good of her baby. They were the most important thing now.

"Okay, give me a few minutes and I'll take some pictures for you." The tech started moving the wand again, then held it in position and hit a few keys. She tried again and started to chuckle. "Your baby's moving around in there and won't sit still. So much for napping."

It took another few minutes but then it was done and the tech gave her a towel to wipe away the gel as the pictures printed. "I'll give you a few minutes to put yourself back together." She handed the pictures to Jeremy. "Congratulations."

Tori wiped off the gel and adjusted her clothing, then got up from the bed and dropped the cloth in the used bin. When she returned, she stopped in front of Jeremy. "Are you okay?"

He nodded. "I think so." He reached out and pulled her closer, so his hand was on her hip and his face was just below her breasts. He cradled her bump and then, to her surprise, placed a kiss on it. Tears stung her eyes at the tender gesture.

"Are you real?" she asked softly, putting her hands on each side of his head. He looked up and into her eyes. "You could have run the moment you found out. You could have offered to buy me off. You could have made demands. But you haven't, and I don't understand, and I'm… I'm afraid that someday soon there's going to be a price I need to pay and I don't know what it is."

He sighed, a heavy, weighted sigh that sounded so weary she wasn't quite sure what to say.

"I'm trying to do the right thing," he finally said. "I'm as responsible for this as you are. There is no blame and if there is, we share it equally. The truth is, that's my child in there. I saw them on the screen and saw their heart beating. It's humbling, Tori. I have no idea how to do this but I want us to try."

"Us," she said, a bit numb from what she thought he might mean.

"We're going to be parents together. We like each other. For God's sake, we kissed the other day."

"You kissed me," she clarified, though her heart thumped against her ribs.

He stood then, so she had to look up the tiniest bit. "If you tell me there's nothing between us at all, I'll drop the subject right now. But if there is, don't we owe it to our baby to try?"

"If we blow it, the stakes are really high," she responded. And yet he was so close she could smell his cologne and feel his warmth. She couldn't lie and say there was nothing between them because there was. Both the attraction from the summer, and the depth of character he'd shown since his return. He'd been far more understanding than a lot of men might have been.

"Look. Look at this picture and tell me this little nugget doesn't deserve us to try at the very least."

She hesitated but couldn't take her eyes off the ultrasound picture. And he'd called him or her a nugget. It was an adorable little name.

Jeremy cupped her cheek, then kissed her forehead. "Let me take you home. Maybe we can talk it over."

Her home. Where she had, in all likelihood, conceived their child. Where they'd spent lazy evenings after a day at the beach. And lazy morning-afters, watching the sunrise.

"Okay," she replied. "Let's go home. And talk."

Because she was really unsure about this step, and they needed to set some solid boundaries.

CHAPTER SEVEN

SHE WAS VERY aware of how small her house was when they stepped in it again, Jeremy for the first time since last July. Just under a thousand square feet meant two bedrooms, a small kitchen with dining area to the side, a modest living room and a bathroom that was smaller than the closet in his suite at the Sandpiper. Still, it suited her well. It was cozy, and it was hers.

He didn't seem to mind as he removed his coat and draped it over the back of her sofa. He slipped off his shoes, too, and left them by the door, stepping inside in his socks. Today he'd worn jeans and a simple sweater, and the look of him in casual clothing, so approachable, made her want to slip into his arms. But she couldn't. Not with what he'd suggested hovering between them.

Could they be more than simple co-parents? More than…friends?

"You're nervous," he said quietly, moving toward her. "Don't be."

"How can I not?" She turned around, folding her hands in front of her. "What you said… It would change everything. I was thinking we could just be friends. Work together as a team. But not…"

Her voice trailed off.

"Not lovers?" he answered, reaching out and putting his hand along her upper arm, rubbing gently.

"Yes, that," she answered, trying hard to keep her breath even. Right now, despite the thread of desire winding its way through her body, she couldn't imagine having sex with him. Her body had changed. Heck, everything had changed. It certainly wouldn't be a summer fling.

He gazed into her eyes for a long moment, then leaned closer, slowly, giving her lots of time to move away, or put a hand on his chest to stop him, or say no. But she couldn't, because the truth was she wanted him to kiss her. Wanted to feel his lips on hers again. His arms around her without mistletoe overhead or staff meters away.

He touched his lips to hers, and she let out a breath. More of a sigh, really, as his arms came around her and pulled her close. Her mouth opened beneath his and she let him guide her, softly, seductively, no rush. Like they had all the time in the world.

She melted against his chest and tilted her head up a bit, hungry for more. Her wordless request was rewarded with a deeper kiss, more urgency, and the desire that had been a slow burn began to blaze brighter.

This was what had gotten them into this mess in the first place. Not that her baby would ever be a "mess," but the situation was certainly complicated.

She pulled back a bit, startled by her response to him, needing space to breathe and think.

"I, uh…" That was as far as she got. Actual words weren't making it from her brain to her mouth.

"I know. It's not what we expected. Well, actually, it is what I expected when I came back. That we could go out again, have some fun. I think it's clear that the attraction is still alive and well. We can't ignore it, you know? Because it'll crop up from time to time."

"I can't deny that, after what just happened." She moved another step backward. His unflinching tendency to state the obvious was at times refreshing and other times vastly uncomfortable. He liked to deal with problems head-on. She did, too, or so she had thought. Still, highlighting the fact that there was still sexual attraction simmering between them threw her off balance. It wasn't something they could compartmentalize in a little box, isolated from the situation.

The sad bit of it was, she wanted him to kiss her again, and again, until her head was swimming with it, and the scent of his cologne, and the feel of his hands on her... Being pregnant hadn't eradicated her libido. Actually, in this moment, she wondered if it hadn't increased. She crossed her arms in front of her and tried to ignore the sensations running through her body.

"We're having a child," she said, and wondered how many times over the last week she'd said those words. "Where do you see this going? Because we're going to be tied together for life, do you understand that? If this goes sideways, it could be a disaster."

But if it didn't...

A secret want bubbled up in her. What would it be like for them to be a family? The two of them together, their child...more children? She gave herself a mental shake. How would that even work? Once again she reminded herself they were from two very different worlds. That the fairy tale had never been in the equation.

"You think we need to set boundaries. Figure out the what-ifs."

"Yes," she said, letting out a huge breath of relief. "That's it exactly."

He went to her, took her hand and led her to the sofa. "Come, sit down. I don't like the idea of us staring each other down like we're in a negotiation."

She followed him and sank into the sofa, the cushions cradling her lower back, which had started to bother her a little after the long day.

"You want to know what happens if we try this and one of us walks away. From a romantic relationship," he clarified. "Not parenthood. We both agree we're in that for the long haul."

"Yes. And there are a lot of things to figure out. I live here. You live in New York. How would it work?"

"I actually have an idea about that," he said, reaching for her hand. He turned on the sofa a bit and tucked his left ankle under his right leg, so he was facing her. "Come to New York with me for a week."

Her stomach plummeted. "A week? In December? Before Christmas?"

He nodded, undaunted. "Yeah. Christmas in New York is amazing. I can show you the sights… Have you ever been?"

She shook her head. She really hadn't traveled much of anywhere. One year, in high school, they'd taken the CAT ferry from Yarmouth to Bar Harbor and gone to Old Orchard Beach. The rest of her travel had been east of Toronto.

Jeremy squeezed her fingers. "I'll take some time off. We can spend it together, figuring things out. With no one interfering."

So this wasn't a ploy to convince her to move there, but to give them time away to evaluate? She sighed. "I don't know…" She pulled away a bit, feeling incredibly overwhelmed with it all. "Jeremy, a week ago I hadn't even decided how and when to tell you, and now you're here, and we're trying to sort out how we're going to do this, and you've kissed me…twice…"

"And you kissed me back," he said firmly. "If it's boundaries you're worried about, then let me put it plainly for you. If for any reason something…more…comes of this, but then either one of us wants to pull the plug, then we can. With the important thing being we do so amicably with the well-being of the baby first and foremost."

It sounded so simple and logical when he put it that way. Could it really be that easy?

Her heart—and her head—said no.

And yet the man sitting next to her, with the earnest eyes and seriously kissable lips, made her believe yes. The idea of a whole week in New York was enticing. She'd only ever seen videos and pictures of things like the giant Christmas tree in Rockefeller Square, the shops on Fifth Avenue...

"I don't know, Jeremy," she whispered. "This—all of this—is so crazy and scary. Everything about my life is changing. Now, talking about going away for a week, together..." She bit down on her lip. "I'm finding it hard to keep up."

He lifted his hand and put it along her cheek. "Don't worry. We'll use it as get-to-know-each-other time. No pressure. No decisions. You're right about one thing. Last summer was so fast, and now we're being thrust into parenthood. If we stand any chance of doing this together, we have to know each other better. Develop trust. I know where you live and your world. But you don't know mine."

It all sounded perfect, which was exactly why Tori was so uneasy. Nothing was ever perfect.

"I'll have to ask for the time off first," she said, surprised she was actually considering it.

"We can go whenever you like. I can work my schedule around you, though I do have a series of meetings on the nineteenth and twentieth I can't miss."

"So I'd be back here for Christmas."

"I'm sure you'll want to be with your mom, won't you?"

She nodded. "Okay. I'll go."

A wide smile lit up his face. "That's great!" He gathered her hands in his and kissed her knuckles. "We're going to be fine. Just wait and see."

Jeremy watched as Tori's eyes widened at the sight of the private jet sitting on the tarmac at Halifax's airport. The option for a direct flight would have taken them only to Newark, with all the other flights requiring a stop. Why would he do that when he could charter something and leave on his own schedule?

Plus he wasn't above trying to impress her a little bit. The woman deserved a bit of pampering and glamour. She worked hard and didn't have a lot to show for it. A cozy little house, sure, and a close-knit work family. But there was a big world out there and he wanted to show her a little bit of it.

"Is this yours?"

He laughed. "No. I chartered it."

Her face relaxed. "Oh. I was having a moment thinking you had your own plane and I was... I don't know."

"I thought about it, and went back and forth about whether I wanted to own one, but in the end, I keep coming back to using charters. It seemed simpler than worrying about where to keep it, having a pilot on call, maintenance... This way I pick up the phone, my assistant books me a charter and I show up." He took her arm as they got to the steps leading to the door. "I like to keep things simple, believe it or not."

It was her turn to laugh. "Jeremy, there is nothing simple about you."

He wasn't sure if that was a compliment or a criticism, but her voice was easy and a smile was on her lips so he was going to take it as a compliment.

She climbed the stairs ahead of him. He watched the gentle sway of her hips, thinking how pretty she looked in jeans and ankle boots with her jacket bundled up around her. She turned and flashed a smile at him when she reached the door and he realized he loved how young and energetic she looked with her hair back in a simple perky ponytail and the minimal makeup she wore, which made her skin look fresh and dewy. Or maybe that was her pregnant glow. It was then that he noticed how snug the jacket was around her tummy. She was only going to get bigger, and the winter was barely begun.

A shopping trip would definitely be on the itinerary.

Once inside, an attendant named Gerry took their coats and got them settled in soft leather seats. The more Tori looked around, the happier Jeremy was that he'd booked the flight. Her lips were open in what he thought was amazement and her eyes flitted over every seat, table and detail of decor in the Gulfstream.

They took off, and her face was fairly stuck to the window as they raced down the runway and left solid ground beneath them.

"This is maybe the coolest thing I've ever done," she said, turning away and smiling up at him. "Is this normal for you? I don't know how I'd ever get used to it."

"It wasn't always. For a while I usually booked first class." He grinned at her. "And some of the commuter jets don't even have a first class." He shuddered for effect, making her laugh.

"I'd be disappointed if I thought you meant that," she replied, sitting back against the comfortable seat. "But you aren't the pretentious type. At least, I don't think you are."

He frowned a little. "That's one of the reasons I suggested the week, Tori. So we could get to know each other better. But I'm relieved you don't think I'm a stuck-up snob."

"Stuck up, no. Used to the finer things? Definitely."

At that moment, Gerry returned. "Are you ready for your breakfast, sir?"

"Breakfast?" Tori parroted, looking from Jeremy to Gerry and back again.

"You didn't think I wasn't going to feed you, did you? It's only ten. If you ate at all this morning, it was hours ago." It was true, because it was over two hours to the airport, and they'd had to return his rental to the agency, then clear security and then customs before boarding.

The meal smelled delicious, and Gerry whisked the cover away to reveal scrambled eggs, a bagel with butter and jam, and heaps of fresh strawberries and raspberries. "Would you like something to drink, ma'am?" he asked.

"Oh, goodness." The low rumble of her stomach was audible, and Jeremy hid a smile. "Maybe some orange juice? Or even just iced water would be lovely."

He took Jeremy's lid as well and Jeremy said, "Water is fine for me, thank you, Gerry."

"This is too much," she said when Gerry had disappeared.

"It's scrambled eggs," Jeremy laughed. "I mean, it's not like it's eggs Benedict or anything elaborate. But I do know that you like eggs in the morning."

Her eyes widened. "You do?"

"You mentioned it one morning when I first arrived. You said Neil made them just the way you liked."

He watched as she took a bite and then turned her amazed gaze to him. "With a bit of cheese and some parsley. I can't believe you remembered that."

The approval in her gaze made him go all warm inside. "Well, I'll confess I asked Neil. Because I get the feeling that you'll just go along with anything rather than voice any preferences."

She put her fork down and her face sobered, her lips

turning downward. "What's wrong? Did I say something?" he asked.

"You're half right. I probably would be happy to just go along with things. But maybe I pick my battles. Scrambled eggs, no big deal. Our child's future…big deal."

She wasn't going to be a pushover. Good. Not that he didn't want to get his way, but he admired strength. "Of course."

Gerry returned with orange juice and water for Tori and water for Jeremy, and left quietly. They ate their breakfast in companionable silence, until Tori sat back with a satisfied sigh. "Okay, so you were right. That was delicious and I needed the protein. Thank you."

"You're most welcome. What would you like to do today? We'll be at my place before noon."

"I have no idea." She laughed. "I guess I figured you'd have an itinerary."

"Sometimes the best vacations don't have itineraries," he replied, and cocked an eyebrow.

She blushed prettily. The last "vacation" for both of them had been those magical days in the summer, when they'd soaked up the sun and each other, with no schedule whatsoever. "Jeremy, if you're expecting…" She swallowed and her blush deepened.

"I have no expectations beyond wanting to show you my town," he replied, then reached over to take her hand. His heart hammered in his chest. There was no denying that the attraction to her hadn't gone away. But it was something he wanted to work with, not against. To acknowledge, not ignore. "You're a beautiful woman, Tori. I'm not going to lie and say that what I'm feeling is totally platonic. But I'm not going to push."

Her eyes delved into his. "Me, too," she breathed. "And

I shouldn't have admitted that, I suppose. I'm not good at holding my cards close to my chest."

"This isn't poker, or some business merger. It's okay. I'm glad you're being honest."

"Me, too. About you, I mean."

The statement left him somewhat uncomfortable, because he hadn't been completely honest with her about what he really wanted. He was more…hoping she'd come around to the same way of thinking without him having to say so. He wanted her to love his place, love New York and to want to be closer. Hell, he'd even consider living somewhere else and commuting. He was saved from saying more as Gerry returned to take their plates away, bring Jeremy fresh coffee and put a tiny pot of steaming water and a cup in front of Tori.

She looked up in confusion and he smiled at her. "Mint tea, ma'am. Mr. Fisher said you preferred it."

"Thank you, Gerry."

She looked over at Jeremy and raised an eyebrow. "Well, aren't you one for anticipating my needs," she said, a hint of sarcasm in her voice.

"Too much?" he asked, sitting back in his seat. He loved it when she had a hint of sass, and his lips twitched.

"I could tell you it's a bit obvious. Or perhaps heavy-handed. But it smells heavenly." She poured from the pot into her cup and the refreshing scent of mint filled the air. "So I should probably just say thank you."

He leaned forward, determined to be honest, at least in the moment. "No, thank you. For coming on this trip. For being so open-minded and for not pushing back when I said I wanted to be a part of our baby's life."

"You're the father," she said simply.

"Yes, but I know you didn't have to tell me, and considered not doing so. I arrived and took that decision out of your hands, and I'm not sorry. But I know it's been difficult and I appreciate you meeting me in the middle."

More than that. He wanted to treat her well because seeing her walk through those grand houses had made him see that he wanted to be able to convince her to be closer. He didn't want to have to fly every few months to see his kid. He couldn't run his business from Back-End-of-Nowhere, Nova Scotia, either. Dictating his desires would accomplish nothing; the right way was to make her want this for herself. His wonderful home in Manhattan. Top schools and opportunities. Weekends away, and no financial stress. In exchange, he'd be there for his kid—the one thing in the world he wanted most. He would never be an absentee father like his own dad had been. His child would never have to wonder if he was loved or if his father even cared at all.

Seeing the ultrasound picture that now lay tucked in his wallet, remembering the steady flicker of the heartbeat on the monitor as they watched... That had changed everything. As had feeling him or her kick against his hand. It had turned an idea into something utterly tangible.

"Likewise," she responded, her gaze soft. "You've been so understanding. Way more than I gave you credit for. I should have told you from the beginning."

"It doesn't matter. It really doesn't. Let's just keep looking forward."

"Deal." She took a sip of tea, then looked out the window for a few moments before turning back to him. "And what about...well...us?"

It was a tough question. He couldn't lie and say he was in love with her. He wasn't. They got along well and enjoyed being together, didn't they? And there was attraction on both sides. There was certainly more warmth between them than had ever been between his parents, obviously, or his mom and stepdad. He wasn't sure he even believed in a burning passion that lasted forever. Hell, his brother was an aficionado of everlasting love and had believed in it so strongly he'd tried it...three times.

So he was as honest as he dared to be. "Tori, you're beautiful, and smart, and you make me laugh. You have this way of lifting one eyebrow that literally makes me hear you say 'Really, Jeremy?' in my mind. You light up when you talk about the baby. Your staff loves you and you love them... And that doesn't often happen with management. It wasn't an accident we connected last summer. And all the things I liked about you then I still like about you now."

She twisted her hands in her lap, as if his declaration made her uncomfortable. She gave an odd laugh and shrugged. "The things you liked about me then? I'm afraid I definitely don't look as good in a bikini as I did last summer."

He remembered, all right. She'd had a red one that seemed to be held together by strings, and then a black one that tied around her neck and made her breasts look—

He clenched his jaw. The image that flooded his brain now was of her in that same bikini, only with the gentle swell of their child curving her stomach. It was no less sexy in his mind.

"I'm not sure about that."

"Oh, I am. My boobs are bigger and wouldn't even fit in those cups—"

"I'm not seeing the problem here."

She stared at him, and then started to giggle. "Oh, I suppose not. But thanks for the laugh."

He wasn't exactly laughing. In fact, he had to shift in his seat to be a little more comfortable.

Gerry reappeared. "Sir, we're going to start our descent soon. In another five minutes or so, you'll need to fasten your seat belts."

"So soon?" Tori looked up with a smile. "Thank you. I think I'll freshen up before I have to get buckled in."

She rose from her seat and made her way to the bathroom. Jeremy ran his finger over his lower lip and tried to get the image of Tori in her bikini out of his mind, but he couldn't.

They'd shared a few relatively chaste kisses in the last week, but clearly the summer had been a lot more heated; the pregnancy was evidence enough of that. He had to admit to himself, at least, that he'd wondered about a sexual relationship with her again. They'd been incredibly compatible…

The more he thought about it, the more he realized that she was near perfect for him. Kind, funny, sexually compatible, she'd be a great mother. Smart and intuitive… there really wasn't anything he didn't like about her.

She checked all his boxes, and a few he hadn't realized he had.

When she returned from the bathroom, he smiled and waited for her to resume her seat and get buckled in. Then, as they approached, he pointed out landmarks through the window, half watching the view and half watching her.

That was it. He'd pull out all the stops. And make her see how perfect their life could be. Her, him and, most important of all, their baby.

CHAPTER EIGHT

TORI'S FIRST IMPRESSION of New York was of noise and traffic. She'd never seen anything like it, and on the drive from La Guardia to the Upper East Side, she'd basically kept her nose pressed against the window of the luxury car that had been waiting for them when they arrived. Not a stretch limo or anything, thank goodness, but a bona fide car service and driver. *Surreal* didn't even begin to cover what she'd already experienced today.

They were dropped off outside Jeremy's building. It didn't look like anything overly special from the outside, but inside was a different story. They took an elevator to his floor, and when he opened the door to his home, she nearly gasped.

What she did immediately was remove her leather boots and place them by the door. There was no way she would track on these floors.

The floor of the foyer gleamed like glass, and just beyond was a kitchen to the left. White cupboards, stainless state-of-the-art appliances, a slate-gray butcher block in the center and an enormous bouquet of fresh flowers made it look more like one of his real estate showings than a home. The concept was open, but a partial wall separated the working part of the kitchen—which looked as if it had never been used—from a dining room. A long table with upholstered chairs was the centerpiece of the space, with a long, silver runner down the middle and a bowl of more flowers sitting in its center. The table had seating for eight, and Tori could almost imagine a dinner party around such a table, with the clink of silverware and tinkle of crystal.

Yep. Definitely out of her league.

"Over here is the living room," Jeremy said from behind her, and she turned to see him holding out an arm. She followed close behind and was bathed in sunlight from the windows. "You can see the park from here," he offered, taking her hand and pulling her forward. She looked out the window... Indeed, there was lots of city around them, but also the huge expanse of Central Park, now covered with an inch of snow, looking cold but a little magical, too.

She was no Realtor but she knew that location was everything. And that he had paid a lot of money for this particular location. She'd looked up his address on the internet, looked at a street view. He was close to the Met, to Central Park, Broadway...

It was nearly overwhelming.

"What do you think?"

She turned to face him and found his face expectant. She glanced around at the impeccably decorated living room. To be honest, it was beautiful but it was missing something. It seriously felt like one of his listings, staged for a potential buyer, made to look wonderful without revealing the personality of the person who lived within.

There wasn't much of Jeremy here. But clearly he was proud of it, so she smiled. "It's gorgeous."

His answering grin made her glad she'd answered as she did. "Come on, let me show you the rest."

The rest included a powder room, plus two more full bathrooms—one main bathroom between two bedrooms and then a luxurious en suite bathroom off the master. The guest rooms were impeccable, of course, and the master bedroom housed a king-size bed with a black leather headboard and a thick silver duvet. The top was turned down to reveal the ends of the sheets beneath, and they were black silk. Chrome-and-black bedside tables held a docking station for electronics and a lamp, and he pulled the drapes aside to reveal another breathtaking view.

He looked at her and smiled again. Were they going to smile their way through the next week? "Whichever bedroom you'd like as yours is fine. The other bathroom is yours, as well."

At least he didn't assume they'd be sharing a room. Not that she'd expected that, but she'd gotten a little nervous on the plane after his bikini comment. As much as the idea of him still finding her attractive was exciting, she needed space and time to figure out if they truly could move forward as a couple. It felt like they kept taking steps that way, and then retreated into the safety of a relationship of utility and co-parenting.

Neither bedroom was overly welcoming. Beautiful, yes, but not…warm. That was it. The grayscale was trendy and definitely classy and elegant, but it was missing warmth.

"The one across the hall will be fine." She knew it had a queen-size bed and the bedding looked thicker and softer there. Like something she could curl up in.

"Great." He clapped his hands together. "I'll put your bag in your room so you can unpack. And then maybe we can go for a walk in the park."

A walk in the park was the perfect way to spend the afternoon. The air was crisp without being frigid, the sky a clear blue, and Jeremy reached down and held her hand as they wandered along. When she said she wanted a hot dog from a street vendor, he obliged, and they sat on a cold bench with cold noses, biting into hot dogs with sweet ketchup and sharp mustard. They wound their way around the paths and he showed her The Plaza, and she told him about one of her favorite children's book characters, Eloise. They had coffee in a little shop to warm their toes and fingers, and then when she looked longingly at the horse-drawn carriages, he obliged and they went on a carriage ride, which he said was eye-rollingly touristy but didn't complain when she got cold and leaned against him, prompting him to put his arm around her and cuddle her close.

The afternoon darkened and it was time to go home. It had been a marvelous first introduction to the Big Apple, and when Jeremy suggested she take a nap before dinner, she didn't put up any fight. She'd been up since five and the fresh air and walking had done its work.

After an hour he woke her and said that dinner was ready. He didn't let her in the kitchen, but seated her at the dining table, where he'd put two place settings at corners to each other, and lit a couple of candles. "Did you have a good nap?"

"The best. I woke up and forgot where I was."

He chuckled. "It's the fresh air. Plus you were up super early this morning."

"And I nap very easily these days," she admitted. "This growing-another-human thing takes some energy."

He disappeared into the kitchen and returned with a plate. "Which is why you need this. You've only had a hot dog and a latte since this morning."

The meal was simple. Chicken, asparagus and pasta were tossed in a white sauce, with a green salad on the side. But it was delicious and Tori ate up every bite on her plate.

"You're a decent cook. Where did you learn?"

"I can't take the credit. I eat out a lot and I have a housekeeper come in once a week. She also brings in a variety of meals and puts them in the fridge with instructions for reheating. I literally just had to put this in the oven, and voilà."

"Oh. Well, my compliments to the chef, whoever she may be." Jeremy was not the domestic type. It was more and more obvious as the day wore on. His apartment... condo...whatever barely looked lived in. There certainly weren't bits that jumped out as being "Jeremy." But he'd fed her and it had been scrumptious, so she patted her belly and said, "There. The baby's happy."

"Is he?" Jeremy's gaze met hers and held. "Is he happy?"

"Maybe it's a she."

"Of course. How about...are they happy?"

"I think so. At least it seems as if they're doing a jig in there."

His gaze deepened, and she thought she caught a glimpse of vulnerability. "May I feel?"

It was sweet of him to ask, lovely of him to want to "Of course," she replied. She pushed her chair out a little, and so did he, and then slid to the edge of his seat so they bumped knees. He put his hand on her belly, his palm wide and warm. But the ripple of feeling was in a different spot, so she put her hand on his wrist and guided him to the left a little. Whether it was arms or legs or somersaults, it didn't take long and the movement thudded against his hand, little taps and rolls.

"Wow," he breathed, staring at his hand, then up at her. "I can't get over that. How does it feel, you know, on the inside?"

She knew he meant the actual sensation rather than her response, but all she could say was, "Wonderful."

He didn't move his hand. But he leaned forward and pressed his forehead to hers. Not kissing, just...connecting. Tears stung her eyes. Maybe this was what had drawn her to him in the first place. Connection. She'd had friends, coworkers. Her mom. But not this kind of connection with another human. Not for a very long time, because she'd always backed away, not trusting that she wouldn't be hurt or duped in the end, as she had been before.

And she'd never had a connection of this depth, because this time they shared a child. His DNA and hers had come together to create a whole other person. It was a huge and sobering thought.

"Jeremy," she whispered. Her throat swelled with unshed tears.

He leaned back and took his hand from her belly and rested it on her cheek. "I don't understand," he whispered back. "You already love this baby so much, and it isn't even born yet. And I don't—" His voice broke off, and he cleared his throat. "Damn, I'm not a little kid. I don't know why this gets to me. I just don't ever remember feeling this much warmth in my home."

Her heart broke a little. "Were there never any fun times? Laughter?"

He shrugged. "I suppose there must have been, but I don't really remember them much. Mom and Dad divorced before I really formed any solid memories. When we were little Mom and Bruce took us to Disney once. And we went to summer camps and that was fun. But I can't remember a single other family vacation that we took together. Mom and Bruce would take off for a weekend in the city, see a show, dinner, hotel. They definitely traveled while we were in school. But never with us."

It was impossible to fathom. "But who cared for you?"

His hand slipped away. "We had staff."

"Shut up! Are you serious?"

She looked so disgusted a smile turned up the corners of his mouth. "It wasn't so bad. Some of the nannies were okay, and I really got along with the gardener who came twice a week."

He had to have been so lonely...and felt so unloved. Her heart ached for the kind of boy he must have been. "That's horrible. And I'm amazed you turned out to be a decent human being, which I know you are, because you've been nothing but kind and understanding throughout this whole thing."

"If I am, it's only because of Merrick. I met my best friends there. Teachers who, for the most part, cared enough to turn us from spoiled, scared brats into actual humans. Not that it always worked, mind you." He chuckled softly. "As a group we were a rich, entitled bunch."

"Materially, maybe."

"I can't complain, Tori. I have had advantages that most people only dream of."

She was glad he realized it, but deep down she knew all the money in the world couldn't buy real affection and love. She thought of all the summers she'd gone camping with her parents to any of the provincial parks. They'd always allowed her to take a friend. There'd been swimming and playgrounds and campfires with roasted marshmallows that scalded the roof of her mouth. Christmases watching movies and drinking hot chocolate. They hadn't had a lot of money but they'd gone on a walk every Thanksgiving Day since she was a little girl, enjoying the fall weather and colors. There had been story time at night before bed, and when she was sick, her dad carrying her to her room and tucking her into bed. There hadn't always been a lot of money, but she wouldn't trade a single moment of it.

Jeremy didn't know anything about any of those things.

Not through any fault of his own, but she wondered how he was going to handle a different kind of parenthood.

It worried her, but she wasn't about to deny him the opportunity to try.

She squeezed his fingers in hers. "It's gonna be okay. I'll help you. I had a great dad." Grief at his loss welled up, but gratitude, too, that he'd been a wonderful father. "I'll share him with you, tell you all about him and the stuff he used to do with me. You don't have to wait for the baby to be born to be a good father, Jeremy. You're doing it already."

His gaze snapped up to hers. "How come you are so great? Why aren't you scared? Freaking out about what's to come?"

"You think I'm not scared? Of course I am. But deep down I believe everything is going to be okay. It has to be."

Faith. It seemed she had some after all.

He squeezed her fingers back. "Okay. I'm going to trust you. At least for now." Clearing his throat, he gave her fingers a final squeeze and then sat up straight. "What do you say we clean up these dishes and then watch a movie or something?"

"That sounds amazing."

The sky was dark but lit by the millions of city lights. After they loaded the dishwasher, Jeremy put down the blinds over the windows while Tori sank into the couch. It wasn't just for looks; the cushions were super comfortable and Jeremy came back with a soft throw blanket from a closet somewhere. "Okay, so regular movie or Christmas movie?"

She was in Manhattan in December. "Christmas, and *Miracle on 34th Street.*"

He laughed. "When in Rome... So, original or remake?" He handed her the blanket and reached for his phone. She shook her head. He could control everything from that thing.

"I know I should say the original…but the remake. Because Richard Attenborough *is* Santa Claus."

"Yes, but Natalie Wood…"

"I know. So my pick tonight, yours tomorrow?"

"Sounds fair."

He scrolled through a streaming app until he found the movie, and then it was on, complete with Thanksgiving Day parade, a drunk parade Santa and Mara Wilson looking adorable. Halfway through he disappeared to make her a cup of tea—apparently said housekeeper had stocked up on a few things before their arrival—and after sipping at the comforting brew, Tori found herself blinking slowly.

She shouldn't be tired. She'd had a wonderful nap before dinner.

Jeremy shifted on the sofa. "Here. Lean against me. You'll be more comfortable and have some support for your neck."

He lifted his arm and she curled in against his side, the soft blanket covering her from waist to toes. He was so warm and stable, and her belly rested against his hip as if it were perfectly suited for the angle. And oh, he smelled good. Like clean clothes and the expensive cologne he always wore. She closed her eyes and inhaled.

On the screen, Dylan McDermott was proposing to Elizabeth Perkins, a huge ring in a red box. Tori opened her eyes and sighed.

"What?"

"I never understand why she's so mean to Bryan in this moment."

"Well, she's afraid."

"I know that. But it makes her stupid."

Jeremy chuckled, low in his chest. "Then there's the

fact that there's still a lot of movie to get through and the happy ending. Why would people keep watching if she said yes?"

She looked up at him. "To see if Kris Kringle is real, of course."

He shook his head. "Uh-uh. You know as well as I do that the love story is the main attraction here. And the question of whether or not Susan gets her house and a dad and a baby brother for Christmas."

"I hate it when you're right," she mumbled, but curled up against his shoulder again, where it was warm and inviting.

CHAPTER NINE

JEREMY WATCHED THE end credits roll and leaned his head back against the sofa. He could shut off the TV right now but he didn't want to disturb Tori, who had finally drifted off just before the courtroom verdict in the movie. She'd missed the happy ending, the perfect house and family and a new brother on the way. Emotion clogged his throat for a moment as he turned his head an inch and looked down at her, lashes against her cheeks, warm belly pressed against his hip.

She would be so easy to love, if he were capable of it.

As it was, he definitely had feelings for her. She was the purest person he'd ever known. Always seemed to find a bright side, a positive angle. Cared about people.

Cared about him.

At least she made him believe she did. And she was snuggled up to him right now, trusting.

He felt pretty damned unworthy of that.

The credits ended and the app went to a home screen with "suggested for you" thumbnails of other holiday movies. It wasn't late, but it was late enough, and clearly she was exhausted. She'd been working long hours for days, and carrying the baby, too.

As carefully as he could, he shifted his hips so that her head was cradled in his elbow, then turned so that he was off the sofa, leaning over her. With as much gentleness as he could muster, he slipped an arm beneath her legs and the other beneath her shoulders, keeping her head snug against him. He lifted her in his arms and adjusted her weight as her lashes fluttered.

"Jeremy?"

"Shh… You fell asleep. I'm taking you to bed."

He got halfway down the hall before she actually lifted her head. "You really are carrying me. You're going to give yourself a hernia."

He couldn't stop the burst of laughter that started in his chest. Lord, but she made him laugh sometimes at the most unexpected moments.

"I'm pretty sure I can handle it," he replied.

He nudged open the door to her room and laid her down on the bed, but she was awake now and scooted up so that she was sitting. "That was very sweet of you."

"I was hoping I wouldn't wake you. You looked so peaceful."

"I was comfortable." She smiled, the edges of it soft from sleep. "You're kind of warm and cozy."

Jeremy went to the bed and sat on the edge. "Honestly? I don't think I've ever been called that before."

"Well, you are. And I need to be awake anyway, because I need to pee and brush my teeth." She put her hand on his forearm. "It was a really nice night. A nice day, when all is said and done. Thank you."

He reached over to pat her hand and ended up taking her fingers in his instead, twining them together, linking them in a way that frightened him just a bit. Still, this was what he'd suggested, wasn't it? Acknowledgment of their attraction for each other? Desire? Affection? His thumb rubbed over the top of her hand, and he met her gaze, saying nothing. The air between them grew heavy with words unspoken, possibilities unrealized.

"You're going to kiss me, aren't you?" she murmured,

but instead of looking away, as she had a tendency to do, she held his gaze.

"Only if you want me to."

She said nothing for a few seconds that felt like an eternity, and he waited, trying to be patient. Wanting to leave this decision in her hands.

"You want me to say it." She bit down on her lip, another thing he realized she did when she was nervous.

"Yeah," he replied, his voice rough. "I do."

Another long moment, and then she said it, her voice barely above a whisper. "Kiss me, Jeremy. Please."

She didn't have to ask twice, or even add the sweet-sounding "please" to the end. "Kiss me" was enough. He squeezed her fingers tighter and leaned forward. "No mistletoe in here," he murmured, only an inch away from her lips.

"We don't need it," she answered, and he closed the remaining distance between them.

Nothing in the world could be as soft as her lips. They opened beneath his, sweet and willing, and an expansive feeling rushed through him as he drank her in. He inched closer, close enough that if he moved his arm at all it would be around her and pulling her close, but tonight she was in charge. She set the pace. He'd kissed her twice already. Tonight he wanted—needed—to know that she wanted him as much as he wanted her.

As the kiss deepened, she leaned forward, moving to get closer to him, and before they lost their balance he put out his left hand and braced it on the bed. Tori curled her hand up around his neck and exerted a little pressure, pulling him closer to her, then shifting so that she was slowly inching downward with him leaning over her from above. Desire surged; last summer hadn't been a fluke, and she still had the power to make him weak and strong at the same time. Their chemistry couldn't be ignored as she made a little sound in the back of her throat. He slid his mouth off hers and pressed his lips to the sensitive spot on her neck where her pulse drummed.

"Oh," she breathed, arching her neck. "Jeremy... That feels so nice."

"Damn right," he growled, fighting to keep his hands gentle.

"Jeremy, I—" Another sigh stopped her midsentence, but she picked up again, undaunted. "Can we just kiss tonight?"

She had to know what she was asking. He wanted to touch her everywhere. Feel her warm, smooth skin against his. But he'd promised himself that she could take the lead and so he dutifully answered, "Of course."

"You're a good kisser."

"Mmm... Likewise."

"You've got SKL. Do you know what that is?"

"Uh-uh." He licked at her earlobe and goose bumps erupted on her shoulders as he slid his fingers along the skin revealed by the slouchy sweater's neckline. It had a V-neck, and with it pulled a bit sideways, a generous slice of cleavage and the swell of her full breast were visible before the rest was concealed by her bra.

"Seriously kissable lips. Not too full, not too thin, really nice and soft. With that little dip in the middle, right here." She slid her hand from his hair down his jaw, then dotted the dip in his upper lip with a fingertip.

"Tori?"

"Yeah?"

"You talk too much."

And then he went to work shutting her up. Because if she wanted to be kissed—and that was all she wanted—he'd give her what she asked for. And he'd do it right.

* * *

Tori rolled over in bed the next morning and stared at the ceiling. The events of last night were crammed in her brain, one on top of the other, until everything was clouded with Jeremy.

She'd intended to be cautious. Said she only wanted kissing. But she'd been mistaken if she'd thought kissing him gave her any sort of protection. Instead, Jeremy Fisher and his clever mouth had sneaked past all her defenses.

It was a good thing that he had no idea how close she'd been to inviting him to stay in her bed. Just when she'd reached the point where she was ready to ask for more, he'd pulled back, kissed the tip of her nose, and wished her good-night.

She supposed she had to add honorable to his list of qualities, too. Instead of being comforted, the thought set her on edge. It couldn't be this simple. There was something about him that had to be flawed, something that was going to go wrong. She wished she had some idea what it was so she could prepare herself for it. She definitely didn't want to be blindsided again.

She got up and went to the bathroom for a refreshing shower, then dressed in tights and a swing-type dress from her "before pregnant" wardrobe that accommodated her growing tummy nicely, at least at this stage. The neckline looked a bit bare, so she found an infinity scarf and wound it around her neck, then put her hair up in a messy bun. She looked in the mirror with a critical eye. Back home this would be dressing up. But here... It was a different atmosphere. Different expectations, too.

Jeremy was in the kitchen, pouring cereal into a bowl. "Good morning. There's decaf if you want it."

Her outfit would be completed with her black boots, but inside she was in her stockinged feet and felt a little vulnerable. She tried a smile, wondering how he could act so normal while inside she was still stuck on last night's kisses and him carrying her to the bedroom.

"I'd like that."

"I'll get it. Help yourself to what you want for breakfast. There's bread for toast, or cereal, and fresh eggs. Or smoothies. I keep stuff on hand for shakes. It's what I normally eat, though today I felt like cereal."

He was quite the conversationalist in the morning, she thought, accepting the mug of coffee he handed over, fixed the way she liked—how had he remembered that?

"You look nice today," he added, touching her arm on his way past her with his cereal bowl. Instead of eating at the dining room table, he perched on a bar stool at a high counter. It was far more comfortable than the huge table and formal setting.

She stuck her head in the refrigerator so he wouldn't see her blush. "Thanks. And there are berries! Excellent."

She turned around and saw Jeremy's eyes flit up to her face. He'd been staring at her backside as she looked in the fridge.

"Sorry," he said, without sounding too sorry at all. "I got distracted by your butt."

Her lips twitched. "You really don't beat around the bush, do you?"

"I try not to."

"Well, then, stop looking at my butt and tell me what's on the agenda today."

She sat next to him on a high stool and arranged berries and melon on a plate. Took a sip of coffee and put the mug down, tried to pretend this was as normal as could be.

"Well, I thought you might like to do some shopping."

"You don't have to buy me things, you know. I have clothes."

"Sure, but how often do you get to shop on Fifth Avenue? Come on, surely there are stores you'd like to go into. Besides, you actually need a few things. Like a coat. Your regular winter one is getting snug already. You're not going to make it through to March or April and still be able to zip it up."

He was right about the coat; she'd already realized it. "Well, I can get one back home."

"And you can get one here. Let me spoil you a little. Besides, I need a new tie."

"Sure you do."

He wiggled his eyebrows. "So, I probably don't. But I can't in all conscience bring you here for a week and not take you shopping. We can walk. And this afternoon I have a surprise for you."

She paused, a piece of honeydew on her fork. "What kind of a surprise?"

"Nope. Not going to get it out of me that easily."

"I don't know, Jeremy. This makes me uncomfortable. I can't ever possibly pay you back."

He frowned. "Why would I want you to do that? Look, Tori. I have more money than I know what to do with, frankly, and rarely have anyone to spend it on. This is a treat for me to do this for you, okay? A gift, nothing more."

"Well, I can't reciprocate, either."

"I don't need you to. Buying you a few clothes, taking you to see a few new things... If I promise not to shower you with jewels, are we okay?"

What could she say? He was right. A day's shopping was a drop in the bucket to him, so why should it bother her so much?

Because it made her feel as if she owed him something.

And she couldn't say that to him without insulting him.

Especially when he'd been so very nice to her already. Never pushing. Not once had he given her any indication he had a hidden agenda or was trying to manipulate her or the situation. She was the one coming up with that scenario, purely out of fear.

Maybe it was as her mom said. Sometimes you had to have a little faith.

By the time early afternoon arrived, Tori was laden with bags, most of which contained what she'd been wearing that morning. Her boots were in a boot box and new ones cradled her feet and calves; she wore the same swing dress and tights of the morning but the scarf was replaced with a new checked one of wool and silk. Instead of her everyday jacket, which was now tucked in another box in a huge bag, she wore a cashmere cape and gloves that Jeremy had insisted he buy her. Add in the sunglasses and she was pretty sure today's ensemble came to more than she'd spent on the down payment for her house.

She felt both glamorous and a fraud, beautiful and a bit not-quite-herself, but today's shopping had been an experience. Brands she'd only ever seen online or in magazines were now on her body.

Jeremy had also insisted she buy some maternity clothes, so he'd taken her into Saks, where he'd slapped down his credit card for two pairs of pants, three tops and two dresses—one that she could wear for any occasion, and the other a cocktail dress. When she protested that one, he'd insisted that sometime over Christmas she might like to dress up. She'd countered by saying she'd be overdressed in something so expensive, and then he'd raised an eyebrow at her and she'd given up. Maybe she would have fought harder if she didn't absolutely love the navy dress, but from the moment she'd put it on, it had been perfect. Then it was off to buy shoes. She'd reached her limit when he came around a corner with a plump, plush penguin in his hand. "And something for the baby, too," he'd said, flashing her a smile.

He carried most of the bags while she held the ones containing the penguin and the dresses. They'd started walking back toward the park—at least that was what she thought if her sense of direction was right—when he stopped and lifted his chin at something over his shoulder.

She turned around and looked. It was the same spot they'd been the day before, just steps away from The Plaza.

"Tea?"

Her mouth dropped open. "Are you serious?"

He nodded. "I got us in for three o'clock, and since we didn't stop for lunch, you must be famished. Today you can be Eloise and have high tea at The Plaza."

"Jeremy."

He laughed at her tone of voice. "Yes?"

"I do not know how you pulled this off. Do people really live like this? I don't believe it."

His eyes shone at her. "Every day? No. Once in a while? Everyone should. Just once in their lifetime, I think."

"I'm afraid I'll get something on me. Seriously." She knew the cape had cost far too much. Right now wasn't life, it was pretending. But she couldn't help it. She'd pretend for a little while longer, because it was amazing.

"Come on. It's ten to three, and we'll get there just in time. You can even freshen up a bit before we're seated."

When they walked in the door, her head nearly swiveled all the way around. The lobby was stunning in and of itself, but when Jeremy led her to The Palm Court, she had to catch her breath.

Light. And elegance. And green palms and the most

amazing ceiling…the iconic stained glass dome. She couldn't believe she was here.

"Tori? Tori." Jeremy was at her side, touching her elbow. "It's going to be a few minutes. Come on, we can leave our bags with the concierge and pick them up when we're done. I'll show you where the powder room is."

She tore herself away from the sight and followed him, her boots clicking on the floor. In the powder room she tidied her hair and refreshed her lipstick. There were roses in her cheeks; partly from the fresh, cold air and partly because of excitement, she was sure. She found Jeremy again and he solicitously took her cape, draping it over his arm for the time being.

When they were led to their table, she looked around at all the other people having tea. Some were dressed more casually than she. Others were dressed impeccably from head to toe, without a hair out of place. At her seat, she placed a hand on her tummy as she sat, tucking the skirt of her dress beneath her.

"So. Surprised?"

"Very," she responded, unable to stop staring. "Oh, look at this place. And how did you ever get a table on such short notice? I've always heard that it takes weeks or months to get in for tea."

"I pulled some strings," he admitted. "While you were asleep yesterday."

Of course he had.

"Look at the menu," he suggested. "I'll say everything's good, but you should make your selections based on what you like. Especially if there's something the baby doesn't like, or you can't eat while you're pregnant."

She lifted her gaze to his. "Has someone been doing some reading?"

"Maybe. When I sent the grocery list to my housekeeper—Melissa, by the way—I wanted to get some things you like and…well, healthy things."

She pointed to the list of sweets on the tea menu. "These are not healthy, and I am going to enjoy several."

He laughed. "Good."

He ordered a plain black tea for himself, while Tori went for a more aromatic Earl Grey. All around them was the clink of silverware on china, the hum of conversations. Tea arrived, and their tray of delights—finger sandwiches of cucumber, salmon, and turkey, perfect scones with Devonshire cream and lemon curd, and a selection of pastries and sweets that nearly made her teeth ache just looking at them. The entire hour, eating and chatting and people watching, was a dream come true. No matter what happened in their future, she'd always have this day to remember.

She'd told him once she wasn't Cinderella, but she was surely feeling like it now. She was in the hotel business, was assistant manager to an upscale resort, but the Sandpiper and all its wonderful amenities paled in comparison to this.

It was like a mansion being compared to a palace.

"Have the last scone," Jeremy suggested. "I can tell you love the cream with the preserves."

They were a bit of heaven for sure. She didn't argue, didn't protest, just reached for the light-as-air scone and smeared it with strawberry, then topped it with cream and popped it in her mouth.

"I love watching you eat," he said, a smile lighting his face.

She nearly choked on a crumb. "Er…what?"

"I just mean you like food. You don't pretend not to."

Oh, goodness. He was probably used to stick women who starved themselves or something. Or perhaps her manners were lacking. How mortifying.

"Don't worry, it's a compliment. You're real, Tori. It's one of the things I like about you."

"Are you sure? Because I'm pretty confident I have scone crumbs on my dress now and sadly when we get home and I take these boots off my ankles are probably going to swell from all the walking and stuff we did today."

"Real," he repeated. "Flesh and blood. No pretending to be someone you're not, no putting on airs to try to impress me. You are who you are and you're comfortable with it. That kind of confidence is rare."

She didn't know what to say. She was very aware that she'd gained a few pounds with the baby and some of it was due to potato chips. And until now, she hadn't really cared. She understood he was paying her a compliment. But she hadn't considered confidence before. "I mean, I guess I just am who I am. I'm not sure I can change for anyone, or be a chameleon."

"I would hope not." He leaned forward. "Because you're normal, you see? And when I'm with you, I feel normal, too."

"Are you lonely, Jeremy?"

"Sometimes. I have my friends and all, and my sister and I are semi close, but it's not the same as being…"

This time his voice drifted off, and he looked away for a moment.

"Intimate with someone?"

His gaze came back to hers. "Yeah. And not just physically, though that's not a problem with you either, it seems."

The baby must have enjoyed the tea as well, because it was moving around fairly consistently. She absently rubbed a hand over the curve, mindlessly soothing. But Jeremy noticed, and his face softened.

"I want us to be a family somehow. You should know that."

Nerves quivered in her stomach. "We will be. No matter what we decide to do. Because we're going to raise this baby together. Okay?"

He nodded.

When their tea was cleared away, he helped her put her cape back on, tenderly buttoning the top button. She picked up her new wristlet containing her phone and cards, and as Jeremy placed his hand along the small of her back, she caught a glimpse of a woman, probably in her fifties, watching them with a soft smile on her face. Tori smiled back shyly and as they passed the woman's table, she said, "Congratulations."

"Oh! Thank you," she answered, pressing her hand on her belly as a reflex.

Right now she felt as if they *were* a family. But the day was pretend. Wasn't it?

CHAPTER TEN

THE WEEK TURNED into a whirlwind, and Jeremy tried to hit every iconic New York experience he could think of.

One evening he took her to the Christmas Spectacular with the Rockettes at Radio City Music Hall, and they watched them kick their way through a dance routine that would have had him winded in about thirty seconds. Tori's eyes had shone as she focused on the stage, her smile bright as she turned to him time and again throughout the show.

Then there were the frenetic lights and sounds of Times Square, filled with tourists. It wasn't his favorite spot, but she'd wanted to see where the ball would drop on New Year's Eve. He showed her, and vowed to himself that one day he'd bring her here on December 31 so she could see it for real.

Of course, no trip to Times Square could be enjoyed without a piece of cheesecake from Junior's, and he bought her pineapple because he thought it was the best. He hadn't been wrong, it seemed, because she'd savored every bite, laughingly proclaiming that it was for the baby.

There'd been pizza one night, sitting on the carpet and finally watching the original *Miracle on 34th Street*, and slow but sweet kisses stolen here and there. A trip up the Empire State Building, where she'd held his hand as she looked out over the city, and a more sobering visit to the 9/11 Memorial.

Alas, he couldn't avoid work altogether, and he'd been

sneaking the odd hour here and there to look after things that couldn't wait. He had to go into his office, though, so he left her the keys and told her to have a relaxing day, wherever that might take her. She'd made noises about wanting to visit the park again, or maybe go to the Met. Both were practically on his doorstep, so he left with no worries about how she'd spend the day.

At one o'clock, he realized he hadn't eaten lunch, so he decided to pop down to the bottom floor and the restaurant on-site. Before he could get out of the office door, however, two familiar faces came toward him down the hall.

"The two of you here together? Something big must be up."

Cole Abbott flashed a grin. "Well, Bran said he was coming to see you, and I was going to be in the city, so I thought I'd tag along."

They exchanged backslapping hugs, then Jeremy turned back around toward his office. "It's good to see you two."

"Bran said you had some news. Wouldn't tell me what it is, though."

Cole scowled at his companion. Bran was smiling, but it didn't quite reach his eyes, and his cheeks still looked hollow from grief. Jeremy knew exactly what had brought Cole to the city. Worry for their friend.

"Bran's bought a house in Nova Scotia. Did he tell you that?"

"Yes, so I know that's not the news. What's up?"

Jeremy took a moment to look out his office window. He had a great view of the Hudson. He had just about everything a man could want.

He faced the men again and let out a breath. "Well, I'm going to be a father."

Branson stared at Cole, who sat heavily in a chair in

front of Jeremy's desk. He let out a curse word and ran his hand over his face. "For real?"

Jeremy laughed. "Yeah. Needless to say, it was a surprise for me, too."

"Who is she? When? How did it happen?"

"Tori, last summer, and the usual way."

Branson laughed, the sound rusty. "Oh, man. Your face, Cole. This is why I didn't tell you."

Jeremy chuckled. "It's not the end of the world, dude."

"Are you sure?"

"We're all nearly thirty-six years old. It was bound to happen to one of us eventually."

Silence fell. Jeremy suddenly wished he could cut out his tongue. It had happened—to Bran. And then it had been ripped away. All his happiness.

"Oh, Bran, I'm sorry. That was thoughtless."

Bran waved a hand. "Forget it."

"I can't. I'm so, so—"

Bran looked him dead in the eye. "It's okay, Jeremy. Really. I can't pretend it didn't happen, and you guys can't tap-dance around it for the rest of your lives. So shut up and tell us what's happening. Because last I heard you were in Canada finding out the news and freaking out a bit."

Jeremy perched on the edge of the desk as the tension in the room dissipated a bit. "Well, she's here, actually. I brought her here for a week so we could talk about what we want to do."

"Are you guys a thing?"

"I don't know. Yes? But no. I mean, we haven't slept together."

"Clearly you did…"

"I mean since I found out." He aimed a "smart aleck"

look at Cole. "But I like her, a lot. And she likes me. And we've kissed…"

Bran nudged Cole. "This is nearly as bad as when we were freshmen and he was telling us about the girl he'd left behind… What was her name? Jill? Jane? Though I think he said he'd felt her up once."

"Again, shut up. I don't know why we're still friends." But a smile curved up his cheek. This was exactly why they were friends, and had been for over twenty years.

"So what, you brought her here? Is she going to move here to be with you? So you can bring the baby up together?"

"We haven't really talked about it."

"But that's what you want, right?" Bran always got to the heart of the matter.

"Yeah." He let out a breath. "I just can't see us living in two different countries and trying to parent. I'm kind of hoping that she'll like it here enough to consider moving."

"Wow." Cole sat back in the chair. "So then what? Marriage? Are you thinking of staying in your place, or buying elsewhere? Your place isn't really one where I can picture kids running around."

Jeremy frowned. "I can always redecorate. And there's room. Plus it's close to everything."

"I don't know, man. It's a lot to ask of a woman. To pack up and leave everything behind." This from Bran.

Cole scoffed. "Yeah, leave behind what? Jeremy's loaded. She's landed herself in clover."

Jeremy pushed away from the desk. "It's not like that. She doesn't care about money. And don't roll your eyes," he said in response to Cole's facial expression. "It's true. If anyone has any ulterior motives here, it's me." He sighed. "Mom and Bruce are having a party in a few days. I'm going to take her. If we do this, she's got to have her eyes wide open." He nodded at Bran. "That was your advice, and I think you're right."

"You're springing the Wicked Witch of the West on her?"

Again, Jeremy couldn't help but laugh at Cole. "Yeah, I am. But Sarah's going, too." He was thrilled his sister had agreed. He hadn't told her about Tori either, but she'd be an ally.

"Damn, brother."

"I know."

There was quiet for a moment, and then Cole said, with a bit of wonder in his voice, "You're gonna be a dad."

"Seems like it."

He got up and clapped Jeremy on the back. "Congratulations, man. You're gonna nail this."

Nope, he wasn't going to cry over this unexpected gesture. Cole was not the touchy-feely type. So he chuckled instead. "You think? Because I had a crappy example."

"Didn't we all? So just do the exact opposite of what your mom and stepdad did and you'll be great."

Bran stood up. "And if the city thing doesn't work out, maybe we'll be neighbors, Jeremy."

Cole looked at them both.

"His new house is less than an hour away from Tori," Jeremy confirmed. "Have you seen it?" He went to his computer and brought the pics up on the monitor. "Look at that. Lighthouse and everything."

Cole tapped his lips. "How much?"

"Just under three."

"You're joking."

"Nope. You looking for an investment property?"

"I might. I've been floating a few ideas around for something. We can talk in the new year."

"Sure."

Bran coughed. "I don't know about you ladies, but I came for lunch. Let's go get a steak somewhere."

"Okay, but I can't be late getting home. I left Tori on her own today."

Bran laughed and clapped him on the shoulder. "And so it begins, bro. And so it begins."

Jeremy took the teasing with a smile. Yeah, they were right and they were ribbing him about it. But it occurred to him that he really didn't mind at all.

Tori had spent the day walking in the park, having a sandwich in a small shop somewhere and then window-shopping. She'd found this little store in Midtown that had an appealing array of housewares in the window, and inside was even better. Now, as she waited for Jeremy to come home, she looked at the items she'd bought and fought against nerves. What if he didn't like the changes? What if he resented her stepping in and doing anything to his space?

She had receipts. She could take it all back.

The kitchen smelled good, too. She'd stopped at a market and bought the groceries required to make her curried chicken and broccoli casserole. She'd made a salad, too.

The casserole was almost ready and she was watching another holiday movie on TV when Jeremy came through the door. "Wow, something smells great in here," he said from the foyer.

Score one. She got up from the sofa and went to the foyer to greet him as he hung up his coat.

"Hi. I made dinner. Not that Melissa isn't a great cook, but I like to cook and since I was at loose ends today…"

"No explanation required. I'm glad you got out today."

"I did! I had fun."

He stepped into the main living area and stopped short. "What the—? You decorated."

"Only a little." She folded her hands in front of her. "You didn't have anything up for Christmas, and it felt a little…monochrome in here."

He unbuttoned his suit jacket and loosened his tie, staying quiet long enough that her nerves bubbled up again. "I think that was the decorator's objective," he said. "To let the space speak for itself."

"Oh." His lukewarm response let all the air out of her joy balloon. She'd wanted it to be a lovely surprise. To see his face light up. Now she was just let down.

He pulled off his tie and stuffed it into his pants pocket while she stood there, unsure of what to do next. She rather liked the little three-foot tree she'd bought, decorated with white lights and red and silver bows. The poinsettia centerpiece she'd had delivered from the florist graced the center of the dining table. The air smelled of pine boughs and cones from the candle arrangement on the glass coffee table. A small gift bag sat on the table, too, and her eyes stung. He didn't like it.

She wouldn't be so obvious as to move his present right away. She'd wait until he moved somewhere else and sneak it away to her room, or perhaps in the drawer of the table. She could return it tomorrow. Return everything.

"I have receipts," she whispered.

"What?"

"Receipts. To take everything back. I know it was presumptuous of me. This is your home. I just thought…it could use some Christmas spirit in here."

He looked at her strangely, then turned his back and went to the kitchen. She rushed over to the table, grabbed the gift bag and tucked it into the drawer where he kept his remotes and magazines.

"There's a rooster in my kitchen!"

Tori froze. Oh, God, was he angry? She pressed her

hand to her chest and pursed her lips, letting out a slow breath. Up until now, he'd been so easygoing. It was one of the things she liked about him. But his living space… It didn't fit with the Jeremy she had spent time with so far. It was colorless and without humor. Without life. She puckered her eyebrows. That made no sense. How could decor have a sense of humor? But it was how she felt just the same. He was larger than life. His apartment was… prescriptive.

She went into the kitchen and prepared herself for, at the very least, an annoyed Jeremy.

He was staring at the ceramic rooster she'd bought, sitting in the middle of the counter. She suddenly felt a wave of irritation sweep over her. All she'd done was add a few holiday decorations and buy a stupid knickknack. He didn't have to be so…cold. It wasn't like him, or at least the Jeremy she knew.

Maybe the problem was she didn't know him at all.

"Your place is boring, Jeremy. You needed a conversation piece, and I got you one." She put her hands on her hips.

His head swiveled and he stared at her for a long moment, and then the most surprising thing happened. He started laughing. A low chuckle, almost despite himself, and her lips twitched. Then harder, and she tried really hard not to laugh back. But when he let loose and bent over, laughing himself silly, she couldn't help it. She started laughing, too, until they were both breathless.

"A…a…conversation piece," he choked out, still laughing. "A rooster. Oh, my God."

Oh, goodness. He was too adorable right now. And not mad. She didn't know what he was feeling, not really, but he wasn't mad at her, and her relief was great.

The oven timer dinged and she took a deep breath. "I have to stop laughing so I can take that out of the oven."

"What is it?"

She looked at the rooster, looked at Jeremy and said, deadpan, "Chicken."

That set them off again.

It wasn't that funny. Maybe the stress of the last few weeks was getting to them.

She got the casserole out of the oven and put it on the stove to cool. Jeremy had finally stopped laughing and leaned over her shoulder to look at the dish. "Hmm. Not familiar. But it smells good."

"It is good. You wait and see." She slid off the oven mitts and turned around. He was close to her, so close her heart started a pitter-patter that she both loved and hated. "Do you really hate the decorations?" She wanted the truth now that the awkwardness had passed.

He shook his head, his gaze sobering. "No, I don't. I just wasn't prepared."

"For what? Christmas?"

"For it to look like home."

The pitter-patter turned to solid thumping. "Why? Why shouldn't your home look like a home?"

"I don't know. And this… Look, Tori. I'm just over-whelmed. I came home to you today. To an apartment with holiday decorations and a woman pregnant with my child and a home-cooked meal. I have no idea what to do with that."

How cold had his life been?

"You must have had Christmas trees."

"Not like this. Not…for me. You did this for me, didn't you?"

She nodded slightly.

Ignoring the hot casserole dish behind her, he put his

hands on the edge of the cold stove and leaned in to kiss her. Really kiss her, with not only skill but with enough emotion that she turned to mush. Could they make this work? He hadn't responded because he was overwhelmed. Because he'd been floored by the idea that someone had done that for him… Her heart broke a little for the lonely boy he must have been. And now he was kissing her as if she'd given him the moon. She'd spent no more than he'd spent on tea yesterday, but she felt as if she'd given him the world.

It would be so easy to fall in love with this Jeremy. Not just the man who'd been a fantastic lover in the summer sun, or the guy who'd treated her like a princess yesterday, but this man, who let her glimpse his heart. Who could be absolutely tender with her when she needed it most.

His body fit so perfectly against hers, even with the baby between them. Over the last week she'd seen a difference in her bump, and the recent snug waistlines had given way to full-on showing. With Jeremy kissing her like she was something precious, and his baby growing within her, she felt both incredibly feminine and extraordinarily powerful in such a beautiful, natural way.

He'd given that to her. And it was worth more than some artificial tree with a few lights and bows.

And when he broke the kiss and hugged her, she felt herself slipping further under his spell.

"Thank you. I'm sorry I didn't say it before. I love that you thought of me and wanted to do this for me. I don't think I've ever really had that before."

"Then I'm glad I did it because everyone deserves to feel seen and important," she answered, holding on to his shoulders. She slid her fingers into his hair. "You're a lot of things, Jeremy, but you're also a man, and you're human."

He kissed her again, long and slow, and she gave herself over to the emotion of the moment. He'd asked her here so they could see where they were in their relationship. What if this could work somehow? What if there really was a happy ending? She tried not to worry about logistics. Those weren't really what concerned her at this point. It was Jeremy, and whether they could parent together, if they could be together. A couple *and* a family.

Right now, all the signs pointed to yes, because he was threading his hands through her hair and she was reaching for the buttons on his shirt.

She was halfway down his chest when he put his hand over hers. "You sure?" he asked, a little hint of sexy gravel in his voice. "You have to be sure."

"I'm sure." She lifted her chin. "I want you. All of you."

Including his heart. And maybe that wouldn't happen today. But she hoped it would someday, because his was a heart worth cherishing.

CHAPTER ELEVEN

JEREMY HAD NEVER once been scared before making love to a woman, but he was scared tonight.

There was a lot at stake. A ton of possibility that could be the best thing ever to happen to him—or he could blow it and they'd be back to square one, just like they were in her office the day he'd discovered she was pregnant.

But more than that, he'd never before made love to a woman where his heart was involved, and it was with Tori. As much as he tried to deny it, she touched something inside him he usually kept locked away. And he'd let her get a glimpse of it. He didn't like being that vulnerable.

She was standing in his room now, facing him, the soft light of a pair of lamps illuminating her pale skin. He moved forward, wanting to undress her, as scared as he'd been his very first time. Her gaze locked with his, her eyes warmed and her lips curved up in a small smile.

"Don't be scared," she said, as if she could read his thoughts.

"I want to see you." His heart clubbed against his ribs as he reached for her sweater, bunching it up in his hands until it went past her waist, over her breasts, over her head. When her hair was free she shook it out, and he dropped the sweater. Her full breasts were cupped by a plain black satin bra, and her leggings came up over her bump. Holding his gaze, she pushed the waistband down until she was standing before him in the bra and matching underwear, the bikini elastic sitting low below where her tummy began to curve.

She was so beautiful. He could stare at her forever, marveling at how gorgeous she was and the awesomeness of her carrying their child.

"Are you going to touch me?" she asked, tilting her head.

He reached out and put his hand on her hip, pulling her closer, and lifted his other hand to her ribs, skimming over her thickened waist, his thumb roving toward her breast. Dammit, his hands were shaking.

She put her fingers on his face, guiding him to look her in the eyes. "I need to know, Jeremy. Need to know that this is still good and real. We have a lot to figure out, but most of all we need to decide how we feel about each other."

"You think I have a choice? That I can decide?"

He was already a goner.

"Maybe *decide* is the wrong word. Maybe *acknowledge*." Her fingers traced over his jaw, the fingernail scraping his stubble a little bit. "Me, here with you, like this… I'm acknowledging that I feel something for you."

"I don't take this lightly," he murmured.

"Nor do I. So when you touch me…when you take me…know that I've made this choice tonight. Knowing the risks and wanting you anyway."

He was afraid. Humbled. He almost considered not going through with it, and then she moved toward him, pressing her lips to the hollow between his shoulder and collarbone. He shuddered and closed his eyes, drinking in the sensation, the tenderness, the heat of it. Their time together in the summer had been nothing short of spectacular. With the news of the baby and walking on eggshells, he'd nearly forgotten. But not now. Not with her so close to him with his shirt spread open and their skin touching, warm and soft.

He let out a shaky sigh, then gathered her against him and shut out the world.

Tori rolled over and felt the sheets gathered beneath her armpits. They were silk, black silk, and caressed her body as she shifted to face Jeremy.

He was still sleeping on his back, his lips relaxed and his lashes resting peacefully.

She was wearing nothing but her bikini panties again, which she vaguely remembered pulling on before sliding back into bed and into his arms, falling into sleep.

That had been two hours ago, around eight o'clock. Right now, her belly rumbled and the baby kicked all at the same time. They hadn't eaten dinner.

"Someone's hungry."

Her breath caught at the sound of his amused voice. His eyes were still closed, but the corners of his mouth twitched.

"I am. And so's your kid. Besides, that casserole is cold now and we should eat it and then put the leftovers in the fridge."

"But you're warm and snuggly."

Snuggly wasn't the word she'd use. Her breasts were heavier now and more sensitive with the pregnancy, and the slippery sheets felt almost like a caress. She was nearly naked in bed with him; that was distraction enough. But she was also starving. And truthfully, she was still reeling from what had happened between them. She needed some distance to make sense of her thoughts.

It had been good between them before. Tonight had been…better. Because it wasn't just a fling anymore. Their connection had been transcendent.

She shook her head and figured that kind of thinking was going to get her into trouble. They still had to figure out this parenting thing with clear heads. Regretfully, she slipped out of the sheets and went searching for her bra.

"Here." He got out of bed and, fully naked, went to the closet and took out a soft robe. "Put this on if you don't want to get all dressed up again."

It was charcoal gray and thick and soft, and she wrapped it around her body while his scent rose from the fabric. "Thanks," she murmured.

And tried not to look at his butt when he went back to the closet, but she failed. It was a rather spectacular backside.

He returned wearing a pair of plaid sleep pants and a sweatshirt. It shouldn't have been attractive, but it made her want to crawl inside his embrace again.

They went to the kitchen and Tori scooped up servings of casserole and put them in the microwave. While they were heating, she put the rest in containers and put them in the fridge, next to the salad that had never been touched. Jeremy filled water glasses, and within moments they were seated at the counter again, chowing down on the chicken, broccoli and rice with creamy sauce.

"This is delicious."

"It's my mom's recipe. I don't know where she got it, but she used to make it now and again, especially for potlucks."

He took a sip of water. "Potlucks?"

She laughed. "Okay, so not everyone in the world caters their functions. A potluck is where you have a gathering of some kind and everyone brings a dish. It's awesome because you get this amazing variety of food. Some people just stop at the grocery store and get platters of veggies and stuff, you know? But then other people bring amazing dishes. We had a neighbor who always made meatballs. A guy from church who came with a ton of hot chicken wings. And don't get me started on the salads and cheeses and appetizers…"

He laughed, scooping up more food. "It sounds fun."

"It is. And if it's a kitchen party, then you also bring your own alcohol and someone is likely to bring a guitar and it gets fun and rowdy."

His face took on a faraway expression. "What?" she asked.

"I don't think I've ever had that in my life."

She patted his hand. "Where I come from, few people are rolling in cash. Everyone chips in, good times had by all. It's what happens in a community."

"In my community, people decorate and cater and send out invitations and try to impress each other."

"Sounds dreadful."

Now his face was downright pensive. "I'm sorry to hear that, because my mom is holding something quite similar to that on Saturday, at our house in Connecticut. I want you to come."

All the warmth that had been flooding through her body froze. "Oh, no. Meet the parents? Not likely."

He pushed his plate aside, and she did, too. She didn't have much appetite left.

"Tori, after tonight, I think we need to start talking about what we plan to do. I mean, really talk about it. This whole week has been amazing and fun. But the point was also to be alone together, to decide what we want to do about us and the baby. We haven't even talked about that at all."

She nodded, looking down at the smears of sauce on her plate. "I know. I've been avoiding it because everything is going to change."

He put his hand over hers. "Would you consider moving here?"

Panic slid down her body. She was still vulnerable from the hours spent in his arms, and her hopes warred with caution. "I don't know. I don't want to say no right off the bat, but while I've enjoyed my week here, I'm not sure I'm the kind of person who can live in the middle of a huge city. Let alone Manhattan."

"We could keep this place and stay here when we want to come into the city. And I'd be willing to look at properties elsewhere that you might like better."

"Like Connecticut?"

He laughed a little. "And be that close to my family? Hell, no. Maybe more like Long Island. There are some particularly good places for young families there." He squeezed her hand. "This is my job, you know. I can find us a place, if you'll consider moving."

Was she really considering it? The idea took her breath away. "You're assuming that I'm okay with picking up and leaving my life. But I like my life. And I like working. I know I wouldn't have to provide an income for us to live off. But the Sandpiper has been my home away from home for years now. I've helped build it into the hotel it is today. It's asking a lot, to leave the life I've built behind."

"I know." He let out a sigh. "But you can work anywhere, right? Especially if it's not about the money. You could find something that you really like."

She thought about it. A big house, their baby, a job she could work at to give her purpose…never any worries about bills. She wasn't sure she trusted a future that seemed so perfect. "After what you said about your mom, I thought you'd want me to be home to look after the baby all the time."

He snorted. "My mom was home all the time and never

spent a second with us. Being a good parent isn't decided on who gets to stay home and who works. Even I know that."

She smiled. "Okay, fair enough." She looked over at him. "And you're sure you don't want to come to Nova Scotia?"

"Don't get me wrong. I love the province. It's beautiful. But the market is so much smaller. I'd be bored out of my mind. And that has nothing to do with you, and everything to do with me not wanting to fall into the trap of the 'idle rich.' I need a purpose, too."

She got that. She truly did.

"There's immigration stuff to worry about. I'm not a US citizen." Especially if a marriage wasn't in the picture.

"We can get a lawyer for that."

"I suppose." She slid her hand out from beneath his. "And problems do go away easier when you can throw money at them."

It was quiet for a few moments, before Jeremy spoke up again, his eyes telegraphing his disappointment. "That's the first time you've thrown money in my face. Are you upset?"

She felt badly, even though what she'd said was true. Solutions to problems came easier when there was lots of money to look after them. Truthfully, though, she was scared. Not angry. Just overwhelmed.

This gorgeous man, sitting in his robe, eating leftovers after making love… She was petrified of making a wrong decision. Because right now the truth was she could envision their life together and it seemed so perfect. She was pretty sure she was falling in love with him, and after what had happened earlier tonight, she thought it might be a possibility that he'd fall for her, too. He'd confided in her. And then they'd been intimate. There had been a moment when their eyes had met and it had felt as if everything clicked into place.

She just had to be brave enough.

"There's a lot of personal risk for me," she said quietly, and swiveled on her stool so she was facing him. Their knees barely touched. "Yes, it would mean both of us being there to parent our child. And yes, this week has been really promising with regards to...us. It's still a leap and a half to think about quitting my job, leaving my country and moving in with you with no guarantees." She patted his knee. "Please don't think I'm looking for guarantees. I'm not. It's much too soon for that."

"We can lay out any terms you want," he replied. His gaze held hers. "You can go home whenever. You know that, right? It's not just about business for me, either, Tori. The opportunities here for him or her... They're huge. I want our kid to have the best of both worlds—the opportunities I had with the love and support I didn't. But I think you did."

Would living here be so bad? Especially if there was money—which there would be—for her mom to fly here, or for her to fly home? It was a fairly short direct flight, after all. And it wasn't as if she hated his apartment; she had loved her week here and all the things New York offered. "You'd really look at moving outside the city and commuting in?"

He shrugged. "Lots of people do it. Besides, I'm not always in the city anyway. We could get a place near the water. Have a boat. Hell, we could travel up the coast to visit your mom if you wanted."

Because money was no object. Except it was all his money, and she knew she shouldn't feel guilty but did anyway.

"I'd want some sort of agreement drawn up," she said

firmly. "Something stating that if this doesn't work out, I can't go after your money. I'm not a gold digger, Jeremy."

His lips dropped open. "I know that."

"I want it in writing just the same."

"Whatever makes you happy." He slid forward on his bar stool a bit. "Tori, I know I'm asking a lot of you. In return I promise to do whatever I can to make sure you're happy and content. If that means you look for a job, so be it. If you want to stay home with the baby, that's fine, too." He put his hand on her belly. "I like you a lot, and I think you like me." That flirty smile was back on his lips. "At least the last few hours give me that impression. I have to do better than my own father did with me, you know? And if that means giving our relationship a try, then what do we have to lose? If it doesn't work, we figure out a new arrangement. But there's so much to gain, sweetheart. So much."

Damn. He'd hit her right in her vulnerable spots. She knew how much his father's abandonment had affected him. And he'd called her *sweetheart*—to her mind, the first endearment to leave his lips.

It wasn't the normal progression for a relationship, but what did that matter? He'd been wonderful from the start. Yes, they had their differences—financially, geographically—but did that mean they couldn't have a future together? Of course not.

"Well, I'm willing to look at some options. No guarantees, but I'm not saying no."

A brilliant smile broke over his lips. "It's a *maybe*, which is way better than *no*. I'll take it. And I can show you some examples of nice properties for us."

She also wanted to ask him about citizenship for the baby, because she couldn't imagine having her baby outside Canada. But that didn't have to be decided tonight.

The fact that they'd come up with the beginnings of a plan was huge.

That she'd be facing a lot of changes meant she had a lot to think over. Work, for example, and how long she'd stay at the hotel before the baby was born. Living arrangements. Possibly listing her own house, if she decided to move.

He got up and took their plates into the kitchen, stopping to load them in the dishwasher. "Come on," he said, once they were out of sight. "Come to bed and get some sleep. We have Mom's on Saturday, but tomorrow I have another surprise for you. Something I haven't done since I was a kid."

"Oh?" Her interest piqued, she lifted her head and peered around the corner at him. "What's that?"

He came back and held out his hand. She took it. "If I told you, it wouldn't be a surprise." He tugged on her hand, and she slipped off the stool. "But I promise you'll like it."

"You haven't steered me wrong yet," she admitted, and let herself be pulled closer, so that his arm was around her as they made their way back down the hall.

At the junction to their bedrooms, he stopped and looked into her eyes. "If you want to sleep in your own bed, I understand, but if you want to stay with me, I'd like that, too. It's your choice."

Spending the night seemed like a big deal, but then, if they were really going to give this a shot, she couldn't keep shying away from intimacy. At some point she had to trust that he was as good as he seemed.

"Your room is fine," she said, butterflies settling in her stomach at this new step in their relationship. "But I'd like to get my pajamas first, if that's okay."

"If it makes you more comfortable," he answered, tapping a fingertip on her nose and smiling. "Don't do it on my account."

Heat crept up her cheeks, but she tried to enjoy it. Sharing a child made the stakes high, but there was no reason why this couldn't turn out to be a good, healthy relationship. Why it couldn't be a real future. It was a dizzying and sobering thought.

She scurried away to get her comfy boxer shorts and top. Tonight they were sharing his room. Tomorrow, some sort of surprise. And then night after that, she was meeting his family.

If that didn't sound like a guy who was serious about moving forward, she wasn't sure what did.

CHAPTER TWELVE

JEREMY KNELT BEFORE Tori and tightened up the laces on her skate. "Is this too tight?"

"No, it feels just right."

He gave the ends another tug, then tied the knot and bow. "Okay, then. Give me your other foot."

Skating at Rockefeller Center was something he'd done as a kid. While his mom had come to the city to shop, their nanny at the time would take them skating and then off to some other adventure—and lunch—since dragging three kids around had cramped his mom's style, and his brother and sister weren't old enough to be left to their own devices. There had always been a trip to see Santa Claus, too. He'd loved that at first; his siblings had been much older and had rolled their eyes. Some years he couldn't remember; he'd been too young. Another, though, he'd asked for some video game system while sitting on Santa's lap.

Christmas morning arrived. No gaming console. His mother had been quite put out at him when he'd complained, and said how was she to know he wanted it? Maybe because he'd mentioned it only a million times and put it in his letter to Santa.

Despite that unfortunate memory, today actually brought back a lot of good ones, including lacing up skates and the hot chocolate that was to follow. Besides, as a kid, the last thing he would have wanted was to be dragged from store to store.

"Jeremy? You okay?"

He lifted his head and met her gaze. "Yeah, sorry. Just got caught up in a memory and forgot to keep tying."

"I hope it was a good one."

He smiled and tugged on the laces. "It was. I came here a lot as a kid." He gave the bow a final jerk and sat back. "There you go. All set."

She waited as he put on his own skates. "I did not expect this for a surprise today."

"It's not Christmas without the tree here and skating. And hot chocolate."

Tori pulled on thick mittens. Today she wore the older jacket that zipped up in front, which was better for skating. But she wore a new hat, he realized, and grinned. It had a hole in the top, and her dark ponytail came out and trailed down the back of her head to her neck.

Adorable was the best word to describe her right now. "You all set?"

She nodded and held out a hand. "Let's do it."

The ice was smooth and the air crisp as they took their first gliding steps. "Be careful," he warned. "I don't want you falling down."

She laughed. "I've been skating since I was three years old. Don't worry about me." Then she twisted a little and pretended to look at her bottom. "And besides, I have lots of cushioning at the moment."

She didn't. She had curves and perhaps her figure had softened since last summer, but he found it even more alluring. Last night he'd marveled at the feel of her against him, around him. The softness of her skin and her sighs. He was in serious danger here. Thank goodness she was considering moving, because he wasn't sure what he would have said if she'd flat out refused. It wasn't just the baby, now. He wanted her with him.

She was right. The apartment was monochrome. His

life was monochrome. Until she'd arrived and brought all the color and life with her.

He gave her hand a small tug, and she did a little flip so that she was skating backward and now facing him. But he held on firmly, slowing them until they were stopped. And then he slid the few inches needed to have her puffy jacket pressed against his.

"Jeremy?"

He kissed her then, on her cold, soft lips, absorbing the taste of her, the scent of her skin, the gentle pressure of her belly against him. He wasn't into showy PDA, so he let her go after a few seconds, but her eyes glittered and her cheeks were rosy.

"What was that for?"

"For being you. For agreeing to come here. For putting decorations in my apartment. For everything."

Goodness, he was feeling all sentimental and mushy, but he wouldn't always be able to hide his feelings, would he? He was sure she wasn't in love with him. She hadn't exactly leaped at the idea of moving here to be with him. But she cared, and he knew she would do whatever she thought was best for their baby. And that made her damn near perfect in his eyes.

"You're welcome. Not that I did anything."

"You've done more than you know, sweetheart."

"Come on. Let's skate. We're just standing here like idiots."

He laughed and took her hand again, and they skated around the rink, enjoying the winter air and the holiday energy and the benefit of physical exertion. They took a break for a bit and Tori took pictures of the giant Christmas tree and the statue of Prometheus.

"It's amazing at night, all lit up," he said, one arm around her waist as she leaned back against him. "But on a Friday night? Busy." He gave her a small squeeze. "Maybe next year we can come back, at night. And bring the baby, too."

The moment he said it something huge opened up inside him. Next year at this time, they would have a seven-month-old baby. They'd be a *family*. He thought about what Tori would look like, their child in her arms, breath cloudy in the frosty air, and his heart turned over. This was the right thing. He was sure of it.

"Oh, Jeremy." She sighed and leaned against him. "Are we gonna be okay? Can we really do this?"

He turned her around and looked her square in the eye. "Of course we can, and we will. Because we both know what's really important."

Her eyes shone, and she gave a sniff. "I'm falling for you, Jeremy. And scared to death because of it. I don't want to screw up the future for our baby and I don't want to set myself up for heartbreak. I'm terrified."

He didn't want to examine his own feelings too closely. Love wasn't something he did or really wanted. Love was what really hurt, and he wanted to be happy with Tori. But he could offer other assurances, couldn't he, without getting himself in too deep? "You can count on me, I promise," he said, and pulled her to him in a hug. "I've never done this before, you know. But I'm going to give you my best."

"That's all anyone can give," she said, her voice muffled against his jacket. "And I'll do the same. And we'll rely on each other, won't we?"

"Yes, sweetheart, we will."

She nodded against him and he closed his eyes as he rested his cheek along her thick hat. She was so honest and kind and willing to think the best of people. He never wanted to do anything to break the trust they had. He'd do anything to protect her and the baby. They were the most important thing now.

She gave a mighty sniff and pulled back. "Oh, I'm such an emotional wreck," she laughed, looking slightly embarrassed.

"No, you're not. If you didn't care so much, I wouldn't l…like you so much."

He'd almost said *love*. It had been right there, on the tip of his tongue, and he could tell by her wide eyes that she'd caught the slip. He couldn't say it, he couldn't give her false hope for something he wasn't capable of giving. What was most important was not repeating his parents' mistakes.

Which reminded him of the following night. The one thing he had left to do was take Bran's advice and take her to Connecticut. He didn't really want to; these days his interaction with his mother was only at special occasions. Still, if Tori was going to understand him, and his feelings about parenting, and if he wanted to have a future with her as well as his child, she had to know what she was becoming part of. Anything else wouldn't be fair.

"Let's skate some more," she suggested, and he shook off his thoughts and smiled at her. Her face was so alight with childish enthusiasm he couldn't resist.

"Okay, but I'm skating backward so you can skate forward and hold on to my hands."

"Overprotective much?"

"Indulge me."

She wiggled her eyebrows. "Okay. Maybe I'll indulge you later, too."

Now that she was starting to drop her guard, he was in even more emotional danger.

They started to circle the ice. Once, he nearly freaked because Tori let go of one hand, then did a half turn so they were both skating backward. It almost felt as if they were…dancing! Then with a laugh, she turned again, faced him, gave a push forward and slid under his arm.

"What the heck are you doing?"

She giggled. "Dancing with you!"

"Be careful."

"I'm always careful!"

In the end, though, it was Jeremy who caught an edge and felt himself go. He was holding her hand and forgot to let go; as he tumbled to the ice, he took her with him. He landed on his hip and he heard her breath leave her body with an *"oof."*

"Oh, God! Are you okay?"

She was sprawled on top of him, and she started to laugh. "Other than having the air knocked out of me? I'm fine."

He scowled. "Don't laugh! You scared me."

Her face grew tender as she looked down at him. "You gave me a soft place to fall," she whispered, and he was a goner.

If he had his way, he would always be her soft place to fall.

After skating, they had hot chocolate and cookies, and then they walked back to his apartment. His hip hurt a bit, but he was more worried about Tori. "I'm just tired," she insisted, but he wasn't so sure. Skating had probably been a bad idea. What if she'd fallen on her belly? What would have happened to the baby?

"Do you have any cramping? Any pain anywhere?"

They reached his building. "Stop fussing. Seriously, I just need a nap. I'm fine, and so is the baby."

He wasn't convinced, but he wasn't going to take chances. Once inside, he tucked her into his bed and called a doctor.

When the doctor arrived, he went in to wake Tori. She was lying on her side, her lips open, a little bit of drool clinging to the side of her mouth. She'd taken out her ponytail and her hair lay in a dark tangle on his pillowcase. Had she been right? Was she just tired? Still, it never hurt to make sure everything was okay.

"Tori?"

"Hmm?" She squeezed her eyes shut tight, and then opened them a little. "What time is it? How long did I sleep?"

"About an hour and a half. I called a doctor to come see you."

She rolled over to her back and frowned. "You called a doctor? And he's here?"

"She's here, and yes. I was worried. You got so quiet. You did have a fall, you know."

"Oh, Jeremy, you didn't have to do that. If I'd had any cramping or anything I would have said."

"Will you let her check you out anyway? It'll make me feel better."

She sighed. "Since she's already here, sure." She pushed herself up to sitting. "Let me put myself together first."

He handed her the elastic from the bedside table and watched as she deftly put her hair up again. Then he handed her a tissue. "You might have drooled a little."

"So attractive," she grumbled. "Okay, send her in. I still can't believe you got someone to make a house call."

What was the sense of having money if he couldn't use it to help the mother of his baby?

He waited outside while the doctor spoke to Tori; he'd made the decision to call but he did respect her privacy. He paced the hallway instead, wondering if there were dangers to the baby that Tori couldn't feel, chastising himself once again for taking her skating in the first place, not thinking of the dangers. Instead he'd been arrogant, thinking he'd keep her from falling when he'd been the one to take the tumble.

If anything was wrong, it was his fault.

Ten minutes after she went in, the doctor came out again. "Mr. Fisher, would you like to come in?"

Oh, no.

Tori was sitting up on the bed, a smile on her face. "I told you," she said triumphantly. "Nothing wrong."

The doctor gave her an amused look. "You still have to watch for anything abnormal, okay? And call if you start cramping or spotting."

"I will. Promise."

"So you're okay? The baby's okay?"

"If you don't trust me, will you trust her?" Tori nodded at the doctor, who was looking rather amused at the whole situation.

"She's had no cramping, no bleeding, heartbeat's steady, and she's felt the baby move. Everything seems fine. But it's always better to be safe than sorry." The doc smiled. "She said you broke her fall."

"We wouldn't have fallen if I hadn't tripped," he admitted. "I'm so sorry."

"Oh, heavens," Tori said. "It's not your fault. You can't keep me in Bubble Wrap for the next four months."

"Are you sure?"

She patted the bed. "Come sit here and listen."

He sat on one side of the bed while Tori scooted down. She'd taken off her sweatpants before sliding under the covers for her nap, so she just had to pull her shirt up as the doctor reached for a handheld machine.

"It's a portable Doppler," Tori explained. "So you can actually hear the heartbeat this time."

His own pulse took a jump. He'd calmed a bit when he'd been assured everything was okay, but now anticipation had his heartbeat accelerating. He still had the ultrasound picture tucked away in his wallet. And he'd seen the little heartbeat on the monitor before, but hearing it…

It took only seconds for the doctor to find the beat and turn up the volume, and a rapid thumping sound touched his ears.

"That's it?"

"That's it, Dad." The doctor turned the unit around so he could see. The number was 137 and the sound coming from it was his baby's tiny heart, beating inside its mother.

Tears stung his eyes and he blinked rapidly. He wouldn't cry at this moment. But he wanted to, his relief was so great. "That's the best sound in the world."

"Yup." After a few more seconds, the doctor removed the tiny wand and Tori used a cloth to wipe away the blob of gel.

The sound was gone, but he could still hear it in his head.

"Now, I've told Tori to take it easy for a day or so, just as a precaution, and the fact that it'll make you happy."

She was right it would. "Forget about my mom's tomorrow. We don't have to go."

Tori sighed. "I'm perfectly capable of going to a stuffy cocktail party for a few hours. And to be honest, I'd rather get this over with."

He couldn't blame her.

"Don't back out using me as an excuse, Jeremy."

"Fine."

The doctor merely chuckled in the background as she packed up her things.

"I'll walk you to the door," Jeremy said, erasing the scowl from his face. Besides, Tori was right.

It would be good to get it over with.

CHAPTER THIRTEEN

TORI DIDN'T KNOW why she hadn't thought to ask if Jeremy had a car. Of course he did. And the next night they left the city and headed to Connecticut, to his family home and the party that would be waiting for them.

She was dressed in the cocktail dress he'd bought her that first day of shopping, and new shoes, and the cape. She carried a little clutch and felt more than ever like Cinderella going to the ball, only this time it felt as if the host wasn't a prince but the evil stepmother.

By the time they left it was dark, so Tori couldn't even focus on the scenery. Instead, nerves bubbled up inside her. Jeremy had said that she had to know what she was getting herself into, and that didn't bode well. She had enough anxiety for the both of them; she didn't need to be absorbing any of Jeremy's. His hands gripped the steering wheel and his jaw was set. He wasn't looking forward to this holiday party, either.

"Just remember that it doesn't matter what my mother thinks of you, okay? Or Bruce, either."

"So why is it so important for me to meet them? I mean, I don't want to say that I think being estranged is a good thing, but I'm just…" She took a breath and let out what she was really thinking. "Are you hoping that it'll scare me off?"

"What? No!" He took his eyes off the road for a moment. "Of course not!"

Then he sighed, a heavy, weary sigh. "I talked to my

friend Bran when we were still back in Nova Scotia. He told me I shouldn't blindside you with my family. That you should know what you're getting into. He's right. And maybe there's a part of me that thinks that maybe it'll help you understand me a little better, too." He looked over again, a grim smile on his lips. "Warts and all."

She tried a small smile. "Kissing frogs who turn into princes?"

"I'm no prince." He smiled back, though it was edged with tension. "Also, a holiday cocktail party means Mom will be on her best behavior, or at least I hope so. Tomorrow morning we'll drive back and it'll be over and done with."

They still hadn't talked about when she'd be returning home, but she did have to be back by Thursday of the following week. She couldn't take unlimited vacation and leave Tom in the lurch with the hotel.

She supposed that meant in the new year she'd be talking to him about resigning and creating an exit plan.

The thought made her sad, and a bit lonely, but she was moving on to big things. And it would have to be done, regardless, because her maternity leave was scheduled to start at the beginning of April.

It was nearly eight when a gate swung open and they pulled into a large, circular drive. The lane leading up to the property was heavily treed, so Tori only saw darkness out the passenger side window. A number of cars were already parked. The party had begun, apparently.

"Cocktails now, dinner at eight thirty," he murmured, turning off the engine. "Phew. Are you ready?"

"No. You're making me nervous."

"I'm sorry." He ran his hand through his hair, a clear sign he was agitated. "I'm being a coward."

She turned in her seat. "Listen, we don't have to go in.

If you're this upset, that tells me all I need to know. Don't do this because of me."

He relaxed a little. "I think it's like ripping off a Band-Aid. Once it's done, I'll feel better. And then I won't have to worry about it again."

"Well, then, let's get ripping. It's going to get cold out here in about thirty seconds." A light snow had started to fall.

He got out and then went around the car to open her door, and held her elbow firmly as they walked to the entrance of the grand home.

At first glance, Tori thought the house was simply a large colonial style—gorgeous but not the imposing mansion she'd been expecting. But as they stepped up to the oversize oak door, she realized that tucked back behind the main house were expansive wings, afforded privacy by the large, sheltering trees to each side of the main building. "Oh," she whispered.

"Nine thousand square feet, give or take," he offered, knocking on the door.

Way larger than even the nicest house they'd looked at back home. And, if she could guess, well over twice the cost, especially when considering currency exchange.

She gripped her clutch even tighter.

The door opened and they were ushered in and divested of their outerwear; they walked only five feet when they were offered a cocktail. Jeremy accepted one while Tori said a quiet, "No, thank you."

Instead of leaving it there, though, Jeremy asked for them to bring her a club soda and lime.

"How did you know what I'd like?"

He leaned closer. "You've been drinking it all week at my place."

He noticed the most mundane things, and she couldn't help but be pleased.

Now they were at the door to a large room, and conversations hummed from inside. His mother was in there. Probably his sister. Stepfather. Their social circle. She was a small-town nobody from Nova Scotia. She couldn't be more out of place if she tried.

She was about to ask him for more time, but then a woman appeared at the door, carrying a glass of red wine, and smiled widely. "About time you got here! I wondered if you'd fed me to the wolves."

"Hey, Sarah." He gave her a hug, but it was more polite than overt affection. "I'd like you to meet Tori."

"Hello, Tori. Nice of you to…"

She'd just noticed Tori's baby bump. "Oh. *Oh.* Well. Congratulations."

Tori placed her hand protectively over the baby. "Thank you."

Sarah looked at Jeremy. "Does Mom know?"

"Of course not."

"Wow, Jeremy, you're going to make her a grandmother. She won't be able to lie about her age anymore."

"Well, cheers to that." The siblings touched glasses.

Sarah relaxed a little. "Seriously, though, congratulations. I'm surprised as hell, but one of us deserves to be happy. When's the due date?"

"April fourteenth," Tori supplied.

"Well, you might as well come in. You can't stay in the doorway all night."

Tori's club soda arrived, so her hands were full of purse and drink as they entered a room that she was sure was nearly as big as her whole house.

The men wore black tie, the same as Jeremy, creating a striking look. The women were dressed in conservative cocktail dresses, with nary a bared shoulder or plunging neckline in sight. Except for one woman, Tori noticed. She had on a little black dress that dipped to the waist in the back, and came to mid-thigh. When she turned around, it was like looking at Sarah all over again, only twenty-five years older and with three times the amount of makeup.

Unless Tori was sadly mistaken, she'd also had substantial work done. Her face had a pinched look that wasn't quite natural.

The woman spied Jeremy and smiled, then her gaze lit on Tori, drifted down to her belly and moved back up with both surprise and distaste in their depths. *Here we go.*

At least the front of the dress was more appropriate than the back. She excused herself and came to stand in front of Jeremy, as if Tori wasn't there at all.

"So good of you to come, Jeremy."

"Mother." He leaned forward and kissed her cheek. Tori wasn't sure the kiss had even made contact with skin. "Merry Christmas. I'd like to introduce you to Victoria Sharpe."

Tori put down her drink and held out her hand. "Hello, Mrs...."

It struck her suddenly. Jeremy never mentioned his mother by her first name, and since she'd remarried her last name wouldn't be Fisher any longer. It would be something else. Something Tori didn't know. She wanted to sink through the floor, especially when the other woman made no move to reduce Tori's embarrassment. She didn't even shake her hand. Tori dropped her hand to her side, feeling sick to her stomach.

"Oh, I'm sorry, Tori. Mom is now Carol Heppner. I can't believe I forgot to mention that."

"Yes really, Jeremy, it's like you don't care who I am

at all," his mother chided, but instead of being hurt she just looked...disinterested.

"Oh, wait." Tori tried a smile and pried open the catch on her purse. "Mrs. Heppner, I brought you something. Just to say thank-you for having me tonight."

She took out the robin's-egg-blue bag and held it out. When she'd been shopping for Jeremy's decorations, she'd seen it and had thought maybe it would be fancy enough for his mother. She hadn't wanted to arrive empty-handed.

Jeremy looked uncomfortable and Carol stared at the bag for a moment before taking it. "Thank you."

She moved to hand it off to a servant when Jeremy's brittle voice came from beside her.

"Aren't you going to open it, Mother?"

With a sigh, Carol opened the bag, then the box inside, and the pouch inside that. She removed the delicate snowman on the red ribbon that Tori had thought so cute and that had taken a substantial chunk of her bank account.

"Isn't that...charming."

She stared at Tori's belly again, then looked at Jeremy and said, "I do hope you enjoy the party. Have you seen Sarah? She's here."

"We saw her on the way in." With a defiant set to his jaw, he added, "She wanted to congratulate us on the baby."

A weak smile touched his mother's lips. "Odd, how you wait until a party to tell your own mother. Oh, well. Let me add my congratulations, then. But excuse me. I do have other guests to attend to."

She walked away. Tori watched as she handed off the ornament to a staff member as if it were nothing at all.

"You got her a hostess gift? Tori, that's ballsy."

"Yeah, well, she didn't look impressed."

"Of course not. She's never impressed." His gaze softened.

"I knew she'd have...exacting tastes. I know it was small. And a snowman... I'm an idiot."

He put his arm around her. "No, you're not. You're incredibly sweet and have better manners than my mother. Come on, let's find Sarah. She's as emotionally stunted as the rest of us, but she tries. And she's an ally."

Tori tried not to laugh but couldn't help it. Emotionally stunted? She didn't think Jeremy was. She thought he covered a lot with smiles and charm, but the last week he'd revealed a lot about himself.

"All right. Could I have another club soda, though? I feel like I need to have something in my hand."

"Of course. And dinner will be soon."

They mingled their way through the room in search of Sarah, whom they found in a corner drinking a glass of wine and holding an animated conversation with a man who looked perhaps thirty. As they drew closer, Tori could tell the conversation was centered on financial stuff she didn't understand. Sarah was clearly schooling the younger man, who was openly flirting back. What was it like to have that kind of confidence?"

"Excuse me," Sarah said. "I'm going to chat with my brother for a few minutes."

She extricated herself from the conversation and turned to Tori and Jeremy. "Oh, my goodness. They get younger every time I turn around. Thanks for the rescue."

"One good turn deserves another. We saw Mom."

"That must have been entertaining. I'm sorry I missed it." She took a big sip of wine. "What did she say?"

Tori looked up. "She said congratulations."

Sarah snorted. "She did not. And if she did, it wasn't in that sweet way that you just did. By the way, I can't place your accent. Where are you from?"

"Nova Scotia."

Sarah looked at Jeremy. "Last summer's trip."

He grinned. "Surprise." Then he leaned over and kissed Tori's cheek. "It wasn't quite what we planned on happening, but life doesn't always go according to plan."

They chatted a while longer and Tori started to relax. Once everyone was seated at dinner, she let out a long breath. "Okay. I think I'm doing okay."

"You are. I told you not to pay any attention to my mom. Everyone else loves you."

Well, everyone except Jeremy's stepdad. The best that could be said of him was that he was utterly ambivalent.

Tori and Jeremy sat together during the meal, which included foods that Tori had never even seen before but bravely tried. She avoided the pâté and soft cheese, but enjoyed whatever the poultry dish was—perhaps duck?— and some sort of fancy potato. And the dessert was delightful, a tarte tatin with cream. Not too exotic, but extra special. Something she'd love to have at the Sandpiper...

Except she wasn't going to be there anymore, was she? Her heart gave a little pang at the thought. Saying goodbye was going to be so very hard. She'd put her heart and soul into the resort.

As the sounds of clinking silverware and crystal glasses slowed, she wondered if this kind of thing would become her life. It was nice for a visit, but she wouldn't want to live like this. Then again, Jeremy didn't live like this. His place was extravagant but his mood was relaxed, his tastes plainer. Like eating casserole two hours late, or ordering in a pizza from his favorite pizza joint. Cheesecake at ten o'clock at night.

She understood now why he'd wanted her to come. This was where he'd come from, but it wasn't where he wanted to be. He'd always be connected to his family, but this wasn't the life he had chosen for himself.

Or for his child.

She leaned over. "This was delicious, but I think I get it now."

"Get what?"

"What you said about me needing to see it. Promise me we won't end up like this. I want backyard barbecues and kitchen parties and people feeling welcomed."

He looked into her eyes. "Of course you do. It's what you've always known."

"I'm sorry you haven't."

"I survived." He flashed her a smile. "Come on, let's go back to the drawing room, as Mother likes to call it. It makes her feel aristocratic."

She laughed and they rose from the table. Now that dinner was over, the mood was even more relaxed in the large room. More wine was poured, and brandy. Tori realized that Jeremy had had his cocktail upon entering and one glass of wine at dinner, but that was it. When she mentioned as much, he shrugged. "I know we said we'd stay the night and go back tomorrow morning, but now I'm thinking we can drive back tonight. If that's okay with you."

She had no desire to stay any longer than she had to. She was a fish out of water here. "Whatever you want to do."

"I'm going to find Mom and let her know. We don't have to stay much longer if you're tired."

He left her with Sarah, who was definitely staying as she'd now switched to gin and tonic. "I know, I shouldn't," she said. "But I am staying the night, and it's the only way these parties are bearable."

"Then why come?" Tori asked. She'd given up club soda and was now drinking straight-up water.

"I don't know. Because it's expected. Because we get the 'you only visit your mother twice a year' guilt trip. And because we can't stand each other, but a few times a year we pretend to and it makes us feel better about our stupid dysfunctional family."

Tori snorted. Sarah didn't have much of a filter after a few drinks.

"But you and Jeremy...you get along okay."

"We muddle through. Out of the whole family, we're probably the closest."

"I'm glad. He talks about you a lot."

Sarah looked pleased at that. "I think you're good for him, if tonight hasn't scared you off."

"We're trying to figure it out." She put her hand on her stomach and sighed. "Can you tell me where the powder room is? I haven't gone all night and the baby's sitting right in a good spot." She smiled at Sarah.

"Outside the door, go right, down the hall. There's a door on the left just across from Bruce's office." She turned up her nose. "He likes to go in there for a cigar after dinner. Gross."

"Thanks. If Jeremy comes back, tell him I won't be long."

She made her way down the hall, away from the noise. The house truly was gorgeous, a real showpiece with creamy walls, white trim and a gorgeous iron railing on the staircase leading to the next floor, which was now bedecked with boughs and ribbon. There wasn't a speck of dust or a thing out of place. No personal knickknacks or photos; just perfectly placed flower arrangements—holiday themed, of course—and pieces of art on the walls. Each one was perfectly level, as if it wouldn't dare be a little bit crooked.

Beautiful, and perfect. But there was no personality, no sense of the people who lived there.

She caught sight of an open door—presumably the

powder room—when she heard voices coming from the room across the hall.

Jeremy's voice. And his mother's in reply.

She went to the door, staying slightly behind. There'd been a strident reply to something from Jeremy, but she hadn't been able to make out the words. Now she strained to hear. She hoped he wasn't getting a lot of grief from his mother. They could just stay over if it was going to be a big deal for them to leave early.

"Why didn't I tell you before? When was the last time you called me, Mother? Asked how I was? I mean, do you even care?"

"Of course I care, Jeremy." Her voice was cold. "I'm going to be a grandmother."

"I highly doubt it. You weren't mother material, you sure as hell aren't cut out to be a grandmother."

Ouch.

"You're so cruel," she replied. "And finding out tonight, in a room full of guests? It was embarrassing. Or was that your intention?"

He didn't answer, so his mother continued in her patronizing voice. "Look, she's probably nice enough, in her way. But really, Jeremy? She's not our kind of people. She's plain, and…uncultured."

"And you know that after sneering at her for two minutes?"

"Seriously. The way you're acting, you'd think you were in love with the girl. You aren't, are you?"

Tori held her breath. Her pride stung from his mother's assessment, but she was angry on Jeremy's behalf. No wonder he stayed away. What a horrible creature.

Jeremy hesitated. Then he said the words: "Of course I'm not. Don't be ridiculous."

Tori's heart plummeted to her feet. The way he'd kissed her. Held her hand. Made love…

It couldn't all have been an act.

She refused to believe it.

"I'm not going to ask you how she got pregnant. We both know that and I don't need the details. What are you going to do about it now?"

"She's here, isn't she?" he snapped, and Tori blinked back tears. He sounded so…harsh. "Look. No kid of mine is going to wonder where the hell his father is. You and Dad…you should never have procreated. He left and you wanted nothing to do with us. And here's what you need to know. I will do anything—*anything*—to make sure I do a better job of parenting my kid than you ever did."

Silence dropped for a moment. Then his mother spoke quietly. "Even pretend to love its mother?"

"Even that. Whatever it takes."

"So you're not in love with her. I knew it."

"Mother, please."

Tori stepped backward from the door, reeling from the pure derision laced in his voice. She hurried back down the hall, determined he not see her. She came across one of the waitstaff and asked where she could find another bathroom. Once she'd located it, she went inside, shut the door and sat on the closed toilet for thirty seconds while she tried to sort out her thoughts. Her feelings.

She'd been played.

Mother, please.

Those words replayed over and over in her head. She'd really fallen for it, hadn't she? All the expensive outings and private flights and sweet words… He'd used his money after all, to get her to do what he wanted. He didn't even have to get a lawyer involved. He'd used her emotions instead, and played her like a violin.

She got off the toilet, turned around and opened the lid. Though she hadn't thrown up for weeks now, her dinner came back up and left her gasping.

Then she flushed the toilet, washed her hands, and patted her face as best she could. She wouldn't cry, not now. But she was more than ready to go home and lick her wounds. And once she'd done that, she'd start making plans to raise her baby.

Hurt threatened to pierce her heart, but she steeled herself and kept it away by sheer force of will. She'd gone along with every single thing he'd suggested, and she'd fallen in love with him. Except it wasn't really him; just a show he'd put on to get what he wanted. And what made her the angriest was that he was planning on working out his childhood issues by using his own child as…what? Therapy? That was no way to bring a baby into the world. Not to solve your own problems.

She still had her clutch with her, and she took out her phone, turned on the data and booked a flight back to Halifax for the next day, on a commercial flight, which left approximately seventy-two dollars of available credit on her card. A knock sounded on the bathroom door just as she was getting the confirmation email. "Tori? Are you okay?"

"I'm fine," she replied, lifting her chin and staring at herself in the mirror. Right now she hated this dress. It wasn't her. It was someone she thought she could be. It was a lie, just like everything he'd said had been a lie.

"Are you sick?"

"I'll be right out." She squared her shoulders and opened the door, unprepared for the shaft of pain she felt upon seeing his concerned face. He wanted her baby, not her. And she rather wished he'd just been honest about that from the beginning, rather than manipulating her.

"Sorry. Turns out dinner didn't agree with me after all. I think I'd like to go…" She hesitated before saying home. "Back to the apartment."

He didn't say much, just watched her with an odd expression as she passed him on her way out the door and led the way to the stairs.

"If that's what you want, I'll get our coats."

It was a long drive back to the city. She didn't relish the idea of being in the car with him for that long, because she wasn't ready to talk about this yet. But it was her only way back to New York. It wasn't like she could ask Sarah. She'd been drinking all night. And Tori refused to cause a scene here.

She didn't bother saying goodbye to Sarah and she certainly didn't say goodbye to the hosts, who hadn't wanted her there to begin with. The snow flurries had stopped, thankfully, and at least they wouldn't be driving back in a heavier snowfall.

She got in the car and he turned on the heater while he cleared off the half inch or so of snow that had fallen earlier.

"Are you sure you're all right? You look flushed."

"I'm fine. Tired." Her heightened color was because she was agitated. Her heart ached and yet she felt outrage. At him, at herself for being so willing to fall for him and his pretty stories of what their life could be together.

She'd been a fool.

And yet she didn't know how to navigate the conversation that needed to happen, so she leaned her head against the car window and stared outside at the darkness. After a few minutes, she closed her eyes and pretended to sleep.

Her thoughts were anything but quiet.

Her heart was broken. Her trust was broken. Her faith was broken. She'd believed him when he'd said he cared for her. When he'd promised not to use his money to fight for his advantage. But he'd used it anyway, in a method far more ruthless.

He'd never said he loved her. He'd used the words *like* and *care*. But never *love*. It was as though his conscience wouldn't let him go that far.

Tears leaked from the corners of her eyes and she fought the urge to wipe them away.

Most of all she was angry with herself, for buying into it all so willingly.

He didn't say anything until they were in the city. "Tori, wake up. We're almost home."

She'd never been asleep but she pretended to perk up, sitting up in the seat and stretching. Her neck was cramped from leaning at an angle on the car door, and her heart felt raw and empty. Now she was minutes away from the conversation she didn't want to have. But she wouldn't run with her tail between her legs as if she had done something wrong.

"Feeling any better?"

"A little," she lied.

"The food was a little rich. Maybe it was just too much."

She didn't reply until they'd reached his building, gone up in the elevator and he was opening the door.

"It wasn't the food that made me sick." She peeled off the cape and put it on a chair in the foyer. She wouldn't take it with her. It was too expensive. A symbol of everything that was wrong with their relationship. She'd take only the things she'd brought with her in the first place. They were good enough for home.

"What was it?" Concern etched the corners of his eyes and she wanted to scream at him to stop pretending he cared.

"I was upset."

"I know it was a hard night—"

"I was upset at you." She kicked off her heels. "I heard you talking to your mother. And just so you know, I'm booked on a flight back home tomorrow morning. Leaving from Newark." It was the only direct flight she could manage, and she did not want to spend two hours in Toronto going through customs and sitting around waiting for another flight.

His face blanked, and a flush crept up his neck. "I don't know what you think you heard…"

Her anger flared now, hot and bright. "Please, do me the courtesy of not lying to my face again. I'm not mistaken. I have excellent hearing."

"My mother doesn't bring out my best qualities."

"Oh, you mean like finding out you're a liar? That you did exactly what you promised you wouldn't do?"

"I don't understand. Why are you yelling at me?"

Because you don't love me, she wanted to scream, but she could hardly do that. It sounded pitiful and she wasn't going to beg.

"It's okay that you're not in love with me. And yeah, we haven't known each other long, despite the fact that we're having a baby together. But you used me, and you pretended to care, because you'd do anything to ensure you show your mother what a horrible parent she was. Even pretend to love me. And those are your words, not mine."

His mouth fell open.

She waited.

"You weren't supposed to hear that," he said, his voice quiet and rough.

"Clearly. But I did hear it, and I'm glad. Because you manipulated me. Tell me, Jeremy, if you manipulate the mother of your child, are you going to manipulate the baby, too? Use him or her to work out all your own mommy and daddy issues?"

His cheeks reddened. "This is so easy for you to say, when you had two parents growing up who clearly loved and cared for you."

Tori took a step forward. "You are a grown man. Do not blame your poor decision-making on your mother. You had the chance to act with integrity. This is on you, and not anyone else." Tears burned in her eyes. "You used my emotions. But more than that, you've lost my respect. And that hurts almost as much as knowing you played me."

His face twisted in pain, and he turned away for a moment. She saw his shoulders rise and fall with a deep breath. Then he turned back. She didn't want to be moved by the look in his eyes. He looked tortured, but she steeled her spine. If he was, it was because he was dealing with the consequences of his actions.

"You've got it all wrong."

"How do I have it wrong? I heard you. Clear as day."

"I lied."

Her traitorous heart kicked a little bit when he said it, but she quickly replaced the momentary elation with doubt. "You lied...to whom? To me? To your mother? How am I supposed to believe you?"

Jeremy ran his hand through his hair, a gesture she now knew he used when he was agitated. "To my mother. Do you seriously think that I would admit my feelings for you to her?"

"Why not? What would happen if you did? It's not like you have a great relationship with her anyway."

"I just... I keep my feelings locked away there. Anytime I tried to talk to her as a kid I was told to get over it or I got a laundry list of all the advantages I had and how I was ungrateful for complaining. It's what I do, on instinct. So does Sarah. We all do." He lowered his voice. "I don't... I mean, it's a vulnerability thing."

She could understand that, but it didn't excuse his behavior. "Again, Jeremy, you're a grown man. You're educated, successful. Powerful. And you can't stand up to your mom? That says a lot to me."

"I don't want her to know how I feel. I don't want her to see any weakness. My feelings for you—"

"What, make you weak?" Hardly a compliment. "When people care about each other, it's supposed to make them *more*, not *less*. And somehow you've got it in your brain that weakness, vulnerability, is a bad thing. It's not."

"It's never been a good thing," he bit back. "For Pete's sake, I don't even think I know how to love anyone. This whole situation terrifies me."

Everything was falling apart. Even if it was true that he'd lied to his mom, that he really did care about her, he considered that a chink in his armor.

She wanted to believe his feelings for her were real. But even if they were, tonight had cast serious doubts on their future. If he was incapable of loving, if he considered that a weakness, how could he possibly love their baby? For all his good intentions, she never wanted her child to feel rejected by its father. Or to have to beg for affection.

"Let me tell you about weakness," she said quietly. "And vulnerability. From the moment I discovered I was pregnant, I knew I was vulnerable because of the power imbalance in our situations. I wouldn't have the resources to fight you for custody of our child if you decided to take me to court. Then you showed up and I was forced to tell you the truth. I figured if we could be on good terms, we could work through something together. You reminded me of the man I met in the summer. You were kind. I started to care for you again. You asked me to come here, and I did. You asked me to uproot my life and I was willing to consider it, even though the job I love and my family and friends are all back in Nova Scotia. I trusted you. I believed in you. And I'm not afraid to say it, even though you are. I fell in love with you."

"Tori—"

"No." She held up a hand. "Just no. I fell in love with the person I thought Jeremy Fisher was. Tonight I discovered he is someone else. He did a great job of faking it, but I don't know you. You wanted me to go tonight so I knew what I was getting into, and boy do I ever. So I'm going home. And after a while, we'll discuss custody and visitation like rational adults, I hope. Financial situation or not, I will fight back if you choose to get lawyers involved. I hope it doesn't come to that."

His eyes dulled and he looked utterly bereft. She didn't want to be affected by his forlorn look, but she was.

"Everything before tonight… It was true. I swear it."

Her insides trembled. "I don't know how to believe you. I don't know which Jeremy is the real one. And that's not something I'm willing to bet my life or my baby's happiness on. I'm sorry, Jeremy."

She moved past him and down the hall to her room, where she started to pack her bags. He came to stand in the doorway. "Please, Tori. I'm trying here." He ran his hand through his hair. "My mom brings out the worst in me, and I'm so sorry. I should have been stronger. Should have been honest."

She looked up at him. "The thing is, I think you were honest. I think your number one priority is to show your mother that you can be better than her. It's not me, and it's not love that's driving that decision. I won't uproot my whole life on that sort of gamble."

For a moment, she thought she saw tears glimmer in his eyes, and her resolve wavered. Then he swallowed and said, "What time is your flight tomorrow?"

"Ten."

"Get some sleep, then. I'll get you to the airport in lots of time."

She opened a drawer and took out some sweaters.

"Tori, I'm sorry. I handled everything badly. I know I messed this up. Wait, and let's try to work through it."

"I just need to go home," she said, not looking at him.

She sensed when he left her doorway, and she braced her hands on her suitcase as her head drooped. Was she overreacting? His explanations made sense, but the fact remained that even if he'd lied to his mother, he hadn't stood up for Tori. And even though he'd said he'd lied, he hadn't said that he loved her, either. Even after she'd admitted her feelings first.

She texted her mom, asking if she could pick her up at the airport the next afternoon, then finished packing. She sat up the rest of the night, unable to sleep.

When six thirty rolled around, she ordered a taxi and quietly made her way out of his apartment and to the bottom floor. She couldn't handle saying goodbye; her feelings were too raw. She didn't want to sit through another ride to the airport, either. When the cab arrived, the driver put her suitcase and carry bag in the trunk and they were off to New Jersey.

She was going home. Alone.

CHAPTER FOURTEEN

SHE WAS GONE.

Jeremy stared at the spare room with disbelief. She'd run. Granted, last night had been a disaster. But he would have taken her to the airport. He'd hoped that they'd get up this morning and be able to talk about what had happened without the high emotions of last night. Maybe even change her mind.

But she was gone.

He wandered to the main living area, his heart sore. The flower arrangement she'd bought was still on the dining table; the evergreen centerpiece in the living room, along with that silly little tree. A few dishes remained in the sink from where they'd had a cup of coffee yesterday afternoon before heading to Connecticut.

She was still here, whether he wanted her to be or not.

Jeremy wandered to the windows and looked out over the snowy city. She'd been right about pretty much everything. He should have stood up to his mother. Why not? It wasn't as if they had a relationship to speak of anyway. But that house... Anytime he was inside he was back to being that little boy again. Protecting himself and his feelings against ridicule and neglect. Poor little rich boy.

He knew very well that rich people could be miserable, too.

It was eight o'clock now. She'd be boarding in an hour, heading back to Nova Scotia and the family and job she loved. After yesterday, he had no right to take her away from that. No matter how much he'd really wanted to try for the life they'd begun to plan.

And his baby… He sank onto the sofa and put his head in his hands. No matter what she thought of him, he wouldn't put either of them through a legal battle. And there was no way he'd take the baby from her. She was going to be a damned good mother.

He wandered through the day aimlessly. Sarah called on her way back from Connecticut and he put her off. Cole texted and he didn't reply. Right now he was licking his wounds.

If only she hadn't heard him in Bruce's office. He could have kept his mom at arm's length and then gone on with his plans. And yet, deep down, he knew that was a coward's reasoning.

He'd been fighting his feelings all week. He'd kept telling himself that he wasn't capable of love. That it wasn't on his agenda. That it wasn't necessary for them to make this work.

But he'd been lying to himself. He did love her. Maybe he had from the beginning, when their connection had been so strong it had knocked him off his feet. When he'd looked for a reason to go back and see her again. Bringing her here to New York.

Making love.

It had been love, too. Not just sex. He just hadn't wanted to admit it because it scared the hell out of him. Love was a weakness that could be exploited.

Except Tori would never do that. He knew that in his heart, and he'd lied to himself until it was too late and she had walked away.

And he could tell her all of that, but she was right. She didn't know which version was true, and she couldn't uproot her life for someone she didn't trust.

She'd loved him. She'd said it. And he'd messed it up by denying what was right in front of his face.

He sat on the sofa until the light turned dark again.

Arrivals seemed to take forever. First, she was seated at the very back of the plane, which meant she was last to get off. Then there was the long walk to customs, and the line to get through. Then waiting for luggage. Finally she cleared the secure area and walked through the doors to see her mom waiting, a smile on her face.

Tori started to cry.

"Oh, honey!" Shelley came forward and gave her a big, reassuring hug while Tori's hand clung to the handle of her suitcase. "Come on. Let's get you to the car and you can tell me what happened."

She had never been so glad to see someone in her whole life.

It took only a few minutes to reach the car in the parking garage and head out onto the highway that would take them first into Halifax, and then down to the South Shore. For the first few minutes, Shelley simply reached over and patted Tori's hand, as if to say, *It's going to be okay*. She kept quiet for ten minutes or so, and then simply said, "So what went wrong?"

Tori sighed. "I don't know where to start."

"Then let's stop somewhere to eat. Neither of us has had lunch. Did you even have breakfast?"

She shrugged. "I had a yogurt at the airport."

"Where do you want to go?"

"I don't care."

Shelley quieted again, and then turned off the highway and drove to a diner in Bedford. "Quieter here than Cora's on a Sunday," she said. "And breakfast all day. Come on."

She wasn't feeling very hungry, but she ordered a

breakfast skillet anyway, to make her mom happy. And orange juice, because it was her favorite.

Once they'd placed their orders, Shelley looked at her with a "tell your mom about it" expression. "Okay. So you came back a few days early, looking like a whipped puppy. What happened?"

She told her mom everything. By the time she finished, their meals had been placed in front of them and Shelley had gotten a refill of her coffee.

"Baby girl," she said, on a sigh. "You're right. You deserve a man who will stand up for you, and for your family. Who will do the right thing."

"I thought he was that man, you know? That's what hurts so much." She picked at a chunk of hash-browned potato in her skillet.

"You think he was pretending the whole time?"

Her fork kept moving the piece of potato around and around. "I did when I first heard what he said. And then... Oh, Mom. I don't know. It's hard to believe that it wasn't real. The whole week was actually pretty magical. And when he heard the baby's heartbeat..."

"You wonder how he could be such a good actor?"

"I...yeah. And I get mad at myself for wanting to believe him. But he never said he loves me. I keep coming back to that. And the fact that I don't know if I could believe him even if he did say it."

She sniffled. Put down her fork. "He had a rotten childhood. He never had a solid family unit like I had with you and Dad."

"Does that excuse his behavior?"

She shook her head. "But it makes me understand it. I know he wants to be a good father, but what if he just doesn't have the ability to let himself love someone? I thought I could go through with it. We were getting along

so well. I could see our relationship growing so that someday maybe it would be…whole."

"But…"

"But it would never be what you had with Dad. And I
don't want to settle for anything less."

Shelley reached for her napkin and dabbed her eyes and
her nose. "Well, I guess your dad and I did something right."

"I miss him."

"Me, too, honey. Every day."

They picked at their food. Tori was hungry, and the
more she ate, the better she felt. Even though she couldn't
finish the large portion, she'd needed the nutrition. So
did the baby.

Shelley looked up at her. "You said before that you
thought you could go through with it. Don't hate me for
asking, but is there a chance you're using what happened
as a way out?"

She wanted to say yes without hesitation, but she
couldn't,

"You hesitated, which means you're thinking about it.
I just think maybe Jeremy isn't the villain he's been made
out to be. Yes, he made a mistake and you absolutely deserve better. You shouldn't settle for less. But you need
to be clear on your own motives too, sweetie. Picking up
and moving countries to be with a man you care about but
who might not love you in return is a big risk."

The meal she'd just eaten churned in her stomach. "And
he gave me a way out without me having to take any responsibility." Ugh, had she really done that? Used his
weakness to justify her own behavior, her own fears?

"I'm not saying you should have stayed. I think I'm
saying this is a big mess, and the only way through it is
for both of you to be completely honest with each other.
You reacted and you left. But now there are a lot of feel-

ings to sort through. I think you should take the time to do it." Then Shelley smiled. "And you can spend Christmas with your mama while you're sorting things out."

"I love you, Mom."

Shelley reached for the bill. "Well, duh. Of course you do. Look, kiddo, since your dad died, I've watched you be afraid. It made you grow up in a hurry. You haven't had a lot of relationships since Riley broke your trust, and I think that trust is your deal breaker. Have you told Jeremy that?"

"Not really."

"Look, your dad set a wonderful example and standard, but you were also hurt when he left."

"He didn't leave us. Not like Jeremy's dad did."

"Not in the same way, but he left just the same. Don't be afraid to love someone, honey. Jeremy lied to his mom. He didn't stand up for you. But that doesn't mean he doesn't love you."

"He didn't say it."

"I know. Just give it some thought, and when you're ready, you and Jeremy need to talk. Even if it's just to decide what's going to happen with visitation."

They got up and Shelley paid the bill, and then they got on the road again. As they merged onto the highway, Tori sighed. "I keep telling myself I'm afraid he'll use his money and power to take the baby. I feel like I need to protect myself and prepare for that possibility. And then my heart says he would never do such a thing. And I think I'm being a fool, again."

Shelley didn't answer, but Tori knew exactly what she would say. Sit on it. Think about it and sort through her feelings. And then talk to Jeremy.

The bar was crowded and noisy, and Jeremy could tell Bran was only going through the motions. Cole, on the other hand, was flirting with their waitress and being his charming self. And Jeremy was running around with his tail between his legs.

Still. He couldn't mope around his apartment forever, and Bran needed to get out now and again. His possession date for the new house was the first of February; then the three of them hanging out would be a rare occasion.

Of course, Bran was going to be close to Tori. And that irritated Jeremy like a scratchy tag on the back of his neck.

"Beer, whiskey, and a rum and coke." The waitress put their drinks on the table. "Can I get you anything else?"

"We're good for now," Cole said, flashing her a million-dollar smile.

She smiled back and was gone with a twitch of her hip.

"Stop that," Bran said, scowling. "You're not twenty-five anymore, Cole."

"What? The day I stop flirting is the day I die."

Bran shook his head. "Yeah, but you have no follow-through. You work too much."

Jeremy shook his head. "Listen, you two, I came out for drinks and a good time."

Cole sipped on his rum and coke. "No, you didn't. You came out because you're being a sad sack since Tori went back to Canada. We don't need to tell you how you messed that up, Jer."

He took a big pull of his beer. "Yeah, sure. I know that."

Bran looked at him. "When we saw you in your office that day, you looked pretty happy. She thinks you were faking it, right? That she was manipulated? But was she?"

The beer didn't quite settle in his stomach. "Of course not. I mean, I wanted to bring her around, but damn, you know?" He scowled. "The way I sounded at my mom's… It was like she wasn't worth loving. I don't blame her for being furious. Or walking away."

Cole saluted with his glass. "Well done, dumbass."

Bran rolled his eyes. "Jer, let me ask you this. What was the moment you first knew?"

"First knew what?"

"That you loved her."

The table went silent.

Bran took a drink of his whiskey and pushed back his shaggy hair. "Look, when I met Becca, I didn't love her at first. But there was a moment. It wasn't even a big moment. She was in my place and she looked over her shoulder at me and laughed and it was just there. *Bam, I love her.* And I'm guessing you had that moment, because you've been dragging yourself around for the last five days, beating yourself up and thinking about nothing but the fact she's gone. So when was it?"

Jeremy's throat tightened. "When we were skating. She did this turn thing and faced me, holding my hands, and she laughed and had this weird hat on with her ponytail out the top, and it was like someone opened my heart and poured in a ray of sunshine."

Cole swore and shook his head.

Bran wagged a finger at him. "Look, he-man. Don't be like that just because it hasn't happened to you."

Then Bran turned to Jeremy. "Dude, I'm telling you right now. You've got to go make this right. I won't have another chance with Becca. She's gone, but Tori isn't. She needs to know how you feel. You've got to lay it on the line, brother. You'll regret it forever if you don't. And she's having your kid. If you want to have a relationship with him or her, if you want to do better than your own father did, you've got to step up."

"She doesn't want to see me."

"Bull. I'm telling you right now, there's no room for

pride at this point. You might have to beg. But if you love her…"

"Of course I do. And my kid, too. Hearing that heart-beat…"

"Then fight for her. You didn't do that when you had the chance, don't you see? And if she loves you, too, that had to break her heart."

Cole took a long drink. "As much as it pains me to say it, I agree with Dear Abby here. We were with you at school. We know you almost as well as you know your-self. You would do anything to not be your dad, and that's great. So stop acting like him. Man, every time you go to that house you act like… I don't know. Like she has some kind of say over your life. You're a grown man."

Jeremy chuckled despite the sting he felt at Cole's words. "That's what Tori said."

"So quit running away and stand up to your mom in-stead of all that polite-distance kind of thing. And go talk to Tori. Tell her how you feel."

"Sometimes manning up means laying your heart on the line, rather than being 'strong,' you know?" Bran fin-ished his whiskey. "I'm telling you guys, I'm a freaking mess, but I wouldn't trade any of the time I had with Bec."

"We know, man." Jeremy put his hand on Bran's shoul-der. "And you're right. I just… I don't know how to do this."

Cole leaned forward. "I think the correct word is *beg*. Or maybe *grovel*."

"Helpful," Jeremy muttered. "I guess…family means everything to Tori. She loves her mom so much, and her dad died a couple years ago, and… I feel like a horrible human, not feeling that kind of connection or loyalty to my own family. Sarah excluded."

"Hey." Bran looked him dead in the eye. "Family is more than genetics. We learned that at Merrick."

"Go Monarchs," Cole and Jeremy said, lifting their glasses.

Jeremy settled back into his chair, while Cole signaled for another round. "Yeah, you're right. You guys are my brothers."

"And it's our job to kick you when you're being an idiot. So get yourself together and figure out how you're going to get her back. It's Christmas. A good present should come with the groveling."

The next round of drinks appeared, and Jeremy perked up. He at least had to try. He'd been miserable the last few days. The apartment was cold and empty. He couldn't focus. He stared endlessly at the ultrasound picture. He'd let the best thing in his life get away, because he couldn't deal with his feelings.

And as Bran and Cole started to discuss ordering some snacks, Jeremy got the first inklings of a plan. Starting tomorrow, he'd have to get himself in gear in order to have it all set for Christmas.

CHAPTER FIFTEEN

CHRISTMAS MORNING DAWNED bright and clear, with a pristine blue sky and a new dusting of snow that made everything look fresh and white but didn't play havoc with road conditions. Tori had slept at her mom's, and would stop in at the Sandpiper later. They kept a very light staff on Christmas Day and Boxing Day, and they had minimal bookings, too. Still, essential staff were away from their loved ones on Christmas morning, so she'd arranged for them all to have breakfast midmorning. The crew would have breakfast meats and eggs cooked by Neil and his sous chefs, and she'd brought in pastries from a local bakery. She'd even made a huge bowl of fruit salad herself and left it in the massive fridge.

Now, though, at barely eight o'clock, she sat beside her mother's decorated spruce tree, looking at the arrangement of presents beneath it.

She had a lot to be thankful for. She was healthy, her baby was healthy, she had a job she loved and a mother who doted on her. And yet the holiday felt lusterless and underwhelming. All because she couldn't get the father of her child off her mind.

"I made you tea," Shelley said, coming in from the kitchen. They were both dressed in fuzzy new pajamas; getting new ones on Christmas Eve had been a tradition for her when she was a kid, and in the past few years they'd taken to buying them for each other. She handed Tori the cup and sat down on a footstool nearby, cradling her own cup of coffee. "So. Have you opened your stocking?"

"I was waiting for you."

"Let me turn on some Christmas music first."

With the sound of carols in the background and the lights on the tree turned on, Tori reached for her stocking. Inside was her favorite chocolate, a three-pack of maternity underwear, some soft and fuzzy socks and the usual toiletries—body wash, deodorant, shampoo. There were some treats, too, like a new kind of tea and a little box of mini-facials. "Mom, this was too much."

"Don't be silly." Shelley was opening her own stocking, with her favorite treats and beauty brands, as well.

There were only a few presents under the tree. Two for each of them from each other, and there was one from the staff for Tori and one from the other nurses on Shelley's unit. Tori oohed over a new maternity outfit in the first box, and then watched as her mom opened her new pressure cooker she'd asked for. Her second gift contained a gorgeous lemon-yellow crocheted blanket.

"Oh, Mom."

"I haven't crocheted in years, but I figured this was as good a time as any to get out the old hook and take it up again. Do you like it?"

Tori ran her hand over the soft, fine yarn. "I love it. The baby will love it, too, because Grandma made it."

"Merry Christmas, sweetie."

"Open your last one, Mom."

She handed the gift bag to her mom. Shelley reached inside and took out a small box, then opened the box and withdrew the Christmas ornament. It was a glass ball with white and gold and the word *Grandma* painted on it with glitter.

"Where in the world did you find this?"

"In a little shop in New York." She had a similar ornament still tucked away in a drawer in her room. The one she'd bought for Jeremy but had forgotten to give him. She'd grabbed it at the last minute and put it in her luggage, hoping it would make the trip without breaking.

She'd been so excited that day. And that night, she and Jeremy had slept together.

"Are you okay?"

"I'm fine." She put on a smile. "Really. We're both fine." She put her hand on her tummy. "And hungry."

They'd picked up the paper from their gifts and were just heading to the kitchen when there was a knock on the door.

"You expecting someone?" Tori called, as she opened the fridge door and got out eggs and ham for omelets.

When there was no answer right away, she straightened and poked her head out of the kitchen. "Who is it?"

Jeremy stepped into the entryway. "It's me."

She shouldn't be so glad to see him. But she was. He was here. In Nova Scotia. In her mother's hall. On Christmas morning.

"Hi," she said, belatedly realizing she was dressed in penguin pajamas with slippers on her feet and her hair in a messy ponytail.

"Merry Christmas."

It was incredibly awkward and emotionally charged. Shelley took a step back and murmured, "I'll just go start breakfast," while Tori and Jeremy stared at each other for a long, painful moment.

"You look wonderful," he said, his voice soft, and she wanted to believe him so badly it hurt.

"What are you doing here?"

"I came to ask for your forgiveness." He stepped forward but only to the edge of the mat; a film of snow was on his shoes. She went to him instead, not necessarily for intimacy but more for privacy. Her mother's house wasn't large, and conversations were easily overheard. She laughed a little as Shelley made an inordinate amount of noise with frying pans.

"You look like your mom," he said gently. "She frowns like you, too. Told me I'd better get it right this time."

Tori's cheeks heated. "Mom doesn't mince words."

"Neither does her daughter. And I've recently discovered that both of you are pretty much right."

She didn't want to hope. But it was Christmas. And he looked so handsome in perfectly fitted jeans and his pea-coat, his hair slightly mussed and his gray eyes focused on her so intently.

His gaze swept down to her belly and back up. "You're feeling okay?"

She nodded, her throat tightening. "Yeah, we're both okay. The baby's been moving around a lot."

"That's good."

"Yeah."

"Tori—" His voice broke off, and then he took a breath and squared his shoulders. "I went to see my mother. And I told her what I should have told her the night of the party. I told her that I love you, and I love this baby, and that I want to do right by both of you. And I owe you such a huge apology, Tori. I never showed my emotions. Not in that house, not with any of my relationships, because every time I did I got punished for it. But you invited me to. You gave me a safe place with no judgment and I used that gift to hurt you. I'm so sorry, Tori. More than you know."

She stood there dumbly, not knowing what to say or do. It scared her how much she wanted to believe him. She'd had time to think over the past several days, and really look at what had happened. He'd hurt her terribly at the party, while she'd still been stinging from his mother's cold reception. And she'd felt incredibly out of her depth. And no, he hadn't told her that he loved her, but he had tried to explain and she hadn't let him.

Because she, too, was scared. And she'd run.

"You love me?" she asked. "And the baby? Not just so that we won't be in separate countries or living in separate homes?"

He swallowed. "I loved this baby from the moment I saw that picture on the ultrasound machine. And I think I loved you all along. But Tori, your family is here. Your job is here. I won't ask you to leave that behind, not if you don't want to."

"And I will stay here, and you'll stay…"

His gray eyes softened. "In New York. We'll work this out on your terms, Tori. I can't force you to forgive me, or love me. But you're going to be a wonderful mother, and I think the best way for me to be a good dad is to make sure you're happy."

Her eyes stung as tears sprang into them. "But you said you love me."

He nodded, and his eyes were bright, too. "I do. Enough to let you go, if that's what you want."

She caught her breath, and it sounded almost like a sob, but she wouldn't let that happen. She wouldn't cry today. "What if that's not what I want?"

The air between them stilled. "Then come over here and put me out of my misery."

She took three halting steps and then threw herself into his arms. His tightened around her, holding her close, the baby sandwiched between them. "You feel good," he whispered in her ear. "I was sure you'd tell me to walk out. Thank you for not doing that."

She nodded against his coat and sniffed. "It's partly my fault, too. I was overwhelmed and feeling like someone's poor cousin, and I wanted you to stand up for me. When you didn't… I just wanted to go home, where it was familiar. I used your mistake as an excuse, rather than talking it out. And I ran away."

"You had good reason. But, sweetheart…" His breath was warm against her ear. "I made a mistake. I didn't stop loving you. I just was too afraid to say it. Loving people has always made me weak, so I told myself I was incapable of it." He pushed back a little so he could look into her eyes. "Until now."

And then he kissed her, a wild welcoming that seemed to put everything right that had gone wrong. It wasn't the kiss of a coward or a pretender; it was the kiss of a man claiming the woman he loved. And when his hand cradled her baby bump, she closed her eyes and let the bit of gratitude that had been missing this morning trickle in.

"I hate to break up this happy reunion, but I have ham and cheese omelets and home fries for anyone who's hungry. That includes you, Jeremy."

He looked into Tori's eyes. "I don't deserve that kind of welcome," he whispered.

"Don't be silly. This is how family works." She clasped his hand. "We mess up and we forgive each other. I was awfully lonely this morning, Jeremy. Wishing you were here. Wondering if I should call you and what I should say. I'd forgiven you for what happened at the party, but I was still afraid, you see."

"You were gone about ten minutes before I started missing you," he murmured, kissing her forehead. "And my real brothers—Cole and Bran—told me I was an idiot for blowing it. It has to be love," he continued, squeezing her fingers. "Nothing else could ever hurt me this much."

Considering the pain he'd been through as a boy, that was saying something. And what was more, she believed him. Because the Jeremy at the party wasn't the real Jeremy. She'd had time to think about that and realize that she'd let one five-minute conversation negate everything else between them. The Jeremy in all the other moments was the real man. And he was something special.

"Let's have breakfast, then."

"Okay. And then I want you to get dressed, because I have something to show you."

"You do?"

"A surprise."

"You and your surprises," she said, making a *tsk* sound. But as they walked to the kitchen, Christmas was suddenly very merry indeed.

While Tori was having a quick shower and getting dressed, Jeremy grabbed a dish towel and started drying dishes for Shelley.

"Mrs. Sharpe?"

She looked up at him, her hands in the dishwater. "You'd better call me Shelley, don't you think?"

"Maybe another time. Right now… Well, since Tori's dad isn't here, I'm going to ask you."

She reached for the dish towel in his hands and dried hers off, then looked up at him. "Ask me what?"

His stomach quivered. This emotional nakedness was all new to him, and he was terrified he was going to get a lecture once he said what he needed to say. But it was the right thing to do.

"Ask you for permission to marry your daughter."

Her gaze bored into him, and he couldn't tell what she was thinking. After what had happened, he rather expected he was being measured and coming up short.

"My girl can make up her own mind."

He nodded. "Yes, she can. But your family is different

from mine, and your approval means a lot. So I'm asking anyway."

Her expression softened. "If Tori says yes, I certainly won't stand in her way."

He sagged with relief. "Okay. Phew. Thanks for not giving me the third degree."

She touched his arm. "Look. Clearly I don't have to worry about her materially, her or the baby. My biggest concern is for her heart. I saw her face when she realized it was you at the door, and I saw yours, too. There's far more between you than just a baby. So I'll leave you two to work out whatever future fits."

"Even if I take her away?"

She nodded. "Even then."

"Mrs. Sharpe?"

"Shelley. And yes?"

"I wish I'd had a mom like you."

To his surprise, she handed him back the dish towel and patted his arm. "Well, now you do."

She went back to washing dishes as if she hadn't just turned his world on its end.

When Tori came back to the kitchen, he and Shelley were talking about Sharpe Christmas traditions. He broke off midsentence when Tori appeared in the doorway. She wore a new outfit of navy leggings and a soft gray sweater that molded to her shape and made her look so beautiful and maternal he thought his heart might burst. "Look at you," he said, putting down the towel.

"It's new. From Mom, for Christmas." She turned in a circle. "See, Mom? Fits perfectly."

"You look lovely." Shelley let the water out of the sink. "Now go on. Jeremy has a surprise for you. I'll expect you back for dinner at five."

"We'll be back before then," Jeremy assured her. "You shouldn't have to cook a whole Christmas dinner yourself."

"Take your time," she said with a laugh. "The prep's done. I'm going to put the bird in the oven and have a nap. Maybe read one of the books I got from the girls at work."

He held Tori's coat for her—still the parka that needed replacing—and then took her hand, leading her to his rented car. "Did you stay at the inn?" she asked, waiting as he opened the door for her.

"No, here in Lunenburg. I didn't want you to know I was in town yet."

"Oh."

"Come on. I've got something to show you."

They drove past Liverpool and toward the Sandpiper, and then past it. He looked over at her face as he turned up the lane leading to the house on the beach, the one they'd looked at after their feed of fish and chips. Her eyes widened.

"What are we doing here?"

"You'll see."

The gate was open, and they drove through, up the drive to the house. A huge wreath was on the front door, and just like at her mom's, a light dusting of snow made everything postcard perfect. He parked and got out of the car, patted his pocket, and went around to open her door. She put her hand in his and got out.

"Jeremy?"

"Come on."

He led her to the bluff overlooking the private stretch of beach. The wind was brisk off the water, but not bitter. The caps were white and the faint sound of the breakers touched his ears. This had been the right choice. No question.

"Tori?"

"Yes?"

"Remember the night we watched *Miracle on 34th Street*?"

She nodded.

"And there was the scene, at the end of the date, where Bryan proposes and she turns him down?"

Tori's eyes widened as she turned away from the ocean and stared up at him. "What?"

It was now or never. "You said to me, I don't know why she's so mean to Bryan. And I said, because she's scared. Plus they had to work to get to their happy ending."

She nodded, just barely, and he reached inside his pocket. "I know you're scared. I'm scared. But we shouldn't let that stop us from being happy. Not if we can be scared together. I'm ready to work toward that happy ending if you are."

And he held out the red ring box, identical to the one in the movie, and opened it.

Tori stared at the ring. It was possibly the most gorgeous thing she'd ever seen, nestled in velvet, winking in the winter sunlight. "You're proposing?"

"I am. I even asked your mom for permission."

She choked out a laugh, imagining how that conversation must have gone. "Oh, you didn't."

"I did. Because while my family is a hot mess, yours isn't. I thought it would mean a lot to you."

She sighed. "It does."

"Tori?"

She couldn't stop staring at the ring. "Hmm?"

"Will you marry me?"

She looked up at him, all gray stormy eyes and wild hair and sexy vulnerability. It was hard to believe that a chance affair months earlier had led to this moment, but it had, and he was standing before her, asking her to be his wife.

And she knew now, without a doubt, that he'd lied to his mom and he'd been honest every step of the way. The proof was in his smiles, in his tender gestures, in the way he made her laugh. In the way they made love. He wasn't perfect. And neither was she. But he was hers, and she was his, and it was time she had a little faith.

So she nodded, said yes, and told him to put it on her finger.

When he slid it over her knuckle, she started to cry. It was beautiful, but what it meant was more so. They'd stopped being afraid and had started facing things together.

He kissed her softly, his lips cold from the wind. "So that's not the only surprise," he said against her mouth.

"It's not?"

"Don't you wonder why I brought you here?"

She looked around. The for-sale sign was gone from the yard. There was a wreath on the door. "I don't know, but don't you think the owners will wonder why we're standing out here on their bluff?"

He reached into his pocket again, and this time he took out a key and placed it in her palm.

She lifted startled eyes to his.

"I doubt it, since I'm the new owner."

"You... What?"

He grinned at her now, excitement flashing through his smile. "You love it here. I love it here. I don't necessarily want to relocate, but can you think of a better summer home? You can be close to your mom whenever you want. We can spend summer days building sandcastles with our kids on the beach. We can put a boat in here and sail down the coast. Have bonfires in the back. Marrying me shouldn't have to mean you leave home behind. Not when we can manage to have you here. And if you want to keep up with your innkeeper roots..." He swept his arm to the other side of the property. "The guesthouse is there. You're right. You could turn it into a vacation rental with no trouble at all. If you want to."

She couldn't believe it. "You bought me...a house? For Christmas?"

He nodded.

She started to laugh. And then she laughed more and more until the sound of it echoed through the winter air.

"What's so funny?" His brows pulled together.

"Just that when we were looking at houses, you said this one wasn't large enough to suit. And now it's yours."

"I said it wasn't suited for Bran. Me? Well, I realized that it's not the house but the love inside it that matters." He spread his arms wide. "I came from a huge mansion with every advantage, but little love. Honey, let me tell you, this house is plenty big enough, as long as you're inside it."

She wrapped her arms around him and hugged him tight. She wasn't sure if fate was a thing, or serendipity, or what, but something had brought him here last summer and turned her world upside down. It was wonderful.

"Let's go inside," she suggested.

"You've got the key."

She went up the walk and turned the lock easily. Inside smelled like pine cones and cinnamon. There was no furniture, but in the corner of the living room, by the fireplace, was a huge decorated tree.

"Merry Christmas, sweetheart," he said from behind her.

She spun in a circle. "It really is. And now is the perfect time to give you your present."

She loved the look on his face right now. He'd thought he'd been in charge of all the surprises today, but she had one more.

"But you didn't even know you were going to see me."

She reached into her handbag and took out the little gift bag she'd hidden in his apartment. The one that had made it through without getting crushed in her luggage, despite being hastily shoved inside without soft packing to keep it safe. And before this Christmas tree was the perfect moment. She handed it to him and smiled. "Merry Christmas, Jeremy."

She stood back while he removed the tissue, then reached inside. The little box was the same as her mom's had been, but what was inside was even more special.

He opened the lid and took out the ornament she'd bought.

It was white, too, but in pink glitter it spelled out "Daddy's Girl" in swooping cursive.

His gaze shot up to hers. "Daddy's girl… We're having a girl?"

She nodded, tears clogging her throat. The look on his face right now… It was almost the same as when she'd first told him about the baby. Terror and surprise but now with an added ingredient: joy.

"I found out a bit by accident, just before we left for New York. I was going to tell you the night I'd decorated your apartment, but then we kind of fought and then we made up and it wasn't the right moment. But now…now it's right. We're having a baby girl, and you can hang that ornament on our very first Christmas tree."

Instead he came to her and crushed her in a hug. "I am not sure what I ever did to deserve you, but thank you. For rocking my world. For loving me. And for giving me a second chance. I'm not going to let you down, Tori. Or our baby."

And when he'd hung the ornament on the tree, they stepped back, held hands and moved into a new future as a family.

* * * * *

BRIDESMAID
FOR HIRE

MARIE FERRARELLA

To
Ellie Melgar,
Not Even Four Years Old Yet
And Already
An Endless Source Of
Inspiration
To Me.

Prologue

"**Y**ou understand that I normally don't like to interfere in my children's lives," Anna Bongino stated emphatically.

Animated, the silver-haired, well-dressed woman was perched on the edge of her chair in Maizie Sommers's real estate office. Anna drew ever closer to the edge as she spoke.

Despite the declaration written in bold black letters on the outer door, the subject under discussion was definitely *not* about real estate.

"You're a mother, Anna," Maizie told the woman in the kind, understanding voice she often used when calming down nervous first-time buyers. "Interfering in our children's lives is written in the bylaws. You'll find it listed right after toilet training and staying up all night."

Sitting back in her chair, Maizie smiled at her friend.

She might have been in charge of a thriving real estate business that she'd started right after losing her husband, but the subject matter under discussion was just as near and dear to her heart. Maybe even more so. To her, matchmaking wasn't just a hobby. Maizie felt it was her calling.

When approached for help, she and her lifelong best friends, Celia Parnell and Theresa Manetti, both successful small business owners in their own right, pooled their vast clientele and were able to hone in on just the right match. So far, they were batting a thousand.

Finding the perfect match had all begun innocently enough. They had decided to take matters into their own hands and find matches for their own children. That successful endeavor had slowly blossomed to the point that their services were sought out by desperate parents or relatives who wanted only the best for their loved ones. They wanted them to have a chance at the happiness that had, heretofore, been eluding them.

Which was why Anna Bongino was now sitting in her office, tripping over her own tongue and trying not to be overly embarrassed as she stated what had brought her here today.

"Gina is a bright, outgoing, beautiful girl," Anna said almost insistently.

"I've seen her photograph," Maizie replied, agreeing, at least for now, with the "beautiful" part of Anna's assessment.

"But she's turning thirty-two soon," Anna practically wailed.

"That's not exactly having one foot in the grave yet, Anna," Maizie pointed out, doing her best to maintain a serious expression. This "advanced" age was clearly a sore point for Anna.

"Well, it might as well be," Anna cried. She drew herself up. "Did I tell you what my unmarried daughter does for a living?"

"No, we haven't gotten to that information yet," Maizie replied.

"She's a professional bridesmaid," Anna all but cried. "Have you ever heard of such a thing? I certainly haven't," Anna declared distastefully, then sighed mightily. "You know that old saying, always a bridesmaid, never a bride?"

"I am familiar with it," Maizie answered sympathetically.

"Well, Gina's taken it to a new level. Professional bridesmaid," she said with disdain. "She made the whole thing up." It was obvious that Anna was not giving her daughter any points for creativity as she went on complaining. "It's Gina's job to make sure that the bride experiences her day without any drama. Gina makes sure to handle any and all emergencies on the 'big' day so that the bride and her bridesmaids don't have to endure any of the hassle."

"That's rather a unique vocation," Maizie commented. "What was Gina before she became this 'professional bridesmaid?'" she asked, as calm as Anna was agitated. Maizie was trying to get to know her subject so that she and her friends could ultimately find the young woman's match.

It seemed clear that she had brought up a sore point. Anna's face fell as she responded, "Gina was an accountant with a Fortune 500 company. She was going places, Maizie. But she said it wasn't 'fulfilling enough' for her.

So she gave all that up to help brides have a wonderful day—as if becoming a bride wasn't wonderful enough."

"Is that why she gave up accounting?" Maizie asked, trying to get as complete and rounded a picture of the young woman as possible. "Because it wasn't fulfilling enough for her?"

Anna huffed. "That's what she said. It also wasn't 'hands on' enough for her. Gina had been a bridesmaid so many times—six," Anna emphasized almost grudgingly, "that she felt she could take this so-called 'knowledge' and parlay it into this 'creative' vocation." Anna shook her head in complete despair.

"Now she's so busy getting other people married off that she doesn't have any time to look around for a suitable man herself." Almost completely off her seat by now, Anna leaned forward over Maizie's desk, her hand reaching for Maizie's. "I need help, Maizie. I need you to throw a sack over my daughter's head and whisk her away to some wonderful hideaway where she can meet the man of her dreams—or barring that, anything close to it," Anna stressed.

The image amused Maizie. "And what's 'he' like, or don't you know?"

"Oh, I know. Or I thought I did. Gina was going out with Shane Callaghan about ten years ago. It looked as if that match was getting serious. I had such high hopes for it. And then, just like that, it *stopped* being serious." It pained Anna to talk about it, even after ten years. "They broke up."

"Why?"

Anna frowned, frustrated. "Damned if I know. Gina wouldn't talk about it. I suspect that she got cold feet, but because I couldn't get her to talk about it, I don't know if I'm right or not."

"Shane Callaghan," Maizie repeated. The name sounded vaguely familiar, but for the life of her, Maizie didn't know why or where she had heard it before. "Do you know where this Shane Callaghan is now?"

Anna shook her heard. "I haven't a clue. If I did, I wouldn't be here. I'd be going right up to him and doing everything I could to bring him and Gina together. According to Gina, he vanished right after college graduation."

Maizie smiled, knowing how frustrating it could be, sitting on the sidelines. That was obviously not Anna Bongino's style. "There are laws against kidnapping in this state."

Anna shrugged. "It would be worth it if it meant that Gina finally had the right man in her life."

"And you think that this Shane Callaghan is the right one?" Maizie questioned.

"Oh absolutely. I'd bet my soul on it," she declared with conviction. "So, will you help, Maizie?" Anna asked eagerly, searching Maizie's face. "Will you help my daughter find the right man and get married?"

"I can certainly try," Maizie promised the attractive woman, shaking her hand.

"'Try'?" Anna asked, a touch of disappointment in her voice.

"Only God gives guarantees, but if it helps, our track record is a hundred percent so far," Maizie assured her friend.

Anna received the news and beamed. "It helps a great deal."

Chapter One

Eight-year-old Adelyn Loren nodded her approval as she watched, mesmerized, as her aunt adjusted a light blue, floor-length bridesmaid dress. There was a touch of wonder in the little girl's soft brown eyes.

"Aunt Gina?" the little girl, known to her family as Addie, asked hesitantly.

The dark-haired little girl jumped off the bed. She had followed Gina into the room when her aunt had asked her if she wanted to see what the dress looked like on her. A fashion buff, even at the tender age of eight, the girl came in eagerly.

She finally had the dress right, Gina thought, looking herself over in her sister's full-length mirror. "What, baby?" Gina asked absently.

Encouraged, Addie's voice sounded a little more confident as she asked, "How many times do you have to do it?"

Gina turned away from the mirror. The dress her latest client had initially picked out had been dowdy and downright awful. With a little bit of subtle hinting, Gina had managed to convince the young woman that being backed up by an attractive-looking bridal party would only serve to highlight her own gown on her big day. That succeeded in making *everyone* happy.

Satisfied, Gina gave her niece her full attention. The little girl had a very serious expression on her face. "How many times do I have to do what, sweetie?" Gina asked.

"How many times do you have to be a bridesmaid before you get to be the bride?" Addie asked.

Gina laughed softly. She knew where this was coming from. "You've been talking to your grandmother, haven't you?"

Addie shook her head vigorously, sending her long, coal black hair bouncing from side to side.

"Uh-uh. Mama said you've been in a lot of weddings and that you were always a bridesmaid so I was just wondering when you get to stop being a bridesmaid and get to be a bride."

Judging by her expression, Gina could tell that it seemed like a logical progression of events to Addie.

Wiggling out of the bridesmaid dress, she draped it on the side of the bed as she threw on an old T-shirt and a pair of jeans. Dressed, Gina sat down on the bed and put her arm around her niece, pulling the little girl to her.

"That's not quite the way it works, sweetie," Gina said, managing not to laugh.

"You mean you're *always* going to be a bridesmaid?" Addie asked, her eyes opening so wide that she resembled one of her favorite stuffed animals. "Doesn't that make you sad?"

"No," Gina assured the little girl, rather touched that the girl was concerned about her. She hugged Addie closer. "It makes me happy."

The small, animated face scrunched up in confusion. "How come?"

She did her best to put it in terms that Addie could understand. "Being a bridesmaid is my job."

But it was obvious that this just confused Addie even more. "Being a bridesmaid is a job?"

"It is for me," Gina answered cheerfully. "The truth of it is, baby, for some people weddings can be very confusing and stressful."

Addie's smooth forehead was still wrinkled in consternation. "What's stressful?"

Gina thought for a moment. She didn't want to frighten the girl, but she did want to get the image across. "You know how when you play your video game and if you're not fast enough, suddenly the words *game over* can come on your screen and your tummy feels all knotted up and disappointed?"

"Uh-huh." Addie solemnly nodded her head.

"Well, that's what stressful is," Gina told her. "Organizing a wedding can be like that."

Addie looked at her uncertainly, doing her best to understand. "Weddings are like video games?"

A warm feeling came over Gina's heart and she grinned. "Sometimes. Your mom almost called off the wedding when she was marrying your dad. Everything suddenly felt as if it was just too much for her."

That had been the first time she had found herself coming to a bride's rescue. In that case it had been her older sister, Tiffany, who needed help. And that had been the beginning of an idea for a career.

"Really?" Addie asked in wonder.

"Really." Gina didn't emphasize how much of an emotional mess her normally level-headed older sister had been a few days before the wedding. "I saw what your mom was going through so I took over and helped her out. It was just a matter of untangling the order to the florist and maybe threatening the caterer," she added as more facts came back to her.

That really caught the little girl's attention. "Did you say you'd beat him up?" Addie asked in an impressed, hushed tone.

Gina laughed. "Worse. I threatened him with bad publicity."

Addie looked up at her in confusion. "What's bad pub-lis-ity?" she asked.

"Something everyone lives in fear of," Gina answered with a smile. "Anyway," she continued matter-of-factly, "I realized that I was pretty good at organizing things and that I could help brides like your mom really enjoy their day and not get caught up in the hassle." She decided that Addie didn't need to know anything beyond that. "And *that's* how your aunt Gina got the idea to became a professional bridesmaid."

"Can *I* become a professional bridesmaid?" Addie asked eagerly. It was obvious that her aunt's story had completely won her over.

"You have to get to be a little taller first," Gina told her, kissing the top of the girl's head. "But I don't see why you can't be one when you're grown up if you want to."

"Will you show me what to do once I get tall enough?" Addie asked seriously.

Gina inclined her head as if she was bowing to the little girl. "I'd be honored."

"Just what is it that you're going to show my daughter how to do once she gets tall enough?" Tiffany Loren asked as she came into the guest bedroom.

Addie swung around on the bed and looked up at her mother. "Aunt Gina's going to show me how to become a professional bridesmaid," she declared gleefully.

Tiffany looked more than a little dismayed. "Just what kind of ideas are you putting into my little girl's head?" she asked.

"I had nothing to do with it," Gina said, disavowing her culpability in the matter. "This was all Addie's idea."

"An idea she got from watching you come over here, parading around in all those bridesmaid dresses," Tiffany said pointedly.

"She could do worse," Gina answered defensively. "I get paid for making people happy and they get to enjoy their big day. Plus I get to eat cake on top of that. Not a bad gig if you ask me."

Tiffany looked at her daughter. This wasn't a conversation she wanted the little girl to hear. "Addie, why don't you go find your cousins? I want to talk to your aunt Gina for a minute."

Addie leaned in and told her aunt in a stage whisper, "Don't let her get you stressed, Aunt Gina."

Tiffany looked after her departing daughter, dumbfounded. "Where did that come from?" she asked her younger sister.

"I'd say she was just extrapolating on what I told her I did as a professional bridesmaid." Tiffany looked at her quizzically. "I told her that I made sure the bride didn't get stressed. I also might have told her that you were stressed on your wedding day—you were, you know," Gina reminded her sister before Tiffany could deny the fact or get annoyed with her.

Gina grinned as she thought about her niece. "I can't wait to hear how this is going to play itself out by the time Addie gets to tell her father about it." She flashed Tiffany a sympathetic smile.

"Terrific." Tiffany looked momentarily worried. "You know how Eddie jumps to conclusions."

"But you know how to get him to jump back and that's all that counts," Gina reminded her older sister. Her brother-in-law had a short fuse, but his outbursts never lasted too long.

Tiffany smiled to herself. "That I do. Can't wait until you get married so that I can pass along that wisdom and knowledge to you, little sister."

"About that, I wouldn't hold my breath if I were you," Gina advised. She saw the doubtful expression on Tiffany's face. "I'm perfectly happy with my life just the way it is."

Tiffany looked at her skeptically. "You'll forgive me if I don't believe you."

"That, dear Tiffany, is your prerogative. Now, if you'll excuse me, I have to prepare to hold a bride's hand and get her through what she'll remember as 'the happiest day of her life,' otherwise known as tomorrow."

"Do you have any more weddings lined up after that?" Tiffany asked her innocently.

"Not yet," Gina replied honestly. "But I will," she added with the confidence that she had managed to build up with this new career of hers.

Tiffany began to ease herself out of the bedroom. "By the way," she added, nodding at the dress on the bed, "you performed a miracle with that bridesmaid dress." She had seen the dress before its transformation. It had been absolutely ugly in her opinion.

"I know." There was no conceit in Gina's answer. There was just sheer pleasure in the knowledge that she was good at her chosen vocation.

Tiffany left the room, walking quickly. She waited until there was a room between her sister and her before she pulled her cell phone out of her pocket. Making sure that she was alone, she pressed auto-dial 8.

The line on the other end was picked up almost immediately.

"Mom?" Tiffany asked just to be sure she'd gotten the right person. When her mother answered in the affirmative, Tiffany declared, "All systems are 'go.' Gina's got nothing scheduled after she's done with this wedding."

"Perfect." The line went instantly dead.

Anna Bongino wasn't about to lose any time in calling her friend with the news.

"Gina has nothing immediately scheduled," Anna breathlessly told Maizie the moment the other woman answered her phone. "Whatever you're going to do, now would be the right time."

"I'll get back to you on this as soon as I can," Maizie promised.

Maizie had already gathered her best friends and comrades-in-arms together to tell them about Anna's daughter and her dissatisfaction that Gina was a perpetual professional bridesmaid. Intrigued, Celia Parnell and Theresa Manetti had gotten to work on the so-called "problem."

Maizie wasn't surprised that they already had a plan ready to go when she called Theresa with the news. A widow like Maizie and Celia, Theresa had built up a thriving catering service and she had found the perfect solution using that service.

"As luck would have it, the young bride whose reception I'm catering in three weeks is about to have a nervous breakdown," Theresa announced, sounding far happier than the news should have warranted.

"Why?" Maizie asked.

"It seems that her photographer somehow accidentally double-booked two ceremonies at the same time, one of them being my bride's. In addition, her cousin dropped out of the wedding at the last minute because her cousin's boyfriend of five years just broke up with her," Theresa explained.

"And we have just the young woman who can handle that for her and smooth out all the bumps," Maizie replied happily.

"Yes, we do," Theresa agreed.

"I admit that this does give us a reason to call Gina so she feels that her particular 'talents' are being utilized, but as far as I know, we still don't have any suitable candidates to play the potential groom to her potential bride-to-be—or do we?" Maizie asked when Theresa didn't immediately respond to her question.

"Hold on to your hat, Maizie. This is about to get even better," Theresa promised.

"All right, consider my hat held. *How* does this get even better?" Maizie asked.

She could almost hear Theresa smiling from ear to ear as she asked, "You know that young man Anna felt was so perfect for her daughter?"

"I remember. Shane Callaghan," Maizie recalled. "What about him?"

Theresa paused dramatically, then said, "Well, I found him."

"What do you mean you 'found' him?" Maizie asked suspiciously.

"Well, actually Celia did," Theresa amended. "He's a client of hers," she explained. "The fact is, 'Shane' has been using another name for his line of work."

This was all very mysterious to Maizie. "The point, Theresa. Get to the point," she told her friend impatiently.

That was when Theresa dropped her little bombshell. "It turns out that Shane Callaghan has a vocation that ties right into our little scenario. The man designs cakes—including wedding cakes—for a living—and he's very much in demand."

"Wouldn't Gina know this, seeing that she's in the business of placating jittery brides-to-be?" Maizie asked.

"That's where the pseudonym comes in. Shane is an 'artiste' known as Cassidy. His bakery is called Cakes Created by Cassidy."

She'd heard of it, Maizie realized. One of her clients had remarked that their son had ordered a cake from this "Cassidy." At the time she'd thought nothing of it.

"Really?" Maizie asked.

"Guess who I'm going to suggest to our bride to 'create' her wedding cake for her reception?" Theresa posed the rhetorical question almost gleefully.

This was playing it close, Maizie thought. "You said the wedding was in three weeks. Are you sure you can get him?"

"Absolutely," Theresa answered confidently. "It turns out that my son's law firm did some legal work for Cassidy a few months ago. It pays to have lunch with your offspring occasionally," she added, although she knew that none of them needed an excuse to get together with their children. Family had always been what this was all about for them, Theresa thought. "That's how I found out who Cassidy really is. It actually is a small world, Maizie," she declared happily. "Now all we need is to get Gina on the scene."

"Well, like I said," Maizie reminded her friend, "her mother just called me and said that Gina has nothing scheduled after this weekend's wedding."

"She does now," Theresa said happily. "I'd better get on the phone and talk to Sylvie—that's the bride-to-be—while she's still coherent. Her maid of honor said she was afraid that Sylvie was going to wind up calling the whole thing off."

"Something that she'll wind up regretting," Maizie predicted. "By all means, Theresa, call her. Tell her about Gina, that she can step in at the last minute and put out any fires that might arise. And then," she concluded, "you're going to have to call Gina."

"All right," Theresa agreed a bit uncertainly. "But why can't you call her?" she asked. After all Maizie was the one with a connection to the girl via Gina's mother.

"I'm a real estate agent, Theresa," Maizie reminded her friend. "There's no reason for me to know about a professional bridesmaid, whereas you, as a caterer with a multitude of wedding receptions to your credit, you could know about her through regular channels. Word of mouth, that kind of thing. If I called her up out of the blue with this offer, I'd have to admit to knowing her mother because how else would I know what she does for a living? She'd smell a rat and politely refuse. Or maybe not so politely," Maizie added.

"Goodness, this matchmaking hobby of ours has certainly gotten more complicated than it was back in the old days, hasn't it?" Theresa marveled.

"I know, but that's also part of the fun," Maizie reminded her friend. "Now stop talking to me and get on the phone to Gina and then to—what did you say was the bride-to-be's name?"

"Sylvie."

"Tell Sylvie you know just the person to step in and wind up saving her day," Maizie told her.

"Wait," Theresa cried, sensing that Maizie was about to hang up.

"What?"

"I need Gina's phone number," she told Maizie. "I can't tell Sylvie about this professional bridesmaid and then not have a phone number to pass on to her if she asks for it," Theresa pointed out. "Plus I'll need it myself if I'm going to set Gina up."

"Sorry," Maizie apologized as she retrieved the phone number from the file on her computer. "I guess I just got excited for a minute," she explained. "I *love* it when a plan comes together."

"So now we're the A-Team?" Theresa asked with an amused laugh. She was referring to an old television program she used to watch while waiting up for her workaholic lawyer husband to come home.

"The what?" Maizie asked, clearly not familiar with the program.

"Never mind about that right now. Just remind me that I have an old DVD to play for you when we all get a few minutes to ourselves."

"Will do," Maizie promised. "But right now, I'm

going to remind *you* that you have two phone calls to make. Possibly three," she amended.

"Three? How do you figure that?" Theresa asked her friend. "Do you want me to call you back once I get Gina and Sylvie?"

"Well, of course I want you to call me back to tell me how it all went. And then," Maizie continued, thinking out loud, "we have to come up with a way to have Gina and Shane get together before the big day. Maybe you can have Gina helping you with the arrangements, kind of like an assistant, and being a go-between for you and this 'in-demand baker.' And then, we can hope that there are sparks."

"A go-between?" Theresa questioned.

"We'll work on it," Maizie promised. "Now go, call while Gina's still free," she instructed her friend just before she hung up.

Chapter Two

Gina carefully hung up the light blue bridesmaid dress in her guest bedroom closet. The dress joined the vast and growing collection of other bridesmaid dresses, both long and short, that she had worn as part of the various bridal parties she'd been in. Because she had come in and in effect—at least in the bride's eyes—saved the wedding, she'd ultimately grown incredibly close to a number of the brides, not an easy feat in the space of two or three weeks.

Some of the brides had actually stayed in touch with her, at least for a little while. The others, though, had faded into the calendar of her life.

Even so, Gina had the satisfaction of knowing that because of her, more than a few women had experienced "the happiest day of their life" without having to endure the proverbial "glitch" that had a nasty habit of cropping up.

And despite what her mother thought of her rather unusual vocation, it did provide her with a nice living. In exchange for her services, she received more than ample compensation as well as another dress to hang in her closet, thanks to the bride, and, after the ceremony had ended and the photographs were taken, there was always a wonderful array of catered food to sample.

Not that she really ate all that much of it. Despite working almost nonstop in the weeks preceding the weddings, on the big day she never seemed to have that much of an appetite. It was almost as if she was channeling the bride's prewedding jitters even though she always appeared utterly calm and in complete control of the situation.

She supposed that was where her very brief flirtation with acting—or at least acting in her college plays—came in handy.

Gina sighed. With the latest wedding now behind her, she was, once again, unemployed.

She knew that she had word of mouth as well as a growing number of satisfied clients going for her, but even so she really needed to give some thought to building up her network, Gina decided. A network comprised of people who could call and alert her to brides in need of her very unique services.

Gina sank down on the bed, willing herself to wind down.

Each time she watched as the happy bride and groom finally drove off to begin their life together—starting with their honeymoon—amid the feeling of a job well done she also experienced just the faintest hint of feeling let down.

This time was no different. She knew her feelings

were silly and she tried not to pay any attention to them, but they were there nonetheless. That tiniest spark of wondering what it might have been like if she hadn't gotten cold feet and had instead agreed to run off with Shane that one wild, crazy night when he had suddenly turned to her and said, out of the blue, "Let's get married."

She supposed that her response—"Are you crazy?"— might have been a bit more diplomatic. But Shane had caught her off guard. They'd dated casually for two years but had only gotten serious in the last six months. When he'd asked her to marry him, the thought of doing something so permanent had scared her to death. She hadn't been ready for that sort of a commitment.

And he hadn't been ready for that kind of a total, harsh rejection. She'd regretted it almost instantly, but by then it had been too late. And she might have even said yes, she thought now. Or at least talked to him and suggested that they take things a little more slowly. But she hadn't been thinking clearly.

They had both just graduated from college that month and life was beginning to unfold for them. There were careers to launch and so many things to do before their lives even began to take shape.

In hindsight, all that uncertainty had frightened her, too. Loving Shane had been a comfortable thing, something for her to lean on. Loving Shane wasn't supposed to contribute to her feelings of being pressured.

Gina sighed. There was no point in going over all that now. By the time she'd worked up her nerve to apologize to Shane, to explain why she'd said what she had, it was too late. He'd taken off, vacating his apartment and leaving for parts unknown, just like that.

Nobody knew where he was.

Stop thinking about what you can't undo, she silently ordered herself. *It won't change anything.*

Dressed in her favorite outfit—cut-off jeans and a T-shirt—Gina went into her kitchen. She took out her favorite ice cream—rum raisin—and carried it into the living room. She settled down on the sectional sofa in front of her giant screen TV to binge-watch her favorite comedy series. She really needed a good laugh tonight.

Just as she turned on the set and pressed the necessary combination of buttons that got her to the first episode of the extensively long-running series—an episode she'd seen countless times before, whenever she was feeling down—her phone rang.

Gina looked at the cell accusingly. It was either someone trying to sell her some insurance—it was that time of year again she'd noticed—or it was her mother to pointedly ask her how "someone else's wedding" went and when did she think she would get around to planning one of her own.

Telling her mother that it would happen when she found someone to stand at the altar, waiting for her, never did any good because that only had her mother remembering how much she and the rest of the family had liked Shane. Shane had managed to endear himself to them in a very short amount of time. That was ten years ago and her mother still nostalgically referred to him as "the one who got away."

No, she definitely wasn't up to talking to her mother tonight.

Gina glanced at the caller ID. It wasn't her mother, or, from the looks of it, an insurance broker. The ID below the phone number proclaimed "Manetti's Catering."

The name seemed vaguely familiar. And then she remembered hearing the name on the radio along with the slogan "Food like Mama used to make."

Curious, Gina set aside the half-pint of ice cream on top of a section of the newspaper on her coffee table and answered her phone.

"Hello?"

"Hello," a cheerful woman's voice on the other end of the call responded. "Is this Gina Bongino?"

"Yes," Gina answered guardedly. "This is Gina."

She was prepared to terminate the call at a second's notice if this turned out to be some clever telemarketer who had matched her name to her cell number.

"Forgive me for bothering you so late on a Sunday, but are you the same Gina Bongino who advertises herself as the Bridesmaid for Hire?" Theresa asked.

Before placing the call, Theresa had everything written down on a yellow pad and it was in front of her now. She didn't want to take a chance on forgetting something or making a mistake. She, Maizie and Celia had covered all the major points before she'd even placed the call to Gina.

"I am," Gina answered, still wondering if this was going to wind up being a crank call, or if this was actually on the level.

"Oh, thank goodness," Theresa declared. "You don't know me, dear, but I'm Theresa Manetti. I run a catering service and I've done a good many wedding receptions. Especially lately."

"Yes?" Gina responded, waiting for the woman to get to the point. She was hoping it involved what she did, but you never knew. Maybe the woman was just looking for some advice. Or even a referral.

"I'll get right to the point," Theresa said as if reading her mind. "The reception I have coming up in three weeks just might wind up falling through. The poor girl who's the bride-to-be is about to have a nervous breakdown and I was wondering—" Stumbling, Theresa took a deep breath and glanced down at her notes. She started again. "Someone told me that you offer a very unique service. You come in and handle any emergency that might come up connected to the wedding so that the bride can enjoy a stress-free wedding day."

"That's right," Gina said, beginning to relax a little. This might be a job after all.

Schooling herself not to sound too eager, Theresa asked, "Just exactly what is it that you do?"

"Essentially, anything that needs to be done in order to make the wedding proceed as initially planned," Gina answered.

"Such as?" Theresa prompted.

Gina thought for a moment before framing her answer. "Such as anything from turning ugly bridesmaid dresses into flattering ones to lining up last-minute photographers to replace the one who dropped out. The same thing goes for hairdressers and makeup artists if the bride planned on having them. You name it, I've probably encountered it."

"Does that include being part of the wedding party? Because one of the bridesmaids suddenly just dropped out, leaving a lone groomsman," Theresa explained, checking off a line on her pad.

"I'm in the background," Gina explained. It was not her intention to take a chance on outshining any bride. "But yes, that's what the title implies. I actually am a bridesmaid for hire," she told the woman on the other end of the call.

She heard a large sigh of relief, something she was more than familiar with.

"Oh, you're a godsend," Theresa declared, and she was only half acting.

"I will need to talk to the bride herself to make sure she's on board," Gina told the caller before things progressed any further. "To be honest, it's usually the bride or a member of her family who hires me. I've never had a caterer ask me to help out the bride before," she said.

"Oh, I quite understand and I realize this is unusual, but then, so's a bridesmaid for hire," Theresa pointed out.

"Can't argue with you there," Gina agreed with a soft laugh.

"I did talk to Sylvie about you as soon as I became aware that there was someone like you who did this kind of thing," Theresa explained. "And she told me to go ahead and see if she could hire you. As I said, the wedding's in three weeks and it seems like everything that could go wrong at this point has."

She'd dealt with situations like that before, Gina thought. "As long as the bride and groom are there, the rest can be managed," she assured the motherly sounding woman on the other end.

"Well, with your help, I'm sure that they'll be there all right," Theresa told her, smiling to herself. This was actually going to work, she thought. Wait until she called Maizie and Celia. "And they're such a cute couple. They're really made for each other."

The woman sounded more like a mother than a caterer, Gina thought. "Sounds good," she told Theresa.

"Now, if you can give me the particulars, I'll place the call to—Sylvie is it?"

"It's Sylvia, actually. Sylvia Stevens, but everyone just calls her Sylvie. She looks like a Sylvie," Theresa told her. There was a fond note in her voice that Gina immediately picked up on.

"Give me her cell number and her address and I'll give her a call first thing in the morning to make the arrangements," Gina said.

Theresa gave her the information, enunciating everything slowly so that Gina didn't miss a thing. "I want you to know that you're the answer to a prayer," she added with just the right amount of feeling. She didn't really have to pretend all that much. After all, Sylvie *was* going to pieces.

"It'll be my pleasure to do whatever needs to be done to make sure Sylvie has as perfect a wedding day as humanly possible," Gina assured the woman.

"Speaking of which, there is just one more thing," Theresa said. She'd saved the most important part for last because she wanted to make sure that Gina was fully engaged in this endeavor before she told the young woman about this part.

Gina had no idea why, but she could feel herself suddenly bracing. What was the woman going to ask for? "Yes?"

"I'm going to be short staffed for the rest of the month—" Theresa began, easing her way into this final chapter.

Gina wanted to quickly stop the woman before this went any further. "I'm afraid that catering the reception is a little out of my league, Mrs. Manetti. Especially if

I'm going to be in the wedding party and seeing to other details," she told Theresa.

"Oh no, dear, it's nothing like that," Theresa was quick to assure her. "The fact of the matter is, the bride requested to have her cake done by this cake designer she heard about. His work is in high demand. Perhaps you've heard of him as well?" Theresa asked, hoping against hope that Gina's answer would be negative. "Cakes Created by Cassidy."

Theresa held her breath, waiting for Gina's response. She caught herself crossing her fingers as the seconds ticked by.

"No," Gina finally admitted. "I can't say that I have," she added, still waiting to find out just what it was that Theresa was going to ask her to do.

Theresa slowly released the breath she'd been holding, being careful not to alert the young woman on the other end that there was anything out of the ordinary going on.

"Well, because I have all these other catering affairs between now and Sylvie's wedding, I was wondering if you could handle ordering the cake from this Cassidy person. Sylvie will give you all her requirements when you talk to her."

The request was doable, but it struck her as being a little strange. "Wouldn't she and the groom want to sample the cake before they put in their final order?" Gina asked.

In her experience, the bride and groom usually sampled a great many cakes before they settled on their final choice.

"Oh no," Theresa quickly shot down the idea. "Sylvie worked furiously to diet down so that she could fit into this dress. Now that she's the right size, she's desperately trying *not* to gain any weight between now and the wedding. That also includes not doing *any* cake sampling."

Theresa paused for a second to catch her breath before continuing. "That would be what she wanted you for, along with an entire myriad of other bride-related things that ordinarily don't add up to that much but right now, as I told you, Sylvie is tottering on the brink of a nervous breakdown. To be honest, no one knows what might just push her over the edge. Would you mind terribly meeting with this cake designer and taking care of this for her?"

"Eating a slice of cake made by an in-demand cake decorator? No, not a bit," Gina answered with a laugh. She glanced over at her melting rum raisin. "Is there anything else, Mrs. Manetti?"

"No, nothing I can think of at the moment," Theresa answered breezily.

"Then thank you for the call and the opportunity. I'll get right on this tomorrow morning," she said again. "And I'll call you once I speak with Sylvie."

"Wonderful. And I look forward to meeting you in person, dear," Theresa told her. "And again, I'm sorry for having to call so late but I just got off the phone with Sylvie and I knew that something needed to be done quickly."

She did have one question. "Who told you about me again?" Gina asked. The woman hadn't been quite clear as to who had given the caterer her name when she'd first called.

Theresa quickly checked her notes, finding the name that she was told to use.

"Virginia Gallagher told me about you, although her

name is Price now. The Gallagher-Price wedding," she threw in to substantiate her story.

Gina thought for a moment. "I was in that wedding party over a year ago," she remembered.

"And Virginia—she's a friend of my daughter's—is still singing your praises," Theresa said, hoping that would seal the deal.

She knew that she and her two coconspirators in matchmaking needed to make sure that Gina didn't suspect anything was amiss as she engaged the professional bridesmaid's services to help smooth out another wedding in possible turmoil. That meant not focusing too much on the additional assignment of selecting the cake. The whole idea here was to get her down to the Cakes Created by Cassidy shop so she could cross paths with Shane after all these years.

From everything that she and her friends had managed to uncover, Gina and Shane had once been the absolute epitome of a perfect match and for all intents and purposes, it seemed that they still were. They just needed to be made to realize that again.

"Oh, and I intend to pay you extra for this cake service you'll be performing since technically, it isn't something you would ordinarily do," Theresa interjected, hoping that would do the trick.

But Theresa hadn't counted on Gina's integrity. "How's that again? You want to pay me extra for procuring the wedding cake."

Theresa hesitated for a moment. "Well, the caterer usually provides the cake unless the bride has other ideas."

"Wouldn't that still come out of the bride's pocket—

so to speak? That makes it part of the package deal between the bride and me," Gina concluded.

"Perhaps, but I don't want Sylvie stressing out any more than she already is," Theresa said, hoping that would satisfy Gina and put an end to any further questions, at least for the time being. "We'll talk more tomorrow, dear," Theresa promised just before she quickly terminated the call.

Strange, Gina thought. But then, so was what she did for a living. Especially in her mother's eyes. The bottom line was that she was employed again.

This was good. This was very, very good.

She could feel herself growing enthusiastic, the way she always did at the beginning of a new assignment.

She looked over toward the coffee table. Her ice cream had turned into soup.

Getting up, Gina picked up the rum raisin container and took it back to the freezer so that she could turn the soup back into ice cream again.

She was whistling as she went.

Chapter Three

Gina felt that her phone call to Sylvie the next morning went well.

Just as she'd been warned, she found that the anxious young woman she spoke to was indeed two steps away from becoming a bridezilla.

Speaking in a slow, calm voice, Gina made arrangements to meet with the woman early the following morning. She promised Sylvie that everything would turn out just the way she wanted, then proceeded to give her a few examples of other weddings she had successfully handled.

Listening, Sylvie seemed to noticeably calm down. She sounded almost eager to look up Gina's website to read what other brides had posted about their own weddings and how potential disasters-in-the-making had been successfully averted, thanks to a few well-executed efforts.

By the time she hung up, Gina was fairly certain that Sylvie had calmed down sufficiently to be downgraded from the level of "bridezilla" to an almost normal, anxious bride-to-be.

While talking to Sylvie, she'd gotten very specific directions about the kind of multitiered wedding cake the bride and groom had their hearts set on—although she strongly suspected that the groom's "heart" wasn't nearly as involved in this choice as the bride's was. She'd even had to promise Sylvie that she'd stop by the bakery to engage this so-called sought-after cake "artiste" known as Cassidy right after she ended their call.

All in all, Gina thought, pressing the end call button on her cell, this was shaping up to be a really productive day.

But before she did anything else, she decided as she grabbed her purse and her squadron of keys, she needed to stop at Manetti's Catering. It was only right for her to thank the woman who had sent this new bit of business her way.

Because of its ever-expanding clientele, the catering company had recently moved out of its former rather small, confining quarters to a genuine homey-looking shop where the shop's homemade pastries and sandwiches-to-go could be properly showcased and also seen through the large bay windows.

Located in the heart of an upscale shopping center, the sight of the food enticed shoppers to come in, sample, and, ideally, be inspired to book a future party ranging from small and intimate to a blow-out bash.

Walking into the shop, Gina was impressed by what she saw and exceedingly pleased that she had managed to catch the attention of someone like Theresa Manetti. She was certain that if she came through for Sylvie, Mrs.

Manetti could be counted on to throw more business her way down the line.

It never hurt to network, Gina thought.

"May I help you?" a soft, almost melodic voice asked, coming from behind the counter.

"Hi, I'm Gina Bongino—the professional bridesmaid," she answered, tagging on her signature label, hoping that would mean something to the older woman.

Coming around the counter, the thin woman with salt-and-pepper hair took her hand in hers. "Gina, what a pleasure to meet you. I'm Theresa Manetti."

Gina's first thoughts were that the woman looked just the way she had sounded on the phone last night. Warm and gracious. And genuine.

Gina found herself eager to please the caterer who she had taken an immediate liking to.

Theresa took out a folded piece of paper from her apron pocket. "I've written everything down for you," she told Gina, tucking the paper into her hand. "That's the baker's name, phone number, the address of the shop and, of course, the kind of wedding cake Sylvie wants at her wedding."

Gina glanced at the paper, nodding. "She already described it to me when I talked to her this morning," she told Theresa.

"Well, it never hurts to have it written down in front of you," Theresa said with a smile. "I'd take care of this myself," she told Gina again, "but as I've already mentioned to you last night, we are extremely busy these days."

As if to bear her out, there was continuous noise coming from the back of the shop. Gina guessed that was where the kitchen was located and the woman's employees were undoubtedly all busy working.

Gina caught herself being very grateful that fate had somehow brought them together. She was *sure* that Theresa Manetti could throw a little business her way down the line.

"Don't worry about a thing, Mrs. Manetti," Gina replied. "I'll take care of ordering the cake and everything else that I gathered Sylvie needed done." She tucked away the paper Theresa had handed her into her purse. "I just wanted to come by and say thank you," she explained.

"I'm the one who should be thanking you," Theresa told her. "My fees are nonrefundable, so it's not a matter of my losing money. But I have to admit I get personally involved with all my clients and I really do want them, if at all possible, to come away happy and satisfied."

Gina could only smile at the woman. It wasn't often she heard someone espousing something as selfless as that. Again she found herself thinking that she liked Theresa Manetti right from the start.

"I have a feeling that this is the beginning of a wonderful friendship," she told Theresa, preparing to leave.

"I certainly hope so, dear," Theresa replied, the corners of her eyes crinkling as she smiled. "I certainly hope so," she repeated as the door closed on the departing enterprising bridesmaid for hire.

Following Theresa's directions, Gina made her way to another, smaller shopping center. This one was located on the far side of Bedford. She briefly entertained the idea of calling ahead but decided against it. She wanted to be there on the premises in case she had to convince this "Cassidy" to accept the order and have it ready by the day of the wedding.

She knew from experience that people who fancied themselves to be "artistes" were, for the most part, temperamental and constantly needed to have their egos stroked. She had learned that stroking was best done in person.

So Gina went over to the Fairview Plaza where the shop was located, parked in the first empty parking space she saw, and set out to find the bakery and this Cassidy who created works of art that could be eaten with a fork.

The store was so small and unassuming, she missed it on her first pass through the center. She was searching for something eye-catching and ostentatious.

The shop, when she found it on her second time around, was neither. It was a small white shop with blue lettering and it was nestled in between a children's toy store and a trendy store selling overpriced organic fruits and vegetables.

Gina looked over the outside as she stood in front of the entrance. "Well, either ego's not his problem or the rent's really cheap here," she speculated.

There were no hours posted on the door, so she had no idea if it was open or not. Maybe she *should* have called ahead, she thought.

Trying the doorknob, Gina found that the door was open. Coming in, her entrance was heralded by the light tinkling of an actual bell that was hanging right over the front door rather than a buzzer or a symphony of virtual chimes.

It was almost charming, she thought. Probably to catch the customer off guard so that they wouldn't think fast enough to protest being hit with an oversize price tag for a cake that could have just as easily been made out of a couple of everyday, standard box mixes.

At first glance, there was no one in the front of the store. She did, however, see a partially closed door that led to what she presumed was the back where "all the magic happened."

"Hello?" Gina called out, raising her voice slightly. "Is anyone here?"

Listening, she heard movement coming from the back. Maybe it was the person who took the cake orders, she thought. Odd that they didn't come out when the bell sounded.

When no one came out to the showroom, Gina tried again.

"I'd like to order a wedding cake for a wedding taking place three weeks from now."

Actually, it was three weeks from this past Saturday, she thought, but that was a tidbit she was going to save until she had someone in front of her she could make eye contact with.

The movement she'd initially heard had definitely stopped. And still no one opened the back door any farther. Weren't they coming out?

This was all very strange, she thought. Maybe this "artiste" wasn't here and she had walked in on a misguided burglar who was caught in the act of trying to rob the place.

She tried one last time. Raising her voice again, Gina called out, "If this is a bad time, I'll come back. You don't have your store hours posted, but—"

She saw the door leading to the back room opening all the way.

Finally, she thought.

And then, when she saw the person walking to the front of the shop—walking toward *her*—her jaw slackened, causing her mouth to drop open. Any other sound that might have come out at that point didn't.

After a beat, Gina realized that she had forgotten to breathe.

Shane.

But it couldn't be.

Could it?

And yet… It was definitely Shane, cutting the distance between them in what now felt like slow motion.

Was she dreaming?

She would have blinked to clear her eyes if it didn't strike her as being almost cartoon-like.

A hot wave washed over her.

Breathe, damn it. Breathe! she silently ordered herself.

When he heard her voice, Shane was almost convinced that he was imagining things. He had come out to see and prove himself wrong.

Even so, he knew he would have recognized *her* voice anywhere.

And he was right.

It *was* her.

Ten years went up in smoke and just for an instant, he was that lovesick kid again.

And then reality, with all its harsh reminders, returned with a vengeance.

"Hello, Gina."

Because for one wild split second, the shop she was standing in had insisted on going for a quick spin around her, Gina grabbed the edge of the counter to keep herself steady. She refused to do something so incredibly hokey as to pass out even though she felt as if she could barely get her legs to support her.

"Shane?" she whispered.

His name slipped out before she could stop herself. It *looked* like Shane, except that it was a handsomer, upgraded version of the man who lived ten years, unchanged, in her past. His face appeared more gaunt now, and more rugged. Some of the boyishness had worn away, replaced, she noted, by an almost arousing manliness.

His hair was still blond, though, and his eyes, his eyes were still that piercing shade of blue that always seemed to go right through her. Time hadn't changed that, she thought.

The corners of his mouth curved ever so slightly at the confusion that was on her face.

"Don't tell me you've forgotten what I look like," he said in response to the questioning way she had said his name.

Oh God, no, Gina thought. Even if she had gotten amnesia, there was no way she could *ever* forget Shane's face. Like it or not, it was and always would be permanently embossed on her brain.

Because she realized that she was staring at him as if he were an apparition, Gina cleared her throat and stumbled her way through an explanation.

"I'm sorry—" she began only to have him interrupt her.

"Nice to finally hear you say that," Shane said.

Gina wasn't able to read his expression, but she instantly pulled her shoulders back, prepared to engage in an unpleasant exchange. Not that, at least from his point of view, she could actually fault him. But in her own defense, she had tried to find him and apologize. But she wasn't able to and that was *his* fault. He was the one who had taken off and disappeared, not her.

"—but I seem to be in the wrong place," Gina continued tersely. "I'm looking for a cake designer named Cassidy—"

Shane inclined his head. For now, he stayed behind

the counter. He didn't trust himself to come any closer to Gina than he was at this moment. Despite the fact that he felt she had humiliated him, despite being angry at her, the woman had still managed to fill his head, not to mention his dreams, every waking minute for more than an entire year.

It had taken that much time for his longing to subside, and then another year for him to pull himself together. That was when he admitted to himself that he didn't want to be a lawyer. That had once been his parents' dream, not his, even though he'd tried to honor it. So one day he just walked away from it, had gone to work with his older brother halfway around the world and ultimately found something he felt he had a passion for. Something unique and unlike anything he had ever done before.

Myriad emotions pulsed through Shane right now as he looked at Gina, although he was able to keep any of that from registering on his face.

Instead, he told Gina in a very calm voice, "I'm Cassidy."

Gina stared at him, her eyebrows coming together almost in an upside down V. What was he trying to put over on her?

"No, you're not," she contradicted, almost annoyed that he was trying to fool her. "You're Shane."

Just saying his name again after all this time sent ripples of warmth and longing undulating through her. Her brain was having trouble computing seeing him after all this time. At the very least, the man should have had the decency to look a little paunchy and worn around the edges, not like some rugged movie star stepping off the big screen.

And why was he smiling at her like that? Was he going to say something sarcastic?

"You don't remember," Shane guessed.

"Remember what?" she asked, feeling more and more confused, befuddled and exasperated.

This morning, she had been happily saving yet another anxious bride's wedding, and now, less than a couple of hours later, she felt as if she was suddenly caught up in the center of a whirlpool, being tossed around and unable to figure out which way was up.

"That my middle name is Cassidy," he went on to tell her. "Shane Cassidy Callaghan," he said, giving her his full name as he watched her face.

Seeing Gina again without any warning just served to remind him how much he had missed looking at that face. How much he had missed the scent of her hair and the feel of her soft body pressed against his.

Get a grip, Callaghan. She did a number on you once, don't leave yourself open for another assault. She's even forgotten your middle name.

But that didn't surprise him. She'd undoubtedly forgotten a great many things about him, Shane thought. And about the two of them.

Things that he *couldn't* forget no matter how much he tried.

"Then Cakes Created by Cassidy is your company?" she asked him, not bothering to hide her disbelief.

Gina was having a great deal of trouble processing any of it. Not just seeing him again, but the rest of it, as well.

A cake designer? Really? Shane?

The Shane she'd known back in college had occasionally slipped her notes with drawings of the two of them at the bottom. She recalled that he liked to draw. But back then the only thing he was capable of doing in the kitchen was opening the refrigerator door.

How had he gone from kitchen illiterate to a master baker?

"It's catchy, don't you think?" Shane asked. There was a touch of pride in his voice that she found hard to miss now.

"More like incredible," she admitted.

"That's a word I usually hear *after* someone has sampled one of my cakes." Before she could say anything, Shane changed the conversation's direction. "When you walked in, you said something about coming here to order a wedding cake."

She was almost grateful to him. It was as if he had snapped his fingers, getting her out of her mental haze and forcing her to focus on the reason she had come here in the first place. The sooner she stated it, the sooner she could get away.

"Right." She took out the paper that Theresa had given her. The cake's specifications were written in the woman's rather striking handwriting. She focused on it now. "I need to have this cake made and delivered to the Blue Room at the Bedford Hilton Hotel by two o'clock." Pointing to the line on the paper, she said, "I need it by that date. That's in three weeks."

He didn't bother looking at the paper. "I know when it is—"

"Good then." She left the paper on the counter for him. "You can send the bill to—"

"—and it's not possible," Shane said, completing his sentence.

Caught off guard, she stared at him, wondering if she'd heard him correctly. "Excuse me?"

"I said that it's not possible," Shane repeated in the same quiet, calm voice.

"What do you mean it's not possible?" Gina demanded. "I'm giving you three weeks' notice."

"I know," Shane responded, unfazed. "And I'm booked solid."

Was he bragging? Okay, she'd let him have his moment. All things considered, he deserved it. She had never wished him ill. She looked around, noticing for the first time that there were framed photographs on the walls. None of him, she noted, but of some of the cakes he had created.

The one that caught her eye was amazingly constructed in the shape of the Eiffel Tower. How did someone even begin to do that? she wondered, stunned.

She looked at Shane, utterly impressed. "You're doing well, I see."

Shane nodded and replied without a trace of bravado, "Very well, thanks."

"And I'm happy for you," she told him—and she meant it, aside from attempting to get on his good side for the sake of her client. "Surely you can squeeze in one more cake."

She couldn't read the expression on his face. But there was no misunderstanding his words. "No," he replied flatly. "Sorry."

Chapter Four

He couldn't be serious, Gina thought.

"But it's just one cake," she argued, unable to believe that Shane, or whatever he chose to call himself these days, couldn't find a way to make this important cake a reality. "It's not even anything especially elaborate, like that tower or bridge," she said, gesturing at the photographs of cakes he had made. "Just a lot of tiers and your signature swirl around the edges." Theresa had told her that Sylvie insisted on the swirls.

But Shane remained steadfast and shook his head again, turning her request down. "Sorry."

He wasn't sorry at all, Gina thought. This had to be his way of getting back at her after all this time. Well, she had no intentions of having her client wind up paying for something that she had done a decade ago.

"Why won't you do it?" she asked. She knew that if

she came back and told Sylvie that she wasn't able to get her cake for the wedding—failing so early in their association—the bride was just going to fall to pieces and most likely fire her. This was becoming a challenge for her. "What if I pay you twice the amount that you normally charge?" Gina proposed. "Will you find a way to do it then?"

But Shane remained unmoved. "Sorry, Gina. You're going to have to just find someone else to bake your cake for your big day."

Was that it? Did he think that she was asking him to make *her* wedding cake? Gina was quick to set him straight. "The cake isn't for me."

"Right," Shane replied sarcastically. "It's for everyone at the reception." He'd heard that approach before.

"Well, technically, yes," Gina agreed. She was right, she thought. Shane did think she was asking for him to bake her wedding cake. She could see how he felt that she was rubbing salt into his wounds, even after all this time. "But if you don't make this cake, in less than three weeks, there is going to be one unhappy bride who will be having a nervous breakdown because she is going to feel that her big day is just crumbling all to pieces right in front of her."

Gina saw something in Shane's eyes that she couldn't quite make out, and then he shrugged, unmoved. "I'm sorry but there's nothing I can do for you, Gina. I'm booked solid. You'll just have to eat someone else's cake at your wedding."

A fresh wave of guilt washed over her. Had she hurt him that much? Over the years, when she couldn't locate him, she'd talked herself into believing that he really hadn't cared.

But he had, she realized.

"It's not my wedding, Shane," she told him quietly.

About to go back into the kitchen area and send out one of his assistants to usher her out, Shane stopped and turned around again.

"Wait, what?" he asked. Was she lying, trying to get him to agree to create one of his signature cakes for her, or was she being truthful?

"I said it's not my wedding," Gina repeated, slowly enunciating every word.

This didn't make any sense to him. Shane was accustomed to having the bride—usually accompanied by the groom—be the one who placed the order for the cake. And this was only after an unusual amount of deliberation and questions, not to mention cake sampling, took place. If Gina wasn't the bride, then what was she doing placing the order for the wedding cake?

"All right," he said gamely. "Whose wedding is it?" he asked.

"The bride's name is Sylvie Stevens," she answered, adding, "Right now, quite honestly, the groom's name escapes me."

Most of the miscellaneous thoughts that usually resided in her head had all inexplicably vanished, leaving her to fend for herself. The reason for that was because she had run into Shane in the least likely place she would have ever thought of seeing him. In a shop that he apparently owned and operated as a creative baker. All of this had left her practically incoherent and totally unprepared to deal with any of this.

"This Sylvie Stevens," Shane said, picking up on the bride's name, "is she a relative of yours?"

There was no doubt about it. Shane felt as if he was

groping around in the dark, trying to find the door so he could get out.

He was fairly certain that he had met all of Gina's relatives during the time that they had been together. As he recalled, it wasn't that big a family. He knew he would have remembered someone named Sylvie.

"No—" Gina began.

He cut her off. "A friend, then?" he asked in disbelief. This was really an unusual circumstance if she was making the decision for a friend. Despite his initial decision to just close the door on Gina the way she had so callously closed it on him, Shane found his curiosity aroused. "Are you here making arrangements for a cake for a friend?"

Saying yes would have been the easy way out, but Gina knew her best bet was to be totally honest with him. "I can't call this bride-to-be my friend, although some of my clients do wind up that way by the time the wedding takes place."

He stared at her. He hadn't a clue what she was talking about.

"You've lost me," Shane told her impatiently.

His choice of words vividly brought back the past to her.

I did, didn't I? Gina thought, a huge pang of regret twisting her stomach. She really wished that there was such a thing as a do-over button she could press.

She took a breath. "Maybe I should explain," she began.

"Maybe you should," Shane agreed crisply.

He silently warned himself not to get caught up in any of this. That meant that he couldn't allow the sound of her voice to get to him or allow the way he had once felt about her to influence him in any way.

But despite everything, Shane had to admit that his curiosity had been aroused in a big way.

Gina took another deep breath before telling him, "I'm a professional bridesmaid."

His reaction was the same sort she had become used to getting. "What the hell is that?" Shane demanded.

"Just what it sounds like," she told him. "Simply put, I hire out my services to prospective brides. I promise them that I will take care of any and all possible emergencies that might arise before and during the ceremony. Emergencies that could derail what the bride had envisioned as her perfect day."

Gina's explanation had almost rendered him speechless.

Almost.

"You're kidding," Shane said, recovering. "You, the woman who couldn't commit herself to the man who foolishly bared his soul to her, *you're* in charge of making other people's weddings a success?" he asked incredulously.

There it was again, Gina thought, that wave of guilt that threatened to all but drown her. "Shane, I can't tell you how much—"

Shane upbraided himself for dropping his guard and allowing this to get personal. Aware of his error, Shane waved away what he could tell was going to be another apology. He didn't want to hear it. The damage had long since been done and they had both moved on.

As possibly a direct result of her rejection, he had forged a better version of himself and had gone on to create a career out of the ashes that was far more satisfying to him than the path he had been set to follow when she'd suddenly stomped on his heart.

"Never mind all that now," Shane told her rather formally. "This cake you're trying to order, it *isn't* for you?" he asked, wanting to be totally sure before continuing.

"No, it's not. And Sylvie really does seem to have her heart set on you being the one making this cake for her." And then she added what she hoped would be the argument that would tip the scales in Sylvie's favor. "If you won't make the cake, it's almost as if the rest of her wedding is doomed."

Shane laughed shortly at the absurdity of what she'd just said. "That's a little dramatic and over-the-top, don't you think?" he asked.

For the first time, Gina laughed in response. He found the sound disturbing in a way he definitely didn't want to be disturbed.

"You'd be surprised what some of these brides are like and what they say when they feel stressed," Gina told him, extrapolating on this momentary temporary truce that they had struck. "The term *bridezilla* is not just some whimsical, weird name that someone dreamed up. It's actually rather an accurate description of the transformation that some of these perfectly sane women undergo when dealing with the one hundred–plus miscellaneous details that comprise pulling off the perfect wedding," she told him.

"Just as an example," Gina went on to say, "suddenly the size and color of the table napkins take on a whole new meaning. Weddings put enormous pressure on the bride and on the people around the bride who are trying to emotionally support her."

He supposed, although he hadn't given it much

thought, he could see that happening. "If that's the case, why not just go to a wedding planner?" he asked.

"Some do," Gina agreed. "But I'm actually less expensive and in many cases, a lot friendlier. I'm more like a paid best friend, there to listen and to hold the bride's hand for the duration ranging from just before the wedding to the three or four weeks leading up to the big day, depending on when I'm called in."

He thought about her description, even though he had never heard of what she did being a profession before. "So this is really on the level?" Shane asked her again as he began to come around.

Gina didn't hesitate for a second. "Absolutely," she assured him.

"Exactly how many of you 'professional bridesmaids' are there out there?" he asked.

She had to admit that she didn't know of anyone who did what she did. She had come up with this on her own while brainstorming one afternoon, going over all the different skills she had developed. Being a bridesmaid all those different times had stood out head and shoulders above the rest.

"As far as I know, there's just me," Gina replied. She saw the skeptical look on Shane's face. "Oh, since there's really nothing new under the sun, I'm sure there might be some other professional bridesmaids out there. But for now, I'm the only one I know of doing this sort of thing. At least in this state." That much she had researched recently. "Anything else you'd like to know?" she asked Shane.

More things than you could possibly begin to answer in the space of time we have today, Shane thought as he tried not to stare at her.

Old memories kept trying to break through and he blocked them.

"No," he replied. "That answers my questions. For now."

An ominous feeling swept over Gina, but she fiercely pushed it away. She couldn't afford to get caught up in anything right now. She needed to focus on the immediate business at hand.

And Shane still hadn't given her the answer she needed. "So, will you do it?" she asked. "Will 'Cassidy' create one of his much sought-after cakes for Sylvie, thereby making her an extremely happy, albeit still anxious bride?" Gina asked, never taking her eyes off Shane's face.

He didn't answer right away. As a matter of fact, he was silent for so long, Gina was beginning to think that maybe she *hadn't* won him over.

If she were to guess what was happening, she would have said that Shane was relishing having to turn her down.

But just as she had resigned herself to the inevitable, he flashed a small smile at her and said, "I'll do it. On one condition."

Gina braced herself. This was going to be something that had to do with her. Shane was going to exact some sort of an act of contrition from her for having turned him down a decade ago. Okay, as long as it wasn't anything incredibly humiliating, she was willing to go through with whatever he came up with, jumping through any hoops he cited.

She owed it to him—and to her client.

"Name it," she said, holding her breath.

"I need to meet with the bride and groom," Shane told

her in no uncertain terms. "Or at least with the bride. Both would be preferable, but meeting with the one is nonnegotiable."

Gina expected a wave of relief to engulf her when she heard Shane's terms. But the relief she would have expected to experience at being taken off the hook like this didn't quite materialize and she had no idea why. Somehow, given all this, she felt as if she'd just been shoved into limbo with the proverbial door being slammed shut on her.

Maybe all this guilt she'd been carrying around in her mind had no real reason to exist after all. It was a possibility, she told herself.

"You want to meet with the bride," she repeated just to be certain she understood what Shane was asking for and there were no unspoken, hidden terms that she wasn't getting.

"Yes, I want to meet with the bride." With a sigh, he explained his reasons behind the term. "I don't just 'bake' a wedding cake. I create it. And creating a wedding cake for a couple is a very personal thing. To do it effectively, to give the couple their proper due, I need to meet with at least the bride to make sure I get it right and capture the essence of the two people getting married."

She wanted to point out that the ingredients would wind up being the same no matter how the couple struck him or what he thought of them. But to avoid any arguments, she kept that to herself. She'd just scored a huge win here in getting him to agree to make the wedding cake at all. She knew she couldn't risk doing something to turn him off and make him change his mind about making this cake for Sylvie.

"Sure," Gina agreed readily. "Just tell me when it's

convenient for you and I'll arrange for Sylvie to come to your shop to meet with you." She paused for a second and then, knowing she was going out on a limb here, she added, "And with any luck, her future husband, too."

There was still part of Shane that thought this was all a creative hoax on her part. That she had made it all up. That meant that there was no "Sylvie," no wedding and definitely not that ridiculous position she had just told him about: a professional bridesmaid.

But he had never been a conceited man and to actually believe Gina had gone to all this trouble just to worm back into his life would be just that, conceited.

No, as absurd as this sounded to him, Shane thought, this had to be on the level. And, if he was being honest, he supposed that her job was no more unusual than what he did—creating extremely unique cakes for people to celebrate all different occasions.

"Wait right here," he told her. "Let me check my calendar."

The next moment, he turned and walked into the back room he had initially been in when she had entered his shop.

Gina watched the door close. She couldn't help wondering if he was stepping out of her life again, just as he had the last time he had walked out and closed the door on her.

She knew that sounded paranoid, but given their history, she couldn't help the thoughts that were rearing their heads in her mind.

When the door opened again a couple of minutes later, Gina almost blew out an audible sigh of relief.

He saw the look on her face before she managed to

sublimate it. "You didn't think I was coming back, did you?" he asked.

"No," she denied. "I was just wondering what was taking you so long." She could feel his eyes looking at her knowingly. "Most people have their calendars on their smartphones, not somewhere in the back room," she explained, saying the first thing that came to her head.

His shrug was offhanded and casual. "I guess I'm not like most people," he told her.

She thought of the way he had been all those years ago and the unusual path his life had taken now. "No," she agreed. "That you definitely are not."

Damn it, why was her heart pounding like this? She needed to get a grip on herself before she said or did something to make a complete fool of herself.

Clearing her throat, Gina forced herself to think strictly about the wedding she was now responsible for and only that.

"So, did you find a date that's good for you?" she asked him cheerfully. "To meet with Sylvie," she added when he didn't respond.

"Well, as I said, my schedule is crowded." As if to prove it, he glanced at his watch and unconsciously took a step toward the back door again. "I've got a cake I need to get started creating even now."

"Then I won't keep you," Gina promised. "Just give me a date and I'll get out of your hair just like that." She snapped her fingers.

I did give you a date. And you didn't want it.

The thought suddenly popped up in his mind, totally unbidden.

This was a mistake, Shane told himself. He should have just referred her to another baker right from the beginning. But he had painted himself into a corner and now he was going to have to live with the consequences.

With any luck, he consoled himself, once this cake was made and delivered, he would never have to see Gina again.

That was what he wanted, right? What they *both* wanted. Right?

Shane realized she was looking at him, waiting for him to say something. Oh right, she was waiting for him to come up with a date.

"Wednesday at ten work for you?" he asked.

She had no idea what Sylvie's schedule was like because she hadn't even met with the woman yet. It didn't matter. Whatever Sylvie had to do could be moved around and dealt with. The bride had implied that this cake was all-important to her and meeting Shane was what it was going to take to make it a reality.

"I'll make it work," Gina told him.

And then she finally fled the shop the way she'd been wanting to from the moment she had seen that Shane and Cassidy were one and the same.

Chapter Five

It wasn't until Gina sat down behind the wheel of her car and closed the driver's side door that it finally hit her. When it did, she felt as if she was experiencing the effects of a ten-megaton bomb going off, catching her dead center.

Shane Callaghan.

Wow. After all these years of wondering what had happened to him, after having him haunt her dreams for at least a year of that time, their paths had finally crossed.

Well, at least he hadn't wasted away in some lonely, one-room hunting cabin, pining for her. That had been one of the concerns that had bothered her over the years when she couldn't locate him.

She had really tried to find out what happened to Shane after she had turned him down and he had totally disappeared. But at the time finding someone to ask about him had been impossible. The friends he'd sometimes spent time with had all moved away after graduation to start their new lives. Shane's parents were both dead. She knew he had an older brother, a doctor, but he was working somewhere on the other side of the world. Shane had said something about his brother being part of Doctors Without Borders. Other than the fact that he was proud of him and that his brother's name was Alan, she had no other details.

And now, without any warning, she had found Shane just like that. And she had absolutely no idea how she was supposed to act toward him.

It was almost as if she would have been better off left in the dark.

Stop it, Gina silently ordered. *You're acting as if time just stood still and you're the same two people you were back in college. Shane Callaghan is a totally different person than the boy you were in love with ten years ago. And so are you.*

Gina pushed her car key into the ignition and turned it on. The car rumbled to life as she put her foot on the gas. But it went nowhere. Belatedly, she remembered to release the brake and put the car into Reverse. She backed out of the parking space and within seconds, she was on the road.

For all you know, Shane's got a wife and six kids, she told herself. *He certainly didn't act as if he was still in love with you. You're the one with the problem, not him. C'mon, get over yourself.*

She let out a deep breath as she headed for Sylvie Stevens's apartment to share the news about the wedding cake.

This whole ordeal surrounding the creation of the cake might be a little uncomfortable, but it was certainly doable. She would wind up seeing Shane—what? One, maybe two more times and then, presumably, that would be that. No reason to suppose she would have any more contact with him than that.

She didn't want any more contact—did she? Gina silently asked herself as she flew through a yellow light. No, she silently insisted the next moment, she didn't. Definitely not.

And yet…

There was no "yet," she staunchly maintained. She turned the radio up full blast, leaving no room for a miscellaneous thought to push its way forward. She didn't want to think anymore.

Sylvie had made no secret of the fact that she was thrilled and relieved when her new bridesmaid had announced that she had been able to secure Cassidy and that he would indeed be creating the "wedding cake to end all wedding cakes" for Sylvie's big day.

"But he does have one condition before he can get started creating your wedding cake," Gina said before Sylvie could get too carried away heaping a profusion of grateful words on her.

"Anything short of my firstborn is fine with me," Sylvie said enthusiastically. "And even that's negotiable," she added with a laugh.

It never ceased to amaze Gina how obsessed some people could become about something they had essentially talked themselves into thinking that they wanted.

"Nothing that drastic," Gina assured her client. "Sh—Cassidy wants to meet you," she said, correcting herself at the last moment. "He mentioned something about creating a wedding cake being a highly personal process and he needs to get a sense of you before he can even begin the process."

Sylvie seemed to find nothing unusual about that. The young woman was beaming as she said, "That sounds wonderful. Did you get an appointment for us?"

"Us," Gina repeated. "Then your fiancé is coming with you?" she asked hopefully. This was good, Gina thought. Shane had said that he preferred meeting with both parties. This would at least give him less to complain about.

Sylvie's answer unfortunately shot her down. "No," the bride-to-be answered, slightly confused as to how Gina had reached that conclusion. "You are."

"Me?" Gina asked, surprised that the woman had inserted her in her husband's place.

"Of course," Sylvie answered as if this was a no-brainer. "You're the one who was able to talk Cassidy into doing this. Between you and me," Sylvie said, lowering her voice as if she was trying to avoid eavesdroppers, "I've heard he can be temperamental, and I didn't think I had a prayer of his agreeing. But you obviously found a way to get him to agree."

Gina tried one more time to get her client to change her mind. "But wouldn't you rather have your fiancé with you?"

Sylvie laughed lightly. "Jeffery said I could have any kind of wedding I wanted no matter how over-the-top it was. He said I could spend anything I wanted on it. His only condition was that he didn't have to be involved in it beyond showing up on the big day. He said he trusts me," Sylvie declared happily.

This Jeffery sounded almost too good to be true, Gina thought. Either that, or totally uninterested in the proceedings. For Sylvie's sake, she decided to compromise in her thinking. "You're lucky to have someone so easygoing."

"Oh, I know, I know," Sylvie enthused. "So when do we go see the wizard?" she asked.

Gina couldn't help thinking that Sylvie sounded as eager as a young child anticipating her first visit to see the legendary Santa Claus.

She only wished that she felt half as excited as Sylvie was. But then, this wasn't her wedding, it was Sylvie's. Besides, it was hard to be excited when your stomach was tied up in the kind of knots that would have made any Boy Scout proud.

Gina forced a smile to her lips. Hard as it was to project an air of happiness, she had no intention of raining on Sylvie's parade.

"There's a meeting set up for us for ten Wednesday morning," she told the future bride.

"You'll come by and pick me up?" Sylvie asked her, then added as an afterthought, "Seeing as how you know how to get to his shop and all and I don't."

In this day and age, with GPS available on practically every electronic device except for the kitchen stove, that was not really an excuse. The way she saw it, Sylvie was asking her to drive because she just wanted someone to hold her hand before she met the heralded "Cassidy."

Well, that was what she was being paid for, Gina reminded herself.

The big question here was, just who was going to hold *her* hand when she walked into Shane's shop, Gina wondered.

"Of course I'll pick you up, Sylvie. I'll be at your place by nine fifteen Wednesday morning," Gina promised. "That'll give us lots of time in case we run into heavy traffic."

Or maybe, Gina thought as she drove home shortly thereafter, if she was lucky, there'd be an earthquake just before they left. Nothing fancy, just something that would be large enough to shake everything up and prevent her from going.

The next evening, because the prospect of having to see Shane again the next day was making her feel exceptionally restless and more than a little nervous, Gina did what she always did when something was bothering her to this extent.

She called Tiffany.

Two minutes into the conversation, or maybe only ninety seconds, it all came out. She told her sister all about running into Shane the day before and how she had arrived at the shop totally unprepared for the shock of seeing Shane because she thought she was going to be talking to someone named Cassidy.

Rather than being on her side and supportive the way her sister usually was, Tiffany sounded almost delighted to hear about Shane's unexpected materializing in her life. She was extremely eager to hear all the details.

"Shane Callaghan? Really, Gina? After all this time? What's he look like?" Tiffany asked.

Gina frowned. Her usually sedate sister sounded as if she could barely control herself.

"Older," Gina said guardedly, determined to dole out her information if she was forced to share it.

"Older? C'mon, Gina, my German shepherd looks

older than she did yesterday. Use your words," Tiffany told her. "The guy used to be drop-dead gorgeous. Is he fatter, skinnier, dilapidated-looking, bald—what?"

"No," Gina answered slowly, picking out her words as cautiously as if they each had thorns attached. "None of the above."

"He doesn't look any different, then?" Tiffany questioned in disbelief.

"Well, his cheekbones are a little more prominent and he might have gotten a little more distinguished-looking," Gina allowed slowly. And then she stopped. "You're sighing, Tiffany," she accused. "I can hear it. Why are you sighing?"

"I'm just picturing him in my mind, Gee. He was pretty damn near perfect-looking when you two were going together," Tiffany recalled.

"You're exaggerating," Gina said, although she secretly agreed with her sister's assessment.

"No, I'm not. And I'm not the only one who thought he was perfect—inside and out," Tiffany insisted. "Mom was looking into wedding venues for you two minutes after she'd met him."

"Why would she have done that?" Gina asked. This was the first she had heard of this. "We weren't *that* serious in the beginning."

"Mom was," Tiffany told her simply.

Thinking back, maybe her mother was at that, Gina conceded. She knew that her mother had certainly been disappointed when she'd told her that she and Shane had broken up.

"Don't remind me," Gina said with a sigh that came from deep down in her toes. "Look, do me a favor. Don't tell Mom about this, okay? Don't say anything about my running into Shane. *Or* that I have to see him again to-morrow to finalize everything."

"Don't worry. Mom won't hear it from me," Tiffany responded.

Admittedly, Tiffany felt a little guilty about being evasive and about keeping this setup from her sister. But, she silently argued, this was for Gina's own good.

Tiffany consoled herself with the thought that in the long run, Gina would thank her for this even though it was their mother who had gotten everything rolling.

At least, she thought, she could hope so.

Tiffany crossed her fingers as she hung up.

This time, as she drove into the older shopping center, Gina knew just where to pull up and park in order to have better access to Shane's store.

She also knew exactly what was ahead of her.

Which was why her knees felt as if they had been replaced by two vats of whipped butter and her stomach was threatening to separate her from her deliberately light breakfast.

"Is everything all right?" Sylvie asked her when Gina turned off the engine and made no effort to get out.

Still seated in the passenger seat, the excited bride eyed her uncertainly.

Gina slowly took in a deep breath, trying to steady her nerves.

"Everything's fine," Gina quickly assured her client. "I'm just working out some details in my head," she said in order to cover up her preoccupation.

Sylvie didn't appear convinced. "Should I be worried?"

"No, absolutely not," Gina told her with feeling. *Me,*

on the other hand, who knows? "It's right here." Gina pointed out the little shop as she got out of the driver's seat.

Sylvie was immediately beside her, surveying the entire area. "It's perfect," she cried.

"It *is* charming," Gina agreed.

Opening the door and holding it for Sylvie, Gina heard the same quaint bell announce their entrance. But this time, instead of walking into an empty reception area, she found that Shane was waiting for them.

Rather than wearing a spattered apron over his T-shirt and jeans the way he had when she had seen him the other day, Shane was dressed in a suit. No tie, but he didn't need one. He looked like the picture of a rakish businessman.

Was that for his client's benefit, or hers?

Dial it back, Gina. This isn't about you, remember?

Coming to, Gina realized that introductions needed to be made. "Sylvie Stevens, I'd like you to meet—"

"Cassidy," Shane said, stepping forward. Taking Sylvie's hand in his, he kissed it lightly, as if he had grown up somewhere in France or Italy rather than Southern California.

Sylvie giggled at the display of bygone continental manners. When he released her hand, she held it to her as if savoring their fleeting contact.

Belatedly, Sylvie found her tongue. "I can't begin to tell you how grateful I am that you're going to be making my wedding cake."

"*Creating* your wedding cake," Gina interjected, sparing a glance in Shane's direction.

He looked mildly surprised, then smiled as he inclined his head at her.

"Oh, of course," Sylvie agreed. "Right. Creating it,"

she corrected herself. Partially awestruck and totally thrilled, the bride-to-be was having a hard time not tripping over her own tongue.

Shane turned his magnetic blue eyes on the nervous bride. "It'll be my pleasure," he told Sylvie. "Now, why don't we all sit down and you can tell me about yourself and your lucky groom-to-be," he suggested, gesturing toward a small table off to the side.

A table Gina could have sworn was *not* there the day before yesterday.

Like a woman in a trance, Sylvie allowed herself to be led to the table. She was Shane's totally captive audience.

"Ask me anything you want to know," Sylvie said, giving him carte blanche to ask her any intimate detail he wanted to.

Shane waited until the young woman and Gina were both seated, then took a seat himself. After politely offering them coffee or tea, he began asking a series of what initially seemed to be totally unrelated questions.

As Gina listened, she realized that this wasn't just for show. Shane was actually asking Sylvie questions that, once put together, highlighted the personality and preferences of both the bride and, by proxy, her groom.

Was this just to justify what she assumed was going to be a high asking price or did Shane consider all this really a necessary part to fuel his "creative" process?

The Shane she recalled was as far from a huckster as day was from night, but people, she freely admitted, did change. If Shane had changed for the worse, she couldn't help thinking that it might be at least in part her fault. Had she wound up crushing his soul after all or was she just reading much too much into all this?

She listened in silence and found she couldn't really

make a judgment. Shane *sounded* as if he was being genuine, but that might all be just part of his act. She didn't know.

The entire session took about thirty minutes and that was only because Shane didn't rush his client to give him answers. In addition he would interject pleasantries throughout the entire process.

When it was *finally* over, Gina allowed herself one comment. "I had no idea so much went into making the right sort of wedding cake."

Shane's lips curved ever so slightly in a patient smile. "Creating," he reminded her. "Not making."

"Right. Sorry." Her eyes met his. There was that same warm shiver again, working its way up her spine, getting the better of her. "I keep apologizing," she said.

"I noticed. No need to apologize," he replied. His voice grew less formal as he turned to address Sylvie. "I think I have everything I need to at least get started."

"You mean right now?" Sylvie asked, surprised and wide-eyed.

His smile was tolerant. "No, I wasn't being literal. The creating part won't take place until a couple of days before your cake has to become a reality. What I meant was that I have enough information to begin *contemplating* your cake."

"Why don't I give you my number so that if you come up with any further questions, you can just call me and ask," Sylvie said, looking around for a piece of paper and a pen. She was eager to make this as easy as possible for Cassidy.

"No need," he told Sylvie. "I have Gina's number. If I need to ask anything, I'll call her. After all, as your professional bridesmaid, that is her function." His eyes slowly slid over toward Gina. "Am I right?"

It felt as if he had actually touched her, just the way he had back when they were a couple. It took Gina a second to catch her breath. This was *not* going to be smooth sailing.

"Yes," she answered. "You are. Now, if you have nothing else," she said, rising to her feet, "I believe I have a fitting for a bridesmaid dress." She glanced at Sylvie for confirmation.

"Oh right. You do," Sylvie remembered.

She was on her feet as well, shaking Shane's hand and once again restating her gratitude for his making time for her.

He just smiled warmly at the bride.

So why, Gina thought uneasily, did she feel as if he was actually smiling at her—with a promise of things to come?

Chapter Six

This was the part of her job that Gina usually hated: going into the bridal shop and trying on the bridesmaid dress. As a latecomer, she technically had no right to give any input about the dress that had been selected by the bride for her bridal party.

However, coming in as a bridal "troubleshooter," she felt that she did.

As she stood in the store, looking at herself in the mirror, none of that really mattered right now. Maybe it was all relative, considering the emotional ordeal she had just been through, but she thought that the floor-length gown that Sylvie had selected for the five women in her party was rather flattering.

Mint green, high waisted and formfitting, with a side-slit that went just high enough to be inviting but was still rather tasteful, it was a dress Gina would have picked out for herself—if she actually went to places where a dress like this could be deemed appropriate. Which, sadly, she didn't.

"What do you think?" Sylvie asked, watching Gina for a reaction. "It was Jennifer's dress—my bridesmaid who dropped out of the wedding party. She never came in for her last fitting because she was just too despondent after her breakup."

I know how that feels, Gina thought. *Shane didn't break up with you, you broke up with him, remember?* she reminded herself.

She looked herself over one last time. "It's as if it was made for me," she said. Gina turned away from the three-way mirror to look at the woman who was very obviously waiting for her opinion. "It's lovely. You have very good taste," she told Sylvie. "Usually, I find myself searching for a polite way to explain to the prospective bride that if her bridesmaids all resembled escaped trolls, that wasn't going to put her in the kind of spotlight she was hoping for." She turned back for one more glimpse in the mirrors—and smiled. "But this dress is extremely flattering. Any bridesmaid would be thrilled to be in your wedding party."

"Really?" Sylvie asked, absorbing the compliment like a water-deprived thirsty puppy.

Gina's smile widened as she assured the young woman warmly, "Really."

Sylvie caught her off guard by rushing up and embracing her as if she were a long-lost sister. "Thank you!" she cried. "I just *knew* you'd be good luck for me."

Gina felt it was only right if she pointed out one important fact. "You picked these dresses out before you and I even met each other."

Sylvie waved away Gina's words. "It doesn't matter. I just *feel* that you're going to bring me luck. Look how you fit into Jennifer's dress." She said it as if that was an omen. "And you got Cassidy to agree to—*create* the wedding cake," she said, applying the proper amount of emphasis on the process. "And you're getting me another photographer. Have you found one yet?" she asked, suddenly realizing that problem had yet to be resolved.

"I have, and I'll be talking to him once I finish this fitting. And," she added, looking over her shoulder at the way the gown was hugging her curves as it made its way from her hips to her ankles, "in my opinion, this fitting is officially finished."

Having made the declaration, Gina looked around for the seamstress who had come to this session fully equipped with straight pins and two tape measures. She had used none of the tools of her trade because once the gown was on, it became obvious to everyone that alternations were unnecessary.

Spotting the older woman standing over by another display, Gina looked at her with a silent query evident in her expression.

The seamstress, with her short crop of gray hair, looked as if she had been lifted from central casting and told to play the part of a capable seamstress. The woman, Olga, lifted her thin shoulders in a shrug.

Olga's solemn expression didn't change as she said, "I hate to say it, but I cannot improve on perfect."

Gina took one final look at herself. She couldn't help wishing that Shane could suddenly materialize and see her like this.

She sincerely doubted that he ever would. Most likely on the day of the wedding, he would have his assistants bringing in and setting up whatever "masterpiece" he was going to ultimately "create" for the happy couple.

In all probability he wouldn't be anywhere around the vicinity of the reception.

Now that she thought back on it, Gina suddenly remembered that she *had* heard the name Cassidy mentioned before. But there had never been any photographs of him posing with his creations. All she ever saw were isolated cakes taking center stage and a swirly signature superimposed on them.

His signature, she thought.

How had she missed that?

"The dress is rather perfect," Gina said, agreeing with the seamstress.

"I was referring to the way it fit you," the seamstress emphasized. "You have a good body to work with," the woman added matter-of-factly.

Gina smiled. She didn't think of herself in those terms. Most days she just thought of herself as a workhorse, a pawn piece to stick in to take someone else's place and to hopefully help pull off yet another bride's idea of a perfect wedding.

This compliment, coming unbidden from Olga, was like an unexpected bonus. For just a split second, Gina allowed herself to bask in it.

But then Gina reminded herself that she had people to see and things to do—and miles to go before she could sleep, she added whimsically.

"Thank you," she said to the seamstress. "I needed that."

Olga looked at her as if she didn't know what she was talking about. With another careless shrug she went on to say, "I just tell you what I see." She straightened, gathering the tools of her trade to her. "If I am not needed here, I have other work to do for bridesmaids who are not as fortunate as you are," she announced, her eyes antiseptically sweeping over Gina.

With that, the woman withdrew from the room.

Gina noticed that Sylvie was looking at her as if waiting for instructions. Gina felt amused, recalling other brides that were definitely *not* this easy to work with.

"Let me just change back into my clothes and I'll drop you off at your place," she told Sylvie as she made her way into the changing booth.

"When we get to my place you can stay if you like," Sylvie said, almost shyly extending an invitation to her wedding "fixer."

"I'm having the rest of the girls in the bridal party over and it'll give you a chance to meet them."

She thought that was a good idea, but right now, the timing was off. She needed to get the photographer on board. Once she did, that resolved all the outstanding issues for Sylvie—at least for the moment. They still had a long way to go before the wedding.

"Sounds good," Gina answered. "But I'm going to have to take a rain check for now."

"Are you sure?" Sylvie asked. She moved closer to the changing booth, as if proximity would somehow make Gina change her mind.

Having carefully taken off the bridesmaid gown, Gina now threw on her own clothes. Dressed, she proceeded to meticulously hang up the gown in a garment bag and then zipped the bag up.

"I'm sure. I have a photographer to sweet-talk," Gina reminded the bride.

"Oh, that's right. I forgot about that. Good thing you didn't," she added.

"Well, I can't really forget now, can I? That's what you're paying me for." Coming out of the booth and carrying the dress folded in half on her arm, Gina said, "I just had an idea. When does your bridal shower take place?"

Sylvie paused, thinking. By the look on her face, that was obviously something else that the still somewhat harried bride-to-be had forgotten to ask about.

Thinking now, she remembered. "That would be next weekend. You're invited, of course," she quickly told Gina, then murmured, embarrassed, "You must think I'm an airhead."

Gina was quick to squeeze Sylvie's hand and soothingly reassure her. "Absolutely not. Just a woman with a great deal on her mind as the big day draws closer. I'm just here to help you manage all that," she reminded the bride-to-be.

Sylvie smiled her gratitude. "It's a Jack and Jill shower," she added, watching to see if that bothered her new savior in any way.

But Gina welcomed the news. "Good, that'll give me a chance to meet the groom. The reason I asked about the shower is because I thought you might like having professional photographs taken of the event. Unless your fiancé gave you a cut-off point as far as spending money on the wedding went," she quickly added. She knew that this wasn't part of the usual expense associated with a wedding, but she thought that the added event might help get a photographer engaged at this late date. Offering him more money to shoot bridal party photographs could be a further inducement to say yes.

"No, no limits," Sylvie told her. "Jeffery just wants me happy. And as for your suggestion, I think it's wonderful." Her smile grew with each word she uttered. "I'd love to have professional photographs taken of the party." She impulsively hugged Gina again. "You have just the *best* ideas," she declared with enthusiasm.

"I just want to make this the best wedding possible for you," Gina told her.

An almost starry look entered Sylvie's eyes. "It really is starting to look that way, isn't it?" she said happily.

"Absolutely."

Gina dropped Sylvie off at her apartment.

The meeting with the photographer she had selected didn't turn out the way she had hoped. Like the photographer before him, the photographer she had wanted to hire for this wedding turned out to have a conflict. He had regretfully told her that he wasn't available.

Disappointed but undaunted because she did have several other photographers to check out, Gina drove home and spent her evening poring over their websites. Eventually narrowing her search down to two candidates, she jotted both names down along with their accompanying phone numbers.

She promised herself she'd call the one at the top of the list first thing in the morning.

Worn out, she finally went to bed.

Exhausted, Gina fell asleep before her head even hit the pillow. And then proceeded to have one dream after another, each one involving Shane in some way.

The dreams, some fragments, some feeling as if they were practically feature-length movies, all involved a wealth of warm emotions that insisted on infiltrating her. All through the night Gina found herself vividly reminded of the way she had felt when she and Shane had been going together.

That, in turn, reminded her just how much she had regretted turning Shane down almost from the very moment that she had. Because once her fears had subsided, allowing her to think logically again, she realized that she *did* love Shane and she wanted nothing more than to face forever with him.

But by then it was too late.

Shane had disappeared as if he had existed only in her mind.

The way he did now in the dreams that kept assaulting her brain.

Gina couldn't help thinking that one stupid wrong move had cost her everything.

Regret left a horrible, bitter taste in her mouth.

"Maybe this is our second chance. We can do this over again." Gina could have sworn she heard Shane whispering that to her.

And then suddenly, he was there, right behind her. Wrapping his arms around her and making her feel safe and protected.

The way, she recalled, that she used to.

She was vividly aware of turning around in the shelter of his arms. Aware of her heart pounding wildly as he slowly began to lower his mouth to hers.

Aware of wanting Shane more than she wanted anything else in this life.

She felt whole.

She felt—

With a start, Gina jerked upright in her bed, her heart

pounding double time, threatening to crack right through her ribs.

The room—her bedroom—was still dark with only whispers of an approaching dawn beginning to infiltrate the darkness.

She was alone.

Alone just as she had been ever since she had allowed fear to speak for her all those years ago, thereby eliminating the best thing in her life.

She had no one to blame for this but herself, she thought.

Gina sat up straighter, dragging a hand through her hair. She was trying desperately to get her brain into focus.

C'mon, Gina. Get with it!

There was no sense in going over the same old thoughts she'd had time and again over these last ten years. This was old ground and if she covered it again, nothing new would come of it. She had a job to do, she reminded herself. Sylvie was paying her to make sure she took care of all things associated with the wedding. She certainly wasn't paying her to mourn over her own stupidity.

Kicking her covers aside, Gina got up and made her way into the bathroom.

Maybe a shower would do the trick and bring her around.

She looked like hell, Gina thought, catching a glimpse of her reflection in the bathroom mirror.

"Time to do a little damage control and get back into the game," she ordered her reflection.

This was her eternal penance, Gina thought as she stepped into the shower and turned on the water.

Cold water hit her body with the force of a thousand needles. It made her focus.

She had callously ruined her own prospects and for that she was going to spend the rest of her life making sure that other women got the fairy-tale wedding she had turned her back on.

Gina met with the photographer she had put in first place on her list after her initial candidate said he wasn't available. Happily, this new candidate *was* free for not just the day of the wedding, but he was also available for the bridal shower, as well.

Closing the deal, Gina left the photographer's studio with a firm commitment—and with a brand-new idea.

She realized that part of the reason she was having dreams about Shane was because she had been racking her brain trying to come up with a legitimate reason to go see him again.

She couldn't just go back and apologize to him again about the way she had turned down his proposal. Thinking it over now, that would just seem like she was rubbing salt into his wound. Besides, if she apologized again, in all likelihood, he would just shut her out. She didn't want to grovel. Groveling sent the wrong message to the man, not to mention that it put her in a position of weakness. That was *not* the image she wanted to project, nor did she think that Shane would look at her favorably if that was the way she came across.

That was if he had any sort of a favorable view of her left, she amended.

What this needed, what they *both* needed, was a fresh start, a clean slate. The one thing they still had in common was confections. Sylvie was having a bridal shower and a bridal shower needed refreshments. From everything she had read about Cakes Created by Cassidy he didn't just make wedding cakes. He could make—*create*, she corrected herself—all sorts of different kinds of pastries.

Since he had agreed to do Sylvie's wedding cake, maybe she could prevail on him to handle her bridal shower, as well.

And if he turned the request down, citing how "busy" he was, well at least she would have gotten another opportunity to see him again. And maybe seeing her a few times would hopefully wear him down, make him remember just what it was that had attracted him to her in the first place.

Maybe it would even make him decide that what they'd had was worth giving a second chance.

One step at a time, Gina, she cautioned, trying not to get ahead of herself.

Even so, she did a quick U-turn and instead of going to Shane's shop, she went home first. Although she always dressed nicely, she wanted to put on something *extra*nice. While she was at it, she also wound up freshening up her makeup.

After checking herself over several times and deciding that if she did anything more elaborate, it would wind up looking like overkill, Gina drove to Shane's shop at the shopping center.

Although the distance between her apartment and the shopping center wasn't very far, her palms were damp by the time she pulled her vehicle up in front of his show window.

This was crazy. She hadn't been this nervous even on her first date with Shane.

But there was a lot more riding on this now, she thought.

Turning off the car engine, Gina gave herself one final pep talk and got out of the car.

The same tinkling sound announced her entrance this time as it had the other two times.

The reception area was empty.

A wave of déjà vu washed over her. And then, suddenly, she heard the sound of laughter. Gleeful childish laughter.

The next moment, the door leading from the back area opened and a little girl of about four or five came dashing into the reception area.

The little girl was holding what looked like a measuring spoon gripped tightly in her hand and there were traces of whipped cream outlining her lower lip. There was also some whipped cream on her right cheek.

She stopped in her tracks when she saw Gina. But instead of being afraid, the little girl looked exceptionally comfortable and secure. She offered her a huge smile.

"Hello," Gina said, her interest definitely engaged. "And whose little girl are you?"

"His," the girl answered, pointing just as Shane walked in behind her.

Chapter Seven

Shane quickly crossed the room and made his way over to the little girl. Placing one hand on her shoulder, he made eye contact with her.

"Ellie, you know what I told you about talking to strangers," Shane told her sternly.

But the little girl didn't seem to be intimidated. "You said not to," she answered.

Ellie was usually either in preschool or with the woman he employed as a part-time nanny. But there was no preschool for her today and Barbara, Ellie's nanny, had a doctor's appointment so he had brought Ellie to work with him. It wasn't really a hardship. The little girl loved the shop and moved through it as if it was her own private playground.

At times Ellie could be a little too brave and that concerned him. While Shane didn't want her to grow up frightened, he also didn't want to have to worry about Ellie going off with the first stranger who was nice to her. He was beginning to learn that this wasn't an easy thing to pull off.

Continuing to make eye contact with Ellie, Shane replied, "Exactly."

Ellie peered around him at Gina. "But she looks friendly," the little girl argued in her own defense.

Turning, Shane spared a glance at Gina. "Looks," he said cryptically, "can be deceiving."

"What's de-de-deceiving?" Ellie asked, pleased with herself for getting the word right after two attempts.

"That's when somebody tries to fool you."

It wasn't Shane who answered her. It was Gina. Shane's words had cut into her like a sharp, jagged knife. She truly wished that there was some way she could make what had happened between them up to him, to prove to him how very sorry she was.

But then he really didn't need her to do that, she thought. Shane had obviously moved on. He had a daughter. He might have other children, as well. Now that she looked at the little girl's face, she could easily see the resemblance. The dirty blond hair, the bright blue eyes, and especially when Ellie smiled. That was all Shane.

Without realizing it, Gina glanced down at his left hand. There was still no ring there, but that didn't mean anything. Some men didn't wear wedding rings. Others took theirs off when they worked because they didn't want to risk getting the ring caught on machinery. In this case, that could include appliances.

Searching for neutral ground, Gina smiled at Shane and said, "She's very cute."

Though he doted on Ellie, he pretended to shrug indifferently. "She has her moments," he replied.

He was still pretending to be stern for Ellie's sake. But he couldn't quite pull that off, not when it came to Ellie. Being the tough disciplinarian never really suited him.

He ruffled Ellie's blond curls and she made a face as she ducked her head away.

"You're messing it up," Ellie complained. She raised her hands and with careful movement, she smoothed down her hair.

Gina couldn't help but laugh. "She's all girl, all right," she said to Shane.

Gina wasn't telling him anything he didn't already know. His eyes narrowed a little as he turned to look at Gina. He hadn't been expecting her. It bothered him that she kept catching him off guard.

"She is that," he agreed. "But you didn't come here just to evaluate Ellie." Up until a few minutes ago, she hadn't even known about the little girl's existence, he thought. "What are you doing here?" he asked Gina bluntly.

Making a fool of myself, Gina thought, although she forced a neutral smile to her lips. *Okay, here goes nothing.*

"You know that woman you agreed to make that wedding cake for? Sylvie Stevens," she said in case Shane didn't remember who she was talking about.

"Yes?" he prompted, waiting for her to get to the point.

He deliberately kept any and all emotions out of his voice. As a result, it sounded almost icy cold. Part of the reason for that was because he didn't want her realizing that he hadn't agreed to make the cake for this Sylvie person, he had agreed to make it for her.

Because, despite everything she had put him through, he wanted an excuse to see her again.

Gina cleared her throat and pressed on. "Well, I know this is probably asking for a lot, but she's having a bridal shower this weekend—"

"Doesn't the lady take showers every day?" Ellie asked, curious.

Grateful for the distraction, Gina looked at the little girl. "It's not that kind of a shower, honey. That's what they call a party for a bride before she gets married," she explained.

"Then she doesn't have to get wet?" Ellie asked. She screwed up her face, doing her best to understand.

Knowing how involved things could get when explaining them to Ellie, Shane tactfully suggested, "Ellie, why don't you go in the back and tell one of my assistants that you need someone to play with you?"

Thinking he was shooing the little girl out for her benefit, Gina vetoed the idea. "That's okay," she told Shane and then crouched down to the little girl's level. "I don't mind explaining things. Bridal shower is really a silly name for it," she agreed with Ellie. "I think they call it that because people come to the party and they shower the bride with presents. That means they give the bride presents," she clarified just in case Ellie still didn't understand.

But Ellie understood just fine. Her sky-blue eyes opened wide as the information penetrated.

"Really?" she asked gleefully, clapping her hands together. Her head swirled toward Shane. "Can I have a bridal shower?"

"Not for a long, long time," Gina told her. "Someone has to ask you to marry them first."

"How do I get them to do that?" Ellie asked earnestly.

Bad example to use, Gina realized. She could literally *feel* Shane looking at her. Was he waiting to hear what she was going to say in response, or was he just going to shoot her down without bothering to listen to her say anything else?

But his silence dragged out so she gave Ellie an answer.

"Well, if you're very lucky, you meet a nice boy and the two of you fall in love. After a while, he asks you to marry him and then—"

"Do I hafta wait for the boy to ask me?" Ellie asked, interrupting impatiently. "Can't I ask him to marry me?"

That caught Gina by surprise. It took her a moment to answer. "You can," she told the girl.

"Good, 'cause I don't like to wait," Ellie informed her.

"Well, I'm sorry, kiddo, but you're going to have to wait awhile longer," Shane told the girl. He didn't want any ideas put into that blond little head. "At least thirty years. Maybe more. Now go in the back and play like I told you," he instructed. Seeing Ellie interacting with Gina took him to places he didn't want to go. There was no sense in allowing that to happen.

Ellie made a face, but even at her tender young age, she seemed instinctively to know when not to push. "Oh, okay."

Gina caught herself looking after the little girl almost yearningly as Ellie all but skipped out of the room.

If things had turned out differently—if she hadn't been such a coward, she upbraided herself—that little girl could have been hers. Hers and Shane's.

"She looks like she has a lot of energy," she commented.

"You don't know the half of it," Shane answered. "It's nonstop all day long."

Myriad questions filled Gina's head, questions she couldn't risk asking right now. Things were still very raw and tenuous between them. If she said or asked the wrong thing, she was afraid that Shane would change his mind and back out of making the wedding cake for Sylvie. She couldn't afford to do that to her client just because her curiosity was aroused.

Besides, maybe she didn't really want to hear about Shane and Ellie's mother. She might not be able to handle it. It was one thing to tell herself that she knew Shane had moved on, it was totally another to actually see living proof that he had.

As it was, she was trying to block the sudden ache she felt in the pit of her stomach.

"You said something about a bridal shower?" Shane prompted, the sound of his voice breaking the awkward silence growing between them.

"Yes, I did," she said, forcing herself to come around. "I was wondering if you could possibly see your way to providing some of your pastries for the bridal shower. Nothing unique," she quickly qualified, not wanting to put any undue pressure on him—or give him a reason to turn her down.

"If you don't want anything unique, why don't you just go to your local Costco and get the pastries there?" Shane asked.

She wasn't doing this right, Gina thought. She tried again. "Okay, maybe we do want something unique," she qualified.

And then, because she felt this wasn't going well, Gina stopped and took a deep breath. She couldn't keep tap-dancing around the very large elephant in the room like this any longer. It was obvious that ignoring it wasn't working. She needed to get it out of the way if she had any hopes of making progress.

"All right," she said, bracing herself, "you want the truth?"

Shane's eyes held hers prisoner. "That would be a unique experience," Shane agreed. "Go ahead, tell me the truth," he challenged.

"The truth is I was trying to find an excuse to see you again. The bridal shower seemed like the right way to go." Gina wanted to look away, but she knew that would be a mistake. She needed to tell him this to his face, not address his shadow. "I thought that maybe the more we saw each other, the less awkward it would be."

The silence threatened to engulf them. And then he said, "I guess you were wrong."

Her heart sank. "I guess I was." Gina gathered her courage together. "But I'd just like to go on record to tell you that I'm sorry. That I behaved like an idiot that day you proposed to me because I was afraid of having anything change between us. I thought if we changed one thing, the magic we had would disappear. I realized how dumb that was practically from the moment I pushed you away.

"And I did try to go back and apologize," she stressed, "but by then you'd taken off somewhere. I asked everyone who was still there and no one knew where you were." Her voice throbbed with sincerity. "I tried everything. Your social footprint disappeared completely. But I kept trying anyway. After a year, I finally realized that you didn't want to be found." She pressed her lips to-gether. "I just wanted you to know that," she told Shane.

It was hard to talk when she could feel tears gathering in her throat. But somehow, she had managed.

With that, Gina turned away from him. She was al-most at the door, her hand on the doorknob when she heard Shane ask, "You looked for me for a whole year?"

She tried but she couldn't read his tone. Was Shane mocking her or did he finally believe her? She couldn't tell.

Gina turned around to look at him. "I did. I tried to find your friends but the ones who were still around hadn't seen or heard from you. They were just as sur-prised as I was that you'd vanished." She pressed her lips together, debating telling him this, then decided there was no point in hiding it. "I even filed a missing person's report."

He stared at her, stunned. "You did what? With the police?" he asked incredulously.

She couldn't tell if he was angry or not, but now that she'd said it, she had to give him the details. "I was afraid something had happened to you. I knew I had hurt you, but I didn't think you would just disappear like that with-out telling anyone. That's why I filed the report. But the police couldn't find you either," she said.

She shrugged helplessly. "Eventually, I suppose the missing person's report was filed with all the other un-solved cases and went into missing person's limbo." She took another deep breath, searching his face, waiting for an explanation for his disappearance.

He didn't say anything.

She gathered up her courage again. "I know that you

don't owe me any explanations, but where were you all that time?"

His eyes met hers. He could still read her, he thought. That was oddly comforting. "You were really worried?"

"I thought if something hadn't happened to you, then maybe you had done something to yourself and that it was all my fault," she said, letting out a shaky breath. She hadn't admitted that to anyone before. It felt good to finally get it out. "You have no idea what went on in my head."

"I guess I didn't," he admitted. "After you turned me down, I couldn't deal with it. I just wanted to get away, so I left. Alan told me that he welcomed any help I could offer. He was a doctor volunteering his services in the poorest region in Uganda," Shane explained. "There was nothing keeping me here any longer so I went."

She should have known. Shane had found something good to do with his life, something that hadn't even occurred to her.

"And did what?" she asked, hungry for any details he could spare her.

He shrugged. "Anything and everything. I cleaned wounds, carried water, drove hundreds of miles for much-needed supplies when they became available. I did whatever my brother's small band of selfless doctors and nurses needed. I guess you could say I was their Man Friday," he added with a touch of self-deprecating humor.

Well, that explained why she couldn't find him. But not how he got to his present position. "So how did you get from there to being a renowned pastry chef?" she asked in wonder.

He wasn't about to get into that right now. He couldn't.

"It's a long story," he told her. "And I have a full sched-ule."

She nodded. She hadn't expected him to tell her as much as he had.

"Right. I won't keep you," Gina told him, pushing her purse's strap up her shoulder.

She was almost out the door again when she heard him ask, "When's the bridal shower again?"

She swung around, grateful for the chance to ex-change a few more words with him. "This coming Sunday. At two. It's local," she added, then crossed her fingers as she told him, "You're welcome to come."

"To a bridal shower?" he questioned, bemused.

"It's a Jack and Jill shower," she said. Thinking he might not know the term, she started to explain. "That's when—"

"I know what that is," Shane said, cutting her short. "But I'll pass. On the shower, not on bringing the pas-tries," he clarified.

At least that was something, she thought. "Really? Sylvie will be thrilled. And I was serious about the invi-tation," she reiterated, giving it another shot. She wanted them to at least be friends. "You could bring your wife."

That caught him totally off guard. "My what?"

"Your wife," she repeated. "The more the merrier." Did that sound as trite to him as it did in her head? she wondered.

Rather than answering, he asked his own question. "What makes you think I have a wife?"

"Ex-wife?" Gina asked. Had she made a mistake, or didn't he want to talk about his situation? When he just went on looking at her, she felt she had to explain why she had assumed he was married. "Isn't Ellie your daughter?"

"Look, I've got a full schedule—" he began, attempting to dismiss this woman who had materialized out of his past.

"I know," she assured him quickly. "I didn't mean to keep you, I just—"

A quick getaway was impossible with Gina. He should have remembered that. "You still don't let me talk, do you?" he marveled. "I was going to say that I have a busy schedule, but if you'd like to get a cup of coffee with me say about six, maybe we can talk then."

Talk? He wanted to talk. Hope sprang up in her chest. Maybe they *could* be friends after all. She needed to re-arrange a couple of things to make the meeting, but there was no way she was going to stand him up.

"I'll be here at six," she told him.

"Not here," Shane told her. "Why don't you meet me at the coffee shop at the other end of the shopping center. Molly's," he told her in case Gina was unaware of the place.

"Molly's at six. Got it. I'll be there," Gina promised. She had an urge to hug him, but she refrained. She didn't want to scare him off.

She walked out of the small shop feeling happier than she remembered feeling in a long time. She had no delusions that having coffee with Shane would lead to anything else. It wasn't going to change anything. The man was married or at the very least had been involved with Ellie's mother and still might be. Knowing his personality, she didn't think that there was any chance that she would be able to suddenly pick up with him after all these years, especially if there was someone else in the picture. And she didn't want to ruin whatever it was that he had going on.

She had missed her chance and she had to make her peace with that all over again. But she did want the man to be happy. That hadn't changed.

"I have wonderful news," she told Sylvie, calling her client once she got into her car. "I talked to…Cassidy," she said, stopping herself from referring to him as Shane. "And he said that he would be happy to make the pastry refreshments for your bridal shower."

"Oh, Gina, you really are a miracle worker!" Sylvie gushed.

"No, not really." She didn't want to take any credit that wasn't due to her. "He wasn't all that hard to convince. Now that he's handling your wedding cake, I think he feels as if he has a stake in your wedding, as well."

"He wouldn't be doing the wedding cake if it wasn't for you. I'm going to tell all my friends about you—some of them aren't married yet," she added. "With any luck, you'll be getting so much business coming your way, you won't have time to breathe."

"Sounds good to me," Gina said.

This way, if she'd be busy she wouldn't have time to think about the one who got away and what a mistake she'd made pushing him out of her life.

Chapter Eight

Gina shifted in her seat and looked down at her watch again. If she didn't know that it was impossible, she would have said that her watch had stopped. But it certainly felt that way because the hands on her wristwatch hadn't moved since the last time she had looked at it.

Or the time before that.

She had made sure that she'd gotten here at five fifty, arriving ten minutes earlier than the time they had agreed upon. It wasn't her habit to arrive early, but she didn't want to take a chance on finding herself stalled in traffic. Granted this wasn't LA with its soul-sucking traffic jams, but Orange County wasn't exactly smooth sailing during rush hour, which wasn't an hour but more like three. Or four.

The last thing she wanted was to have Shane walk into the coffee shop at six and not find her there. With her luck, he would wind up jumping to the very logical conclusion that she had decided not to come and see him after all.

He didn't come in at six.

She had been sitting here at this table for two for almost thirty minutes now, Gina thought, staring at the analog numbers that were flashing across her watch. What if *he* wasn't coming? What if Shane had thought better of having her meet him for coffee and had just decided not to show up?

How long did she have to sit here before she finally gave up?

There were a million reasons why he wouldn't show up. But none that she could come up with that would keep him from calling and letting her know that he wasn't coming.

Maybe it was just a simple matter of getting even, her mind whispered.

No, Shane wasn't like that, she argued the next moment.

She was thinking of the *old* Shane, Gina reminded herself. What did she know about what the new Shane was like?

Maybe this *was* payback. Maybe he wanted to pay her back for breaking his heart the way she had when she had so abruptly and thoughtlessly turned him down.

She saw the server behind the counter who had made her coffee drink looking at her with pity in her eyes. She was so obviously waiting for someone.

What was she doing here anyway? Gina silently demanded. If she had a lick of sense left, she'd get up and walk out instead of sitting here like some kind of a mindless robot.

But despite her silent pep talk, she just couldn't get herself to get up and leave, couldn't get herself to give up the hope that Shane was just running late. After all, he *had* told her that he had a busy schedule.

In addition to his work, there was that little girl of his. What if the reason he was late had something to do with her?

So she remained sitting at the table, silently making up excuses for Shane and all but jumping out of her skin every time the entrance door opened. And each time it did, she could feel her heart sinking, dropping down into her stomach with a thud because it wasn't Shane.

This couldn't go on indefinitely, she told herself. She could only nurse her overpriced coffee for so long. It was almost all gone and she couldn't just continue sitting here once it was finished. She knew that the store had a strict policy about loitering. She supposed she could always order another container, but she had never developed a taste for these high-caloric drinks.

And then, at six forty-two when she had finally convinced herself to get up and leave the shop, the front door opened and this time it wasn't some stranger coming in. It was Shane.

Maybe it had something to do with the fact that she had consumed a large container of designer coffee while she'd waited, but her mouth suddenly went incredibly dry. So dry that she was worried her tongue was hermetically sealed to the roof of her mouth.

She raised her hand halfway so he could see where she was, although the place wasn't *that* big.

He'd quickly scanned the area. Seeing Gina, Shane crossed to her small table over in the corner. He nodded at her and spared her the barest hint of a smile.

"Sorry I'm late," he told her.

She was about to say something flippant about just having gotten there herself, but she decided against it. She didn't want to start off their renewed relationship with a lie.

So instead Gina merely nodded at his apology. "I'm sure you have your reasons for being late, and besides," she stressed, "this isn't anything formal. It's just two old friends getting together for coffee." She watched his face to see if he agreed with her, but she couldn't read his expression.

"Is that what you think?" he asked her. It wasn't a challenge, it was a simple question. "That we're old friends?"

Gina felt as if she was trying to make her way across a tightrope. Determined, she pushed on. "I think we could be. We were once," she reminded him.

"Were we?" Shane questioned. And then, with a shrug, he changed the subject. "I'd better go get some coffee. They don't like people just sitting around without buying anything."

With that, Shane got up and walked over to the counter. He placed his order, then, to her surprise, he came back to the table to wait for that order to be filled. She would have thought that he'd use the excuse of waiting for his drink to continue standing by the counter rather than to sit with her.

Maybe there *was* hope, she thought.

Which was why she said, "We were," as Shane sat back down.

He looked at her blankly. She realized that he had lost the thread of their conversation—or was pretending he had.

"We were what?" Shane asked.

"Friends. You asked if we were friends just before you went to place your order. I'm answering your question. We were." Her voice grew more confident as she went on to make her point. "We were friends before anything ever developed between us."

This was killing her, this limbo she suddenly found herself lost in. Did he forgive her? Hate her? She couldn't tell and the not knowing was seriously adding to this agitated state she felt growing within her. One minute she was hopeful, the next she was courting despondency.

"Why did you ask me here?" she asked. She thought she had convinced herself that just being able to see him was good enough, but it wasn't. Not when she wasn't sure where she stood with Shane.

He was quiet for a moment, as if deciding whether to answer her or not. And then he asked, "Did you really file a missing person's report on me?"

At least this she could address. "Yes, I did. I was desperate and I'd run out of ideas on how to find you. You'd just packed up and disappeared," she reminded him. "It was like you didn't exist, like I had just conjured you up in my mind. Except that I hadn't."

"And you felt what, guilty?" Shane guessed, his eyes intently on her.

The server at the counter called out his name and he rose. "Hold that thought," Shane told her as he went to get his drink.

When he returned, Gina answered his question. "Guilty, scared, angry. You name it, I felt it," she said honestly. "It was like everything suddenly stopped and wouldn't start up again until I could find out what happened to you."

"But you just said you didn't find out," he reminded Gina.

"No," she agreed. "I didn't. One day I realized that my living in limbo was getting to my mother and the rest of my family, so I forced myself to snap out of it." She sighed. None of this had been easy at the time. "I pulled myself together, got a job, then got another job until I finally decided that what I had studied in school really wasn't me. None of that was me. So I found something else to do with my life."

He took a sip of his drink before saying anything. When he did, it wasn't exactly a revelation. "And you became a professional bridesmaid."

She couldn't tell if he was mocking her choice or if he was surprised by it. In either case, taking offense wouldn't get her anywhere, so she decided to poke fun at herself instead.

"You know the old saying. Those who can, do, those who can't, teach," she told him.

He nodded. And then he took her completely by surprise as he told her, "I guess I wanted to see you so I could apologize."

She weighed her words carefully, knowing that if she responded the wrong way, she would succeed only in chasing him away. But she did need to know why he thought he needed to apologize to her.

"For?"

"For disappearing without telling you where I was going." He understood now that it must have been hard for her to deal with. "In my defense, I didn't think you much cared."

"Of course I cared." It was an effort to keep her voice down, but what Shane had just said was completely ridiculous. "Just because I didn't want to get married the second we were out of school didn't mean I didn't care, that I didn't love you." For the first time, she looked directly into his eyes, searching for the man she had loved. How could he have doubted that even for a second? "The exact opposite was true."

"And you decided to show me how much you loved me by turning me down," he told her. He was highly skeptical of her protest.

"I didn't turn you down, not really. Not in the forever sense." She could see he didn't believe her. "I was stalling," she explained.

His brow furrowed as he tried to make sense out of what she was saying. Despite the number she had done on his heart and his ego, heaven help him but he did still love her.

"Stalling?" he questioned.

"I was afraid that if we changed the dynamic we were in, you'd eventually realize that you'd made a mistake." She could tell by the look on his face that he didn't understand, but she went on. "That you'd realize that you really didn't want to be married to me and then I'd lose you. I just wanted to keep everything the way it was a little longer."

"What kind of twisted logic is that?" he asked, shaking his head at what he felt was the sheer mind-boggling stupidity of it all.

"My logic," she said simply. "Don't forget, I was twenty-two, fresh out of college with no real-life experience."

Shane gazed into his cup and at the fading foam for

what seemed like an inordinate amount of time. And then he finally looked up at her.

He supposed, seeing it from her point of view, he could sort of understand what she was saying. But she should have come to him with that, not made him feel as if she was throwing cold water on his plans.

They had both made mistakes. And their lives had changed because of it.

"In hindsight, maybe I should have left you a note," he conceded. "But I was so hurt by your flat-out refusal that I just wanted to get away from the scene of my disaster. I wanted to put as much distance between us as possible." An ironic smile curved his mouth. "And then my brother showed up on my doorstep. He'd come for my graduation."

"I don't remember meeting your brother at graduation," Gina said.

"That's because Alan's flight got delayed. He wound up arriving two days late—just after you had turned me down."

Gina winced. With all her heart, she wished she could be able to relive that day. She'd do it all differently now.

"Alan saw something was wrong. Instead of giving me a pep talk, he offered me a way to see beyond my own small world. He asked if I wanted to come back with him to Uganda and help people who really needed help, people who had nothing. Before I knew it, I said yes and I was on a plane, heading for Uganda."

"You could have written," Gina told him.

Her voice wasn't accusing, she was just pointing out the fact that he could have found a way to get in contact with her and let her know what he was doing. He didn't even have to call. Just a simple note would have been enough. A simple note would have spared her a world of grief.

But then, she had also caused him grief, Gina reminded herself. So maybe in his mind, that made them even.

"I could have," Shane acknowledged, and looking back, he knew he should have. But at the time, he wasn't thinking clearly. "But I was angry and hurt and thought you didn't care. And then, once I got there, I was just too caught up in what needed doing to take the time to write. Life in that country is totally different than what we're used to over here. I found I had no time to think about myself. Or you."

He paused for a moment and looked at her. "I guess that was the whole point, not to think about you."

His words reverberated within her. Though she wanted to fault Shane, she really couldn't. Gina now understood why he had felt the way he had.

There was something about his story that didn't quite add up as far as she was concerned. "How long have you been back?"

"Three years," he answered.

And if she was any judge of ages, his daughter was four. Which meant that he had gotten together with the girl's mother almost five years ago. Not exactly the solitary life he was painting.

"Well, it seems like you must have had time to think about someone," Gina said.

He finished the last of his coffee and set down the container. "I'm not sure what you're getting at."

"Ellie's mother," Gina answered. She deliberately kept any accusation out of her voice. But for her own sake, she needed to get this straightened out. "You must have found time for her. Was Ellie's mother a nurse?" Gina was trying to piece together his life as best she could. Shane wasn't exactly a font of information.

"Yes," he replied, recalling the woman. "Ellie's mother was a nurse."

It was like pulling words out of his throat, she thought impatiently. "And did she come here with you when you left Uganda?"

"No." The word rang with finality. And then he told her, "Ellie's mother is dead."

Gina was instantly filled with regret. Here she was, being jealous and Shane was dealing with a tragedy. "Oh, I'm so sorry, Shane. What happened?" The moment she asked, she realized how intrusive her question was. "You don't have to tell me if you don't want to, but no matter what you think of me, I'm here for you if you want to talk. You have to believe me when I tell you that I have always wanted you to be happy. You deserve to be happy."

Gina paused, but he wasn't saying anything. Shane wasn't answering her questions or commenting on anything she'd just said. Had he decided to give her the silent treatment?

"Is that why you're back?" she pressed. "To try to make sure that you give your daughter a better life over here?"

Shane debated just letting her go on thinking that, but now that they were finally attempting to clear the air, he couldn't allow the lie to continue. It wouldn't be fair to his brother.

"Ellie's not my daughter," he told her.

She looked at him, stunned. Why was he saying that? "Sure she is," she told him. Maybe she'd believe what he was saying if the little girl didn't have all his features. "Ellie looks just like you."

"That might be," he allowed. "But she's not my daughter. Ellie's my niece."

Now Gina was really stunned. "She's your what?"

"My niece," Shane repeated. "She's my brother's daughter."

It still wasn't making any sense to her. "And your brother's all right with you bringing Ellie back to the States?"

Shane laughed dryly. It surprised him that Gina was so concerned about his brother, seeing as how she hadn't even met Alan. "He probably would be if he had a say in anything. But he's not saying anything these days. Alan's been dead for three years." He saw the stunned sympathy on Gina's face and just for a moment he felt close to her the way he had all those years ago. But then that feeling faded. "He and his wife were both killed on their way to bring medicine to some of the villagers."

"Car accident?" she asked in a hushed voice.

He shook his head. "No, it was as a result of an uprising. The locals were challenging the people currently in power. As it turned out, Alan and his wife, Mandy, were caught in the crossfire. The old jeep they were driving exploded when a stray bullet hit the gas tank." He walled himself off from the details he was telling her. He couldn't function otherwise. "I buried their charred bodies, grabbed Ellie and got on the first plane back to the States.

"I was lucky because our parents had set up a large trust fund for both of us. When I came back, I used my share to help set up my business and finance it."

"Cake creating?" she questioned. She was still having a hard time wrapping her head around that. "How did you come up with that?"

"I found out I had a knack for baking while I was over there with Alan and his wife. The locals only thought of food as a way to survive. Cakes and pastries were unimaginable treats for them. My first efforts weren't too great," he recalled with a smile. "But I got better at it. And I got hooked on the mesmerized expressions on their faces when they devoured what I'd baked for them. So whenever I could—and we had the supplies—I'd bake something. I found that it helped fulfill me.

"When I came back with Ellie, I knew I needed something that would make me feel whole again. My own business where I could keep her around so that she wouldn't feel abandoned. After all, she'd lost her parents when she was only a little more than a year old and I was the only family she had. Her mother, Mandy, had been an orphan," he explained. "It was one of the things that she and my brother bonded over. That and their desire to help people," he added with pride.

"Anyway, creating cakes seemed like the perfect solution to me as far as having my own business went," he concluded. "Any more questions?" he asked.

Gina shook her head. For once in her life, she found herself utterly speechless.

Chapter Nine

Given Gina's personality, Shane was surprised when she didn't say anything in response. "Did I overwhelm you?"

Managing to collect herself, Gina said, "No. It's just a lot to process." She let out a long breath. "But you did answer all my questions." She thought about everything he had just told her. "You do have a lot going on," she freely acknowledged. "What with running your own business and being a single parent—did I get that right? You *are* a single parent?" she asked, having really no idea how he saw himself in this situation.

Did Ellie think he was her father, or had he told the little girl that he was her uncle? Gina didn't want to take a chance on messing anything up for him by making the wrong reference around the little girl.

"Single uncle," Shane corrected. "Ellie knows I'm her

uncle. I've shown her pictures of her dad and her mother ever since she was old enough to recognize faces. She knows all about how she came to live with me here in Southern California."

That must have been hard for him in many ways, Gina thought. It had to be painful talking about his late brother's death and yet he'd had to have kept it simple enough for his niece to understand.

"That's very progressive of you," Gina told him.

Shane merely shrugged. For him there had been no other option. "Lies have a way of bogging you down. It's much easier in the long run to stick with the truth. And if that was your subtle way of asking me if there's someone currently in my life over three feet tall," he said with just a hint of a smile, "there isn't. Between raising Ellie and running my business, there's just no time for anything else."

After saying that, Shane rose to his feet. He'd done what he came to do. He'd wanted to apologize to Gina for being so cold and abrupt with her earlier. Now that he had, it was time to leave.

Gina took the hint and got up from the table. Grateful that Shane had finally opened up a little to her, she didn't want this to be the last time that they talked like this. Yes, he was taking care of the pastries for Sylvie's shower and the cake for her client's wedding, but she really didn't want that to be the end of it. There had to be a way for them to stay in touch.

She thought of the little girl he was raising. If he was anything like some of her friends, half the time he probably had no idea what he was doing. Maybe he could use a little supportive help. After all, he had said that there was no other family for him to turn to for help or emotional support.

"Listen, I enjoyed clearing the air like this," Gina began. Shane nodded and turned to walk out. She put her hand on his arm to stop him for a second longer. "If you find that you ever do need help with Ellie, you have my number. Don't hesitate to call me. I'm really good with kids."

Shane didn't respond. He walked with Gina to the shop's entrance, then held the door open for her.

"I thought you were so busy," he finally said once they were outside.

"I am," she assured him. "But I always find a way to make time for the important things."

"I'll keep that in mind," Shane responded.

Gina didn't know if he meant it or if Shane was just trying to placate her. She searched for something more to say, wanting him to stay there with her just a little bit longer.

"I appreciate you taking the time to get together with me and answering all of my questions." She knew she was repeating things, but for the moment it felt as if her brain had completely dried up. "I really did enjoy talking with you."

They were outside just beyond the coffee shop now and Shane was standing very close to her. So close that she could feel her skin warming as that old feeling that only he could create within her began to churn, taking possession of her entire being.

He was so close to her, she could feel his breath on her face—or was that wishful thinking?

Even so, for a split second, she thought Shane was going to kiss her. The very idea made her pulse begin to accelerate, causing her heart to pound. She found herself willing him to kiss her.

But then, as if breaking the spell, Shane took a step back from her. And just like that, the moment was gone.

"Yeah, well, I decided that you deserved an explanation," he said very casually. Rousing himself, Shane told her, "I guess I'll be seeing you at the shower."

Gina smiled at him widely, doing her best to sound nonchalant. "Absolutely. I'll be the woman running back and forth, doing my best to make sure everything is going smoothly," she said with a laugh.

The sun was so bright where they were standing, it was weaving golden streaks through her hair. For just an instant, Shane found himself catapulted back a decade. Feelings were attempting to work their way in.

He forced himself to block those memories. That trusting man with the loving heart was gone now.

"That sounds pretty exhausting," Shane commented on her description.

"It is," she agreed. "But it's also pretty rewarding in its own way."

Gina had almost slipped and used her usual line about helming the weddings: that there was nothing like knowing that she helped make someone's dream of a perfect wedding come true. She knew that would only remind Shane that she had torpedoed *his* dream of their wedding as well as their future together.

So she forced a cheerful smile to her lips and said, "Tell Ellie I said hi and that she's a very lucky little girl."

He knew where she was going with this and he wasn't about to let her flatter him. "I'm the lucky one," Shane contradicted. "Taking care of her gives my life purpose."

And then, like a polite stranger, he was putting his hand out to her. "Goodbye, Gina."

"Goodbye." The words all but stuck to the roof of her mouth.

She put her hand in his and shook it, thinking how painfully civilized this all seemed.

As they parted and went their separate ways, she was back to wondering if perhaps Shane still hadn't forgiven her.

Or, if he had, for some reason he hadn't done it completely.

She needed to find a way to have Shane look at her the way he used to before she'd allowed her insecurities to ruin everything. Gina desperately wanted to turn back the clock because somewhere along the line, in that brief encounter they'd just had over overpriced coffee, she realized all too clearly that she still loved him.

It wasn't just a matter of wanting something she couldn't have, thereby making it more desirable. This was a matter of bringing to attention what she had known all along in the back of her mind. That when she had fallen in love with Shane the first time, it was meant to be forever.

Maybe that was what had frightened her so badly, causing her to make the worst mistake of her life. She loved Shane so fiercely, she was afraid that he couldn't possibly love her the same way. And when he had impulsively proposed to her right after graduation, she was certain he'd regret it before the ink had time to dry on their license.

Afraid of having her heart broken, she'd turned down the proposal. But not the man. However, all he knew was that she had turned him down and that was where all their trouble started.

It was suddenly all so clear to her now, like an epiphany coming out of nowhere and dawning on her.

Now all she had to do was find a way to explain it to Shane. In order to get Shane to listen to her, she needed to get him to be open to what she had to say.

That would require finesse.

She bit her lower lip. Right now, the way to Shane's heart was through Ellie. Since she thought the little girl was adorable, this wouldn't really involve any deception on her part—just a clever approach.

Gina was smiling broadly, humming to herself by the time she got home.

Her smile lasted long enough for her to open her front door and walk in. That was when her cell phone suddenly began playing the first few bars of "Happy Days Are Here Again," letting her know that she'd just received a text message.

Hoping that Shane had had a change of heart and wanted to get together, Gina opened her phone to discover that the text wasn't from him at all.

It was from Sylvie.

Her current client had texted "9-1-1" followed by five exclamation points.

Rather than exchanging a whole slew of text messages, she thought it would just be simpler to call the bride-to-be instead.

"Hi, Sylvie, it's Gina." Anything else she was about to say was tabled when she heard the sob coming from the other end of her call.

"Oh, Gina, thank God! This is awful. You've just got to help me!" Sylvie cried.

The way Sylvie's voice was rising and falling in between sobs, Gina guessed that the woman was pacing, which only seemed to add to her agitation.

"That's what I'm here for," Gina told her cheerfully, her soothing voice cutting through the sobs. "What seems to be the problem?"

"It's not a problem, it's a total disaster!" Sylvie wailed.

Okay, Gina thought, rephrasing her question. "What is the disaster?"

Sylvie took a moment to get her voice under control before proceeding. "Well, you know I was supposed to get married in St. John's Church," the woman said, her voice still bordering on hysterical.

"Yes?" Gina encouraged.

"Well, Father Joseph said we can't use the church. Gina, it's too late to get another church. The wedding's in less than three weeks!"

Sylvie sounded as if she was on the verge of having a complete meltdown. Gina summoned her calmest voice and spoke gently to the young woman. "I know when the wedding is, Sylvie. Take a deep breath," she counseled, "and then tell me exactly what Father Joseph said to you. *Why* can't you use the church? Whatever the reason is, I'll fix it." She knew the unrealistic promise was the only way to at least partially calm the woman down.

"Because there's a huge hole in the roof!" Sylvie cried.

Well, that definitely was a reason, Gina thought. But this wasn't making any sense. Holes don't just suddenly appear.

"How did it happen, Sylvie?" Maybe the bride was exaggerating, she thought hopefully. She just needed to get to the bottom of this.

"You know that big wind that picked up after midnight last night?" Sylvie said, her voice hitching as she explained. "The big elm tree next to the church, one of its branches broke and went right through the roof. It's a disaster," she sobbed again. "Father Joseph said it wouldn't be safe to conduct the wedding in the church. He's even suspending all the masses at the church until they can come up with the funds to pay for someone to repair the roof."

Gina waited for more. When Sylvie didn't add anything, Gina said, "And that's it?" Surely there had to be an insurance policy to cover this, she thought.

"What do you mean 'and that's it?'" Sylvie cried, stunned. "That's *everything*! All my life I've dreamed of having a big church wedding and now it's not going to happen." She was sobbing again. "The wedding's off!" she declared miserably. "I can't get married!"

"Don't go canceling anything yet," Gina warned her soothingly. "Let me see what I can do."

"You fix roofs?" Sylvie questioned in disbelief.

She thought of Tiffany's husband. Eddie was a contractor. He had to be able to get someone for this job. "Not directly," Gina answered, her mind going a mile a minute. "Just hang in there. I'll get back to you in the morning."

"What am I supposed to do until morning?" Sylvie cried, back on the edge again.

"Sleep comes to mind."

"Sleep? How am I supposed to sleep when my wedding's disintegrating right in front of me?" Sylvie wailed.

She was really earning her fee this time, Gina thought. "Sylvie, getting worked up isn't going to change anything. Let me handle this."

"And you'll call me to tell me what's happening?" the overwrought bride asked nervously.

"Yes. As soon as I can get it to happen," Gina told her pointedly. "Now please, get some rest and let me do my job."

Gina paused, waiting to see if Sylvie had anything else she wanted to ask or say. For the moment, the bride-to-be's ragged breathing had subsided. She was breathing evenly and, for the moment, she was silent. Gina took that as her cue to terminate the call.

The second she ended the connection, she initiated a call to her sister. She counted the number of rings in her head, hoping she wasn't going to wind up talking to Tiffany's voicemail.

She heard Tiffany come on the line just after the fourth ring. Thank goodness!

"Tiffany, I need your help," Gina told her. "I have a four-alarm emergency on my hands."

Tiffany was perplexed when she responded. "A personal emergency or a professional bridesmaid emergency?" her sister asked.

"The latter," Gina told her.

"And just how does this professional bridesmaid emergency involve me?" Tiffany asked.

She knew she had to word this carefully. "How would your wonderful husband want to have his spot in heaven guaranteed?" Gina asked.

Tiffany sighed. "Well, to begin with, it would help if you spoke English."

Gina gave her the short version. "The church where my latest client was all set to get married has suddenly closed its doors to everyone because, thanks to that freak storm last night, they have a huge hole in their roof where the tree branch landed." She was hoping the situation was better than it sounded, but until she went out to investigate it herself, she had to rely on what Sylvie had told her.

"Well, unless that hole is the size of an abyss, I'm sure they can have it fixed," Tiffany told her.

"They probably can," Gina agreed, "but I got the impression that the congregation needs to raise the funds first and if that's the case, that's going to take time."

It dawned on Tiffany where her sister was going with this. "And you want Eddie to fix it for free," she guessed. "Gina, I can't ask him to—"

"Not for free," Gina insisted. "It's probably covered by insurance. But if there's a problem, I'm sure that Father Joseph is an honest man. Once he gets those parishioners back in their pews and starts passing around the collection plate, Eddie will start seeing the money come rolling in. In the meantime, he'll have the good feeling of knowing that he did something noble for his local church. I've seen his people do work. It takes them three days for a whole roof. This is only part of a roof. Piece of cake," she pleaded.

"I don't know, Gina…"

She could hear her sister biting her lower lip in indecision the way she did when they were kids. Gina tried to close the gap. "Did I mention it's an emergency?" she stressed.

"You did," Tiffany answered.

"I can come over right now and talk to Eddie myself about this," Gina offered. She liked her brother-in-law and for the most part, they got along well.

"Please don't," Tiffany said, vetoing the idea. She was being protective of her husband. The last thing she wanted was to be caught in the middle. "You're like a pit bull. Once you clamp your jaws down on something, you don't let go until you've worn the person down."

Gina laughed at the image. "You say that like it's a bad thing."

"All depends on what you're clamping down on," Tiffany answered wearily. "Let me talk to Eddie about this. I'll wait until he's receptive and then broach the subject with him."

"Don't wait too long," Gina cautioned. "We're fighting the clock on this one."

"What's your alternative?" Tiffany asked. "Doing it yourself?"

"I am handy," Gina pointed out.

"Right," Tiffany scoffed. "Hold on to your tool belt, Gee. There's a world of difference between banging a nail into a wall and repairing a roof. I'll call you after I talk to Eddie."

"Tell him a lot of people's happiness is at stake here," Gina added, hoping that would do the trick. Eddie was a good guy.

Tiffany laughed. "I guess Mom's not the only one who knows how to wield guilt like it's an ancient saber," she said to her sister.

"Not guilt," Gina corrected. "In this case it's just simple fact. If the roof isn't fixed, the church'll remain closed. If the church remains closed, then my bride and her groom have nowhere to get married. I gathered that neither city hall nor a backyard are alternative venues in this case. So, if they don't get married—"

"I get the picture," Tiffany said wearily, stopping her sister before she could get too carried away. "Now hang up so I can go and nag my husband into doing this."

"No, not nag. Put him in a good mood and *then* ask him to do it, remember?" Gina said, reminding her sister of what Tiffany had told her more than once.

"Since when did you get so good at playing the husband/wife game?" Tiffany asked.

"I've been taking notes, watching you," Gina teased. "Now go and plead my case with that skillful contractor of yours before I decide to do this job myself."

Gina found herself talking to dead air. Smiling, she put her phone down. "Thanks, Tiffany," she murmured. "I owe you one."

Chapter Ten

Why was it that she had all this fortitude and the courage of her convictions when she had to sell her unusual abilities to total strangers, but when it came to approaching Shane and his niece, Gina felt her steel backbone suddenly dissolving until it had the consistency of lukewarm water?

After all, she wasn't coming to see him in order to ask Shane to do anything other than what he had already agreed to do. As a matter of fact, she thought as she slowly made her way from her parked car to the entrance of his shop on extremely rubbery legs, she wasn't asking him to do anything at all.

She was coming by to bring a peace offering of sorts. It wasn't even for him. It was for his niece, Ellie. Granted it was a thinly veiled attempt to make friends with the little girl.

Kids, especially those under ten, had always been her

weakness. Maybe because she'd longed to have kids of her own almost from the time that she was old enough to be able to have them.

Yes, she admitted, stepping up to the sidewalk, there was a small part of her that thought if she made friends with Ellie then talking with Shane would become that much easier, but that wasn't her primary focus for coming here. The little girl looked as if she needed something to play with, something to divert and hold her attention while she was here at the shop. The last time she was here, it occurred to Gina that Shane was obviously too busy to spend the kind of time with his niece that she needed.

In any case, what did she have to lose giving Ellie this gift? At the very least, Shane would just shoot her down and make her leave, although she hoped that he'd keep her offering and let Ellie have it.

Unless, of course, he was still secretly harboring a grudge.

Gina shifted the gift to the other side, putting her hand on the doorknob.

Okay, here goes nothing.

Taking a deep breath, she opened the door and walked into the airy shop.

The bell overhead tinkled, announcing her presence, although that wasn't necessary this time. Shane was out in the showroom, talking to a heavyset woman who was punctuating every word she uttered with a profusion of animated hand gestures. Gina saw him looking in her direction when the bell announced her entrance and for a second, she thought that Shane almost looked relieved to see her. And then he raised his eyebrow in an unspoken question, nodding at what she was holding.

She caught her lower lip between her teeth, wondering if that was a signal for her to come forward and say something.

And then she didn't have to.

"Why don't I give you some time to look through these photographs taken of some of the cakes I created for other weddings, Mrs. Watkins. Maybe you'll see something that will inspire you," he told the woman in an even cadence, "while I see what I can do to help this lady."

Mrs. Watkins didn't look as if she welcomed sharing his attention with someone else, but since she obviously still hadn't made up her mind, the woman grudgingly inclined her head.

"Go ahead," she murmured coldly.

"Looks like 'Cassidy' has his hands full," Gina observed with a smile, keeping her voice low as she referred to him by the name she assumed he used in the shop.

"So do you," Shane commented, nodding at the large stuffed dog she was carrying. It looked like an oversize Labrador. "New friend?"

For a second, watching Shane with the woman, she'd forgotten she was carrying this large stuffed offering. "This? It's not for me," Gina answered. "But I thought that maybe Ellie might like him." She shifted the toy to look down at its face. It was almost life-like. "I thought I could give it to her to keep her company while she's here. Unless you'd rather I didn't give it to her," she said, backtracking.

She didn't want Shane thinking she was presuming anything. She was clearly giving him the option of refusing the toy, although why he should was totally beyond her.

Shane looked the stuffed animal over and then smiled. "Thank you. That's very thoughtful of you."

She offered the Labrador to him, but he didn't take it. Instead, he walked back toward the rear door and pushed it slightly open.

"Ellie, can you come out here, please?" Shane called to his niece.

The next moment Ellie bounced into the showroom as if she had literally launched herself from a trampoline. Mrs. Watkins stopped looking through the album of photographs and appeared startled. Her round face transformed into a mask of disapproval.

"You have *children* in here?" she questioned, saying the word "children" in the same disdainful tone she would have used to say "rats."

"Not children," Shane corrected, smiling at Ellie. "Just her."

Mrs. Watkins sniffed. Gina found herself pitying any child the woman might have raised. "Isn't that disruptive in a place like this?" the woman asked, clearly showing that *she* thought it was.

"On the contrary, I find having Ellie around inspiring," Shane said, addressing his words affectionately to his niece.

Ellie shifted so that she could look up at her uncle and beamed.

"Oh," Mrs. Watkins huffed, and then she visibly retreated.

Ellie, meanwhile, was oblivious to the exchange going on around her. Her eyes were almost saucer wide as she stared at the stuffed dog that Gina was holding. The little girl who had literally bounced into the room now took a tentative step toward the stuffed animal.

"Can I touch it?" she asked Gina almost shyly.

"You can do anything you want with it," Gina told Ellie with a broad smile. "It's yours."

Ellie's mouth dropped open. "Mine?" she asked in almost a hushed voice. The next second, her head swiveled toward her uncle. "Really?" she squealed.

"That's between you and Miss Bongino, peanut," Shane told his niece.

"Miss Bon-Bongee—" Ellie was obviously having trouble saying Gina's name.

Gina tried not to laugh. She didn't want to hurt the girl's feelings. "Just say 'Gina,' Ellie. It's much easier," Gina told her.

Ellie looked at her uncle. "Is that okay?" she asked.

"That's up to Miss Gina," he said, sticking in just a small sign of respect for the girl to use. "If it's okay with her, it's okay with me," Shane told her.

It was easy to see by the look on his face that although Shane was trying to raise the little girl with some rules, he completely doted on her.

"Well, now that we've got *that* out of the way," Gina said to the little girl, "I think that it's time that you and Robby got acquainted."

"Is that his name?" Ellie asked, still looking at the stuffed animal as if she expected him to take off at any second.

"Unless you'd like to change it," Gina said, offering Ellie the option to do just that.

Ellie looked as if she thought that was sacrilege. "Uh-uh," she answered, emphatically vetoing any kind of a name change. "He might not like that."

"I see," Gina said, trying hard not to laugh.

Accepting the incredibly soft stuffed dog into her

arms, Ellie looked slightly overwhelmed by it. The little girl buried her face in the dog's side.

"It's so soft," she marveled. And then she looked up at Gina. "I can really keep him?" she asked in awed disbelief.

Gina nodded, offering an encouraging smile. "Absolutely."

Ellie squealed, burying her face against the stuffed dog again. And then, without any warning, she propped up the dog against the counter on the floor—it was almost the size of an actual small Labrador—and threw her arms around Gina, giving her a really fierce hug.

Gina was surprised at the amount of strength the little girl exhibited.

"Thank you!" Ellie cried.

How those simple words affected her. Gina thought her heart would burst. "My pleasure, baby. My pleasure," she assured the little girl, stroking her blond head.

The other woman in the showroom cleared her throat rather loudly. When Shane looked in her direction, she coldly announced, "If you're through humoring the child, I'm ready to tell you what I want for my daughter's wedding cake."

Shane was quiet for a moment, as if debating what he was about to say. And then he decided to say it. "You know what, Mrs. Watkins? I just rechecked my schedule again when I ducked into the back and I'm not going to be able to create that cake for your daughter's wedding after all." Mrs. Watkins's face fell, but he went on talking as if he hadn't noticed. "I'm just too booked up."

"But you have to," Mrs. Watkins insisted, completely appalled.

"No, I don't," Shane countered, his voice firm, his position steadfast.

The gray-haired woman was utterly stunned. Momentarily at a loss for words, she finally cried, "Well, what am I supposed to do now?" Her tone was totally accusatory.

"I'm afraid I haven't the vaguest idea," Shane replied, beginning to guide her toward his door. "But I am sure that a resourceful woman such as yourself will be able to figure it out."

Mrs. Watkins sputtered several times, although nothing intelligible sounding came out of her mouth. Finally, seeing that "Cassidy" was not about to change his mind, she stormed out, slamming the door so hard in her wake that it reverberated throughout the small, tidy shop.

Gina watched the door, holding her breath. Afraid that Mrs. Watkins would come stomping back in. Or, at the very least, that the glass in the upper portion of the door would shatter.

But the glass remained intact as the noise slowly abated. And then another, less threatening sound replaced the sound of the slamming door. It was the sound of Gina clapping her hands.

Ellie looked up at her new friend quizzically. "Why are you clapping?" she asked. "There's nobody singing or dancing like the shows I get to watch on my TV."

"I'm clapping because your uncle did something very brave," Gina explained to the little girl.

Ellie's small face was a mask of surprise and wonder as she looked from Gina to her uncle and then back again. It was clear that she didn't understand and she wanted to.

"He did?" she questioned.

Gina's eyes met Shane's. And then her lips curved as she nodded.

"Yup, he did. Can you afford to turn business away?" she asked him, worried about what the noble move might have cost him.

"I can if it means working for someone like that. I have to at least like the person I'm creating the cake for," Shane told her. "I have a feeling that Mrs. Watkins wasn't going to allow her daughter to have a say in any of this. The woman is a dictator with a mean streak a mile wide. It was obvious that she wants to be involved in the process from start to finish." He shook his head. "I can't work like that."

Ellie seemed oblivious to her uncle's explanation. Instead, she had a question for him out of the blue. "Do you like Gina?"

Shane looked down at his niece, stunned. Where had that come from? He knew he hadn't said anything to make Ellie think that he had any sort of feelings about Gina one way or another. Maybe he'd misunderstood her.

"What?"

"Do you like Gina?" Ellie repeated. "'Cause I like her," she told him matter-of-factly, wrapping her arms more tightly around the stuffed dog.

Now he understood. "That's because she just bought you off with that mutt," Shane said with a laugh.

"I wasn't trying to buy her off," Gina protested. "I thought that if Ellie had something fun to play with, you could get more work done," she explained.

"So you did have an ulterior motive," Shane concluded.

Gina didn't know if he was just kidding or being serious. She certainly couldn't tell by his expression.

She decided to sidestep his insinuation altogether and only said, "I'm just trying to be helpful." Feeling that it was safer, she shifted her focus to Ellie. "You know when I was your age, Ellie, I had a stuffed tiger I took everywhere."

Ellie looked up, interested. "What was his name?" she asked.

"His name was Timmy," Gina told her.

She answered his niece's question so easily, Shane thought that maybe Gina had actually had a stuffed tiger by that name.

"Where's Timmy now?" Ellie asked, then added hopefully, "Maybe he and Robby can play."

Gina flashed the little girl a sad smile. "I'm afraid I don't have him anymore."

Ellie's face drooped in disappointment. "Where is he?"

"Timmy went to stay with some kids in a hospital oh, about twenty years ago," Gina answered. She saw the little girl's confusion and added, "Timmy liked cheering kids up and we both thought he'd be happier there where he could play with kids."

"But what about you?" Ellie asked.

Gina smiled fondly at the little girl. "I wasn't a kid anymore."

She could feel Shane looking at her but for the life of her, she couldn't begin to guess what he was thinking. Did he think that she was somewhat demented, talking about a stuffed animal as if it was real with actual feelings and the ability to think? There was a time when she *had* felt that way about some of her toys, but that had been a very long time ago.

Gina smiled, unable to help herself. That had always

been her gift. Her ability to remember what she had been like as a little girl. It helped her easily relate to children like Ellie.

Of course, that same "gift" probably made other adults think that she was slightly crazy or at least a little strange.

"What do you say to Miss Bongi—to Miss Gina?" Shane corrected himself as he prompted his niece.

If possible, Ellie's arms tightened even harder around the stuffed dog she was holding.

"Thank you, Miss Gina," Ellie declared, a smile all but vibrating in her voice. She was beaming at her as she held on to the stuffed dog.

Just hearing the little girl sound so happy was more than payment enough as far as Gina was concerned. She ran her hand over the small blond head.

"You're very welcome, Ellie," Gina told her with feeling.

Gina straightened slightly. It was time to leave. She couldn't very well just hang around here like an extra appendage, even though, secretly, she was more than willing to stay.

But she had done what she had come to do: she'd made friends with Ellie and that, in turn, had gotten Shane to see her in a better light. With a little bit of luck, she could build on that and maybe, eventually, she could work her way back to how things had once been between them. Or, at the very least, to the point where he felt less hostile to her than he had felt before this wedding had miraculously come up.

"All right then," Gina said to the little girl. "I'm glad you and Robby have hit it off so well." She turned toward

Shane who was still silently watching her. "And I'll come by on Saturday to pick up the pastries for the shower."

"There's no need for you to come by on Saturday, Gina," Shane told her in a subdued voice that set off all sorts of alarms in her head.

Oh Lord, had he changed his mind again? He couldn't do that. She'd already told Sylvie he was handling the desserts.

She needed to find a way to get him to change his mind back.

"You're not going to make the pastries after all?" Gina questioned, making no effort to hide her disappointment.

"I didn't say that," Shane pointed out quietly after a beat.

Okay, maybe she was getting ahead of herself. Gina forced herself to calm down before she asked, "All right, what *are* you saying?"

"That you don't have to come by to pick them up because I'll be delivering the pastries to the shower myself," he told her.

Yes, Virginia, she thought as relief and happiness suddenly flooded all through her insides, *there is a Santa Claus!*

Gina felt the corners of her eyes growing damp. The man just kept on surprising her.

Chapter Eleven

There were no new panicky calls from Sylvie—for which Gina was extremely grateful because that meant she had no new fires to put out. Knowing this could change at any moment, Gina decided to go see her brother-in-law and find out firsthand if Eddie was going to be able to fit in making the necessary repairs on the church's roof in time for the wedding.

Thinking she needed better information herself, she drove by the church first. She wanted to get an idea of how bad the damage actually was.

It was bad.

That was the first thought that hit her as Gina drove into the church's near-empty parking lot.

She could see the damage even before she came to a full stop. More than fifty years ago, someone, presumably a well-meaning parishioner, had planted a California pepper tree next to the church. Pictures of the area indicated that it had been little more than a sapling when it had been planted. But it had long since become an accident waiting to happen.

And then it did.

Getting out of her car, Gina slowly walked around the church and surveyed the damage. It was lucky that it had happened at night and not during the daytime, or on a Sunday when there might have been a lot of people attending a service.

Someone really could have gotten hurt then. At least this way, the only thing that had suffered was the roof and part of the inside of the church.

"Could have been worse."

Caught off guard, Gina didn't jump when she heard the deep voice coming from behind her. She'd recognize her brother-in-law's rumbling cadence anywhere.

Turning around to face him, she smiled up at the tall, lanky man with his permanently unruly chestnut hair.

"Hi, Eddie. Thanks for coming out. Can you fix it?" she asked him hopefully.

Her brother-in-law had his clipboard in his hands and was writing things down even as he talked to her. "Of course I can fix it," he answered. "The problem is, do I have the time?"

"If you need an extra body, I can help," she quickly offered.

He laughed dryly. "That'll take me twice as long, then."

Gina pretended to be offended, although she knew he was teasing her. She also knew that he was better off using trained workers than taking her up on her offer. "I'm not that bad," she protested.

Eddie looked up from the clipboard and rolled his eyes. "All I need is you falling off the roof and I'll have my wife and your mother on my case for the rest of my natural life. Maybe longer. No thank you, Gee."

Gina nodded. "All right, what *can* I do to help?"

He went back to working on his notes. "Just let me make my assessment of the damage and what it'll take to fix it. Then you can go and make arrangements with the local padre—"

"Monsignor," Gina corrected.

Eddie waved his hand. "Whatever. The head guy," he said, using the all-purpose term, "to give my company the authorization to get the job done."

She knew she should just back off and leave him to his estimate, but she was anxious. "When do you think you can finish it?" Gina asked.

Eddie never looked up. "In a month," he answered.

"Eddie!" Gina cried, distressed.

He raised his head, briefly focusing on his sister-in-law. "The job'll take four days. Finding the time to do it in, however, is going to be trickier," he told her honestly.

Gina moved around so that she was able to get into his face. She gave him her most soulful expression. "I'm counting on you, Eddie."

"Great. Pressure. Just what I need as an incentive," Tiffany's husband murmured under his breath. And then he said more audibly, "All I can say is that I'll do my best."

That was as good as a promise, Gina thought. "Knew I could count on you," she cried, giving Eddie a quick, grateful kiss on the cheek. "Tell Tiffany I said she married a great guy."

He laughed dryly. "I tell her that all the time. She doesn't seem to be convinced," Eddie told her, walking away.

Tuning his sister-in-law out, Eddie continued making notations to himself about the job.

Gina left him to it and slipped away quietly.

"It's all under control," Gina informed Sylvie for the third time in as many days.

It was the day of the bridal shower and the nervous bride had confronted her in person the moment she had walked into Sylvie's sister's house. Sylvie's sister, Monica, was her maid of honor and the Jack and Jill bridal shower was being held in her house.

"You're sure?" Sylvie asked, and her voice went up so high, it was almost a squeak. Gina winced as the piercing sound penetrated her ears. It was going to undoubtedly haunt her dreams for a good while to come, if not forever.

"Very sure," Gina assured her as serenely as possible. "I was there yesterday and I spoke to Father Joseph who, in turn, had spoken to Monsignor McGuire about the whole thing." She smiled broadly. "The upshot is that they gave the go-ahead for the work to commence and the church will be ready in time for your wedding. My brother-in-law's company is handling the repairs and you couldn't be in better hands," Gina guaranteed.

"Relax, Sylvie," she calmly instructed the bride. "If you keep this up, you're going to worry yourself into a hospital bed before the wedding ever takes place."

"You're right," Sylvie agreed, blowing out a long

breath. "You're absolutely right." She flashed a spas-modic smile that vanished as quickly as it had appeared. "It's just that—"

"It's just that nothing," Gina informed her, putting an end to any further protest from the bride-to-be. "In the blink of an eye, this will all be over and you will have missed it because you wound up worrying yourself to a frazzle," she told her client. "This is your wedding shower, Sylvie. Enjoy it."

Gina saw Sylvie's face suddenly brightening.

"There, that's better," she congratulated her client—and then she realized that the woman was looking at something over her shoulder.

Turning around Gina could see Shane walking in through the front door. He was carrying a very large box embossed with his logo on it: Cakes Created by Cassidy.

"If you'll excuse me," Gina said, stepping away from Sylvie. "I think the pastries for your shower have ar-rived."

Weaving around the several guests who had arrived early and were in the process of mingling, Gina made her way over toward Shane.

"Hi! You made it," Gina declared, smiling up at his handsome, chiseled blond features and beautiful blue eyes.

Shane turned toward her. He wasn't surprised to see Gina there ahead of him. "Didn't you think I would?" he questioned.

"Of course I did," she answered, scrambling to cor-rect any misimpression she might have created. She didn't want him thinking that she didn't have any faith in his word. "It's just that, well, things happen in my line of work. Sometimes the best laid plans, etcetera, etcetera…" Gina said, allowing her voice to trail off. Changing the subject, she said, "That smells wonderful." Gina nodded at the box.

In all honesty, she meant that *he* smelled wonderful, although she knew that she couldn't say that. She'd caught a faint whiff of cologne when someone opened the door just now. Unless she had totally lost her mind, Shane had on the same cologne he used to wear when they were going together. The scent always made her feel nostalgic.

Every so often, whenever she caught a hint of the cologne while passing someone in a restaurant or in a store, old memories would come flooding back to her. Memories accompanied by that longing she always experienced whenever she thought of Shane and all the things that might have been.

If only…

"Where do you want this?" Shane asked, nodding at the box he was holding.

"I just got here myself," she told him, looking around. "But my guess would be over there." Gina pointed to a table that was set up against one of the family room walls.

The next moment, the question of where to put the pastries was solved.

"Hi, I'm Monica," a tall, statuesque brunette said, introducing herself as she came over to join them, or rather Shane, Gina thought. "I'm Sylvie's maid of honor in charge of this little shindig and yes, that's where all the food is going." Putting one hand on Shane's wrist to hold him in place, Monica used her other hand to lift the lid on the box he had brought in. "That looks really tempting," she told him with an appreciative sigh.

Something told Gina that from the way Monica was looking at Shane, she wasn't really talking about the pastries.

This was no time to give in to jealousy, Gina silently upbraided herself. She was here in a professional capacity, despite the pretty invitation that had arrived in the mail. Besides, she didn't own Shane. He was certainly free to pay attention and receive attention from anyone he chose.

"There're more boxes of pastries in the car," Shane replied.

"Oh, I can help you bring them in," Monica quickly volunteered.

If her smile were any wider, Gina thought, Shane was in serious danger of falling in.

Shane didn't seem to take note of the fact that the woman's eyes were gleaming at him.

"That's all right," he told Sylvie's maid of honor. "Gina already volunteered to help me with them. Gina?" he asked as he turned toward the doorway and began heading back outside again.

"I'm right here," Gina assured him, picking up her pace in order to keep up with Shane.

The man had eight inches on her and it was all leg, she thought, hurrying.

"I hope you don't mind helping out," Shane said to her as soon as they had cleared the house. "It's just that I think the bride's maid of honor had more than just pastries on her mind and I don't like things getting complicated."

Gina struggled not to laugh. Instead, she said playfully, "Always happy to help you beat them off with a stick."

Shane cleared his throat, although he didn't appear embarrassed. "I didn't mean to sound conceited."

"You didn't," she quickly assured him. "You can't help it if women are attracted to your tall, blond good looks." She wasn't teasing him. She meant what she was saying.

Shane's laugh was self-deprecating. He shook his head. "I guess I deserve that."

"No," Gina told him. *But I do. I deserve you*, she thought. *I just have to get you to realize that.*

There were four more boxes filled with the pastries he'd made for this occasion. They were carefully arranged in the back of his SUV.

Gina looked in. "You certainly brought a lot."

"In my experience," he told her, "people tend to get very hungry at these things. Better to bring more than not enough."

She lifted out a box, then waited for him to do the same. "You are staying for this, aren't you?" Gina asked him. She had learned that taking anything for granted was always a mistake.

There was a slight frown on his face which told her that Shane was far from happy about the demands this situation placed on him.

"Only until it's politely acceptable for me to make my exit," he told her. About to reach in to take a box, he paused and looked at her, searching her face. "Why?"

She didn't try to sound clever. Honesty was her best policy when it came to Shane. "Because I have to stay," she told Shane, "and it would be nice if I had a friend to talk to."

He surprised her by laughing. "As I recall, you never had any trouble when it came to talking."

"I said *a friend* to talk to," Gina pointed out, repeating what she'd said.

Rather than taking Gina up on her offer, he pointed out, "You don't have to stay."

"Oh, but I'm afraid that I do," Gina contradicted. "My job is to make sure that no emergencies—big or small—arise from the moment the bride hires me until she and the groom have their last dance and make their escape to begin either their honeymoon or start their blissful life together."

"Blissful, eh?" Shane repeated. Was it her imagination, or did he look amused? "Is that part of your guarantee, too?"

"No, that part is up to them," Gina told him seriously. "I just try to make sure that everything leading up to that point paves the way for that to happen for them. If it doesn't..." She lifted her shoulders in a careless shrug. "Well, at least I know that I tried my best."

For the first time since she ran into him, Shane's mouth curved in a lopsided grin. She'd forgotten until this moment how much she used to love seeing that.

"As I recall," he told her, "your best was more than good enough."

It was a moment of weakness and Shane knew it. But he couldn't seem to help himself. As they stood next to his SUV right over the two boxes of pastries they were about to carry into the house, Shane leaned over and kissed her. The second he did, he was instantly propelled back through time and space, back to when there had been no hurt feelings, no rejections, no oceans separating them and all the things that might have been.

The second his lips touched hers, Gina felt as if her heart was going to explode right then and there.

She had *never* thought she would feel like this again, never thought she could be this happy again. And yet, here she was, being swept away the way she always was whenever he had kissed her.

Her heart went into double time. She could barely catch her breath.

And then, just as quickly as it had happened, it was over.

Shane drew back, the look on his face all but telling her that he felt he had made a mistake. When he spoke, he just compounded the jagged, painful sensations she was feeling.

"Sorry," he told her. "I didn't mean to do that. I guess, just for a second, I forgot who we were." The words were stilted. Awkward. "It won't happen again."

Her eyes searched Shane's face, looking for a trace of the man who had once loved her. The man who she still loved.

He wasn't there.

"Even if I want it to?" Gina asked, addressing the words to his retreating back.

Shane stopped walking for a moment. She thought he was going to turn around and say something to her, maybe even answer her question.

But he just continued walking as if he hadn't heard her. Or worse, didn't think that she deserved an answer.

Taking a breath, she willed her feet to move and followed Shane into the house.

"Here, let me help you," Monica said, suddenly meeting them in the doorway. "These must be heavy." She raised her eyes to his face. "It took you a while to carry them in."

Her words were for Shane, not her, Gina realized.

The maid of honor took the box from Shane. "You can get the rest—if there's more," she added with what Gina was certain the woman thought appeared to be an attractive pout.

"There's more," Shane answered.

"Wonderful!" Monica gushed. "I'll tell Allison to make room on the buffet table." The woman strode quickly with the big box. Putting it down, she looked ready to escort Shane back out to his SUV.

Gina was tempted to put the box she'd brought in down on the first flat surface so she could go back out and rescue Shane, but then she rethought the matter.

Maybe he didn't want to be rescued, she told herself. Maybe Shane preferred someone who he had no history with. Someone with a clean slate, at least where he was concerned.

In any event, she silently told herself, Shane was a big boy and could more than take care of himself. After all, he had just proved it with her.

Chapter Twelve

For the next few hours, Gina remained at the bridal shower, keeping to the background as she watched to make sure that everything at the party went off without a hitch. She felt that it was her job to make sure that everyone had a good time.

She managed to do it all while staying close to Shane. What made it even better was that he remained with her by his own choice, not hers.

Because of that, Sylvie's maid of honor threw her a number of dirty looks, but Gina fended them all off with a smile. She acted completely impervious to them as well as to the scowl on Monica's face as the latter shot daggers in her direction.

"I have a feeling that when I leave this party, the maid of honor is going to try to run me over with her car," she confided to Shane in a low voice. When he looked at her, his eyebrows raised in a silent query, Gina found herself laughing. "I'm just kidding, although I'm pretty sure I won't be making Monica's Christmas card list this year."

Sitting off to the side, out of the way, Shane took in what was going on around him. He could remember a time when parties were a prominent part of his weekends, but now he preferred to spend his time more quietly.

He was well aware of the way that the maid of honor was looking at him. Like she was a hungry cat and he was the last morsel of food left in the area.

Inclining his head toward Gina, he said quietly, "Thanks for doing this."

She knew he meant, in essence, having her behave like a roadblock for him. "Hey, I'm the reason you're here to begin with, so I kind of owe this to you," she said, shrugging off his thanks.

"Well, you can get back to mingling in a few minutes," he told her. "It looks like no one has any complaints about the pastries, so I'm going to be leaving soon."

"So soon?" Gina asked, not bothering to hide her regret.

"Soon?" Shane repeated, glancing at his watch. "I've been here over two hours."

"*Almost* two hours. That's really not very much time. You could stay a little longer," she coaxed, trying her best to sound casual.

"Maybe I would under normal circumstances," he allowed, "but Ellie was coming down with a cold when I left today and I like being around when she's not feeling well."

He had really become a homebody. Who would have guessed? "Does she have a temperature?" she asked him.

"It had gone down when I left, but you know kids." The inference in his voice was that he assumed she knew all about the fevers they could run at times.

"Only by reputation," Gina quipped. "And, of course, there is my niece. You know," she recalled fondly, "when I was a kid, any time I was sick, my mother made me chicken soup—from scratch, not out of a can. And she always gave me comic books to read. It got to the point that I used to look forward to being sick." Gina grinned at him. "One time I tried to fool my mother by holding a thermometer over an open flame on the stove. It registered really high and I got busted—when the thermometer did."

Shane's laugh blended with hers. Gina felt a warm shiver washing over her.

"Can't fool mothers," he murmured as if it was a private joke that just the two of them shared. Taking a breath, Shane set the glass of punch he'd been nursing for the better part of the last two hours on the table. "I'd better get going." He hesitated for a moment, then said, "Give me a call in case someone finds the pastries not to their liking."

All Gina heard was that he was asking her to call him. It wasn't easy to keep from grinning from ear to ear. "So you're really serious about taking in complaints?"

"I'm open to constructive criticism," Shane told her.

For a second, she debated keeping quiet. He might just think she was trying to flatter him. But not saying anything just wasn't her way, so she asked, "Want my opinion?"

He looked at her, not sure what to expect. "Go ahead."

"You know you're really good at what you do," Gina told him. She'd sampled a few of his creations and each one was better than the last. "Those pastries are out of this world. You don't need to hear some person who's trying to build up their own ego by coming down hard on what is clearly a wonderful effort. The only way those pastries you 'created' could taste better is if they were served in heaven."

Shane laughed at that, really laughed. And just as he took his leave, she noticed that the wariness she'd detected earlier was gone from his eyes. The walls between them were finally breaking down, Gina thought with relief. There really was hope!

Though it wasn't easy, she curbed her desire to walk with Shane to the front door. She didn't want him to feel that she was crowding him.

Just as she was holding herself in check, Gina saw Monica come hurrying over to Shane as he reached the front door. The maid of honor looked as if she was attempting to draw Shane aside under some pretext, but she saw him shaking his head and then leaving within a couple of minutes despite all of Monica's efforts to the contrary.

Gina's triumphant feeling faded as she glanced at her watch. She couldn't leave yet. There were at least two more hours of this to go.

Putting a smile on her face, Gina made the best of it.

It wasn't easy, but she refrained from calling Shane when she finally left the bridal shower some three hours later. Fighting the impulse to fly out of there, she adhered to her obligations. That meant remaining at the bridal shower until the last of the guests had trickled away.

On the plus side, she knew her client was extremely happy. In addition, keeping her ears open, she was also able to collect a large number of flattering comments about the pastries that Shane had created and brought to the party.

No one, it seemed, had a single negative thing to say about them—unless she counted the fact that a couple of bridesmaids lamented that the pastries were "sinfully delicious" and impossible to stop eating. Gina had a feeling that there would be several bridesmaids whose dresses would be severely stretched to the limit.

She resisted the urge to call Shane with her "report." She even thought about skipping the call altogether and just driving up to his house to tell him in person.

Giving in to her curiosity, she had done a little research on him and apparently Shane was living in the house where he had grown up. She had always assumed that it had been sold years ago, but apparently he had hung on to it, maybe as a way of keeping the memory of his parents and brother alive. He had mentioned that there was a trust.

Gina had gone so far as to pick up her keys and head toward her car, but she talked herself out of it. Because going there now would be seen as stalking.

No, she could call him tomorrow to tell him what she'd heard people saying about his pastries. Calling him tomorrow would seem far less desperate than calling today—or showing up on his doorstep.

She knew she was doing the right thing, waiting like this. But being right wasn't nearly as much of a comfort as it should have been, Gina thought with a sigh that went clear down to her toes.

Being there with Shane in that party setting proved

to her just how much she'd really missed him all these years.

Just then, the phone in the kitchen rang, startling her. The landline sounded so much more demanding and business-like than the cell phone she kept in her pocket did.

Hurrying over to the landline, she picked up the receiver and put it against her ear. "Hello?"

"Is it over?"

It was Shane.

She basked in the sound of his voice for a second before answering. He had to realize it was over because she was here to answer the phone, but she didn't bother pointing that out.

"Yes. It ended half an hour ago. I just walked into the house this minute," she told him. Glancing around, she spotted a chair, pulled it over and sat down.

"Half an hour," he repeated as the words sank in. "And you didn't call because there were complaints," he guessed, obviously assuming the worst from her silence.

"No, I didn't call because I didn't want you to think I was stalking you," she told him honestly. "I was going to call you tomorrow—to tell you that everyone in the wedding party is cursing you."

"Cursing me? Why?" he cried, surprised.

"Because if they don't fit into their bridesmaid dresses in two weeks, it's all your fault," she told him. "You made pastries that they, no matter how good their intentions were, couldn't resist." There was silence on his end. Was he worried that she was saving the worst for last? She was quick to relieve his concerns. "There wasn't so much as a crumb left and believe me, several of the bridesmaids, not to mention the mother of the bride, checked. They even asked me if I was hiding more somewhere. Some of them saw me coming in with you, carrying one of the pastry boxes," she explained. "I'm lucky that I managed to get away from there without being tortured."

"Tortured?" Shane questioned, puzzled.

"In case I *was* hiding more pastries somewhere," she answered.

That same wonderful laugh she loved echoed against her ear, all but engulfing her. "I forgot how much you liked to exaggerate," he said.

"I'm not exaggerating this time. I think you don't realize just how good those creations of yours really are," she told him. Because she knew that Shane had always had a hard time with compliments, she changed the subject. "How's Ellie doing? Did her fever go away?" she asked him.

"That all depends on what time you're asking about," Shane told her. "When I came home, it was almost back to normal. Then an hour later, it started to climb up again. I've had three different readings since I got back. If it's like this tomorrow, I might have to take her to the walk-in clinic. Or the ER," he said, thinking that the acclaimed hospital right in the area might be his best bet.

While Gina loved the fact that he was concerned about the child, she didn't want Shane worrying to the point that he was all but wrapping the little girl in cotton.

"When they're harboring a cold, kids under the age of seven tend to run high fevers at certain times of the day, especially in the evening. It can be high when they wake up, drop to normal around noon and then go up again by six."

"You have kids?" he questioned, surprised. Shane

thought she'd said that she didn't, but maybe he'd misunderstood. Maybe there was even more about Gina that he didn't know.

"No, but I have a niece and I was there when my sister went through this." Maybe she was butting in where she wasn't wanted. This was all very new territory to her. All she could do was tell Shane the truth. "I just wanted you to know this isn't all that unusual."

"Thanks," he told her and he sounded as if he meant it. "I appreciate the pep talk."

"Anytime," Gina replied. She didn't hear a childish voice calling in the background. "Sounds quiet."

"It is," Shane agreed. "I gave Ellie some baby aspirin and she fell asleep about fifteen minutes ago."

"I'd better let you go, then," she said although she was reluctant to end the call. They were really getting along rather well at the moment. She was afraid that the second she hung up, things would revert back to what they had been just a little while ago, but that would be selfish of her. "It's important to get your rest when you can."

"That makes sense," Shane agreed. And then she heard him say, "Gina?"

About to say goodbye she stopped and held on to the phone with both hands. "Yes?"

"Thanks for calling."

Gina hesitated, torn. She didn't want to spoil the moment and correct him, but if he remembered this later, he'd know that he'd gotten this wrong. She hadn't called him, he had called her. She needed to say something now before it got too awkward.

"Um, Shane?"

"Yes?"

"You were the one who called me," Gina told him.

There was silence on the other end. And then he said, "You're right. I totally forgot. Maybe I *should* get some rest."

Gina felt her smile widening. He didn't take offense at having her correct him. She took that to be a good sign.

"Good idea," she told Shane. "I'll talk to you later."

It was only after she hung up that she realized she'd all but told him that she was going to be calling back. And he hadn't objected.

So, this was what progress felt like, Gina thought, pleased.

For the first time since she had walked into the bakery and had her world blown apart when she saw Shane standing there, Gina spent a restful night.

She woke up early because that was a habit she'd developed from the time she was in grade school. Back then it was because life was an exciting adventure to her and she was afraid of missing anything, even a moment of it. She grew up, but she never outgrew that feeling.

Taking a quick shower, she made herself a slice of toast and then got down to work.

She checked her refrigerator to see what she needed to get at the store—and found that she didn't need to get anything. Her shelves were full.

"You have *got* to get another hobby besides me, Mom," she murmured. But for once, she wasn't upset about her mother dropping by with groceries. It saved her time. She found that she had all the ingredients she needed—carrots, celery and a whole chicken.

She was going to make old-fashioned chicken soup just the way her grandmother had taught her. It wasn't going to be anything elaborate, just basic ingredients, mixed in an oversize pot with water, salt and love.

Smiling, Gina got to work.

Dutifully, she turned up the flame on her stove, brought everything she'd put into the pot to a boil, then turned the flame down again until it was on medium. She partially covered the pot, then sat down in the kitchen to keep vigil for the next hour and a half. She knew the old adage about a watched pot never boiling, but she was also aware of the practical fact that unattended pots sometimes had a way of boiling over and then having their contents boil away.

Finding the timer she had stashed in a drawer, she set it for ninety minutes, then forced herself to be patient.

It was much easier said than done.

While the ingredients she had thrown together were busy becoming soup, Gina searched for something to carry it in once it was finally finished cooking and had cooled down enough to transport.

Finding something appropriate to use took her more time than putting the soup together had. But she finally found a clear airtight container she could use to bring the soup to Shane.

If Ellie was all better—and kids really did bounce back with amazing resilience—then Shane and the little girl could have the soup for lunch anyway. And if Ellie was still sick, then if the little girl was anything like she'd once been, Gina was confident that the soup would be incredibly welcome.

Gina dug a box of egg noodles out of her pantry and prepared them to go with the soup. The noodles were ready a lot sooner than the soup was. Straining the noodles, she packed them up in a separate container and went back to waiting.

Once the soup was ready and was placed, along with shredded bits of chicken, into its own container, there was only one thing missing from this meal.

But for that, Gina knew she needed to stop at a book-store.

She glanced at her watch. Today was Sunday. The bookstores in her area didn't open until ten thirty.

Perfect timing, she thought as she moved around and got ready. Everything would be packed up and ready to go by ten thirty.

Chapter Thirteen

"But I'm all better, Unca Shane," Ellie protested, her lower lip protruding in a pout as she looked up at her uncle.

In an effort to strike an acceptable compromise with Ellie, Shane had told his niece she didn't have to stay in her bed as long as she remained on the sofa he'd made up for her in the family room. He'd placed three multi-colored pillows at her back, propping her up into practically a sitting position. Shane had also tucked Ellie's favorite princess blanket all around her small body.

To keep his niece occupied, there was a collection of popular cartoons playing on the TV courtesy of the Blu-ray disk he had inserted earlier.

"Humor me, sweetie," Shane requested, ruffling her soft, silky hair. "You weren't all better last night," he reminded her.

"But that was then. This is now," Ellie insisted with the budding logic of a little woman. "I wanna play, Unca Shane."

"You can get up and play tomorrow," Shane told her. He finished his sentence quickly because he could see that Ellie was already starting to throw off her princess blanket. She gave all the signs of being ready to hop off the sofa at the slightest provocation.

"But tomorrow's school," she complained as he tucked the blanket back around her.

The sharpness of Ellie's mind never failed to amaze him. Half the time Shane felt he had trouble keeping track of what day it was, yet this little munchkin whose care he'd found himself entrusted with always seemed to be on top of everything.

"Preschool," he corrected, although he knew that to Ellie it was one and the same. "Tell you what. You stay on the sofa today like a good girl and you can stay home from preschool tomorrow."

Shane knew he had to make arrangements with Barbara, the nanny he usually had watching his niece when he worked, but that was really the easy part. Getting Ellie to stay put today was definitely going to be the difficult part. Luckily, since it was Sunday, the bakery was closed and he could stay with Ellie.

"So do we have a deal?" he asked his niece in all seriousness.

Ellie puckered up her mouth as if she was thinking over his proposition. And then she nodded, announcing with a resigned smile, "Okay, deal." Having made her declaration, she put out her hand to her uncle, wanting to shake on it.

Caught off guard, Shane realized that Ellie felt it was

part of the agreement because she had witnessed him shaking hands with one of his suppliers after a delivery had been made. He knew that reinforcement had become very important to the little girl. She needed it to make her feel secure.

Smiling at Ellie, Shane shook her hand. Just as he did, the doorbell rang. Surprised, he glanced over toward the front door.

"You expecting someone, Ellie?" Shane asked his niece, doing his best to keep a straight face.

Ellie appeared to seriously think about his question, then shook her head, her blond hair swinging about her face. "No."

"Stay there," he instructed when he saw that, prompted by her boundless curiosity, Ellie was starting to get off the sofa again.

He heard Ellie sigh mightily as he walked to the door, as if he were trying the last of her patience.

She was going to be a handful when she got older, he thought.

Preoccupied, Shane didn't look through the peephole when he reached the front door. Instead, he just opened it, and then stared in absolute surprise at the woman on his doorstep. His surprise doubled when he saw that she was holding what looked like a picnic basket and using both hands.

"Can I come in?" Gina asked when he didn't say anything. "This is getting heavy."

Coming to, Shane reached for the basket. "Here, let me take that." The first thing that hit him was that Gina wasn't exaggerating. The basket really *was* heavy. Stepping to the side, he let her in, then turned to follow her.

"Did I forget we were supposed to meet today?" he asked Gina, confused.

"No, you didn't forget anything," she replied, hoping that she hadn't made a mistake and overstepped some invisible boundary line Shane had drawn. They were making progress and she didn't want to take a chance on ruining that. But at the same time, she did want to go with her instincts. "I just thought, since you said that Ellie was sick, that I'd bring her—and you—some chicken soup. Homemade," Gina added quickly. She didn't want Shane to think she had just opened up a few cans of soup, warmed them up and then dumped them into a container. "That always made me feel better when I was Ellie's age and got sick."

He looked down at the basket he was carrying. The scent of hot chicken soup was beginning to waft up to him through everything.

"You mentioned that," he recalled. "You also said something about a comic book."

Smiling, now that her hands were free, she pulled out several comic books she'd stopped to pick up at a nearby bookstore. She had painstakingly pored over them to find just the right, age-appropriate ones to give Shane's niece.

"She doesn't already have these, does she?" she asked him.

"She doesn't have any," Shane told her.

"No comic books?" Gina asked, surprised. But then, she supposed that things like that were probably no longer in vogue for the short set. She could remember spending hours reading all sorts of comic books as a kid, everything from the adventures of a park bear and his faithful sidekick, to the ongoing crusades of an entire slew of superheroes. "Well then, she's in for a treat," Gina promised him.

"Who's there, Unca Shane?" Ellie called out, craning her neck and getting up as far as she could on the sofa without actually coming off it. She knew her uncle wouldn't be happy if she did.

"Hi, Ellie, it's me," Gina answered, peeking into the room.

The little girl's eyes lit up as soon as she heard Gina's voice.

"Gina!" Ellie cried, overjoyed. And then her eyes shifted to what her uncle's friend was holding in her hands. "Did you bring me something?" she asked Gina eagerly.

"Ellie," Shane admonished. "What did I tell you about asking that?"

Ellie dropped her head. "Not to," she mumbled in reply.

Gina pretended not to pay attention to the exchange between Shane and his niece.

"Of course I brought you something," she told Ellie, walking into the family room. "I brought you chicken soup."

Ellie's face fell. "Oh." Then, because her uncle had made it clear how important manners were, the little girl politely said, "Thank you."

Wow, Gina thought, clearly impressed. Shane should be giving parenting lessons.

Ellie was still staring hopefully at what Gina was holding in her hands. Not wanting to prolong the torture a second longer, Gina said, "And when you're finished eating your chicken soup, I brought you these comic books to read."

Ellie's forehead wrinkled, conveying that the little girl was slightly confused by the term she'd used. "Comic books?" Ellie repeated.

Gina sat down on the edge of the sofa, facing Ellie. "Comic books," she repeated, holding up one as a visual aid. It was a copy of the adventures of a band of friendly dogs who helped people. "See?"

Clapping her hands together, Ellie squealed her thanks, then she took the comic book from Gina. "This is for me?" she asked hopefully.

"All yours," Gina assured her.

Ellie's eyes crinkled as she leaned forward and hugged Gina. "Thank you!"

Looking on, Shane realized that he was still holding the basket Gina had brought.

"I'd better put this in the kitchen and get a couple of bowls. Three bowls," he amended, correcting himself.

"Three?" Gina questioned. Was he entertaining? Had she come at a bad time?

"Sure. You're going to have some with us, aren't you?" Shane asked.

"There's not all that much soup," Gina pointed out. "And I made it for you."

"Stay and have some," Shane urged her.

She didn't want Shane to feel obligated to share it with her, but she wasn't about to argue over it either. After all, this was what she secretly wanted. To become part of his life again and he part of hers. Ten years had passed since they'd been together but all that meant was that she had a loss of ten years to make up for.

"Can I help?" she called out.

He didn't answer her. Instead, he came back a couple of minutes later carrying a tray with three servings of soup and three spoons. He set the tray down on the coffee table that was right next to Ellie's sofa.

"I'm perfectly capable of ladling out three bowls of chicken soup," he told Gina.

"Of course you are," Gina replied. "I just like to help, that's all."

He looked down at the bowls, then back up at her. "You already did," he told her quietly.

There was that warm feeling again, Gina thought, reveling in the way it washed over her.

All three of them had soup for lunch. Her appetite nudged, Ellie even had seconds, although her bowl was slightly smaller than theirs was.

Clearing the bowls away, Gina wound up reading the comic books she had brought out loud to Ellie. After she had finished reading all of them to the little girl, they went on to play a board game. Shane attempted to beg off, but Gina and Ellie ganged up on him and he had no choice but to agree to play, too.

He was a reluctant participant at first, but Gina watched his resistance dissolve when Ellie looked up at her uncle with her big, soulful eyes.

With a sigh, he murmured, "I can't say no to you." Triumphant, Ellie clapped her hands in delight.

After that, they played one game after another until, completely tired out, Ellie fell asleep with one of the characters they were using on the board game clutched in her hand.

Gina rose slowly, taking care not to wake the little girl. She waited until she had walked out of the room before she risked saying anything to Shane.

"That little girl has more energy than any three people I know," she told him.

Shane smiled fondly as he looked back at Ellie over his shoulder.

"I wish I could tap into that," he confided honestly. "Thanks for bringing the soup and the comic books. And for helping out today," he added.

"I didn't do anything out of the ordinary," Gina protested, although truthfully, she liked being on the receiving end of his gratitude.

"You kept her entertained," Shane pointed out. "Ellie was just about ready to jump out of her skin when you got here just like the cavalry."

"Then I'm glad I could help keep her in her skin," Gina teased, loving the warm feeling that was spreading all through her just because of the way he was looking at her. "That's a wonderful little girl you have there. You've done a great job raising her."

"Half the time I think she's just raising herself," he confided.

"Don't kid yourself. I can see you in her," Gina told him. "The way she holds her head when she's thinking. That crooked smile on her lips when she's about to spring a surprise. She even phrases things the way you do. There's a hint of a lisp, of course," she added with a grin, "but it's definitely you."

"You're imagining things," he told her.

"No, I'm just very good at observing things. And at remembering," Gina added.

Because the moment had gotten so serious, it made her a little uneasy. She was afraid of having any sort of a serious conversation with Shane, afraid of any recriminations he might bring up.

Clearing her throat, she turned away, saying, "I'd better get my picnic basket so you can take advantage of the moment and get some rest. Something tells me that ball of fire in the next room will wake up raring to go."

"You're probably right," he agreed. "It was all I could do to convince her to rest one more day. We compromised on the sofa, but she was about to abandon it when you came over."

In the kitchen, he took a look at the container she'd brought. It was less than half full.

Gina saw the way he was looking at it and guessed at what he was thinking. "No need to transfer anything. You just keep the container until Ellie finishes the soup. I will take back the basket, though."

"Hold on. I can't have you leave with an empty basket," he told her. He opened the refrigerator and rummaged around.

Because his back blocked her view, she didn't know what he was doing until he was finished taking things out and putting them into the basket. Shane closed the lid before he turned around so that she wasn't able to see what he was doing.

Curious, Gina opened up the basket and saw that Shane had put about half a dozen pastries into the basket, just like the ones he'd brought to the bridal shower.

She raised her eyes to look at him. "You want me to get fat, don't you?" she asked. Gina was only half-kidding.

"It'll take more than half a dozen pastries to make you fat," he told her.

"Maybe, but it's a good start." Debating, Gina made up her mind and pushed the basket back toward him. "I can't take these."

Shane didn't understand. He thought she liked them. "Why not?" he asked.

"Because Ellie might want to eat them." It certainly wasn't because she didn't like them.

"It's not like I can't make any more of them," he told Gina. He nodded at the pastries in her basket. "I was just practicing with these."

That didn't make any sense to her. "You have to practice?" she questioned.

"Sure. Concert pianists have to practice," Shane pointed out, then shrugged. "Chefs aren't any different."

"I never thought of it that way," Gina admitted. In her opinion, you couldn't improve on excellence.

The room felt as if it was getting smaller to her. And warmer. Gina realized that somehow, Shane was standing closer to her than he had been a few moments ago.

Or maybe she was the one who was closer to him than she had been before.

However the logistics had gone, the end result was that her skin was beginning to tingle and desire was firing up within her like a newly lit display of fireworks against the darkened sky.

Gina knew she was asking for trouble because things were going so smoothly, but she found herself wishing Shane would kiss her again the way he had yesterday in the parking lot.

Except longer this time.

And then, the next moment, she wasn't wishing any more.

Because he was.

Chapter Fourteen

Gina wasn't aware of the basket sliding from her limp fingers. All she knew was that her hands were now free to go around Shane's neck.

Her heart pounding, she threaded her arms around his neck. Rising up on her toes, Gina allowed herself to sink into the kiss, reveling in the heated sensations that were being released throughout her entire body.

Feeling suddenly incredibly hungry for more, Shane wrapped his arms around her, drawing Gina closer to him as he deepened the kiss. Just for a moment he lost himself not only in the kiss but in all the old, wonderfully familiar feelings that kissing Gina had once again brought back to him in all their vivid glory.

He could have sworn that those feelings had all died long ago, lying buried in some forgotten grave where broken dreams went to die. Yet here they were back again, just as strong as ever.

Stronger.

Feeling insatiable, Shane slanted his mouth over and over against hers, each kiss deeper and full of more longing than the last.

Heaven help him, he wanted her, wanted to recapture all those emotions that had once pulsed so vividly between them.

Shane's heart quickened as his pulse raced faster and faster. And then, from some deep, distant nether region, common sense pushed its way to the foreground. Strengthening, it took hold of him.

With effort, he drew his head back and slid his hands from her waist up to her shoulders. Exercising extreme control, he held her away from him.

"I should get back to Ellie," he said, his voice tight, hoarse.

"Right," Gina heard herself agreeing.

Her brain caught up half a beat later. What had she been thinking, kissing him like that? It wasn't as if she could lure him into making love with her, not with his niece sleeping in the family room and liable to wake up at any second.

"You can't leave her alone," she said, embarrassed that for a few moments, she hadn't been thinking of Ellie, only of how it had once been for Shane and her. "Go," she urged him, waving him toward the family room. "And thanks for the pastries," she added belatedly. Her brain was having a lot of difficulty processing what had just happened out here to her.

"Thanks for the soup—and the comic books," he added with a smile that quickly burrowed straight into her chest.

She nodded, reluctant to see Shane leave despite what she'd just said about his going to his niece.

"Don't mention it. And please let me know if there's anything else you need," Gina added. She was stalling and she knew it.

C'mon, Gina, get those feet moving toward your car. Go home.

"I will," Shane told her.

The look in his eyes told her more than that, but Gina was afraid that she was letting her imagination read far too much into it.

Shane had kissed her, she thought, kissed her the way he used to, with abandoned passion, and that was enough for now, she told herself.

She could build on that.

Gina didn't remember driving home. Didn't remember walking from her car into her apartment. All she was aware of the entire time she was going from here to there was the golden glow that was radiating within her.

The golden glow began to dissipate the second she saw the light blinking on her landline. Someone had left her a message. It was probably Sylvie calling with another mini-emergency for her to handle. Gina closed her eyes. She was certainly earning her money with that one.

Why hadn't Sylvie called her on her cell? Gina wondered, opening her eyes again. Oh well, she'd find out soon enough.

Sighing, she kicked off her shoes, got comfortable and played the single message on the phone.

She stiffened the moment she heard the voice. It wasn't Sylvie calling her, it was her mother.

"Hi, Gina. Haven't heard from you for a while now. Just checking to see how you are. I'll talk to you later."

Gina sighed again, louder this time.

Her five-foot-two mother was the only person in her world who could say those words—"I'll talk to you later"—and make them sound like a threat.

She pressed her lips together, thinking. Just as she was debating whether or not to call her mother back— "not" was winning—the landline rang. Caller ID identified the number as belonging to Anna Bongino.

"Not really the patient type, are you, Mom?" she murmured to the telephone.

Gina knew that if she didn't pick up the receiver, she was fairly certain that her mother would have the police dragging the nearby lake for her body. Taking a deep breath, she brought the receiver up to her ear.

Summoning a cheerful voice from somewhere deep within, Gina said, "Hi, Mom."

"Hello yourself, Gina," her mother responded. Gina knew something was off immediately. "I just thought I'd call and ask what's new in your life."

And that confirmed it. She knew that all-too-innocent tone of voice. Rather than beat around the bush and try to feel her mother out, she went straight to the question at the heart of this call.

"You know, don't you?" she accused.

"Know what, Gina?" Anna asked, taking her innocent tone up an octave.

Gina rolled her eyes. Her mother knew. Knew about Shane suddenly reappearing in her life. This was all her own fault. She should have never said anything to her sister.

"Mom," she said, doing her best to see the funny side

rather than lose her temper, "your abilities as an actress really leave a great deal to be desired."

Rather than become defensive, Anna merely said, "I'm sure I have no idea what you're referring to, Gina."

She wasn't about to drop this. "Yes, you do," Gina responded. "You're calling me because you're hoping to pump me for information about Shane."

"Shane?" Anna repeated so innocently Gina almost believed her, emphasis on "almost."

"Do you mean that really nice boy from college who would have made such a wonderful husband for you? *That* Shane?" she asked.

And now she oversold it, Gina thought. "Yes, Mother," she replied, at the end of her patience. "*That* Shane."

"Are you telling me that he's back? He's here in Bedford?" Anna cried.

Gina sighed. "Still not cutting it as an actress, Mom."

Ignoring her daughter's sarcasm, Anna plowed ahead. "When? How? Are you seeing him again?" her mother asked with enough enthusiasm to make Gina harbor a sliver of doubt, just enough to give the woman the benefit of possibly not knowing about this supposed "happy" development in her life.

"Slow down, Mom," she cautioned. "Oddly enough, I ran into him while helping my latest client with all her wedding requests."

There was silence on the other end of the line. Eerie silence. And then her mother almost wailed, "Don't tell me he's the groom."

Okay, maybe her mother really *was* on the level, she thought. "No, Mom, Shane actually 'creates' wedding cakes. That's how I 'ran into' him. My client sent me to him to ask that he do her wedding cake. It seems that Shane is very much in demand."

She heard her mother chuckle. "I'll bet," Anna interjected. "So, did you talk? Did you catch up on old times?"

She really wished that her mother would drop this. "It's not that easy, Mom."

"Of course it is," Anna insisted. "Talking was always easy for you. You said your first sentence when you were nine months old," she said proudly.

Gina closed her eyes. "So you've told me, Mom," she said wearily. "But this takes a little more finesse than that."

Anna seemed to be unfazed by her daughter's protest. "So? You've had thirty-two years of practice. Finesse already," Anna urged. Then, before her daughter could say anything she wouldn't welcome hearing, Anna went on with her sales pitch. "He really was such a very nice young man. Maybe I should invite the two of you over for dinner sometime."

And so it starts, Gina thought. Maybe she could put the skids on her mother's plan, at least for now. "You'd have to set three places at the table."

"You don't want your father there?" Anna questioned, confused. "I know he can be irritating at times, but still, he's your—"

"No, Mom, that's not it," Gina protested, stopping her mother before this got completely out of hand. "I'm saying that you'd need to set three *extra* places if you invite us over."

Her mother was quiet for a moment again. Then, in almost a hushed voice, unhappy voice, she asked, "Shane has a wife?"

She should have just taken her chances and not answered, Gina thought. "No, Mom, he has a four-year-old niece. And before you ask, he's her guardian."

"Oh my lord, he's even nicer than he used to be," her mother enthused.

Okay, she knew her mother meant well, but this was just agitating her at this point. "I've got to go, Mom. I've got a lot of details to see to if this wedding is going to be a success."

"Let me know how it's going!" She could hear her mother's voice practically radiating from the receiver as she started to hang it up.

"If there's anything to report," Gina replied and then quickly disconnected the call before her mother had a chance to say anything further that was just going to annoy her.

Gina took a deep breath, willing herself to get her agitation under control. She really couldn't blame her mother for being like this and taking up Shane's cause. Shane had charmed the woman from the first moment her mother had laid eyes on him.

Same as her, Gina thought.

Although she tried to will herself to go to sleep, she just couldn't seem to manage it.

Gina had finally managed to drop off to sleep when her alarm went off. The shrill alarm mingled with the sound of her ringing cell phone. Bleary-eyed, she reached for the alarm clock, shut it off and glanced at the time.

Seven o'clock.

By her calculation, she had gotten under five hours' sleep. Lord, she hoped she didn't look it, she thought.

Pulling herself together, she reached for the cell phone and brought it up close to her face.

"Hello?" she mumbled into what she hoped was the right end of the cell phone.

"I'm sorry, did I just wake you up?" she heard Shane apologize.

Her eyes flew open. Instantly, she could feel her brain scrambling in a frantic attempt to focus itself. She dragged air deep into her lungs, praying that would do the trick.

"No, I'm up," she protested, then repeated, "I'm up. I've been up for hours."

"Your voice doesn't sound like it," Shane told her.

Gina sighed. "That's because I'm lying," she admitted. "I had trouble falling asleep last night." Then, realizing what that had to sound like to him—that she was telling him that he was the reason she couldn't sleep—she quickly said, "My mother called when I got in and, well, you know how she is."

"Charming, as I recall," he answered with an amused laugh.

"No," she contradicted. "That's just my mother's gentleman caller facade. Her real persona is a lot different," Gina insisted. Not wanting to go into any further explanations about the woman—or what they'd discussed—Gina changed the subject back to the reason that he had called her in the first place. "What can I do for you?"

Shane got down to business. "I usually do a trial-run cake before I create the actual one for the wedding," he told her. "And since you told me that the bride was being extremely careful about not eating anything that she feels might make her gain weight, I was wondering if you'd like to be her stand-in."

All sorts of ideas ran through Gina's head, none of which really made any sense to her in this particular context.

"Excuse me?"

"What I'm asking you is if you would like to come in and sample the wedding cake I'm creating for Sylvie? Provided that you're not too busy," Shane added. He sounded completely serious.

"I'm never too busy for you—um, for your cake," she managed to amend at the last minute. "When would you like me to come by your shop?"

"How does two o'clock sound?"

Perfect. But then, any time he would have suggested would have been perfect, she thought.

"I'll be there," she answered brightly. "How's Ellie doing?" she asked, wondering if the little girl was still sick.

"Great," he answered. "She bounced up out of bed early this morning like she was never sick."

"I told you," Gina said, pleased.

"You did," Shane acknowledged, "and deep down inside, I knew you were right, but I still couldn't help worrying."

"That's because you're a good dad, I mean good uncle," she corrected herself.

"Actually," Shane confided to her, "a lot of times I feel as if I'm both an uncle *and* a father to that little girl."

There were a thousand things Gina wanted to say to him. She came very close to blurting out that her mother had asked about him, but she felt she was still in uncharted territory. That meant that she needed to be as cautious as possible so as not to endanger any progress that might have been made so far. She was intent on building things up between them, not in having them disintegrate.

So Gina curbed her desire to say all sorts of positive, possibly over-the-top things to him and just went with something relatively neutral.

"There should be a way to hyphenate that in your case," she told him. "You know, like Uncle-Dad."

He laughed. "Like that's not going to confuse Ellie at all."

Gina grew serious. "Does she know what happened to her parents?"

"Yes. I told her the first time she asked about them. I put it in terms she could understand—that Mommy and Daddy had been in an accident and they went straight up to heaven to keep God company. That seemed to satisfy her at the time. She doesn't feel that they abandoned her if that's what you're asking."

"No, I wasn't thinking of that," Gina said honestly. "After all, she's only four."

"A very bright, precocious four," Shane pointed out. "She certainly keeps me on my toes."

"Oh, I'll bet." She could listen to the sound of his voice against her ear all day, but she knew he had work to do. Just as she knew she needed to let him get to it. "All right then, I'll see you at two—unless you call and tell me that you want me there later."

"No, two will be fine. Unless the stove blows up. I'm kidding," Shane assured her when he heard silence on the other end. "That hasn't happened to me for a while now."

"You're still kidding, right?" Gina asked uncertainly.

"Actually, it was this ancient stove that I used when

I was in Uganda and no, I'm not," he told her. "It really did blow up."

"Okay, my cue to leave," she said. She knew that if she didn't force herself to hang up now, she never would. "Bye."

"Goodbye, Gina."

The sound of his voice echoed in her head for the rest of the morning, keeping her company and whispering of things that were to come.

Maybe.

Chapter Fifteen

"You look exhausted."

It wasn't what Shane had intended to say to Gina when he saw her walking into his shop that afternoon at exactly two o'clock on the dot, but her wearied appearance caught him totally by surprise.

Gina swept into the shop and went straight toward one of the two tables in the showroom. "Flatterer," she quipped, dropping her shoulder bag on the table.

"No, I'm serious." Shane came around the counter and joined the woman on the other side. He searched her face. "Is everything all right?"

"It is now—I think," she replied uncertainly.

"And before?" he asked, waiting to hear the explanation behind why she looked as if she'd been on a forced march for the last eighteen hours.

She sighed. "Before it was like being in a canoe, pad-dling madly while trying to navigate in the middle of a torrential storm."

Shane pulled out a chair, silently urging her to sit down. He waited until she did, then he dropped into the one opposite her before he said, "You are going to translate that into English so that the rest of us can understand, right?"

She sighed. She supposed she was carrying on a little bit too much, but she had earned it after what she'd gone through.

"I can't wait until this wedding is over with," she told him with a sigh.

He got up and poured her a cup of tea from the stand he had set up to the side for his customers. "I kind of thought it might have something to do with that. What happened?" he asked.

She looked up at him with a smile. "Well, aside from my having to sweet-talk a wedding cake from the much sought after 'Cassidy'—which turned out to be a good thing," she quickly added, "and finding a contractor who could repair an unexpected large gaping hole in the church roof in time for the wedding, not to mention securing a decent photographer to replace the one who suddenly remembered he had a conflict—two weddings at the same time taking place in opposite directions— I just spent the whole morning negotiating with a florist who tried to tell me that carnations made a better statement decorating the church than the lilies that the bride wanted."

She paused to take a sip of the tea, then sighed as the hot liquid curled its way through her system. "I had no idea that florists could be so temperamental and hard-nosed."

Listening, Shane nodded and looked properly sympathetic.

"Who won?" he asked when she paused to take another breath.

About to take another sip of tea, Gina raised her eyes up over the rim of the cup. Her eyes met his. "Who do you think?"

Shane laughed. "I don't have to think, I know. You always were persuasive," he recalled fondly. She really did look wiped out, though, he thought. "Look, if you want to go home and unwind, we can do this tomorrow. There's no huge rush."

"I *am* unwinding," Gina informed him. Being here with him like this was having an oddly tranquilizing effect on her, she realized. She had gotten past the tense, nervous stage with him, so that was a good thing. "Right now, what I need most is a friendly face." She smiled at him. "You qualify."

Setting the small delicate cup back in its saucer, she looked around the showroom. It was just the two of them out front, although she did hear the sounds of activity coming from the back area where all the baking was done.

"Where's Ellie?" Gina asked him. "I expected to see her out here."

He could see why she would have thought that, given what he'd told her about why he had gone into this line of work to begin with.

"I needed to concentrate this morning so I gave Ellie a choice of going to preschool or staying home with Barbara," he said, referring to Ellie's nanny. "She picked Barbara—big surprise."

Gina put her own interpretation to his explanation. "Ellie doesn't like going to school?"

"Ellie loves learning new things well enough—as a matter of fact, she likes reading her storybooks to me. What she doesn't like is having to follow rules. She finds them 'not fun,'" he said, quoting his niece. "I guess she thinks they're too confining."

"Wonder where she gets that from," Gina said, doing her best not to laugh. She didn't succeed.

He looked at Gina in surprise. "Hey, I followed rules."

"Funny, I seem to remember you cutting classes and talking me into cutting them, too, so that we could spend the afternoon just hanging out together."

Shane shrugged. "That was a unique set of circumstances," he told her. "And besides, I was a kid then."

"You were twenty," Gina reminded him. "And Ellie's only four," she added as if that explained why the little girl was acting rebelliously in his eyes.

"Oh, but at four I listened to the adults in my life."

"I wouldn't know," Gina replied. "I didn't know you when you were four. You could have been a hellion at that age," she teased.

"Well, I wasn't," he told her. "I was a quiet, mousy kid back then. Ellie's nothing like that," Shane pointed out. And then he looked concerned. "Ellie's so smart for her age, there are times she sounds like an adult trapped in a little person's body. She worries me," he confessed. "There is such a thing as being too smart."

He was serious, Gina realized and tried to reassure him. "Not if she has someone looking out for her, guiding her."

"You're talking about me," he concluded.

"No, I'm talking about my imaginary friend, Sam," Gina said, gesturing about at the empty air. "Of course I'm talking about you. Hey, you're kind, patient, creative and have a very level head on your shoulders. If you ask me, I'd say that Ellie's future couldn't be in more excellent hands."

Shane waved her words away. "There's no need to flatter me, Gina. I've already agreed to create this cake for your client's wedding."

She was insulted that Shane thought she would do that. "I'm not flattering you," she said with an edge in her voice. "I'm telling it like it is."

Shane raised a brow, looking at her. She could feel herself squirming inside. She always did whenever Shane looked at her that way.

He was getting to her and she needed to hold it together. She didn't want him feeling that she was coming on to him in his workplace. Shane had kissed her, and she'd kissed him back. Twice. He had to know how she felt about him. The next move was up to him and she had a feeling it wouldn't happen here, in his place of work. Not with his people only a few steps away in the back. They were liable to walk in at any second.

"You said something about sampling the wedding cake you created," Gina prompted, looking toward the back where she assumed he had it.

"Right." He rose again, nodding toward the back area. "It's in the back. Let me go get it."

"I'll be here," she told him cheerfully.

The second Shane left, she whipped out her small mirror from her purse and quickly looked herself over. Gina winced. He was right. She looked as if she'd been fighting off dragons for the last forty-eight hours. Damage control involved doing a quick pass through her hair with her comb and freshening up her fading lipstick.

She barely finished the latter when she heard Shane returning to the showroom.

Throwing the lipstick back into her purse, she deliberately straightened in her chair as if assuming better posture helped somehow.

Gina thought she would just be sampling a slice of cake. She wasn't prepared for what he brought out. It was a complete, detailed miniature wedding cake like the one he proposed to make for the actual event.

Nor did she expect to be totally blown away by it. The cake was comprised of five tiny tiers, arranged to look like wedding gifts piled one on top of another. The "gifts" came with ribbons made out of what she assumed was intricately decorated icing. There was also a cascade of pink roses, also made out of icing, spilling down one side of the "gifts."

Visually, it was incredible.

"It's beautiful," Gina whispered to him in utter awe. "A total feast for the eyes," she added, looking up at Shane.

"All right, so it looks good," he responded. "But the true test here is how it tastes." Cutting a slice of off-white chiffon cake for her from the bottom, he slid it onto a plate. She noted that the filling had cherries in it. Shane handed the plate to her along with a fork. "Tell me what you think."

"What I think is that it's a sin to cut up such a work of art and put it into my mouth," she told him honestly.

"Then you'd be missing out on the best part—provided that everything turned out the way it should," Shane added. He nodded toward the plate. "Tell me what you think," he repeated.

"I think you could give humble lessons to the florist," Gina responded.

"Not interested in the florist," he told her, dismissing the man. "I'm interested in what you think of the cake."

She expected to like the cake. After all, she had already had some of his pastries—more than she should have, she knew, but they were very difficult to resist. She assumed the same would be true of the cake Shane had created for Sylvie's wedding. It would be delicious.

Delicious was a paltry word in this case.

The moment she slid the fork into her mouth, Gina knew that the bar of her expectations had been set much too low. This was by far better than anything she had thought it would be. There was an explosion of magnificent taste in her mouth.

She sat there, taking in a deep breath as she savored what was in her mouth.

"Well?" Shane prodded gently when she hadn't said anything.

Gina looked at him. Rather than answer, she took another forkful and put it into her mouth. Her lips closed over it, savoring the exquisitely seductive dance that was occurring on her tongue.

She swallowed and smiled. "What I think is that you are *definitely* in the right business. I also think that my tongue is in love." She eyed her plate, tempted to stuff the rest of it into her mouth. It took effort to restrain herself. "Where did you *ever* learn how to do this?"

He shrugged dismissively at the implied compliment. "You can't help picking up things along the way if you keep your ears open. So, you really like it?" Shane asked again, just in case Gina thought she had to be nice and wasn't being totally straightforward.

"Like it?" Gina repeated. "This cake is a whole new reason to get married."

The second the words were out of her mouth, she realized what she had said and the memories that those words could very well have unearthed.

Idiot!

Clearing her throat, Gina tried to walk her words back. "I mean—"

Shane held up his hand to stop the apology he knew was coming before she could attempt to form the words for it.

"That's all right, Gina, I know what you meant. Thanks." He smiled. "It's good to know you liked it."

"You don't need me to verify your efforts," she told him. "You know you're good."

"I know I *try* to be good. But there have been failures. And just because something works for me doesn't mean that it's going to work for someone else—visually or taste-wise," he added.

"So I'm your test guinea pig?" Gina asked with a laugh.

"I wouldn't exactly refer to you as that," Shane told her. "But I can't very well ask anyone who works for me to give me their 'honest' opinion because I sense that they're afraid if I don't like what they say, I'll terminate them."

He wasn't like that and she knew it, but she decided to tease him a little. The situation had grown far too serious. "Would you?"

"Of course not," Shane told her with feeling, and then shrugged. "But you can't change the way people think. And anyway, what I wanted was the opinion of someone who had it in them to be brutally honest—like you."

Gina blew out a breath. The remark stung. She hadn't expected that. But there was no sense in getting defensive about his comment, even though it really bothered her that that was the way Shane thought about her.

"I guess I had that coming," she allowed.

Shane saw the look on her face. He'd said too much, he thought.

"I didn't mean it that way," he told her. "I meant that you're not afraid of saying what you think."

She drew back her shoulders, unconsciously bracing herself for what might be coming. "I've also learned that saying the first thing that pops into my head is something that I had to temper because it wasn't always what I really *wanted* to say." Her eyes met his. "I did pay a price for that. I think I already told you that."

She needed to leave, Gina thought. Now, because she was afraid that she might say something she was going to regret again. Either that, or just break down in tears. Neither was something she wanted Shane to see or hear.

Gina rose to her feet then. Picking up her purse, she slid the strap onto her shoulder, securing the purse with a tug.

"Your wedding cake exceeds any expectation I had and I'm sure that Sylvie will say the same thing. Don't change a thing—about the cake," she emphasized, looking at him pointedly.

Shane silently upbraided himself. The tight rein he had kept on his emotions while being around Gina all this time had slipped and he had allowed those hurt feelings he'd been suppressing all this time to come spilling out. And he didn't feel any better by doing it; he just felt worse.

"Gina—" he began, trying to find a way to apologize for allowing his pettiness to take over.

She was already at the entrance, one hand on the

doorknob. All she wanted to do was get away. "I forgot I promised the bride I'd see her today and give her a progress report on everything."

He knew that was an excuse. Shane tried again. "Gina—"

The corners of her eyes were stinging. She had to get out of there before she broke down. She kept her face averted.

"I'll give her a five-and-a-half-star rating out of five for your cake. That'll make her very happy," she told Shane as she hurried out the door.

Moving quickly, Gina got into her car. She slammed the door just as she heard Shane coming out of his shop. He was coming for her.

Gina gunned the engine. He was going to try to apologize, or maybe say that one bad turn deserved another, she didn't know. In either case, she didn't want to hear it.

Most of all, she didn't want to let him see her crying. Crying was a sign of weakness and she had sworn to herself that she wasn't going to be weak. Not ever again. She'd made her apologies and he really hadn't taken her at her word.

Fine. She needed to move on now.

No matter how much she wanted to be with him, her rejection—her stupidly worded, baseless rejection—would always be there between them and he was never going to let her forget it.

Well, what was done was done and she was through trying to atone for it.

It was time to forget about him.

Chapter Sixteen

It had been a long, grueling day. At one point, Gina didn't think that it would ever come to an end. She'd even seriously entertained the idea of throwing up her hands and quitting, but in her heart she knew she couldn't do that. Quitting would have gone against everything that she was.

But she had to admit that the idea was nonetheless awfully tempting.

Sylvie had needed a great deal of hand-holding today. Her latest client had gotten into an argument with her maid of honor last night and hurt feelings were still very much alive and well today. Monica had actually threatened to hand in her title and her gown and be a no-show at the wedding.

The cause of the argument was so petty, Gina couldn't even get the two women to talk about it. Nevertheless, through sheer grit Gina had managed to get them to patch things up. It had taken her the better part of four hours to smooth things out and to get the two women to call a truce. She embarrassed them into realizing that they would be sacrificing one of the most important days in not just Sylvie's life, but in Monica's, as well.

"Mine?" Monica cried in a shrill voice. "How can it be mine?"

"Because not everyone gets to be asked to be a maid of honor," Gina informed the woman in a voice that bordered on no-nonsense. "There's a lot of unspoken love that goes into making that choice. You don't want to allow an inconsequential argument to make you lose sight of that, do you?"

Using that, and similar arguments, Gina managed to intimidate both women into calling a truce.

After she got the two women to grudgingly agree with her, they wound up crying and made up. And then Sylvie and Monica *celebrated* making up. Gina, being instrumental in making them resolve their differences, perforce had to remain for that part, as well. The women had insisted on it.

It was close to eight o'clock by the time Gina was finally able to pull into her parking spot. Getting out of her car, she crossed the parking lot and made her way to her ground-floor apartment.

She didn't see Shane sitting in front of her door until she was almost on top of him. By then it was too late for her to retreat unnoticed.

He had obviously been waiting for her for a while now. The second he saw her, Shane scrambled to his feet, his body partially blocking access to her door.

Gina's fingers tightened around her keys, momentarily at a loss as to what to do. She raised her chin defensively. "What are you doing here?"

"Waiting for you." Shane was tempted to leave it at that, but that didn't begin to explain what had forced him to come here in the first place. So he told her the truth and completed his answer. "Thinking of all the different ways to tell you I'm sorry."

No, damn it! She wasn't going to allow herself to let him into her life again. She'd finally talked herself into putting him out of her thoughts. She couldn't go back to square one again.

Why was he doing this to her?

But he was just standing there, looking at her. Waiting for her to say something.

Almost grudgingly, Gina asked in a stilted voice, "Where's Ellie?"

"She's home," he answered. His smile was self-deprecating. "I asked Barbara to watch her at double her rate. When I got to triple, she was more than happy to accommodate me and stay. Even told me to take all the time I needed." Shane's expression turned serious as he looked at her. "I figured I'd need a lot of time." He searched her face, looking for some indication that he had some small, slight chance of making amends. He nodded at the door. "Gina, can I come in?"

She knew she should say no. Knew she should tell Shane that they had nothing to talk about and just send him on his way.

Turning from Shane she almost said it, almost told him to go.

But then she unlocked her door and walked into her apartment. She left the door standing open behind her.

He took the open door as consent on her part. Grateful, he walked into the apartment behind her.

Easing the door closed once he'd crossed the threshold, Shane repeated his apology. "I'm sorry that things got out of hand today. I didn't mean for them to—"

Gina swung around to face him. Her face was a collage of all the mixed emotions churning within her. "You've been back in Bedford, what, three years now?" she asked, cutting into his apology.

"Yes," he replied, never taking his eyes off her face.

He saw anger creasing Gina's forehead as she asked him in an accusatory voice, "Why didn't you look me up when you came home?"

"I didn't think you wanted me to," he explained haplessly.

"You didn't know *what* I was thinking," she countered. "You never gave me the option of telling you." She was struggling to keep contained the anger that had been unearthed in the aftermath of what had happened in his shop today.

She could actually feel it growing, swelling in her chest. Seeking release.

He needed to phrase this right, Shane thought, searching for the right words. He didn't want this to turn into another argument. He hadn't come here for that. He'd come for forgiveness.

"Maybe it hasn't really occurred to you yet, but by the time I came back, my whole situation had changed. It wasn't just me anymore. I was responsible for the care and welfare of a little human being. I was then and I am now," he emphasized. "And I felt that if you didn't want me when I was alone, I *knew* you wouldn't want me with a little kid to raise. I couldn't stand to hear you turn me down again."

Gina had fisted her hands on her hips, her eyes flashing not just at what Shane had said but at the terrible waste that had been created because of all the miscommunication that had gone down.

Not to mention all the time they had lost because of the thoughtless rejection that she had said to him in fear.

"Sorry, smart guy," Gina informed him, "but you were wrong. You didn't know anything." Tossing her head, her eyes narrowed as she said, "I would have loved to have been there to raise that little girl with you."

He didn't believe her. "You're only saying that."

She threw up her hands, uttering an unintelligible noise in her sheer frustration. "How do I get you to believe me? Should I get all three of our names tattooed somewhere on my body, linked in hearts? What?" she demanded. "Tell me what to do and I'll do it!"

The corners of Shane's mouth curved. "I admit that would be interesting," he acknowledged.

She stared at him, shaking her head. She didn't know what to think.

Was he being sweet? Did she drop her guard and believe him, or was he waiting for that so he could get back at her for what he felt she'd put him through with that rejection years ago?

She didn't know and she was afraid of making the wrong choice.

"Damn you, Shane," she cried, "you're the only one who's ever made me crazy like this."

"Oh no," he contradicted. He was grinning at her now and the grin was working its way into her system, seducing her. "I can't take credit for that. You were this way long before I ever came along. A 'self-made woman' I think was the way you once referred to yourself."

Exasperated, not to mention frustrated, Gina doubled up her fist and swung it back, ready to punch him in her agitation.

Shane caught her hand, blocked the punch and pulled her to him.

Pinning Gina's arms against her sides, he brought his mouth down to hers and kissed her. Kissed her long and hard, until she stopped struggling and kissed him back.

Her hands loosened, no longer fisted, she raised them up and threaded her arms around his neck as the kiss continued growing in intensity and depth.

Gina sighed as Shane drew his lips away. "I don't want to fight, Gina," he told her softly.

Her mouth slowly curved into a smile. "Oh, I don't know," she responded. "Wrestling's got some things going for it."

But he shook his head. "Me, I always liked that old slogan from the sixties. Make love, not war." He grew serious as he searched her face, wanting to make sure that he hadn't misjudged the situation. "Make love with me, Gina," he urged in a low, seductive voice. "It's all I've thought about for the last ten years."

Gina paused and for one awful moment, he thought she was going to turn him down. That she was going to tell him that they had lost their chance and shouldn't reopen old wounds.

And then, her eyes locked on his, she whispered, "Prove it."

That was when he finally knew that it was going to be all right. That they had both paid for his rash proposal and her equally as rash refusal.

"With pleasure," he answered, pressing his lips against her throat. He felt the pulse there jump in response and the desire he'd felt building within him increased tenfold.

Holding himself in check despite the fact that he ached to take her right then and there, Shane made slow, deliberate love to every inch of her body, causing Gina to yield to him as he crisscrossed her skin with a network of hot, ardent kisses, branding her body everywhere he touched.

Making it his.

Shane only vaguely remembered stripping Gina's clothes from her body.

What left a far greater imprint on his brain was feeling her fingers traveling along his chest, his shoulders, his torso. Touching him everywhere.

Arousing him to an incredible degree.

Every time her hand passed over another part of his body, Shane could feel himself responding to her, feel himself aching and wanting her the way he had never wanted another woman before.

Because in his soul, he knew that he had never loved another woman, not the way he loved her. Even while he kept denying it to himself over the years, he knew he loved Gina.

Always had.

Always would, Shane now thought silently. Even if all he ever would have was this one night with her, he knew himself well enough to know that he would never love anyone else the soul-branding way that he loved the woman here with him now.

A white-hot passion wrapped itself around Shane as

he blanketed Gina's body with a burning array of kisses, spreading them all up and down her heaving skin.

He had her back pressed against the sofa cushions when Gina surprised him by suddenly pulling him to her, reversing their positions. Determined to return the favor. Pressing her mouth against his throat, his shoulders, his chest, Gina all but devoured him, startled by the amount of passion that had been unleashed within her. Every place she touched became a burning, erotic area, moist and throbbing. Desire just continued mounting and she acted on it.

Because he could hold himself in check for only so long when she did that, Shane flipped their positions again, laying her on her back. From there he began to anoint all the regions of her body, working his way from her mouth to the hollow of her throat, down her breasts, then on to her quivering belly.

She thought he would stop there and she tried to wrap her legs around his torso, arching against him. But he was too quick for her.

His mouth went questing farther and farther, until, before she realized it, his tongue was mining the very core of her.

Gina suddenly arched her back, seized by an exquisite sensation that exploded within her. It sent shockwaves to every nether region.

Stunned, she stared at Shane, her heart pounding from the climax she'd just experienced.

She had no time to regroup because Shane began to move up along her body again, following his journey in reverse until the face that had filled so many of her dreams was looming right over hers.

Shane slipped his fingers through hers, joining them before he moved her legs apart with his knee.

Breathing hard, she pressed up against him, silently inviting him in.

"Look at me," he whispered.

Until that second, she hadn't realized that her eyes were closed. She opened them and that was when he entered her, creating one unit out of two.

Her heart was pounding wildly and she heard herself telling him, "I've missed this."

She thought she heard Shane say, "So have I," but she wasn't sure. Adrenaline was racing through her whole body, the rush she was experiencing blocking out everything except for the two of them and the myriad desires and passions throbbing demandingly throughout her entire being.

Shane began to move, slowly at first despite the urgency that propelled him. Gina matched each move he made, going faster and faster the second he did until it became a race to see which of them would be gratified first.

It was a tie.

Shane brought her up and over the summit of sensations just as it exploded all around him.

Euphoria showered down all around them, embracing them in its grip. Gina held on to it for as long as she could, trying to push the wave of pending sorrow as far back as she could.

It came anyway. Sorrow because the euphoria had receded.

But he was still there, still lying next to her, with his arm wrapped around her, holding her close. It pushed back the darkness. She listened as Shane's heart beat against hers, slowly returning back to its normal rhythmic beat.

She was afraid to move, afraid if she did, she would wind up chasing away all these delicious feelings, sending them back into some deep, dark cave where she couldn't reach them, couldn't touch them.

Gina felt him shifting, but Shane wasn't getting up. Instead, he just raised his head and pressed a soft kiss against her hair.

"You're awfully quiet," he commented. "Something wrong?"

She laughed at his question, at first softly and then with growing gusto until the sound echoed throughout the room.

"Wrong?" Gina repeated, raising her head so that she could look at his face. "For the first time in ten years, everything is absolutely right."

"Oh," he said and she could have sworn she heard relief in his voice. And then he confirmed it by saying, "You had me worried there for a minute. I thought maybe you were having regrets."

"Regrets?" she questioned.

"Yes, over what we just did," Shane elaborated.

"Regrets," she repeated as if it was a strange, foreign word that she was trying to make sense of. And then she laughed again. "My only regret is that it took so long for this to happen again."

Before he had a chance to comment on her words, Gina proceeded to take the lead so she could show him how much she didn't regret what had just happened there between them. She pushed him back against the sofa as she kissed every square inch of him, a prelude to another round of lovemaking.

Chapter Seventeen

Gina felt gloriously exhausted. She and Shane had made love two more times that evening. That was a total of three times, and she was amazed that she could still move. The temptation to curl up in Shane's arms and fall asleep was almost overwhelming. But Gina knew that she couldn't in good conscience give in to that.

That would be selfish, and she was determined not to ever put herself in the center of anything. Turning toward Shane, she murmured, "I'm going to get up and make you some fresh coffee."

"I'm not sure coffee will help," he told her, pulling her back into bed as she began to get up. "You have completely exhausted me."

"No, not for that," she laughed, brushing a quick kiss to his lips. "Coffee to wake you up so you don't drive off the side of the road while you're going home."

"I'm going home?" he asked.

"Yes. You want to be there in the morning when Ellie wakes up, don't you?"

He was surprised that she had even thought of the little girl. "And you're okay with that?" Shane questioned.

"Why wouldn't I be?" Gina asked. "She's not a rival, she's a sweet four-year-old girl—and your niece," she underscored. Funny how everything seemed to have changed now. "I think you wanting to be there for Ellie and take care of her is one of your more attractive qualities."

He would have been lying if he hadn't admitted that this was in the back of his head, wondering how all this was going to work out between them. "And you really don't mind my leaving to be with Ellie?"

"If you must know," she told him, pausing to give Shane one more quick kiss before slipping on a T-shirt to cover herself before she went to the kitchen, "right now I feel so absolutely wonderful, I think I could probably walk across water if I tried. Besides, I don't want to be the bad guy who keeps you away from Ellie." She made her way toward the doorway. "This way, you might be more inclined to maybe come back for seconds."

"Seconds and thirds and fourths," he added, calling after her as she left the room.

Gina smiled. That sounded good, but she wasn't about to hold him to what he had just said. Taking her opened coffee container out of the refrigerator, she measured out just enough to brew a superstrong mug of coffee the way she knew he liked it.

Setting the measuring spoon aside she poured a mugful of water into the machine. She wasn't going to allow herself to start dreaming about forever and risk being disappointed again. Once had been incredibly difficult for her. Twice would undoubtedly come close to killing her—or at least kill her spirit.

"Let's take it one day at a time and see where this goes," she told Shane as he came into the kitchen.

He had put his clothes on again and looked as if he was ready to leave. Well, that hadn't taken much persuading. She reminded herself that it had been her idea, so of course he was ready to go.

"Here's your coffee," she said, putting the mug on the table. "Why don't you sit down while you're having it," she coaxed.

Shane sat down and picked up the mug, looking at her thoughtfully. Gina was being cautious again, he thought. But he supposed, when he got right down to it, he couldn't really blame her. Not after the way things had gone down between them the first time. Granted, it had initially been her fault, yes, but he was the one who had taken it upon himself to go away. Looking back, he had to admit that had to have been hard on her.

He raised the mug, as if he was trying to toast something. "To one day at a time," he said, his eyes on Gina's.

He vowed to himself that he was going to tread lightly, but in the end, he was fully committed to convincing Gina that they belonged together. Whether she knew it or not, she had already passed the first hurdle. She had put Ellie ahead of not only herself, but also ahead of their rekindling romance.

It could only go well from here.

When Gina smiled at him after he'd made his "toast," he knew that he was on the right track.

Funny what reviving a romance could do for a person's spirit, Gina thought several days later. In her case, it gave her the strength and fortitude to handle any crisis and bear up to it all with surprising humor and an astounding amount of energy.

Nothing daunted her.

Not even the fact that she had to deal with Sylvie and her current client's never-ending cavalcade of mini-emergencies.

This time Sylvie's newest emergency was courtesy of the bride's pet cat, a calico named Cinnamon. Apparently, Cinnamon had managed to pull down Sylvie's veil from where she had it hung up in the closet and then the nimble cat proceeded to attack it in a frenzy, shredding parts of it as if it were some sort of a gauzy enemy.

Reviewing the damage, Gina was temporarily speechless. But she was quick to rally—and in part she credited that to Shane's influence. She managed to calm down the hysterical bride, then she told Sylvie that she knew someone who could restore the veil to practically its original state.

"You do?" Sylvie sniffled. "That would be nothing short of a miracle. I had it handmade and flown in from Switzerland."

Of course you did, Gina thought. "Trust me. I know a miracle worker," Gina had told her, gathering up the veil and depositing it into the large box it had originally come in.

Anna Bongino stared at the torn veil that Gina had brought to her, then raised her eyes to her daughter's face.

"Is this some sort of a joke, Gina?" she asked her daughter.

"No, not a joke," Gina assured her, trying to sound

cheerful. "Think of it more as a challenge, Mom." She smiled at her mother. "I just talked you up to my latest client. You were a seamstress at that high-end bridal shop for twenty-three years, right, Mom?" Gina reminded her mother.

"Seamstress, yes. Miracle worker, no," Anna replied, taking the torn veil out of the box. She shook her head, totally astonished. "Besides, I took that job so that one day I would be able to sew your wedding dress and veil, not repair a veil that some girl's cat mistook for its dose of catnip."

Gina put her hand on her mother's arm. "Please, Mom. This means a lot to me."

Something had changed, Anna thought. She could *feel* it. She secretly blessed the woman she had sought out with her problem. She knew that Maizie and her friends were behind this. There was a lightness to her daughter that had been missing for years.

Looking at the veil again, Anna pretended to take a dim view of the veil's chances. She frowned, shaking her head. "I'll see what I can do, but I can't make any promises."

Gina threw her arms around her mother, totally surprising her. After a beat, Anna allowed herself to close her arms around her daughter and return the hug.

This was worth everything.

"You seem rather chipper, given that you're working with a crazy woman," Anna said. She couldn't resist adding, "Anything I should know about?"

"Nope, not a thing. I just love life, that's all," Gina answered as she began to leave. She paused at the door for a moment and said, "And for the record, I don't think of you as a crazy woman."

Anna drew back her shoulders. "I wasn't talking about me," she informed her daughter.

"I know." Gina laughed. "Thanks, Mom, you're a lifesaver. And I'll give you a call later to see how you're doing." She opened the front door, about to leave. "By the way, I'll need you to finish fixing the veil by Tuesday at the latest. Earlier if possible."

Anna's mouth dropped open, but she forced herself to swallow the first words that came to her. Instead, she just shook her head.

"It's going to take a miracle," Gina's mother murmured in disbelief. But she knew that she was talking to herself by now.

Having temporarily taken care of Sylvie's latest emergency and then checking on all the other recently handled pseudoemergencies to make sure that everything was progressing on schedule and that no new developments had taken place, Gina decided to reward herself and swing by Shane's house later that day.

Gina started talking the second that Shane opened the door. "I hope you don't mind my stopping by. But I was passing by this bookstore today and saw this big picture book in the window with that cartoon, *Happy Hound Puppies*, on the cover. I thought of Ellie because she said she liked watching that cartoon, so I got it for her." She indicated the shopping bag she had in her hand. "I hope that's okay," she added as an afterthought.

Shane took the bag from her. It felt heavy to him. "You did say one book, right?" he asked, looking into the shopping bag. "It looks like there are several in here."

Gina shrugged a little sheepishly. "Well, once I went into the store to buy that book, I saw a few others that I thought Ellie might like. I really couldn't make up my mind, so I bought all of them," she concluded with a smile.

Shane laughed at her explanation, touched that she was motivated to buy gifts for his niece. "I can see that."

Ellie had obviously heard Gina talking and came running in from another room to join Gina and her uncle. "Hi, Gina!" she cried. "We're having dinner. You can eat with us if you'd like. We have plenty—especially vegetables," she confided, lowering her voice when she came to the word *vegetables*.

Shane looked amused. "Ellie doesn't really like vegetables," he told Gina needlessly.

Ellie tossed her head, negating his statement. "I like mashed potatoes."

"You need green vegetables, munchkin," Shane reminded her.

Ellie pursed her lips in a frown. "My stomach can't see. It doesn't know the mashed potatoes aren't green," she informed her uncle.

Delighted by Ellie's spirit, Gina laughed. "Can't argue with that."

The next thing she knew, Ellie was grabbing her hand and pulling her toward the kitchen.

"Come to the table," she coaxed, echoing something she'd heard her uncle say to her.

Gina looked over her shoulder at Shane to see if this was all right with him.

Following behind them, Shane gestured toward the kitchen. "You heard the munchkin." He smiled at Ellie. "Come and eat with us."

She didn't need her arm twisted.

Gina stayed for dinner, which turned out to be pork loin. There were also two servings of vegetables, spinach and mashed potatoes. She saw Ellie deliberately avoiding the spinach on her plate.

"Did you know that if you mixed potatoes into the spinach, it doesn't taste like spinach at all?" Gina told Ellie. She proceeded to mix the two on her plate, then offered a small forkful to Ellie. "Try it," she coaxed.

Ellie made a face, then took the tiniest of bites, moving her head in and out like a small bird taking a drink of water.

"Not bad, eh?" Gina asked. "My mom used to do that to get me to eat my spinach."

"You didn't like green vegetables either?" Ellie asked, surprised and also pleased that she had something in common with Gina.

"Nope. Would you like some more?" Gina asked. She was aware that Shane was silently observing all this play out.

Ellie's head bobbed up and down. "Yes, please. It tastes like crunchy mashed potatoes."

Gina nodded, preparing the two vegetables for the little girl. "Good description."

After dinner, Ellie begged her to stay so that they could "read these books together."

"If it's okay with your uncle," Gina qualified, glancing toward Shane.

"Oh sure, he won't mind," Ellie confidently assured her. "He's a good guy."

Which was how Gina wound up helping Ellie read the books that she had brought over. Ellie insisted on reading all of them. Or at least most of them. Ellie's eyes began to droop by the time they had finished four books. By the middle of the fifth book, she finally lost her battle with her eyelids.

"You wore her out," Shane said. "Good job. It usually takes me a lot longer."

Moving aside the storybooks Ellie had surrounded herself with, Shane slipped one hand underneath his niece's body and slowly picked her up, taking care not to wake her up. Gina followed behind him as he carried the little girl up to her room.

"Want me to change her into her pj's?" Gina asked him.

"No, just take off her sneakers. If you start to change her out of her clothes into her pajamas, she might wake up and you would be amazed how recharged Ellie can get by taking a simple ten-minute nap."

"Taking off sneakers it is," Gina responded, slowly slipping off first one sneaker, then the other and placing them side by side at the foot of Ellie's bed.

Shane covered his niece with the princess throw she had at the edge of her bed, turned on her nightlight, then tiptoed out as he eased the door closed.

"You did that like a pro," Gina couldn't help telling him.

"I should. I've had more than three years of practice doing it." He stopped in the hallway and turned toward her. "With any luck, she's down for the night. What would you like to do now?" he asked Gina.

She knew that she should call it a night herself. She didn't want him to think she'd come here so they could pick up where they had left off the other night.

But for some reason, she couldn't seem to get her legs to work. Couldn't seem to make herself walk out unless he told her something that would make her feel she should go.

So rather than do what she felt was the right thing, Gina looked up at Shane and said, "Surprise me."

"I don't think," he told her, moving closer to her, slipping his fingers into her hair, "after the other night, that anything I did would surprise you."

She could feel his breath along her lips, feel anticipation instantly rising up, full of demands, within her veins.

"Why don't we test that theory?" she proposed.

He cupped her face in his hands as her heart continued to beat wildly in her chest. Her breath froze as he slowly lowered his mouth to hers. When he made contact, it felt like there were multicolored flares going off in her head.

Stifling a moan, Gina slipped her arms around his neck, rising up on her toes to further lose herself in his kiss.

After what felt like a blissful eternity, he released her and drew his head back.

"Too forward?" he teased.

"Just shut up and do it again," she told him.

Humor curved his lips. "If you insist," he said just before he kissed her again.

The kiss lasted longer this time, eroding what little there was left of her resistance. And when he drew his head away a second time, something inside of her almost let out a mournful cry.

"You know," he told her in a low, seductive voice, "if you're interested, my room's just down the hall. We'd have more privacy there, provided of course you want more privacy."

This would have been the perfect time to pretend that it didn't matter to her one way or another. A perfect time for her to play hard to get.

But she wasn't interested in playing any games. She was interested in soothing this ache that was building up inside of her, making wanton demands on her. If making herself available to Shane was the wrong way to play this, so be it. Despite the vocation she'd chosen that required her to hold jittery brides' hands, she wasn't versed in the games people played. She wanted there to be nothing but honesty between them because at bottom, honesty was all any of them had.

"Funny man," she quipped. "Take me to your lair," she told him.

His eyes were already caressing her. "I could carry you off," he offered. "Like Tarzan. Maybe even find a couple of trees to swing from."

"Just walk," she told him.

He grinned. "Yes, ma'am."

He took her hand in his and brought her into his bedroom.

The room all but reeked of masculinity with its sleek, straight lines. There was a framed portrait of a couple with two little boys on the bureau. She assumed that was a family photograph taken when he was a little boy. But other than that, and one framed photograph of Ellie, there were no other pictures, no other personal touches in the room.

She turned to ask him why the room was so devoid of other photographs of his family but found she couldn't. Shane had found something better for her mouth to do. And her heart rejoiced over it.

Chapter Eighteen

The wedding that Gina had seriously felt would never arrive finally did.

Her mother, bless her, had lived up to her reputation and had somehow brought the bride's semishredded veil back from the dead, although it had taken longer than anticipated.

Gina presented it to Sylvie just as the bride had finished getting into her sleeveless, floor-length wedding gown.

Carefully placing the veil on the bride's head, Gina kept her fingers crossed that Sylvie wouldn't notice that the veil was a little shorter than it had been before Cinnamon had gone to work on it.

"Oh, it's perfect," Sylvie cried with enthusiasm. "Thank you! I never would have been able to survive all this chaos without you."

She carefully looked herself over from every possible angle in the floor-length mirror. The mirror was set up in the chamber that had been set aside for the bride and her bridesmaids.

There was no hiding the pleasure throbbing in Sylvie's voice.

It was a quarter to one o'clock in the afternoon and the wedding in the newly repaired church would be starting in fifteen minutes. Gina herself had been up since six, working nonstop almost the entire time. She had been checking and double-checking a thousand and one details so that there were no unexpected surprises, otherwise known as emergencies, cropping up before the festivities had a chance to get underway.

They were almost at the finish line, Gina thought.

She would have liked to demur to Sylvie's comment about not being able to survive without her services, saying something to the effect that Sylvie was stronger than she'd thought and was up to handling whatever emergency came up. But that would have been an outright lie. Sylvie, Gina had come to realize over these last three weeks, was too high-strung to handle a hangnail, much less anything that was more stressful than that.

Not wanting to insult the woman on her big day, Gina merely replied, "That's what I'm here for, Sylvie." She smiled at the bride. "Glad I could help."

"I'm telling all my friends about you," Sylvie promised, looking herself over one last time. "Get ready to have your cell phone start ringing nonstop."

Gina merely smiled at the bride's comment. Most likely, once all this was over, Sylvie wouldn't remember this conversation.

The beginning strains of the wedding march wove

themselves into the room. "That's your cue," Gina told Sylvie. Turning toward the other bridesmaids, including the maid of honor, Gina asked, "Everybody ready? This is it." She turned back to look at Sylvie again. The latter suddenly began to look pale. "Sylvie, what's wrong?"

"I think I'm going to throw up," the bride wailed, pressing her hand to her stomach.

"No, you are not," Gina informed her in a stern voice, then, looking Sylvie in the eye, she instructed, "You're going to walk down that aisle on your father's arm and you are going to marry the man of your dreams. Do you understand?"

Sylvie acknowledged the question with the barest nod of her head.

"Yes," she said in a hoarse voice.

"All right then," Gina announced, placing one arm around the bride's waist, guiding the young woman through the door, "we all know our positions. Let's have a wedding!"

The five bridesmaids all filed out. Gina hung back until she could create a space for herself right in front of the maid of honor. Sylvie clutched at her one last time, mouthing the words "Thank you," before she released Gina's arm.

The music seemed to swell as Gina walked into the church directly in front of the maid of honor. Moving slowly, Gina kept her eyes focused on the altar. Even so, she still managed to do a quick scan of the immediate area.

She was looking for Shane.

According to her schedule, Shane and his assistant should have brought the wedding cake to where the reception was being held an hour ago. That would have given him plenty of time to set up the cake, then change into a formal suit and come to the church. Shane was her plus one.

Right after the ceremony was over and the photographs were taken, Gina intended to spend the rest of the reception with Shane.

Provided, of course, that he hadn't decided to leave after he had set up the wedding cake, she thought. She was beginning to suspect that might very well be a possibility as she came up to the altar and took her place with the other bridesmaids on the left side of the church.

Temporarily facing the congregation now, Gina quickly scanned the faces of the people waiting for the bride to reach the altar and her destiny.

Shane was nowhere to be seen.

Had he changed his mind after all? Gina struggled to contain her disappointment. She had to hold it together. This wasn't about her. This was Sylvie's day and she had to keep smiling for the bride's sake. The photographer was moving around, snapping pictures. Nobody needed or wanted a sad bridesmaid ruining the pictures.

If nothing else, she reminded herself, Sylvie had already paid her for her services.

Just as she was moving in closer to the right of the altar and the other bridesmaids, the sound of the outer door, the one leading into the church proper, caught her attention. Sparing one glance to the rear of the congregation, Gina thought she caught a glimpse of Shane. Her heart literally skipped a beat. He looked dashing, dressed in a dark suit.

She allowed herself one more look as the minister began the ceremony.

It *was* Shane.

He'd kept his word. The smile that took over her face was genuine this time.

As a relaxed sigh escaped her lips, she allowed herself to enjoy the wedding.

The photographer, Andre, a small nimble man with a sharp eye for composition, was extremely thorough and he seemed to be everywhere, almost at the same time. Although she was the one responsible for finding him and bringing the photographer to Sylvie, Gina began to think that Andre was never going to stop herding them from one spot to another, never stop issuing orders and snapping photographs.

By the time Andre was finally finished, Gina felt she was wilting. But it turned out that the photographer had just finished this part of it. He and his assistant were coming to the reception hall to continue preserving the wedding with his camera. In addition, a videographer named Suzanne was making sure she was preserving everything that happened at the reception on video, as well.

Despite all this going on, all Gina saw was Shane. The first moment she was able to, she made her way over to him, a broad welcoming smile on her lips.

"You made it," she cried.

"Barely," Shane answered. "The traffic getting here was an absolute bear," he told her. "Some driver decided that his SUV belonged in two lanes at once. Driving like he owned the road, it was only a matter of time before he caused a minor pileup. Luckily, it happened right in front of me."

Gina blinked. Had she missed something? "Luckily?" she questioned, stunned that Shane would phrase it that way.

"Well, if it had happened a mile ahead of me, I'd probably still be on the freeway, trying to get here. And, even luckier," he continued, "the guy missed me."

She smiled, shaking her head. "Leave it to you to bury the headline."

The band was playing a familiar slow dance. Shane leaned into her, a warm look in his eyes. "Dance with me?" he asked.

"I'm not all that good at dancing," she warned.

Gina wanted only to sit with him and just spend the time talking. Having him here had sunbeams bouncing around inside of her. Part of her had doubted that he'd actually show up. Granted they had made love several times in the last week, but that was a private thing. Dancing with him was far more of a public thing.

"C'mon, Gina," he coaxed. "All you have to do is sway from side to side. Nobody's grading you on this," Shane assured her as he took her into his arms. Just as he closed his arm around her, he drew back his head to look at her. "You're trembling. Are you cold?" he asked, although it didn't feel cool enough to warrant her reaction.

She shrugged off his question, then decided to be honest with him. "I was just thinking of you getting crushed by that SUV, that's all."

A smile played on his lips. "Well, if that had happened, there wouldn't have been a cake for the reception."

Gina closed her eyes, searching for strength. She banked down the urge to shout at him. "That's not what's important here," she told him, gritting her teeth.

Shane smiled at her. "No point in thinking about what might have happened, Gina. It didn't," he stressed, brushing the incident aside. Changing the subject, he looked around as they continued dancing. "You put together a nice wedding."

While his compliment warmed her, she didn't feel right about accepting it. "The wedding was already put together when I took over. I just tweaked it in order to get it on track."

"All right," he allowed, "you do a good job tweaking." Shane's eyes crinkled as he grinned at her. "Although it's a little too grand for my taste," he had to admit. "I prefer something small and intimate." The look in his eyes seemed to take her prisoner as he asked in a far more seductive tone, "How about you?"

"Small and intimate is good," she agreed, the inside of her mouth growing suddenly dry.

"You mean it?" he asked, surprised. "You'd be satisfied with a small church wedding? With just a few friends and family members in attendance?"

"Yes," she answered, suddenly afraid to breathe because the next breath would undoubtedly dissolve the dream she realized she was entertaining at this moment. "Why?"

"Before I answer your question, I think we should stop dancing," he prompted. When she looked at him quizzically, he pointed out, "The music's stopped."

"Oh." She'd been so intent on listening to what Shane was saying, she had managed to filter out everything else. Including the band.

Embarrassed now, she moved from the small space set aside for dancing and started to hurry back to her table. She wanted the shelter provided by the guests who were seated there. Shane couldn't laugh at her if there were other people present—could he?

Shane caught up to her in a couple of strides. Taking hold of Gina's arm, he stopped her escape.

"Don't you want me to answer your question?" he asked.

Trapped, she relented. "All right. *Why* were you asking me if I'd be satisfied with a small wedding?"

"Because," he answered, "if you wouldn't be satisfied, then I'd opt to go with the whole package." He gestured around the large ballroom to get his point across. "With this," he specified. "Although it would mostly be up to you to fill it up."

"And we're back to 'why,'" she said. "Why would it be up to me to fill up a large room?" Her brain felt as if someone had shaken it like one of those snow globes. There were falling snowflakes all around her and nothing was clear. "Did you skip a step or did I miss something?"

She was utterly confused at this point. Moreover, she was really afraid to jump to a conclusion because she was afraid it would be the wrong one.

Shane took her further aside so that they were away from the other guests. "No, you didn't miss something. I'm the one who skipped a step." He took in a deep breath before continuing. "Mainly because I'm afraid that you'll shoot me down again if I ask."

Gina discovered that it was really difficult to talk with her heart in her throat, but somehow, she found a way. "I won't shoot you down," she promised, then whispered, "Ask."

It's now or never, he told himself. And with that, he started talking. "I have been in love with you for the last twelve years. Even after you laughed in my face and demolished my ego, I didn't stop loving you. I didn't want to love you," he admitted, "but there are some things that a person just doesn't have any control over." And loving her fell into the category.

"I didn't laugh in your face," she insisted. "That was just nervous laughter. I told you, I turned you down back then because I didn't want to get hurt."

"That still doesn't make any sense to me. I don't understand," he confessed.

Gina shook her head. "It doesn't matter. The only thing that matters is that I should have said yes then, the way I'm saying yes now—that is," she qualified nervously, "if you're seriously asking me to marry you now."

"Seriously, laughingly, I'll ask you any way you want me to, as long as your answer is yes," he told her. "I'm tired of missing you, Gina. Tired of regretting the life we should have had, but didn't. I don't want to waste any more time like that." He took her hands in his, looked into her eyes and quietly said, "Marry me, Gina."

"With my whole heart and soul, I want to say yes," she told him.

He caught the hesitation in her voice and the phrasing she had used. "But?"

Her response wasn't the one he expected.

"Did you tell Ellie about this? I'm not just marrying you, I'm marrying her, too. She belongs in this decision, Shane. What if she doesn't want you to get married?" she asked, clearly concerned.

Shane laughed with relief. "As a matter of fact, she gave me her blessing. Not in those exact words, of course, but I talked with her about this last night and she's very excited about the prospect of the three of us living together. She's got the whole thing planned out," he told Gina. "So, you see, if you turn me down, you'll also be disappointing Ellie because you'll be turning her down, too."

The wave of relief that flooded over her was unbelievable. "Then it's a good thing I won't be turning her down," Gina told him.

"So it's yes?" Shane asked her, wanting to be a thousand percent sure before he allowed himself to celebrate.

"It's yes." All of her was smiling now, inside and out. "Yes to both of you," Gina told him, wrapping her arms around his neck.

"That's good," he told her. "Ellie will be overjoyed."

She cocked her head as she looked up into his face. "And Ellie's uncle?"

He laughed. "That goes without saying," he said, about to lean in and kiss her.

But she drew her head back, trying to look serious, but not managing to quite pull it off. "Humor me, Ellie's uncle. Say it."

"Oh, I'll do better than that," he told her. "I'll show you."

And he did.

He showed her for a long, long time.

Epilogue

"I don't know how to thank you!" an elegantly attired Anna Bongino cried, throwing her arms around Maizie's neck. The floor-length silver mother-of-the-bride gown caught the light, shooting out bits and pieces of sparkling rainbows around the church. "You truly are a witch—the beautiful, good kind," Anna quickly clarified. She definitely didn't want to risk insulting her friend. "How did you ever manage it?" she asked. "How did you find Shane and bring them together?"

Celia smiled her pleased, mysterious smile. "Well, we could tell you, but then we'd have to kill you," she deadpanned.

"Don't pay attention to Celia," Theresa told Anna, waving a hand at her friend. "She's been watching way too many mystery thrillers on TV lately."

Glossing over Anna's question—they never liked

going into the details involved in their process—Maizie told her friend, "It's really very nice of you to have Gina invite us to the wedding."

"Nice?" Anna echoed. "Without you, there would *be* no wedding. I don't know how you did it, but I will be grateful and indebted to you until my dying day," she told the three women. "And whatever you need, whatever you want, all you have to do is ask."

Maizie's eyes shone as she smiled at her friend's enthusiasm. "We're just happy we could finally bring these two together."

"I hate to interrupt this, but I think we should find seats," Celia told the others. "I can see the organist getting ready to start playing."

Anna placed her hand over her heart, as if to ensure that it remained in her chest. She looked like a child on Christmas morning after being told that Santa Claus had been there, Maizie thought.

"It's happening," Anna cried excitedly. "It's really happening."

"Yes," Maizie replied with the pride of someone who had once again accomplished what she had set out to do, "it's really happening." Placing a hand on Anna's shoulder, she urged the woman, "You'd better take your seat up front."

Anna snapped to attention. "Oh right, of course. I'll see you all at the reception," she told the trio just as an usher approached her side, ready to escort her into the front pew.

"It isn't often we see a mother of the bride acting even more excited than the bride," Celia commented, amused, as she and her coconspirators filed into a pew on the bride's side of the church.

"I think it's kind of cute," Theresa said.

"Yes, it is," Celia agreed.

"Well, ladies," Maizie whispered to the others as all three sat down. "Mission accomplished. Again," she added with a twinkle in her eye.

Theresa chuckled. "Was there ever any doubt?"

Finally, Gina thought as she heard the organist begin to play the wedding march—*her* wedding march. After being a bridesmaid in so many weddings, it was finally her turn. She almost had to pinch herself.

It didn't seem real.

"Ready?" her brother-in-law asked, peering into the room.

Gina smiled at Eddie. Because her father had passed away several years ago, her sister's husband had volunteered to give her away.

"Ever so ready," she replied. Scooping up the ends of her veil, she walked out of the room, joining Eddie. "Thanks for doing this," she told him.

He carefully led her toward the inner doors of the church. "It's good practice for when I have to give Addie away," Eddie answered.

Gina wanted to run into the church to make sure that Shane was up there at the altar, waiting for her. But she forced herself to move slowly. And then they were in position, just behind the pint-size flower girl, ready to proceed to the altar.

Ellie turned around to flash a huge grin at Gina, then instantly adopted a very serious expression as she turned back around. Moving slowly with a surprising level of maturity, Ellie carefully scattered rose petals in front of her.

Shane's niece was out of petals by the time she reached the altar and it was clear she felt she had completed her job well. Winking at Gina, Ellie allowed herself to be led off to the side where the bridesmaids were gathered.

Gina's breath caught in her throat as she came to the end of her short journey. Her eyes met Shane's.

"You're on your own, Gee," Eddie told her affectionately, pausing to brush a quick kiss on her cheek.

Gina was barely aware of her brother-in-law or what he had just said. Every fiber of her being was totally focused on Shane.

Shane's smile was warm and welcoming. "You came," he whispered.

"Wild horses couldn't have kept me away," she answered just as the priest began to recite the time-honored words that would forever bind them together.

The warm, pleased smile on Shane's face burrowed into her heart.

This time, Gina thought, it was going to be all right. Finally.

She wanted to memorize ever single nuance and syllable of the ceremony, but the words the priest was reciting kept buzzing in and out of her head like bees filled with adrenaline. Gina found herself waiting to hear the ones that counted.

And then she did.

"I now pronounce you man and wife," Father Scanlon declared. Smiling, he told Shane, "You may kiss the bride."

Shane lifted up the veil from her face, the veil she had just discovered her mother had lovingly made for her ten years earlier in anticipation of her wedding.

"I've been waiting to kiss the bride for a long, long time," he told her just before he followed the priest's suggestion.

The kiss, they both thought, was well worth waiting for.

* * * * *

COMING SOON!

We really hope you enjoyed reading this book. If you're looking for more romance, be sure to head to the shops when new books are available on

Thursday 31st October

To see which titles are coming soon, please visit

millsandboon.co.uk/nextmonth

MILLS & BOON

MILLS & BOON

Coming next month

THEIR FESTIVE ISLAND ESCAPE
Nina Singh

An appealing, successful, handsome man was asking to spend time with her on various island adventures but his only objective was her business acumen.

That shouldn't have bothered her as much as it did. But that was a silly notion, it wasn't like she and Reid were friends or anything. In fact, a few short days ago, she would have listed him as one of the few people on earth who actually may not even like her.

"Why me?" Celeste asked. There had to be other individuals he could ask. A man like Reid was unlikely to be lacking in female companionship.

She imagined what it would be like to date a man like him. What it would mean if he was sitting here asking her to do these things with her simply because he wanted to spend time with her.

What his lips would feel against hers if he ever were to kiss her.

Dear saints! What in the world was wrong with her? Was it simply because she'd been without a man for so long? Perhaps it was the romantic, exotic location. Something had to be causing such uncharacteristic behavior on her part.

Why hadn't she just said no already? Was she really even entertaining the idea?

She wasn't exactly the outdoors type. Or much of an

athlete for that matter. Sure, she'd scaled countless fences during her youth trying to outrun the latest neighborhood bully after defending her younger sister. And she'd developed some really quick reflexes averting touchy men in city shelters. But that was about the extent of it.

Reid answered her, breaking into the dangerous thoughts. "Think about it. Between your professional credentials and the fact that you take frequent tropical vacations, you're actually the perfect person to accompany me."

Again, nothing but logic behind his reasoning. On the surface, she'd be a fool to turn down such an exciting opportunity; the chance to experience so much more of what the island had to offer and, in the process, acquire a host of memories she'd hold for a lifetime. It was as if he really was Santa and he had just handed her a gift most women would jump at.

Continue reading
THEIR FESTIVE ISLAND ESCAPE
Nina Singh

Available next month
www.millsandboon.co.uk

LET'S TALK
Romance

For exclusive extracts, competitions
and special offers, find us online:

f facebook.com/millsandboon

🐦 @MillsandBoon

📷 @MillsandBoonUK

Get in touch on 01413 063232

For all the latest titles coming soon, visit
millsandboon.co.uk/nextmonth

JOIN US ON SOCIAL MEDIA!

Stay up to date with our latest releases, author news and gossip, special offers and discounts, and all the behind-the-scenes action from Mills & Boon...

 millsandboon

 millsandboonuk

 millsandboon

It might just be true love...

GET YOUR ROMANCE FIX!

MILLS & BOON
—— *blog* ——

Get the latest romance news, exclusive author interviews, story extracts and much more!

blog.millsandboon.co.uk

MILLS & BOON
MEDICAL
Pulse-Racing Passion

Set your pulse racing with dedicated,
delectable doctors in the high-pressure
world of medicine, where emotions run
high and passion, comfort and love are the
best medicine.

be watching the word for a while.
village shop scene to a little boy
along looses to her feet
tered around her